THE UGLY SECRETS OF
PRIVATE ROY

A YOUNG MAN STRUGGLES WITH HIS LOYALTY TO AMERICA DURING ONE OF THE MOST TUMULTUOUS PERIODS IN AMERICAN HISTORY

by Mr. Edward Roy

ISBN: 145643859X
ISBN 13: 9781456438593
Library of Congress Control Number: 2010918376
CreateSpace Independent Publishing Platform,
North Charleston, South Carolina

Dedication

This novel is dedicated to Dale, my girlfriend, business partner and wife of 44 years for her unselfish support and dedication to our children, grandchildren and me.

To my son Teufelshunde Doktor (Devil Dog Doc) HM1 Tareem Tebri who continues our family's honorable service to America, by serving as an US Navy Hospital Corpsman with the US Marine Corps.

To Sergeant Lonzo one of America's brave Black fighting men whose courage, dedication and service will never be forgotten.

To Malcolm X (El Hajj Malik El Shabazz) whose encouragement and life's example has inspired me for a lifetime.

To President John Fitzgerald Kennedy, whose stand against injustice in America and in the world caused him to pay the ultimate price, not by a foreign hand, but by hands of our own.

Contents

Acknowledgements

This novel is based upon true events and is written in the memory of millions of American Soldiers of African Slave Decent, whose unheralded sacrifices for America are buried in battlefields and in cemeteries on every continent of the globe. Additionally, I wish to thank my publishers, contributors, editors, translators, on-line resources and individuals from New York City, New Jersey, St. Thomas-USVI, Atlanta-Georgia and California.

1

The Original Black Panther

I watched as Sergeant First Class Lonzo marched his phantom platoon repeatedly up and then back down 115th Street in Harlem.

"Hut haw, yo left, yo left, yo left right left. Hut haw, haw, hut haw, haw, yo left right left. Jody got yo girl and gone, Jody got yo girl and gone, am I right or wrong?, yo right. Rear hut, wake up Jones because Jerry (the Nazis) will shoot your balls off, hut haw, haw."

I am Edward Roy, it was August 20, 1962, about 7 am and in a few hours the black pavement would be so murky and hot that my Converse All-Stars sneakers would disappear into the tar that was once a street.

Yep! It was shaping up to be a hot summer in America as the end of August approached. It had been hot all summer and I am just not talking about the weather either. There were sit-in demonstrations throughout the South. Rev. Dr. Martin Luther King Jr. was in Albany, Georgia demonstrating against segregation and arrested. Negro churches were being firebombed, Freedom Riders were beaten and their buses burned for protesting separate and unequal public facilities.

"I will stop James H. Meredith from attending the University of Mississippi; because he is a Negro," Governor Ross R. Barnett said.

When President John F. Kennedy told him he would send in federal troops, the governor told President Kennedy to go fuck himself. I couldn't understand racist white Americans. Why should any rational thinking white American put Negroes through this kind of torment after suffering so much pain themselves? During the Civil War, ninety five percent of Southern whites could not afford slaves, yet Southern white folks lost one out of every four of their sons trying to defend slavery and the South. Yep! It appeared as if America was bubbling from the summer's heat. In spite of this, Negroes were some of the bravest and most loyal Americans in defending white American's freedom, but not their own; until now.

I had been procrastinating for days. I was due to ship out to Army Boot Camp at Fort Dix, New Jersey. The fence that I was walking on was giving way on the side of not going into the US Army. If I didn't take the oath, I didn't have to go, I was only seventeen. Was I crazy for wanting to defend an America that wasn't loyal to me?

It was a chore waking up on those hot muggy mornings to walk my dog Spot. It was made easier by SGT 1st Class Lonzo's wakeup call. I loved to hear his rhythmic cadence calls reverberating off the ceramic tile hallway walls just outside of our first floor apartment. Lonzo loved Spot as much as I did and always had a warm hug for him each morning as we joined him and his phantom platoon. Spot was a beautiful dog; he was jet black with a white spot on his neck and chest. He was a full-blooded Mongrel, mixed with a bit of Terrier-Pit Bull type. We marched up and down 115th until Spot found a fireplug to his liking and Lonzo would bring his platoon to a halt until Spot finished his business.

Lonzo never told me his last name and no one else on the block knew it. It was his secret; possibly an ugly secret. I had no idea that gaining knowledge of his and his friend's ugly secrets would cast me into the middle of the most tumultuous events in American history. That knowledge would shower me with my own ugly American secrets, laying bare my very soul, radically changing my thinking, my vision of America and causing me to question everything including myself.

"You no good son of a bitch"

WHAM! A flowerpot exploded in the street between Lonzo and me. I quickly tightened up on Spot's leash and darted us both back into the doorway of 112 West 115th St. where we lived.

WHAM! The second pot hit. In that instant, this crouched, half-dressed figure ran from the building's doorway across the street. He leaped two garbage cans and shot pass Lonzo and me. He ran so fast that his wake straightened up Lonzo's leaning body. In a mild panic, Lonzo instinctively reached for his back pocket, containing his wine bottle, to protect the fuel for his battered soul.

My eyes followed the second flower pot's dust trail through the air, back across the street and up the side of the building to the fifth floor fire escape. There a huge half-naked woman stood defiantly blocking out the morning's sunlight. Clad only in her panties, she was throwing any movable object within her reach at her latest escaping overnight lover. She was spitting, cursing and her breasts were swinging like bowls of Jell-O in opposite directions of one another. It was Sis.

WHAM! The third flower pot hit the top of a Cadillac owned by Steve, the numbers man.

"Grab his ass, Lonzo," she hollered, "You cheap son of a bitch, don't you ever bring your cheap, yellow, black-ass here again."

About this time, this poor fleeing soul leaped two additional garbage cans; beating Bob Beamon in the long jump. Then, he disappeared around the corner of 115th St. and Lenox Ave, like a thief at a diamond convention.

Lonzo picked up the lid from a garbage can and held it above his head. "Incoming, prepare to load, load, fire and withdraw." He was finding safe refuge in his Sherman Tank. He served in the 761st Tank Regiment in WWII. The 761st was General Patton's crack, Negro tank regiment and one of the first allied tank regiments to cross the Rhine River into Nazi Germany during WWII.

"The Fighting 761st," Lonzo would often add, "The right fighting 761st, The Black Panthers."

Spot became very, very nervous. I tugged on his leash, but he wouldn't respond. He began pulling me feverishly towards the freshly painted fireplug down a few doors from our building. I guess he wasn't nervous enough to let Sis's flying flower pots drive him back into the house without making his daily contribution to the City of New York.

"Spot, hurry up man; I don't want to get my head busted open by a flowerpot, and you don't either."

Walking Spot with Lonzo in the mornings started my motor. Outside of Lonzo calling cadence, the mornings usually were the quietest time of the day in Harlem. My Spot wasn't your Dick and Jane's Spot in your first grade reader. He played no "Street Games" at all. There was no, "See Spot run" or "See Spot fetch" in this dog. He paid no attention to loose balls, or sticks, no matter how much you encouraged him. He didn't run or fetch anything, but food. On the other hand, strangers couldn't pet him, because they would lose their fingers. He wouldn't let anyone pet him, but family and Lonzo. He was the best guard dog on the block.

He hated junkies with a passion, because he could smell the dope in their bodies as they exited the drug shooting gallery in the basement next door. If the junkies got too close to him, he would leap at them without warning. I had to be very careful with him. I'll be walking him down the street minding my own business when, suddenly, he would lunge at somebody. Nine times out of ten, that person was a heroin addict. If I put a muzzle on him, it just made him act crazier.

My family had great difficulty trying to figure out why Spot hated Junkies so. One afternoon we found a junkie lying one story down in the airshaft of our building, bleeding from his hands and with a broken leg. He refused to tell my mother how he had got there; so she left him there for him to figure out how to get himself out.

The next day we found blood and bits of torn clothes all over the floor near the window that opened to the airshaft. We punished Spot for that, because we thought he had gone in the closet and destroyed a pair of my brother's pants. We didn't "put two and two together." A few days later, we concluded that the junkie had been trying to break into our apartment when Spot attacked him and he fell off the window ledge. The torn clothes by the window were his and his bloody hands were the work of Spot.

It was easy to allow yourself to be caught up in the entertainment on the block, but you did so at your own peril. Briefly, the excitement of flowerpot mortar attack caused me to forget that I had a very important decision to make. I had wasted a lot of time enjoying Lonzo, Sis and her latest streaking lover; all starring in Harlem's version of General Hospital. I couldn't make up my mind. Was I going to take the ride downtown on the Iron Horse to Whitehall Street and take the oath for Uncle Sam's Army or not?

Lonzo was the Super of my apartment building, 112 West 115th Street. I lived on the first floor in apartment 1C. Lonzo lived in the murky, damp, basement full of coal dust and large "water cockroaches." The roaches were so big they could sign up for welfare checks. Every now and then, a few would trek up into our apartment; I was deathly afraid of them.

As old as I was, I would run terrified calling for my mother. I would throw things at them, hit at them with a broom, TV antenna or with anything I could lay my hands on. In the process, I would destroy half of my mother's possessions. One time, I was so terrified of one that I pushed my little brother Bernard into the kitchen to kill it and he almost set the entire apartment on fire. My mother demanded that I do nothing, when I saw one, until she was available to take care of it. This would keep me from burning down the entire apartment building.

Lonzo's job was to keep heat and hot water in the building, mop the halls, pick-up trash and put it out for pickup. My mother never let him in our apartment to fix anything, because she felt he didn't have any fix-it-man skills. He often begged my mother to let him fix something-anything in our apartment. She wouldn't let him touch a thing. She made him tell our Jewish landlord to send a carpenter, plumber or electrician-somebody with real maintenance skills.

Lonzo did his Super's job well between bottles of cheap wine. The floors were always mopped and cleaned. He kept the furnace fired with coal, which produced too much steam heat in the winter and life threatening steam heat in the summer. It didn't make a damn bit of difference to Lonzo what season of the year it was. In the summer, you could fry eggs on the radiators in our apartment.

My mother liked Lonzo – one reason was he didn't use drugs other than alcohol – but, I sensed she didn't trust him around her children. He lived alone in the basement. He didn't have a family, a girlfriend or anyone he considered a friend, but me. He stayed drunk most of the time and pissed on himself a lot. He only had two changes of clothing and both reeked of urine. He didn't have a bathroom in the basement so he couldn't take regular baths. Mrs. Mae, who lived by herself in 1A, the front apartment on the first floor, allowed him to use her bathroom when he requested.

When my mother wasn't watching me, I would sneak down into Lonzo's room or his "foxhole" as he put it, just to hear him talk. He applied the right name to his dusty, roach and rat incubator. I loved to hear him talk when he was sober. He had a strong, clear voice. He was very precise with the words he used. His vocabulary was limited, but he made good use of the words he knew. When he wanted to make an important point to me, he would use two or three verbal expressions; making sure that I understood. Also, he made sure that I always remembered the points he was making.

He loved to sing the blues, especially the naughty blues. Millie Jackson, Bessie Smith and Big Maybelle were his favorites. Big Maybelle was a frequent visitor to the drug shooting gallery next door. After shooting up, she would break out in a song in the middle of 115th Street that would light up the whole block. He would often break into a blues song; sometimes during a conversation utilizing the song's lyrics to bring home a point. I began to sing many of his blues songs myself. "Put on your red dress baby" was one of his favorite. Neither of us could sing very well.

He didn't have a radio, TV, clock or watch. His room only had one back-less chair, a dirty sheet-less mattress and a broken dresser. On top of the broken dresser was an electric hot plate; harboring a pot containing fossilized food with a rusty spoon imbedded in it. On the other side of the dresser was an old cover-less telephone book that he wrote cryptic notes in. Sometimes, unannounced, I would walk in on the rats having a party in his pot on the hot plate. When they saw me, they wouldn't flee, so I plugged in the hot plate. For some reason, I was not as afraid of rats as I was of those huge water roaches. Rats, I guess, were just cute and cuddly. Water roaches were creepy.

Hanging up in the corner of his room was the remains of a US Army Eisenhower Jacket loaded with medals and campaign ribbons lined above the left breast pocket. A battered Ranger patch was still visible on the left shoulder and dark triangular spots on the sleeves where sergeant stripes once resided.

There were no locks on Lonzo's door. I would hide in his room when my mother was looking to deal with my rear end for my frequent misbehavior. I would sit on his bed quietly; simply staring at his uniform jacket hanging in the corner. I tried to remember what he said all those ribbons and medals represented; while my mother called my name in vein upstairs with her belt in her hand.

Many times, I would enter Lonzo's room while he slept in a drunken stupor. I would sit quietly listening to his snoring and his frequent in-sleep chatter. Much of it was too incoherent to understand. Lonzo didn't like for me to sit and listen to him sleep. He knew that he talked in his sleep and he might reveal something he shouldn't; a secret-possibly an ugly secret. He caught me once. It wasn't pretty; he grabbed me by the arm and asked,

"What did you hear me say?"

I said, I didn't hear you say nothing. The truth was I didn't understand what he was saying. It all sounded like one of the blues songs he would sing to me. I did remember a few numbers that he repeated frequently, the 24th Infantry and the 38th parallel in Korea.

I knew not to get him riled-up. He kept a loaded 1911-Colt 45 pistol under his mattress. I sat on the pistol a couple of times. He actually pulled it out once when he was drunk. I thought he was going to shoot me with it. He handed it to me butt first, my eyes got big, because it scared me to death. It was the first time I ever held a loaded pistol.

Lonzo said, "The reason Samuel Colt made the 1911-45 ACP (Automatic Colt Pistol) was the 38 caliber pistol used by US Forces at the time was too light. Also, the Smith & Wesson six shooter was too clumsy to reload in a hurry. During the Boer War in China, US Marines fired point-blank, at charging Chinese guerillas hopped-up on opium and they kept coming. It was like slapping them in the face with a fly swatter.

Now, if I shot you in the foot with my 45, you aren't going any place, but straight to hell. The 1911 Colt 45 is the best pistol ever made. Even Mr. Luger, the famous WWI German pistol maker, made 45 versions of his Luger for the US Army right before the start of World War I. Kaiser Wilhelm of Germany stopped the full production of the 45 Luger, because he knew they were being made for the American Army; the Army he might have to fight one day.

Two 45 Luger test models were made for the US Army. Mr. Luger made the pistols himself. The US Army destroyed one of the 45 Luger pistols in a testing competition with the 1911 Colt 45. The US Government sold the other unfired. Some people say the 45 Luger pistols are the most valuable pistols in the world. I actually had one sometime ago. Roy, did I tell you about the first German girl I made love to."

Sober, he was the most intelligent and coherent person on the planet. Drunk, he would change the subject in the middle of a sentence, but I didn't care, I liked to hear him talk. I loved for him to tell this one and would always listen intently, as if it was the first time he had told me the story.

"Roy, a Hard-Johnson has no conscious.

My platoon of tanks just crossed the Rhine River into Germany and began to move through a small German town called Bitburg or something, I really don't remember. I was amazed; the Germans were cheering, dancing in the streets and waving small American flags. I was in the lead tank as I slowly led my tank platoon through the center of town. So many Germans were jumping on the tanks that I slowed my platoon down to a crawl for fear of running somebody over. Out of nowhere, this healthy built blonde climbed onto my tank and planted a long sloppy kiss on my mouth. She spoke almost perfect English.

'My name is Gretchen. I will be waiting for you at the guest-house that my family owns. It is the only guesthouse with unbroken stained glass windows left in village. You will find it at the end of this street.'

I told her that I had to find a place to bivouac my tanks on the other side of town and I would meet her back at the guest-house later that evening after I squared-away my tank platoon. Roy, my Johnson was so hard, that I couldn't get it and me back through the tank's main turret hatch. I was embarrassed that I let her arouse me so easily in front of the whole town. I was very glad to get her off my tank so my Johnson would stop pounding the turret like a drum. My tank driver was laughing so hard he almost ran over a little German kid.

I ordered my tank platoon to bivouac on the edge of the town. I still couldn't stand up straight because my Johnson was throbbing. I took a GI shower in my steel helmet and sprinkled on some of the cheap French perfume that I had taken off a dead German in France. I loaded and chambered the first round in my 45, returned it to my holster as I walked slowly down Main Street with my right hand teasing the trigger.

In France, the women flowed like French wine. Some Negro soldiers "got-over" with a candy bar and a kiss. The French girls told us not to make love to the German girls when we got there. They said, 'Those German bitches are cold as snakes and they make love the same way.' Frankly, I hadn't expected such a warm welcome from German women anyway.

I found the building she had directed me too. The guest-house that she said her family owned. There she was sitting in a secluded corner next to the bar wearing a traditional German dress. It had beautiful pink and blue embroidered flowers attached to little frilly shoulder straps that covered a charming, hand-sewn white blouse. But, frankly, she looked out of style with most of the other German women in the guesthouse.

Roy, a Hard-Johnson has no conscious.

She recognized me immediately. She waved me over to sit with her at her secluded table. She asked if I was hungry, I said no. I knew food was scarce for them. She asked if I wanted to share a bottle of wine with her. I also refused. I learned in France, that canon fire shakes the wine cellars and causes the wine to go bad inside the bottles. We settled on a couple of beers, which were made at the town's local brewery.

I was delighted she spoke English. I spoke no German except "Haultenze schwine" (stop pig). It was the only warning that I gave to those German bastards before blowing their asses off. She was very tall, a natural blond, big boned and blue eyed. She was very clean for a woman whose town's water plant had been serenaded by George Patton's 55MM cannons.

She said she had to leave the University in Berlin due to the allied bombing and that she took over her parents' guesthouse, here in town, after they were killed in an auto accident. Gretchen's conversation was very lively, interesting and intelligent. But, I only had one thing on my mind and that was to get into her panties as quickly as possible. I hadn't made love to a woman in three weeks.

Roy, a Hard-Johnson has no conscious.

She moved the conversation to me, asking why was I fighting for a country that enslaved my parents and still mistreated me at home. I said to her, I really can't answer that question. I haven't given much thought to the issue with the war going on and all. The true reason was General Patton left little space in anyone's mind for thinking about anything, but killing Germans. I only had room in my mind for four things, killing Germans, keeping my tanks running, sometimes eating and sometimes sleeping. Making love was optional and catches as catch can. General Patton made sure you didn't forget the right order to place them in either.

I told her that things weren't great at home for Negroes, but they were getting better. And, things will definitely get much better after the war is over. I said to myself, under my breath, bullshit those American redneck bastards are still lynching Negro soldiers in their uniforms when they return home."

I wanted to move the conversation to a more romantic subject, so I pulled the small bottle of French perfume from my pocket and presented it to her. She lit up like a roman candle on the 4th of July.

Roy, a Hard-Johnson has no conscious.

Throughout my conversation with her, I never noticed that I was the highest-ranking soldier in the guesthouse. We had lost our white lieutenant three days earlier when his tank hit a mine. After a few beers and some creative begging, she finally invited me into her small apartment in back of the guesthouse. Her apartment was very clean yet sparsely decorated; almost like a military barracks. I paid little attention to the details, like the small Jewish charm a "Mezuzah," that was attached to right side of the door frame as I walked into her apartment.

Roy, a Hard-Johnson has no conscious.

She asked me to get undressed and to wait by the mirrored dresser while she went into the bathroom to get ready. I was so excited that I pulled off my shirt and pants without unbuttoning them. I threw them on a chair in the corner of the room along with my pistol belt and holster containing my 1911 Colt 45 pistol.

She peeked at me several times from behind the bathroom door. Finally, she slowly slid her left leg out through the opening. It looked like someone poured sugar out of the bathroom. She dangled her toes at me and told me to take off my underwear. I did as she instructed. I was now standing "butt-naked" with my back turned to her.

Once again, Roy, a Hard-Johnson has no conscious.

Men do dumb things in the name of sex. She told me not to turn around as she slipped into the bed between the sheets. As I turned, she flicked her tongue at me while motioning me over to the bed with her left index finger. As I pulled back the covers to get in the bed with her, my eyes bulged as I glazed upon her beautiful, almost flawless, well-proportioned body. Her skin looked like it was bathed in goat's milk. The hair down-there looked like it was manicured. I got so excited that I started to climax.

Then instantly, she produced a dark object from under the pillow and fired once, "bam," point-blank, hitting me. I fell backwards across the room grimacing from the pain. The bullet hit me in the left shoulder. Now, I could see it was a Luger she hid under the pillow. It was the biggest damn Luger I had ever seen. I knew no nine millimeter Luger could hit like that; it had to be a much larger caliber. My body began to go numb from the tremendous pain. Man, my whole life flashed before my eyes. I had killed a number of Germans, even killed a Soul Brother in a bar fight in Kansas City. I fathered two children in Oklahoma that I denied. I began to make peace with my maker. I had never been stunned like this before.

She rose slowly from the bed with her cold steel blue eyes focused on me; hell bent on sending me off quickly to my maker or to hell, whichever one I reached first. She raised the Luger again and fired a second shot, "bam!" it missed, but the blast of the second shot spun me around and knocked me back across the room. I stumbled pass the mirrored dresser, piling my body like a dishrag over the chair that held my clothes.

I watched, helplessly in the mirror as she walked butt-naked and purposefully over to me. She raised her right hand at arm's length. She slowly squeezed the trigger of her Luger to fire the final fatal shot in the back of my head. Somehow, my Colt 45 miraculously appeared in my right hand as if God placed it there himself; forgiving me of all my transgressions and sins. I released the safety with my thumb, turned and fired one shot, "bam!" The shot hit her square in the middle of her deranged head, knocking her back onto the bed. I pulled myself up using the chair as a brace. I stumbled to the bed, pulled the tangled covers off her body and fired again. Bam! I made sure that witch would never pull a trigger on another American soldier again and especially a Negro one.

Bleeding badly and all over her, I checked her neck for a pulse. That's when I noticed the two tattoos on her left thigh. They were two lightning bolts (Nazi-SS). I picked up her pistol from the bed and discovered it to be a 45 Caliber German Luger. As far as Americans knew, Mr. Luger only made two. This one had the serial number of 3. She tried to kill me with a "Third 45 Caliber German Luger." What an honor, maybe I am the only American still living to have been shot with a 45 Caliber German Luger."

Each time Lonzo reached this point in the story, he would stop and pull open his shirt to show me the bullet wound, I guess to confirm he wasn't lying. The first time he told me the story, I asked him, "Lonzo you told me at the beginning of the story that this was the first German woman you made love to, but you killed her before you got a chance to make love to her?"

He turned to me with malice in his eyes and said, *"Roy, a Hard-Johnson has no conscious.* It was the coldest and bloodiest piece of behind I have ever had in my life."

I laughed so hard that I couldn't breathe. To this day, I haven't figured out if Lonzo was telling the truth about her shooting him and him screwing her after he killed her. But, it was clear to me, he was one of the most courageous and patriotic individuals I knew. Several times, he came within a hair on a gnat's ass of donating his life for this country.

Lonzo was very proud he had served in the US Army and with General Patton in Europe during WWII. He said he also served in Korea, but he avoided talking about Korea for some reason. I figured out that the bad dreams he often had were due to his service in Korea. Korea was his ugly secret. Some mornings, before he started to drink, Lonzo and I would just talk and walk Spot, sometimes all the way to Central Park. Those days were special when you could hold a sober conversation with him.

He would often say "When allowed, Negro soldiers fought with honor, distinction and courage in the Pacific, Africa, Italy, France and Germany. There was American Negro soldiers buried on every continent on this planet. When properly trained, equipped and led, there is no finer a fighting man in America or on the face of this globe."

He often told me that many good American Negro soldiers died for me and I had a responsibility to make sure that America didn't allow their lives to be wasted in vain. He would tell me the same war stories over and over again. I would listen intently as if he was telling me the stories for the first time.

"After we landed in France," Lonzo told me one time, "General Patton himself climbed up on my tank, "The

Mighty Mouse," and told the entire 761 Tank Regiment, "I don't give a damn what color you are. You are serving with me, because you are the best damn Tankers I could find. I want you to use the guns on your tanks to kill every damn German you see. Shoot up haystacks, graveyards, church steeples, old ladies and children, this is war damn it. And, as long as you kill fucking Germans, I won't have any problem with you and no one else better fuck with you either; if so, I will shoot their damn balls off.""

Lonzo briefly mentioned that his tank platoon had liberated a German concentration camp, but he said it was too horrible and too difficult to talk about. I guess this was another of his ugly secrets. He would tell this story only in pieces, while drunk, until he realized what he was talking about; then go silent. He said he saved a Jewish kid from a concentration camp. And, with his help, the kid had made his way to America, joined the Army and followed him to Korea. He was also harboring something very deep, something very ugly, and something very secret about Korea. Lonzo said my looks reminded him of the Negro lieutenant that commanded his platoon in Korea. But, he never mentioned the kid's name that he saved or the Negro lieutenant's name he had served under. He never mentioned the name of the rifle company or the company commander that he served with while in Korea.

Some people on 115th Street said that old pissy drunk Lonzo was just shell shocked and his stories were all lies. They said, the only ones on the block that could stand the smell of his urine soaked body long enough for him to tell his stories, were Spot and me. But, his exploits seemed truthful to me and made me feel real good inside. They provided me with a sense of warmth and confidence on a global scale that was rarely experienced in my neighborhood. Most people in Harlem never ventured pass the rivers on each side of Manhattan. Lonzo provided a historical foundation upon which I could build my decision on whether to join the Army and serve America, my country.

I learned from Lonzo who the Black Panthers truly were. The knowledge he transferred relieved me of my fears of facing white American racists who I would face in the Army; that were ignorant of their own history and wanted to fight the Civil War over again. Yet, on the other hand, his exploits cemented my fears not to trust racist white Americans with my life by joining the Army.

While drunk, Lonzo told me that he wanted to make a career out of serving in the US Army. He had remained in the Army after WWII was over, because of the changes President Truman made. He felt things would be very different in the new post war Army. The Negro vote carried Truman over the top in his close election defeat of William Dewey. President Truman then signed Executive Order 9981 directing equality and equal treatment in America's Armed Forces. This order integrated the Army and other branches of the armed services in 1948. Truman grew tired of Negro soldiers and veterans being attacked, lynched and killed; sometimes in their uniforms by Southern white mobs.

Lonzo was promoted to Sergeant First Class after the war and sent to Japan in 1950. He volunteered to join the first US Army Ranger Battalion stationed overseas. He said it was a great unit, but he developed a stomach infection and didn't ship out to the Korean front with his unit.

When he recovered, he was sent to a new unit in Korea. His new unit was formerly an all Colored Infantry Regiment, the 24th Infantry Regiment. This unit was the descendent of the famous Buffalo Soldiers. The new unit wasn't truly integrated yet. Harry Truman had signed the order to integrate the Army two years earlier, but those redneck Army Generals took their damn time about it. When the Korean War broke out, the 24th Infantry Regiment was all Negro with white Officers. There was one or two low ranking Negro officers thrown in with a few white enlisted soldiers, who served as clerks for the white company commanders. Still, the unit was basically segregated.

He received a number of medals and citations in WWII - a Silver Star, two Bronze Stars, and two Purple Hearts - but he received nothing during the Korean War.

I noticed several burn marks on his back when he shoveled coal into the furnace in the summertime. When he saw me staring, he would stop shoving and put a shirt on. He never answered my questions how he received those burns.

My times with Lonzo were very special. He was majestic, remarkable and heroic, with his pants steaming from his drying urine; wildly barking orders and stumbling as he marched his phantom platoon to the cadence of his raspy drill sergeant voice. Whenever he stumbled, he quickly and calmly moved his hand to his back packet to protect his little soldier, his bottle of Gypsy Rose wine peeping out of its pouch like a baby kangaroo.

As encouraging as Lonzo was, I was still very unsure about joining the Army. On one hand, there was the opportunity to serve my country with courage, honor, the same dedication as Lonzo and so many other Soul Brothers before him. There was also the sense of pride, excitement, respect of continuing the glorious American Negro military traditions and achievements that generally went unheralded.

Yet, was I truly an American, was America truly worthy of my trust, loyalty and dedication? Should I turn over to America the most precious gift that I received from God, my life? Young Brothers like me were considered dangerous in America. I had survived America's fetish for eating her Negro young, like my friend Teddy who was strung out on heroin. I had avoided and overcame the mountains of obstacles that she placed in my way. America had serious flaws that would consume me, flaws that I could not address nor correct alone, and the same flaws that had consumed the original Black Panther.

***

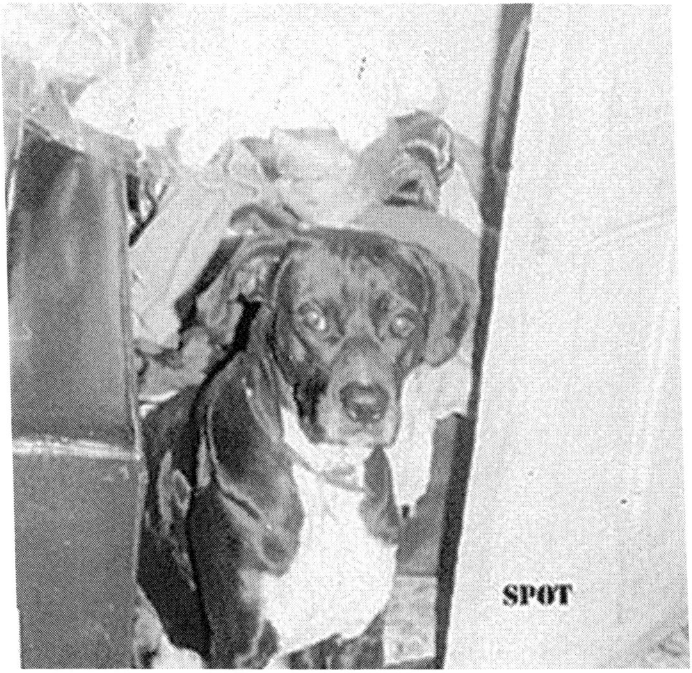
SPOT

Roy on the Block

The Street Games

2

THE UCLA

"No more Black blood should be spilled in defense of America until America lives up to the promises she made to all of its Black citizens; as well as to herself."

Malcolm X took you to school at every opportunity he could. I was sure that I was NOT going to join the Army each time I heard him speak. Was I crazy for even thinking about volunteering? No one was forcing my hand. I wasn't even draft age yet. Malcolm X was doing everything he could to help me make the right decision, and that was not to join the Devil's Army.

I ran into Minister Malcolm X once or twice a week. Sometimes, he would stop to shop at Garden Supermarket, which was directly underneath Mosque No. 7 near the corner of 116th Street and Lenox Ave. I worked there part time after school and on the weekends bagging groceries, stocking shelves and cleaning-up after the store closed. One evening he was in the store just before closing. It was one of the few times I saw him without his menacing Fruit of Islam bodyguards. He was inspecting the fresh vegetables and he asked me in his low baritone voice.

"When are you coming upstairs to the Temple?"

I sort of nodded my head and shrugged my shoulders.

"Have you finished high school?"

"This is my senior year and I am thinking about joining the Army."

He almost had a stroke. "I want to see you, young Brother, in the Temple this weekend."

I didn't go to the Temple. When he came into the market again, I went to the back of the store to avoid him. But, I couldn't escape. Sometimes, after work I would run into him as he spoke to huge crowds on the corner of 116th St. and Lenox Ave. It was called the UCLA, "The University Corner of Lenox Ave."

Malcolm X would quietly walk out to the corner with a ladder on his shoulder flanked by two or three of his Fruit of Islam bodyguards. Inside of 5 minutes, he would have over 300 hundred people standing on the street corner eagerly awaiting him to rain hell's fire down on white folks. I had to push my way through the large crowds that assembled to hear him speak. He called it "fishing for souls."

At that time, Malcolm X's approach to resolving the "white problem" in America was total Negro disengagement (segregation). If white folks wanted to be segregated from "so-called Negroes," then Malcolm X wanted to give them what they wanted.

Malcolm X was a Black Nationalist, which meant he felt Black Americans should have their own country and govern themselves right here on the North American Continent. He courted defiance and aggressive self-defense in the face of white racism and oppression. His tactics were unlike those of the Rev. Dr. Martin Luther King's who called for nonviolent engagement of racist white folks.

Malcolm X said, "King appeals to white folk's better nature, their sense of justice and fair play. They have none. Dr. King's non-violent tactics are stupid and suicidal. More Black people are killed under Martin's leadership than under Muslim leadership. In America's Declaration of Independence, it states, "We hold these truths to be self-evident that all men were created equal." What white folks really mean is all white folks are created equal, everyone else is fair game for white folk's treachery, oppression and abuse."

He seldom read from prepared text and his humor always drew blood, white blood. And, he always touched on his favorite subject, which was legally encouraging so-called American Negroes not to join the American military or allowing them to be drafted.

"The American government wants to turn you against your own kind, they want you to think you have no place else to go. You will never have peace here. You will never have security here. You will never have hospitality here. You will spend another thousand years here exposed to the hypocrisy and false promises of the white man.

We, the Black Muslims, don't tell you not to go into the US Army, because they will put us in jail for sedition. I wouldn't be that dumb.

But, if you are dumb enough to fight for something that you have never gotten or will get; go right ahead.

If you are dumb enough to let the white man stick his uniform on you, for you to go overseas to fight, then you go right ahead.

If you are dumb enough, like your brothers who went to Korea and then came back home, and caught more hell here than they did in Korea, go right ahead.

If you are dumb enough, like your brothers in WWII, like Isaac Woods, who served in the South Pacific and got his eyes punched out by a white policemen here at home, go right ahead.

If you are dumb enough with what you know about the white man today, go right ahead.

Black Americans fought in every war that this country was engaged in, from the Revolutionary War to Vietnam currently. The so-called Negroes received nothing for it, but a free ticket to hell.

Don't ever put me in your airplane full of bombs and tell me to go find the enemy, because I won't have far to go. Give us a piece of this land and we will have something to fight for. Those days are gone; if you think, you can draft this little Black man, sitting up here in the slums and ghettos of Harlem getting the worse schools, education and can't even get a decent job.

That Cracker is out of his mind, if he thinks we are dumb enough to go running after him to fight in some war that he started after some mercenary instinct, those days are over. If you and I can't fight in Mississippi, we can't fight over someplace else. If we are going to be non-violent at home then we are going to be non-violent abroad."

Malcolm X knew that a former American slave, Crispus Attucks, was the first to die for America's freedom when he led fellow white patriots against young British soldiers in the infamous Boston Massacre. Boston, Massachusetts was a city that Malcolm X remembered well. He was jailed there. Yet few white Americans knew Crispus Attucks name or gave him the credit for being the first true American.

Malcolm X had a point. "Stop serving America until America starts to serve you."

But, Lonzo's also had a point. "If we don't defend a wrong America then there may not be a wrong America to make right."

The two different points of view added to my dilemma making my decision to join the Army very, very difficult. Most of the time, I was more interested getting "next" on the basketball courts across Lenox Ave in the Steven Foster Projects' playground than trying to solve my American dilemma. When I got off from work, the large crowds that gathered to hear Malcolm X speak were always an obstacle preventing me from getting there. Quietly, I would try to sneak through the huge crowds on my way to the basketball court, but the basketball in my hand would give me away every time. I knew he remembered that I told him that I was thinking about joining the Army and had not showed up in Mosque #7 as he requested.

"Young Brother, you with the basketball in your hand."

He never asked me my name and I never volunteered it to him either. I was reluctant for him to get too close to me. He could be intimidating at times.

"Don't you know that the Blue Eyed Devils invented that game just for you?"

The crowd turned towards me in laugher.

"Yes, young Brother, just for you and other young Brothers to entertain them, to amuse them; by running, jumping and hanging from iron rims in arenas like trained monkeys. You scramble around, half-naked, looking like apes in a zoo; zoos that were built especially for you.

"Young Brother, you are too busy having a good time, wasting your time, having no respect for time, and too blind to see the importance of time. You're ignorant of the fact that you are doing nothing for yourself, and in time, you will destroy yourself.

"Young Brother, clean-up yourself, clean-up your mind, clean-up your bad habits, stop eating that pork, stop drinking that liquor, stop fornicating and abusing your Black Women.

"Young Brother, take yourself into the Muslim Bookstore behind you and educate yourself on the devil's real game.

"Young Brother, put down that basketball and come into the Nation. Submit to the will of Allah."

By this time, the crowd made a pathway for me to get through and they were in an uproar, chanting "Malcolm X, Malcolm X," over and over again. Crying out, "Down with the devil, down with the devil."

Malcolm X was a towering figure, almost 6'5", I was no midget at 6'2", but he seemed to grow taller with every chant. Yet, he never played basketball or maybe he wouldn't admit it to me and especially to the crowd. The white policemen standing nearby on the corners surrounding the crowd placed their hands on their guns, out of fear, when the crowd started to chant. They started to move back from the crowd in unison, putting more space between them and the angry crowd. I think Malcolm X got a kick out of seeing that.

Almost every time he spoke, if he spotted me in the crowd, he would hit me with the same routine as if I was his straight man in a comedy act. The crowd would go wild in the same manner and the white policemen would become fearful again. Both the policemen and I became a part of his routine. But, it was a serious routine. He was dead serious about America's abuse of its Black citizens.

At one point, Malcolm X almost convinced me to join the Nation of Islam, but I didn't, because I would have had to give up too many of my bad habits; bad habits that I just begun to enjoy. After being used as the straight man, I eventually decided to take him up on his invitation, at least partially. I went into the Muslim Bookstore and began to read and I never told him. I guessed, deep down within, I liked getting the attention at those rallies.

I was not about to give up eating pork or drinking cheap wine with the boys to become a Muslim. My Mother's pork chitterlings tasted too good and we didn't eat them that often anyway, maybe on Thanksgiving or New Years. Even though I wasn't old enough to drink, my 6'2" frame was "all-the ID I needed" to make a purchase in most liquor stores. Give up sex, no way; I just started making love to my girl Jenny Rodriquez. So, I only took Malcolm X up on one thing, The University Corner of Lenox Ave (UCLA).

I visited the Muslim Bookstore, usually during the weekdays, when Lenox Ave was quiet and none of my Homeboys would see me. I was always in total amazement at the magazines, books, artifacts and information I found there. There were newspapers from all over the world, Africa, Asia and the Middle East. There were books that the Muslim Brothers said were banned in America. Books the FBI said were subversive. They had tremendous books on global Black history, global Black military and little known global Black heroes. My interest peaked with Black military history partly, because of

SGT 1st Class Lonzo's unheralded exploits, which were encouraging me to join the Army.

I'd had no idea that the stuff I was reading existed. No one in the New York City's Public School System had ever told me that historians like John Hope Franklin, J. A. Rogers, or Artuno Alfonso Schomburg were collecting and producing volumes of work, contradicting European/American historians' assertions that African peoples had no global history; especially military history.

After a few visits to the Muslim Bookstore, my hunger for Black Military History exploded and grew like a cancer. I became obsessed with Black Military History, not only American Black Military History, but European and Global Black Military History. After much reading, it became very apparent to me, that it was the guy with the victorious army that wrote the history books.

But, was Malcolm X right? By joining the Army, would I be condoning America's misconduct purposefully, disgracefully, distorting and hiding historical truths concerning the American Negro fighting man? Would I be leaving Lonzo's heroic military struggles at the curbside? Would I be contributing to white America's ill treatment of me and peoples around the world?

Malcolm X's answer, "Yes"

His prescriptions for change were love yourself, educate yourself, defend yourself, work for yourself and be yourself. All these prescriptions summed up into one phase, "Do for self." The medicine Malcolm X prescribed begun to work on my psyche. I was having serious problems with my American identity and joining the Army.

The clerks in the Muslim Bookstore would let me read as much as I could absorb, as long as my legs held up. There were no seats in the bookstore and they wouldn't let me take the books out of the store. I would stand there reading for hours, I could not afford to purchase the books. Some cost a whole eight dollars. I began my college education in a Muslim Bookstore, the same way Malcolm X began his college education in a Massachusetts's prison library.

Malcolm X felt, that America had gone to the well one time too often with the loyalty of its Negro citizens. He felt it was time for white America to pay the piper for the 300 years of suffering bestowed upon its Negroes. The paycheck was a piece of America for Black peoples. We deserved a place of our own; separate from white folks.

It became very clear from the historical material in the Muslim Bookstore that too many, so-called Negroes, gave their very lives in the hope that their children would experience the same America as their white brethren. They and their children received nothing, but disrespect, neglect and racism. I suspected that Lonzo and his ugly secrets were a living testament to that.

The one thing that Malcolm X and Lonzo had in common was an honest vision of America and love of Black Military History. They had different perspectives on how to correct America's sins, yet they shared the common view that America could be saved with some "arm-twisting."

Additionally, I loved Malcolm X's fire, his strong sense of direction, and his uncompromising willingness to stand up to white America. Yet, deep within myself, I sensed a flaw, a weakness, and vulnerability in Malcolm X. This tall good looking Brother might not be as strong and self-confidant as he appeared. He might also have his own ugly secrets.

He helped me grow immensely. Yet, I felt that I was in need of additional development, improvement, and preparation for tomorrow's challenges. I felt the portrait I was painting of myself was incomplete, unfocused and sometimes confused. I wondered whether joining the Army would provide the sledgehammer I needed to break out of the confining box that my mind lived in. Would the Army give me the opportunity to grow into manhood as the recruiter said? Would it provide the answers I needed to understand America better as well as my American self and how the two fit together? I did not know.

Malcolm X had complicated my quest by tying knots in my head that were mushrooming into cantaloupes, clouding my vision and having profound effects on my ability to make a decision. At night I had recurring dreams of being attacked by a gorilla. It always appeared to be something else until it got close and revealed itself.

How was I to know that I must untangle them before they consumed me?

How was I to know that untying these knots would reveal a host of ugly secrets binding him together with his nemesis, President John Fitzgerald Kennedy, for eternity?

I had been procrastinating for days and had to make up my mind in short order. I was scheduled to ship out to Boot Camp at Fort Dix the next day. The fence that I was walking was giving away on the side of the Army. In the end, the tipping factor wasn't Lonzo's sense of duty, honor or country.

I had originally signed up under the buddy system with my high school friend Harvey Cross, but Harvey wore Coke bottles for eyeglasses and couldn't pass the physical.

My eyes' weren't much better. My vision was 20/20 in my left eye, but 20/200 in my right eye. But, the Army said I had one good eye and that was good enough. Actually, it would keep me out of front line combat units. I asked Harvey what I should do. He said he didn't know.

My girl was Jenny, a fine Rican. She was almost as tall as I was. She had long black silky hair and long slender shapely legs to match. She was very bright in the head and went too Stuyvesant High School, one of the best high schools in the city. She liked Afro-Cuban Jazz, as I did. Some called it Salsa; white folks called it Latin Jazz. Jenny and I were into the music no matter what you called it. Our favorite artists were Tito Puente, Mongo Santamaria, Willie Bobo, Johnny Pacheco, Joe Cuba, with some Calypso artists thrown in.

I was going to ask her the question after the PAL (Police Athletic league) Basketball Street Games Championship on 115th street. But, she said she wanted to go home early, because she had got into an argument with my mother. My mother didn't like me dating Puerto Ricans. So, I walked her home. She lived on the eastside in Spanish Harlem - El Barro, only a few blocks away.

We talked on the way and she said, "We should break up now, because you are going into the Army for three years. And, it is going to be difficult for us to stay to together."

I said, "No, we can make it, Baby. My mother doesn't control me."

She said, "Bullshit, you're a Mama's Boy."

She was eighteen years old and I was seventeen. She could drink legally, go into adult clubs, and rent a hotel room, I couldn't. I kept saying to her, we can make it, Jenny.

"I want to continue to get it on with you, Ed, but you don't have your own bed much less a place where we can be alone. You should go into the Army."

As we entered her building, Jenny's older brother gave me a dirty look as we passed him. He didn't like me, a Brother, going out with his sister either. I walked her upstairs to her apartment, calmed her down by kissing her on her neck and slowly massaging her behind. She gave me a long tongue kiss, unzipped my fly, reached her hand in my pants, and began to stroke my Johnson. I ran my fingers slowly up her thighs, parted her panties, and stuck my index finger into her juice filled privates. She began to gyrate up and down as our tongues fought for dominance in each other mouths. She started to climax and then we heard her brother coming up the stairs. We stopped; I kissed her goodbye and said that I would write her. I knew I was lying, because I hated to write.

She said, "Bye Ed, you will have your own bed now and no more Street Games for you at UCLA."

***

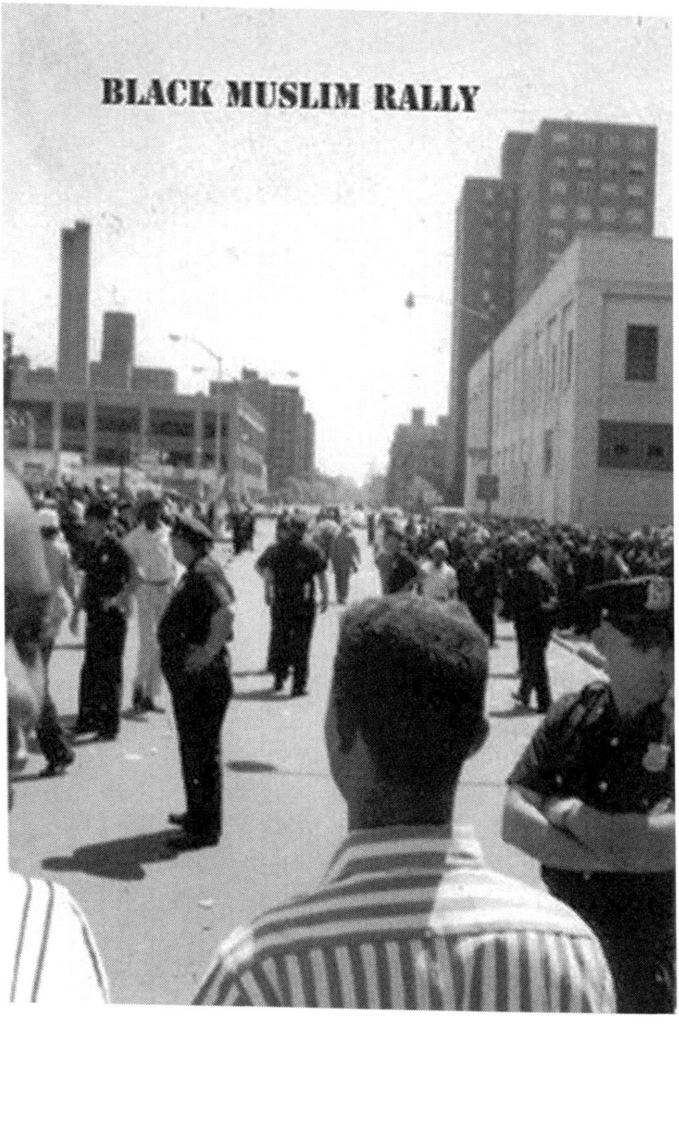
BLACK MUSLIM RALLY

3

The Ultimate Weapon

As usual, the next morning, I woke up to the cadence calls of Lonzo echoing off the hallway's walls. I was lying in a puddle of my brother's piss; it would be my last, I would have my own bed by night. I was joining the US Army.

Spot was scratching at the door. Mom was in the bathroom, because I heard the toilet flush. I jumped out of the bed and dashed for the bathroom and pushed my way in. Mom did not make eye contact as I squeezed pass her. She just held her noise and smiled.

She never said much to Bernard about pissing in the bed, because all of her children had the problem at one time or another, including me. I grew out of my habit just in time for Bernard to perfect his. I took a shower and oiled myself down to minimize the itching from my bad case of psoriasis.

I threw on my white button down collar shirt, slid into my green high water pants, which displayed my monogrammed socks underneath and fumbled into my pair of dark brown cordovans. I kicked the side of the sofa bed for Bernard to get up and walk the dog. I grabbed my new green flight bag that mom purchased as a going away gift two days earlier. I gave Mom a big hug, tapped Bernard on the head and said good bye to my baby sister, Verna.

I didn't touch Spot; if I had, he would have started to pee. I threw the piece of toast, I had in my hand, down the hallway into the kitchen and Spot took off after it. I unlocked the door and made my exit before he realized I opened it. Mom still couldn't make eye contact as I left.

I saluted and hugged Lonzo and then ran down the street towards Lenox Ave; headed for the Subway. The Muslim Bookstore was closed, but I could see J.A. Rogers' three-volume set of World's Great Men of Color setting majestically in the window. I had read most of it standing in the middle of the store. I smiled thinking maybe someone would write a book about me one day.

I heard a rumbling sound coming from the street below. I may have touched two steps in the whole flight of stairs hopping down to meet the approaching iron horse racing below the street. I dropped a fifteen cent token into the turn style as the number three train pulled into the 116th Street Station. I was having difficulty breathing from the excitement. It appeared to me that the twenty minute trip took twenty hours to reach the Bowling Green Station at the tip of downtown Manhattan.

As I exited the Subway, I could see a line of young guys forming in front of 110 Whitehall Street. On line were so-called Negroes, whites of every persuasion, Chinese, and Puerto Ricans. As I approached the line, out of breath, the line started to move into the door marked Army Induction Center. For the first time I started to think about war; the Cold War.

Earlier in the year, Captured U2 Pilot Frances Gary Powers had been exchanged for Soviet Spy Rudolph Abel in a deal with the USSR. John F. Kennedy had visited Berlin, Germany and made his rousing, Ich bin ein Berliner speech in April condemning the USSR construction of the Berlin wall. The USSR countered by accusing the United States of fighting an undeclared war in South Vietnam. The Russians and the Americans were playing their own version of the "Street Games" all over the world. Those countries and individuals that were caught in the middle of the games seemed to be the losers.

But, what I was most concerned about was a Daily News story about a, crazy ass, Marine Corps Drill Sergeant marching his new platoon of young recruits into a river in the middle of the night; drowning half of them in Parris Island, South Carolina.

We all moved into the auditorium and it filled up quickly. A tall tan looking captain marched briskly on to the stage.

"Gentlemen, I am Captain Marshall Tooney and you are about to begin one of the most important journeys in your lives for your country. Please raise your right hand and repeat after me: 'I solemnly swear to uphold the Constitution of the United States of America and to defend it against all enemies both foreign and domestic'."

As I swore, all I could visualize was Malcolm X's stern face peering directly at me; saying nothing.

The captain then said, "Welcome to the United States Army."

After signing some paperwork, all of us were given a box lunch and told to board buses at the front of the building. The sign on the busses read Fort Dix, New Jersey. I found a seat in the front of the second bus. I didn't sit in back of anybody's bus; not after so much was given up by Freedom Riders in the South for the privilege.

I sat down next to a talkative white kid from Brooklyn. He introduced himself as Roger Moreland. His father was a NYC garbage man. He said, his parents told him it was time for him to leave home. His father and mother were retiring, selling their house and leaving the neighborhood. He said, they wouldn't tell him where they were moving. He said he majored in Chemistry in high school. He was accepted to some "big-time" college in Massachusetts-MIT or something, with a partial scholarship, but his family wouldn't or couldn't help him with the balance of the money to go. He went to work in a dry cleaning store, part time, because he loved to mix and play with chemicals. His part time job at the local cleaners didn't bring in enough money for him to pay for an apartment, so he joined the Army.

"With the right chemicals, I could clean anything," he said.

I could see why it was difficult for his parents to get along with him. I couldn't get a single word into the conversation. He said that after basic training, the Army was sending him to the Chemical, Biological and Radiological (CBR) Warfare school. He was really excited about it. Only one problem lay ahead for him. His MOS (Military Occupation Specialty) required a top secret clearance, which he said was in the works, but he wasn't sure if he was going to get it.

There was plenty of chatter on the bus as it turned the corner on Canal Street and lumbered down into the Holland Tunnel. One of the recruits let out a horrible screech. We all turned to give aid. It was the first time in that "cruit's" life that he ever left Manhattan and gone underneath the Hudson River through a tunnel. He felt it was going to collapse and drown him.

The bus drivers flew through the New Jersey Tollbooths without stopping and pass the cesspool of fowl smelling oil refineries that choked both sides of the highway. For forty-five minutes we rode. The driver didn't say anything to us during the whole trip, as if he knew we were on our way to hell and he didn't want to spoil the surprise. As I slid down into my seat, enjoying the scenery of poorly maintained oil storage tanks and fuel refineries, I heard President Kennedy's words ringing through Moreland's chatter in my ears.

"Ask not what your country can do for you, but what you can do for your country."

I also thought of Malcolm X pointed comments.

"Your real enemy is right here at home, not somewhere overseas."

I asked myself whether or not Kennedy's statement applied to me since the Constitution didn't. I started to doubt again whether I had made the right decision to join the Army. My Mother's thoughts began to provide some comfort. They were instilled in me since I was five.

"You must always finish what you start, if you start a fist fight, then punch like hell until you win the fight. If you are running from a fist-fight, then run like hell until you get away, but always finish what you start."

The bus turned into the main gate at Fort Dix, about 50 miles south of New York City. Fort Dix was named after Major General John Adams Dix who served in the Union Army during the Civil War. He later became a Senator from New York and thereafter the Governor of New York State. Why didn't they name an Army base after him in the State of New York instead of New Jersey? You figure it out.

The bus crept up a long straight driveway that disappeared between neatly stacked white buildings on each side and then came to a stop. A young Puerto Rican corporal boarded the bus and hollered, "I am Corporal Persio Ramirez, welcome to Fort Dix, New Jersey, The Home of the Ultimate Weapon."

Some guy on the bus replied, "What's an ultimate weapon?" Most of us turned and laughed. Still, quite a few guys on the bus scratched their heads in ignorance.

The corporal ordered us off the bus and form two lines on the gravel pathway. Then he ordered Roger and me to help our bus driver off load the bags. Finally, he ordered the "cruits" to collect their bags. As we picked up our bags, we noticed that some guys were not moving, they had come with no bags at all just the clothes on their backs, and some had cardboard in their shoes. This was the first ugly secret knot I untied in the Army. American poverty comes in all colors. There are more white Americans in poverty than non-whites. Some people said I was poor. I really didn't know what poor truly meant or what it felt like. I don't ever remember missing a meal or going without clothes or shoes, even though we lived partially on monthly welfare handouts from the City of New York.

So, being labeled poor usually meant you were being defined by someone else's standards. Everyone on 115th St. had about the same material things, so being poor must have another meaning. Maybe a spiritual meaning, such as a Church Sister pointing out a poor weary soul or an object of pity in need of spiritual help, strengthening or resurrection in the congregation. That definitely was not my family or me.

Former President Eisenhower said, "We were poor, but never knew it."

Former Vice President Nixon said, "We were poor and I never forgot it."

I always wondered if Nixon would make a good President someday, if he could ever be elected.

The corporal began to call our names while two privates handed each recruit his own folder. We all proceeded down the gravel path to a long white building, which bore a sign stating Medical Intake. As soon as we opened the door, Army medics attacked us like ants at a Baptist Church picnic.

They began to examine us in mass. It reminded me of pictures I had seen of Jews getting off trains at Nazi Concentration Camps being processed for the gas chambers. I instinctively lifted my nose into the air to smell for burnt remains. I didn't smell any, but I was temporally overcome with the smell of alcohol. Shaking my head to clear it, my eyes circled the large room suspiciously, thinking that the rough treatment that I was receiving may have been reserved just for Negroes as Malcolm X indicated. I forgot that most of the recruits with me were white. What a relief!

This was my first time seeing medics at work. They were busy sticking thermometers in our mouths and up the asses of those who didn't know that you weren't supposed to eat them. They were taking our blood pressure, timing our pulses, giving us shots and asking us all kinds of dumb questions.

When you volunteer for the Army, you can choose your MOS. I choose to become a medic. I hoped what I saw wasn't what I would be doing for the next three years. Still, I was questioning why I joined the Army. Maybe becoming a medic, "a warrior without a weapon," was my compromise for joining the Army against Malcolm X's wishes. I also wanted to be the best soldier in the Army, like Lonzo, but without having to kill anybody in the process. Maybe becoming a Medical Corpsman would also allow me to do that, or so I naively thought.

When the medics finished reaming out our asses, the corporal ordered us out of the building on to the gravel pathway again. After falling in, CPL Ramirez said, "Most of you look like shit warmed over, and should be Sectioned 8 (mentally unfit for military duty) out of the Army, right now."

He walked over to me and asked, "What is your name, Private?"

I replied, "Roy, Private Roy Corporal."

"Private Roy, your face looks like a pussy, a virgin pussy at that. Do you shave Private Roy?"

"No, Corporal."

"By tomorrow morning, I want your face to be as clean as a gnat's ass; do you understand me, Private?"

"Yes, Corporal."

"Each of you will go to the PX tonight and purchase all the personal items you need; up to 10 dollars' worth. That amount will be deducted from your first pay, whether you purchase something or not. Private Roy, you will buy a razor. I have a soft heart and I really want all of you to be successful in this man's Army. I am giving you, your first marching commands. But, before I do, I want to ask you country boys to identify your left hand. OK, all at once, you raise your left hand."

Two poor farts raised their right.

"There are two or three in every new bunch that are retarded, with their brains wired backwards. You two jerks get at the back of the line. "Le-e-eft" face, forward march, left, left, left right, left."

He marched us towards an opening between the last two buildings in the group.

"Column halt"

We halted in front of the post's flag which was about to be retired for the day. I began to think about Lonzo and the over two million Black American soldiers that fought for what that flag stood for; many died and the rest never tasted its fruits.

Corporal Ramirez turned to us and pointed, "You see those soldiers standing at attention in front of the flag pole? They are being inspected for guard mount. The sharpest will be given the honor of being the Supernumerary. He will act as the Sergeant of the Guard and supervise the other soldiers for the next twenty-four hours.

"As I said before, I have a soft heart. I am going to help you cruits out. One day, each of you will stand guard mount, if you are able to stay in the Army long enough. The most frequently asked question on guard mount is, who is the highest-ranking man in the Army? Does anybody know?"

Roger hollered out, "A four star general." Most of the other guys nodded their heads in agreement.

The Corporal laughed, "No, numb nuts, it's the President of the United States. Now, the second most asked question. Don't go to sleep on me now! Who is the President of the United States?"

I looked at Roger. He knew the answer, but he waited for someone else to answer. I heard nothing, but silence. Finally, I hollered out, Kennedy, President John Fitzgerald Kennedy.

Malcolm X had called President Kennedy every ugly name printed in the dictionary in the Muslim Bookstore. He said that JFK was a bleeding heart liberal who wanted to do everything for so-called Negroes except get out of our way. John F. Kennedy was elected President in 1960. Kennedy was elected by one of the smallest vote margins ever in American history for a US President. Like Truman, It was Negro Americans that provided the margin of victory that put JFK over the top in his election. But, almost two years had passed, acknowledgment and support for Negroes causes was slow in coming from President Kennedy. Malcolm X said he refused, outright, to address the pressing issues of the Negro community as he promised during his election campaign. He turned his back on us, Malcolm said.

Taps started to play over the loud speakers. The Sergeant of the Guard hollered "atten-hut, present arms," as two of the guards slowly lowered the flag. The remaining guards presented their weapons at attention like toy soldiers in a kid's game. None of us cruits knew how to salute. We all followed Corporal Ramirez's lead and we were a pitiful sight to behold.

"Order arms" the Sergeant of the Guard shouted. We watched in silence as the Officer of the Day (OD) and the Sergeant of the Guard inspected each of the guards. One by one, they were eliminated until only one was left. We all clapped and hooted for him without really knowing why or how he was selected as The Supernumerary. We made so much noise, that the OD turned and gave us a dead-man's stare to silence us.

Corporal Ramirez ordered us back into formation and marched us back through the group of buildings. This time he halted us in front of the building across the street from the Medical Building. Its sign read Quarter Master-Clothing Issue.

He ordered us into the building single file. As we marched into the building, we were immediately set upon, this time, by soldiers with measuring tapes slinging underwear, socks, shoes, shoe laces, uniforms, caps, bass insignia, belts, buckles, blankets, sheets, and pillows. We attempted to stuff as much as possible into our duffel bags. Not all of it would fit.

He then marched us at double time out the back door into the last building on the block. He followed us into the building with an arm full of items we had dropped on the way. He dumped them all in the middle of the barracks floor.

"You girls better find every piece of your Uncle Sam issue by the morning. Anything you have lost by morning, you will pay for out of your first pay." He then assigned us bunks and told us to change into a pair of our Army fatigues for chow.

We were all tired and hungry, but we hit that pile of military issue like Harlem roaches on a leftover birthday cake. After we determined what was whose, we settled down helping one another figure out what this Army stuff was used for. Some guys knew how to spit shine boots already. I, the former Boy Scout, knew what Brasso was used for. My Boy Scout belt buckle was almost identical to Uncle Sam's. We managed to get into our fatigues without taking showers. We didn't have enough time to take one-though we all badly needed one.

It was about eight o'clock, (2000 hours) when Corporal Ramirez hollered, "fall-in" and marched us over to the Mess Hall. The first ten guys on line were told, "Volunteer for KP." Roger Moreland was number 11 and I was right behind him. As he opened the door to the Mess Hall, an awful smell knocked his head backward. He hesitated to enter for a moment, but the other guys were about to storm over us. As we entered, I handed him one of the large stainless steel trays. It still had grease on it from the last person who ate out of it. The GI that cleaned it did so by simply dripping it into the soapy water without wiping or rinsing it and passed it on. I just shook my head.

Corporal Ramirez give both of us a chilly stare and said, "Move on, privates."

There were six compartments on the tray, five small ones surrounding one large one. As we moved down the serving line, each server slapped food in the single large middle compartment, piling food on top of food as we went down the serving line. At the last station, the dessert, Jell-O was slapped right on the top of the entire mess. I now know why they call it a Mess Hall.

As the cruits passed by him, Roger just stood there staring at his food. I saw Corporal Ramirez homing in on him like a hawk in heat. In a very soft voice, Ramirez said to Roger, "Oh! Is there something wrong Private?"

Roger replied sarcastically, "I can't eat this."

Ramirez agreed, "No you can't eat this, Private Roy. That is your name, Roy, isn't it?" (We hadn't sewn name tags on our fatigues yet)

"No its PVT Moreland, PVT Roy is standing over there."

"Standing, OK, PVT Roy you come over here and stand next to PVT Moreland."

He then shouted in a loud voice, "Atten-hut!" Everyone in the Mess Hall stopped eating and snapped to attention.

"PVT Moreland here and his homeboy PVT Roy think there is something wrong with good Army food. Does anyone else in the Mess Hall feel that way?"

All the recruits in the Mess Hall mumbled, "No, Corporal."

Ramirez replied, "I can't hear you."

"No, Corporal," they shouted.

"These two clowns feel Army's food is not good food. They think there is something wrong with Uncle Sam's Kitchen. It appears they are the only ones, right!"

"Yes, corporal," they all shouted.

"Since you two clowns are the only ones who have a problem with Uncle Sam's food, you don't have to eat it. Go dump your trays in the garbage and report to the kitchen. Now! When you get there, I want you to tell the mess sergeant, Sergeant First Class Coles that you didn't like Uncle Sam's food that he prepared."

We cleaned pots and pans until 2 am in the morning. When we got back to the barracks, it was 2:30 am. We got half hour sleep before the Corporal woke us up at 3:00 a.m. for bus transport to our training companies. The corporal gave us fifteen minutes to wash, dress in our fatigues and fall out on the gravel pathway. Corporal Ramirez told us that we had ten minutes to eat chow before we boarded our buses to our training companies. I ate everything on my plate without saying a word to Moreland.

The buses were waiting. Corporal Ramirez began to read off the training company assignments. Moreland was assigned to Company M. I was assigned to Company Q. Both companies were a part of the 4th Training Regiment. Lucky for him, Moreland and I were not assigned to the same training company, because I was about to choke the life out of him.

Lieutenant Colonel George Melowisky was the 4th Training Regiment's Commander. It started to rain as I said goodbye to Moreland. I slapped him five as I tossed my over-stuffed duffel bag on the bus. They were school buses painted in olive drab or better known to GIs as shit green. There wasn't a luggage storage compartment below or above on the bus. Seating was very tight and GI's duffel bags were everywhere. Finally, the buses took off for the training companies. I could not believe that I was sitting in a bus loaded with America's Ultimate Weapons.

***

4

Terror in the Rain

The heavens opened and pissed down on us, giving us a grand welcome to Army Boot Camp; as if God himself was going to the bathroom for the first time in months. The bus ride was very short as we pulled up in front of a group of white buildings identical to those that we left. The windows of the bus were frosted over from the rain.

A tall stocky figure in an Army raincoat and a white striped helmet liner boarded the bus and said, "I am Sergeant First Class Talco. Welcome to Company Q of the 4th Training Regiment, Fort Dix, New Jersey. You scum have 30 seconds to get the hell off this bus. This man's Army is too damn good for you. The last one off this bus is "gonna" get my foot stuck in his ass. I am gonna put my foot so far up his ass that he's gonna need a half-track to pull it out. I wear a size thirteen, which is gonna-be a bad luck number for the last SOB getting off this Bus."

Before the sergeant completed his statement, the front door of the bus immediately became jammed with green clad bodies. GIs began to throw their duffel bags and themselves out of the bus windows. I went out the emergency back door.

At the front of the bus stood a row of angry drill sergeants lining a rain-soaked pathway. They were kicking and screaming at us as we crawled, scratched and kneed our way up to the assembly area between the white buildings. A river of mud flowed down the pathway as the bodies began to pile up blocking it.

I managed to drag my duffel bag and my muddied remains up to the assembly area. There, a second set of drill sergeants were hollering, cursing and spitting, "fall-in, atten-hut" and "look straight ahead." We stood in the rain at attention as the remainder of the cruits sloshed their way into formation.

I could see boot prints all over the GIs in front of me. On one GI, a boot print was planted square in the middle of his ass. Which drill sergeants boot print it was? I didn't know and I didn't want to know either. But, it looked so funny, a big brown mudded boot print, planted right in the middle of that GI's ass. I was turning red, trying very hard not to laugh. Then, the same fiery-faced drill sergeant, that had ordered us off the bus, surprised me from behind.

"Wipe that damn smile off your face, Private. What-in-the-hell are you laughing at, Private?"

"Nothing, Sir."

"Are you saying that I am a nothing, Private, or are you saying that all sirs are nothing?"

"No, Sir."

"I am not a sir, Private, Army Officers are sirs. Are you saying that I am an Army Officer, or are you saying that Army Officers are nothing?"

"No, Sergeant."

"Drop down and give me twenty."

"Yes, Sergeant."

"Count-em off, Private"

After I counted off the tenth push up, the mud and rain backed up in my fatigue jacket like a toilet at Yankee

Stadium. I barely made twelve with half of the dirt of Fort Dix clinging to my chest. I fell headfirst into the mud and I heard a bubbling sound. I began to think of those Marine Corps recruits that drowned in a river at Parris Island, South Carolina.

"Get up, Private, before you drown."

We stood in the rain for what appeared to be two hours wet, muddy and shivering. Finally, the Company Q commander came out of the headquarters building and walked into the center of the assembly area. He pulled back his rain soaked poncho, revealing a clip board in his left hand, and said:

"Good morning recruits, I am First Lieutenant George Doughty. I wish to welcome you to Company Q of the 4th Training Regiment at Fort Dix, New Jersey. You have just experienced the harsh terror that can befall you. There are two ways of doing things here, the wrong way, and the Army way. If you do things the Army way, you will succeed.

You are going to be the best trained soldiers in Fort Dix. I will accept nothing less from you and you will accept nothing less from yourselves. If you pay attention, follow your sergeant's orders and perform your assigned duties well, you in turn may never witness this terror in the rain again. If you don't follow orders, I will assure you, this will get much worse. Have I made myself clear?"

The cruits mumbled in response, "Yes, Sir."

"I can't hear you"

"Yes, Sir" they replied in a loud unified voice.

"Standing in front of you is your Company Q staff. Your Company's First Sergeant is Hans Hosaner. Your

Platoon Leaders are Sergeant First Class George Talco, Staff Sergeant Edmond Rives, Sergeants True Potter and Roman Dooble. Your Senior Training NCO is Staff Sergeant Juan Gomez. The Company Clerk is Private First Class Donald Jonathan. 1st SGT Hosaner will now assign you to your Training Platoons."

Hosaner then stepped into the middle of the mudded formation and began to call the names of the terrorized horde; assigning us to platoons. I was assigned to SGT 1st Class Talco's Second Platoon. Boy, I was striking out big time. He kicked us in the ass getting off the bus, he gave me twenty push-ups in the mud and now he was my platoon sergeant. I was dead meat for sure.

The Top Soldier, Hosaner ordered us to fall out into our platoons. SGT 1st Class Talco immediately ordered us into Second Platoon's barracks; to get us out of the rain. The other platoons were still standing in the rain as we entered our barracks.

I could not believe he was the same guy. His personality went through an instantaneous transformation. He politely assigned us bunks in alphabetical order and asked if anyone in the platoon had any ROTC or Boy Scout training. I thought to myself, "If I confessed that I was a Boy Scout, they might kick me out of the Army." My Scout friends and I had done some foul things while in our Boy Scout uniforms. After Scout meetings we would raid the local newsstands and rock New York City buses.

Two guys raised their hands. He named one of them Acting Barracks Corporal. He told us to get out of the wet fatigues and into dry ones, but the fatigues in our duffel bags were wet also. So we simply stood "at ease" in our underwear while he explained what we were expected and required to learn in three mouths of basic training.

"You will become proficient in the art of killing and you will learn to do it as a team. If you don't become proficient, you will be recycled into a new platoon in the next training class. There will be no individuals in my platoon, no kings and hopefully no queens, just knights. You had-better learn to depend on one another to get through your training. It makes no difference to me if your serial number starts with US (drafted) or RA (volunteered), if you are tall or short, educated or uneducated, rich or poor, good looking or bad looking, Negro or white. I expect the best from each of you at all times."

"I always have the top platoon in this training company. I expect the same out of this platoon. By tomorrow morning, you had-better memorize your individual serial numbers and your orders of the day. Each day you will be given a color to memorize. This color is the password for the day. If a guard on duty challenges you, you had-better know the password or you may get shot. The password for tomorrow is Red."

SGT Talco then instructed the acting NCO to pick men for the all night fire watch. Each man was assigned two hours of watch during the night.

He continued, "Anyone caught sleeping on watch will cut every blade of grass in Fort Dix with a pair of scissors, and that's for starters. Finally, there will be no weekend passes during basic training. You will be allowed to make one phone call home tomorrow. You had better tell your folks at home what a good time you are having here at Fort Dix. I had-better not get any letters or phone calls from your mamas stating that I am mistreating you. Have I mistreated you?"

"No, Sergeant"

"I can't hear you."

"No, Sergeant"

"The call will be for three minutes on Uncle Sam. Now! If anyone has any drugs, alcoholic beverages, knives, guns, ammunition, brass knuckles, pornographic books or pictures, cards, dice, pets or thermonuclear weapons. I will leave a garbage can in the middle of the barrack's floor. They had-better disappear or are placed in the garbage can by tomorrow morning. Do I make myself clear?"

"Yes, Sergeant"

"I can't hear you."

"Yes, Sergeant"

Over the next few days, I began to settle into my own individual bed and my first semi-permanent home since we arrived at Fort Dix. I was so focused on keeping SGT Talco's feet out of my ass, that I forgot there was a world outside of Fort Dix. Deep down inside of me, I wanted to become a Ranger like SGT 1st Class Lonzo and join the Special Forces. On the other hand, Malcolm X would scold me for sleeping with enemy.

The first few weeks of basic training focused on drill, teamwork, discipline, and physical fitness. I was in good, but not top shape. Playing basketball had developed my legs for running, which was my forte. I needed to work on my upper-body's strength with push-ups and pull-ups or I would eat a lot of mud. A perfect PT score in the

US Army was 78 push-ups in 2 minutes, 78 sit-ups in 2 minutes and run 2 miles in 13 minutes. I was far from it except for running.

Running the confidence courses, which consisted of various obstacles to overcome, was a piece of cake. Swinging on ropes over ponds, crawling through muddy ditches and climbing walls were fun, but the horizontal ladder crossing consistently exposed my upper-body weakness. These courses were designed to simulate obstacles a soldier would have to overcome in a combat situation.

It was like training to cross 7th Ave., no man's land, in Harlem. The Englishmen's territory began on the West Side of 7th Ave., where I went to school and the Imperial Knight's territory began on the East Side of 7th Ave. where I lived. I didn't belong to either gang and I was red meat for both.

My competitive juices began to flow. For the most part, I felt comfortable that I could compete with any GI on the base. Yeah! I could talk all the shit that I wanted to, but the real test would come when I was willing to put money on it like we did in the "Street Games" back on the block.

The Platoon woke-up at 0400 hours to "Triple-S"-shit, shower and shave. The peach fuzz on my face was giving me a problem, because I hadn't started to shave. The cheap razor that CPL Ramirez ordered me to purchase from the PX was cutting more skin than hair on my face. Getting cleaned up in the morning and falling out for a 2-mile, double-time run was great. I loved running in the morning. It was like walking Spot with Lonzo calling the cadence. It was always dark when we started and we would run into the morning's light. We always wanted to look and sound better than the other platoons that were also running in formation.

The key was to keep the guys in step and motivated to complete the run together. Cadence calling was the glue. SGT Talco did a good job with his old army standards like "Jody got your girl and gone" and "I want to be an Airborne Ranger", but they needed updating. I loved to call the cadence, Lonzo had taught me how. It reminded me of sounding on someone's Mama back on the block. I would lie awake in my bunk at night, piecing together the calls for the next day. Sometimes I made up the calls as we ran. Some I altered from classics.

About a mile into the run, SGT Talco would run out of steam. He was the oldest NCO in the training company, and not in the best of shape. "Private Roy," he would holler, and I would take over as he took a shortcut that allowed him to catch up with the platoon at the end of our run,

I don't know, but I've been told.

Platoon: "I don't know, but I've been told."

That, polar bear pussy is mighty-cold

Platoon: "That, polar bear pussy is mighty-cold"

I shipped out to Alaska to see if was true

Platoon: "I shipped out to Alaska to see if was true"

There, I met a polar bear whose name was Sue

Platoon: "There, I met a polar bear whose name was sue"

She told me her boyfriend went out to sea

Platoon: "She told me her boyfriend went out to sea"

But an Airborne Ranger she'll screw for free

Platoon: "But an Airborne Ranger she'll screw for free"

Am I right or wrong?

Platoon: "You're right"

You know it won't be long

Platoon: "You're right"

I don't know, but it's been said

Platoon: "I don't know, but its' been said"

Those Russian soldiers are not being fed.

Platoon: "Those Russian soldiers are not being fed"

Our Army spies say that it's true

Platoon: "Our Army spies say that is true"

Then we'll give-them some of our GI stew

Platoon: "Then we'll give-them some of our GI stew"

If GI stew won't kill-em in their tracks

Platoon: "If GI stew won't kill-em in their tracks"

Then we'll finish-em off with a fart attack

Platoon: "Then we'll finish-em off with a fart attack"

Am I right or wrong

Platoon: "You're right"

You know it won't be long

Platoon: "You're right"

The entire platoon's right feet would hit the ground with a simulations hard stomp that could be heard over the entire base. We would run a few minutes clapping our hands and grunting, "Uh, ah, uh, ah, second Platoon coming through." Every training company on the base knew Second Platoon of Company Q by our cadence calls. As we passed other platoons in formation, we broke them up laughing at our cadence calls. We were on the case. SGT Talco didn't approve of my lyrics, but he never stopped me.

It's a funny thing about military discipline; I don't remember SGT Talco ever raising his voice again during basic training. I don't remember guys goofing off or not paying attention after the first week of basic training-unless they were too tired to keep their eyes open. We all seem to understand that every bit of knowledge and expertise he was giving us was important and may have to be used against other individuals taking similar training elsewhere on this planet, like in Cuba and Russia.

We had a surprise inspection every week by the CO. our barracks was cleaned so often that you could eat out of the toilets any day of the week. The toilets were the only place in the barracks where you could truly be alone. When GIs wanted to be alone, they would go sit on the spotless toilets and write letters home or to their girlfriends.

I wrote to my girlfriend Jenny once and she wrote back once. When you are in the Army and away from home, you change your focus very fast. I was so focused on the task at hand that I wasn't motivated to write. Needless to say, I hated writing anyway, but I had some hot wet dreams thinking about her.

We were being taught how to kill and I wanted to be the best at it. It wasn't that I was a blood thirsty individual or disrespected life. I was raised in a culture that didn't respect losers, and if you lost the contest, you won the fight after. And, we were learning how to win. There were GI's that truly didn't understand why they were here or what they were being taught. They thought we were playing a game of cops and robbers. The NCO instructors repeated their instructions over and over until everyone in their platoon understood them. Now, I saw why Lonzo talked the way he did.

When a GI was thick in the head, and couldn't understand the material, the NCOs assigned that failing GI to a buddy who assisted him with his training. I was assigned to help a white guy named Jeffery Tobin from Pennsylvania. He had two lefts of everything, feet, hands, eyes. SGT Talco told him he would be recycled to the next class if he didn't shape-up. This was another ugly secret knot I untied. Not all whites are smart, I suspect it, but Tobin confirmed it.

By the second week, our Platoon's drill became excellent. We were clicking liked a well-oiled machine. Even PVT Tobin improved. In the third week the excitement begin to build, we were about to be issued or M1 Rifles. One evening SGT Talco called us to attention in our barracks. He unlocked the rifle rack and personally handed each recruit his weapon.

"I would like to introduce you to your new girlfriend. You will treat her with respect, like a queen and be faithful to her. You will give her a name, you will hold her, stroke her, kiss her, sleep with her and you will never let her out of your sight. You will keep her covered and warm. You will take good care of her by cleaning her, keeping her well-oiled and feeding her properly. If you do these things well, she will protect your life."

He ordered PVT Tobin to immediately name his weapon and sleep with it in his bunk that night. Tobin named her Alice. We were all ordered to name our weapons by the morning. I named mine Brown Sugar. The next morning, we began to drill with our weapons. We were constant practicing the Manual of Arms; right shoulder, left shoulder, port, sling, inspection and present arms. Tobin was having serious difficulty. He didn't know his left shoulder from his right. I would work with him after chow in the dark, below the single barrack's light, like I use to play basketball in the park.

Before we fired the weapon, we had to learn how to break her down and take her apart, clean her and reassemble her, all in good working order blindfolded. Naturally, Tobin couldn't get it right. We began our marksmanship training about the fourth week of training and I was assigned to help Tobin again. There were three levels of shooting proficiency, Marksman, Sharpshooter, and Expert. When we fired for record, I had to struggle with Tobin for him to qualify at the lowest level of Marksman. I scored Sharpshooter, missing Expert by a few points.

The M1 Garand rifles we were issued were of WWII vintage. It was considered the single most important weapon in the big one. German Field Marshal Erwin Rommel once said, "That weapon will cause Germany to lose the war." It weighed 9½ pounds, was 43.6 inches long, gas operated and held an 8 round, top fed clip. The M1 Garand fired a 30.06 caliber round, which could not be used by other Allied Forces infantry weapons and vice versa. What made the M1 so popular with American soldiers? It would fire accurately dirty and wet. After you ran out of bullets, you could beat the hell out someone with it and it wouldn't break.

At the end of WWII, the Russians began developing a new rifle and not much was known about it except its name, the AK47. American military experts didn't think very highly of the weapon or the Russian's ability to produce a top of the line infantry weapon. Bullshit, the AK47 was a worldwide hit straight out of the factory box.

After the Korean War, the US Army improved the MI with the new M14 model. With the M14 all NATO forces could use the same ammo, a 7.62-mm round, even if they had different weapons. The troubling fact was that the Russians invented the 7.62-mm round and guess what, our ammo could be fired from a Russian AK47.

With the AK47 in mind the Army began developing a completely new infantry rifle in 1956, the AR-15. It was lighter than the M1 and the M14, almost carbine in size. It could fire automatic as well as semiautomatic. We heard through the grape vine that the AR15 was picking up a bad name for unreliability in Vietnam.

Some days, I fired so many rounds that I would have a headache, a helmet full of brass jackets and a sore shoulder to boot. My marksmanship was getting better and better each day I fired. As I became more proficient with the M1, for some reason, my gorilla attack nightmares began to diminish.

You and your weapon truly became one. The crackle of the round leaving the barrel no longer caused you to flinch. The kick of the weapon simply reminded you that whatever came out of the front end of the weapon would kick the shit out of someone else much harder than the weapon kicked you. It was more like playing basketball on 115th in the street games, the more shots you took at the basket the better you became.

And we continued to fire; we fired from the prone position, the kneeling position, the standing position and the sitting position. We fired from concealed positions in the bush, from foxholes, advancing on the enemy and retreating from the enemy. When you moved from one concealed position to the next you never exposed yourself for more than three seconds. Three seconds was the average amount of time necessary for an enemy soldier to get you in his sights to fire a fatal shot. I wondered what if he was above average.

The most important skill of disciplined squad firing was determining when to fire and when not to fire. We learned what our weapon could do and more importantly, what it could not do. We learned to move and attack as a squad, a team, and not to rely on any one individual to get any task accomplished. This training tested the squad's ability to deal with stress, surprise and unfamiliar situations quickly. Aggressors would pop up from unsuspected positions fire at you and then disappear. You only had a few seconds to respond by taking cover or firing back. We fired blanks on this course to ensure that we didn't kill one another.

The foliage in the woods began to show a little blaze of color here and there, whispering to us mud men that fall was upon us. It was starting to get a little cold in the evenings, so the DI told us to dress in layers.

I was assigned to my first guard mount in the third week of October 22, 1962. We heard through the grapevine that President Kennedy was going to address the nation that evening at 7 p.m. The drill sergeants tried to scare us by saying that Cuban spies had been spotted near the post. It was to be my first shot at winning Supernumerary. I was determined to win my first time out. I spit shined my boots, my fatigues were pressed, my brass buckle was shined to a mirror finish and my weapon was cleaned and oiled. I was ready, so I thought.

I reported to the post's flagpole at 1600 hours. The OD shouted, "atten-hut" and we fell into formation for inspection. I was number three to be inspected. The OD was from Company P. and the first guard in formation to be inspected was from Company P. The OD inspected that GI for all of ten seconds and moved on to the rest of us grunts on the guard mount.

He approached me, took my weapon for inspection, and said, "There is dirt in the chamber."

I said, "Where, Sir?"

He pointed and I saw no dirt. He walked around my rear, looked at the back of my neck and said, "You need a haircut, Private."

"I just had one, Sir."

"Get another one tomorrow."

Well! You know who didn't win Supernumerary. All is fair in love and war, especially in the US Army.

We were not allowed to look at TV, but this was an important occasion. The OD allowed one of the NCOs to bring one into the guardhouse. There was plenty going on in America and in the world. We learned what was going on through hand me down newspapers left lying around by the drill sergeants.

The USSR had launched their third astronaut, Maj. Andrain G. Nikolayev. Their fourth was launched three days later, Lieutenant Colonel Pavel R. Popovich. Russia resumed testing nuclear weapons in the 40 mega-ton range in its arctic regions. In West Berlin, East German border guards marked the first anniversary of the Berlin wall, by shooting and killing a fleeing East German youth. They left him hanging on a barbed wire fence to bleed to death. Secretary of Defense John McNamara warned that the United States was ready to use nuclear weapons to protect its vital interest in Berlin, if the Russians invaded West Berlin. The Soviet Union was sticking it to JFK. They appeared to be winning the propaganda war.

The number of Russian soldiers in Cuba was steadily rising. Some estimates said there were over 4,000 in Cuba and more on the way. Kennedy said he would use "any means necessary" to stop Cuban "aggression" and defend America.

It was remarkable that JFK used the same expression that Malcolm X used. He would get support from the American people for his, "by any means necessary" policy. Yet, Malcolm X would be ostracized for making the same statement to Black Americans; encouraging them to defend themselves against white American racism. I had heard Malcolm X make the same statement on the corner of 116th St. and Lenox Ave.; many times. Malcolm X was taking heavy criticism from the white newspapers for making "by any means necessary" his motto for acquiring human rights for so-called Negroes here in America. It all seemed very hypocritical to me and caused me to question again, why was I here at Fort Dix. Who should I really be learning to fight? America has a different standard for white leaders versus Black leaders.

JFK was also taking a lot of heat from American right-wingers for being soft on Communism and Negro demonstrations. Additionally, he took a lot of heat from Malcolm X and other Black leaders for his timid civil rights policies here at home. America had a double standard, freedom for European Americans and pseudo-freedom for American Negroes.

Meanwhile, in Mississippi, Governor Ross Barnett and his Lieutenant Governor Paul Johnson continued to disobey federal court orders to enroll James Meredith into the University of Mississippi. JFK made good on his threat and sent 25,000 federalized U.S. Soldiers into Oxford, Miss. to enforce the federal court order. The former Army Major General Edwin A. Walker, a devout segregationist, had to be led away at bayonet point by soldiers he formerly commanded. Over 50% of the Army's white officers were from the South and they didn't let any Negro soldier forget it either. I was lucky my company commander was from Vermont.

While sitting in the guardhouse waiting for my turn for guard duty, I overheard, the NCOs talk about President Kennedy and what a lousy job he was doing. They said he punked out on the Bay of Pigs invasion by not providing air-support for the Anti-Castro Brigade "2506." One suggested that someone should put the president and his brother Bobby out of their misery. President Kennedy addressed the nation at 7:00 p.m. Eastern October 22, 1962, announcing the presence of nuclear missiles in Cuba. I was scared to death. This playing soldier was for real now.

Two days later, we learned to fire rifle propelled grenades. It was like learning to fire your own personal mortar. Tobin did well with rifle grenades to my surprise.

Things began to pick-up quickly. Our next stop was the Infiltration Course, which was designed to prepare you for receiving and avoiding enemy machine gun and mortar fire. That would be your enemy throwing everything at you including the kitchen sink. We were taught how to crawl like a snake on our bellies and backs; it was difficult until you practiced a few times. Up to now, we were the only ones doing all of the simulated killing. Now it was someone else's turn to try to kill us.

You never know what situation will cause you to lose it and panic. It was during the day Infiltration Course, that I met my 600 pound gorilla nightmares face to face in broad daylight. I was crawling on my back under barbwire when an officer began throwing CN-Tear Gas Grenades at me. As the CN-Gas began to replace the air that I was trying to breathe, I tried to remove my gas mask from its case attached to my leg, but the barbwire caught my field jacket and prevented me from reaching it. I started to choke from the gas. There was a machine gun firing over our heads and I lost it. I began to throw up all over myself. I couldn't get my gas mask on even after I got it out of its case. So, I stood straight up in the barbwire. The officer who threw the gas at me stepped though the barbwire and approached me with his mask on, sticking it directly in my face.

"You're dead soldier, if that damn machine gun was firing live ammunition, you would have been killed instantly. Now put on your mask, pick up your weapon and catch up with your platoon."

During the Night Infiltration Course, fifty caliber machine guns were firing live tracer ammo over our heads with real explosions going off around us; showering us with hot gravel. This course gave you a real taste of what real shrapnel feels like. It definitely would be a deadly mistake to stand up in this course in a panic.

Tobin stopped in the middle of the course crying out to me that he wasn't going any further until they stopped shooting at him. I helped him get back to the starting point and I continued on the course without him. I thought they would kick him out of the Army for sure, but they gave him another chance the next night to repeat the Night Infiltration Course. I crawled the entire one hundred yards with him this time.

We were hearing all kind of rumors that things were not getting better in Cuba. Soviet Foreign Minister Andrei Gromyko warned in the UN that an American attack on Cuba would mean war with the Soviet Union. The NCOs were really dogging President Kennedy. They quoted the President saying in September that he would kick Castro's ass, if he took offensive action against any nation in American hemisphere. Did the President waffle? Learning that JFK didn't enjoy the confidence of the military brass was a huge ugly secret.

SGT Talco said, many times during our training, that American soldiers killed one another by accident as much as the enemy did in combat. Because of that, a great deal of attention and care was given to hand grenade training. Our first throws were under the direct supervision of a NCO. This was the training area were the most injuries and deaths accrued. After practice throws with dummies grenades, you dropped into a foxhole on the grenade range with a drill sergeant for the real thing.

The Range Officer said, "Ready on the left, ready on right, number "X" is cleared to throw."

Then the sergeant in the hole handed you a live grenade and gives you the commands to proceed.

"Ready."

You place the grenade in your throwing hand. Then you place your opposite hand's index finger through the grenades' ring attached to the grenade pin. The pin acts as a safety device that will not allow the grenade to explode unless the pin is removed.

Then the sergeant gives you the next command, "pull pin."

Then he tells you to "throw."

The release lever is activated when the grenade leaves your hand. The grenade will explode in three seconds after you throw it.

The NCO's instructs you to throw the grenade from your crest, more like a push than a throw. The reason for this is to prevent any obstacles around you from hitting your hand and causing the grenade to fall short or land on you instead of the enemy. If something goes wrong and the hand grenade falls back into the foxhole with you. You and the NCO have 3 seconds to get out of the hole. If something goes wrong and the grenade lands a few feet from the foxhole. You get as deep into the foxhole as possible. Under no circumstances do you try to retrieve the hand grenade.

Everything was going great. The whole platoon completed their throws except for Tobin. The sergeants left him for last. SGT Talco was in the foxhole with him. Tobin was very nervous. He had to pass this course or he definitely would be recycled. When SGT Talco gave him the order to throw his hand grenade, he panicked and dropped the grenade into the foxhole.

SGT 1st Class Talco immediately jumped out of the foxhole. He told Tobin to follow him, but Tobin tried to retrieve the grenade. I rushed over to the foxhole and tried to pull him out of the hole. I had him halfway out when the grenade went off. The blast blew him completely out of the foxhole with me in tow. We landed ten feet away. The blast mangled both of his feet and one lower leg. The medics were already on the Grenade Range and they rushed him to the base hospital. The doctors were able to save his leg, but he lost both feet.

When things like this happen, it makes you think about the weirdest shit. What motivates people to learn how to kill? I had my reasons, but others had theirs. I remember reading in the Muslim Bookstore that during the Civil War the newly arrived Irish immigrants joined the Union Army in large numbers to fight. They formed whole regiments. The New York 69th Regiment was one of them.

They were not motivated to fight to end slavery or to save the Union. What they really wanted was to learn the skills of warfare, so they could return home to Ireland and drive the British out of their homeland; as we did. And some tired just that after the war.

The buildup in Cuba was masked by Russian assertions that their weapons were only "defensive." At Fort Dix, President Kennedy continued to be severely criticized by his military officers for his lack of decisive action. The criticism made me feel uncomfortable. Not, because I had not heard Kennedy criticized before, but never from individuals that reported to him.

I could feel the tension in the air. JFK was being pushed to the wall by his top military brass to invade

Cuba, and he would have invaded Cuba if he was pushed just a little further. There was too much whispering going on amongst the NCOs. I was asked by SGT Talco to go to the HQ building to pick up an accident form for Tobin. I walked into the HQ building, no one was in there, but PFC Donald Jonathan and me. I made eye contact with him and I asked him for the accident report form. He turned around to retrieve it and he just started talking.

"That was a hell-of-a-thing that happened to PVT Tobin. PVT Roy, good job. The companies' training is going to be intensified. All of you may be extended an extra week so you guys can get some additional time to improve your squad tactics and marksmanship. Our entire basic training company will be sent to Cuba, as an Infantry Company, after attending a week of Advance Infantry Training in Florida."

I asked if this meant we would not be attending the scheduled schools.

He stared at me and went on, "Most of the officers don't like the President, his policies or Bobby Kennedy."

We were in deep shit, if war broke out. Our officers would be battling with the Kennedy brothers not the Cubans.

I ran over to the Post Exchange to get a copy of any current newspaper. I wasn't interested in President Kennedy or the Cuban situation. When I become upset, I like to read the comics to calm myself down. Snuffy Smith was my favorite cartoon character. He had a down home humor matched with a quick trigger finger, especially when he was guarding his moonshine still. He reminded me of Lonzo and laughing at him calmed me down quickly.

After I joined the Army, I didn't spend much time with the political stuff, except for now, because now I was directly in the middle of it.

Kennedy acted. In an international telecast, he announced a quarantine of Cuba, because the Russians had established a nuclear missile base in Cuba. Our reconnaissance planes photographed the missile sites. The missile sites were capable of hurling atomic bombs at the United States, some fifty times more powerful than the bomb we dropped on Hiroshima, Japan. After receiving various reports that the United States was about to invade Cuba, Nikita Khrushchev sent a letter to JFK suggesting a resolution of the crisis. Castro sent a letter to Moscow suggesting that Nikita Khrushchev order a preemptive nuclear strike against the United States. The same day Castro ordered his SAM batteries to open fire on an American U-2, piloted by Major Rudolf Anderson, downing the U2 and killing him. Ignoring Cuba's Premier Fidel Castro veto, the Russians agreed to withdrawal all of their offensive weapons from Cuba. The agreement said that the withdrawal would be carried out under our inspection and the United States would lift its naval blockade and not invade Cuba. President Kennedy won against the Russians, but he loss with his own military brass. They were not impressed.

Castro released 1,113 Cuban prisoners from the Bay of Pigs invasion of 1961; furthering the humiliation of JFK. They were flown to the United States in exchange for over two million dollars in cash and fifty three million dollars in medical supplies that were donated by American pharmaceutical firms. Fidel Castro also agreed to release 1,000 relatives of the prisoners.

One NCO said, "The Kennedy Brothers bark was bigger than their bite. Kennedy was just a young liberal Harvard whiz kid with a hotheaded brother; both too immature to run the White House. The Bay of Pigs fiasco and now the Cuban missile crisis debacle made them look like wimps."

We went on with our training with a renewed sense of urgency and maturity, almost without intervention or direction from our platoon NCOs. Most of our training now was very specialized, often given by Specialist NCOs outside of our training company, first aid by medics, CBR by chemical warfare specialists and communications by the Signal Corps.

I was released from basic training a week before Company Q's graduation, because my medic class at Fort Sam Houston, Texas was starting early due to the Cuban Missile Crisis. I didn't get a chance to say goodbye to Tobin, who was still in the base hospital. I wanted to stop home to see Mom, Lonzo and Jenny before I took off too Texas. My plane ride was out of Idlewild Airport in Queens, NY. So, I took the bus into NYC to see them.

When I walked up 115th St., Lonzo was sitting on the stoop wearing a coat that looked like he had slept in it. His whole face lit up at the sight of me and he gave me a big hug. He said my uniform was too big for me and my shoes were not spit shined. He teased me about the lack of ribbons on my chest. He escorted me down into his foxhole. As we set down on his filthy bed, he offered me a drink. This was the first time he ever offered me a drink of his cheap wine. I was still seventeen years old and not old enough to drink in New York State. The only place I could legally drink liquor was on an Army base, no place else in America.

Lonzo said to me, as he poured the glimmering liquid into a paper cup. “If you are old enough to die for your country then you are old enough to drink with me.” I touched my cup to his wine bottle and I saluted him.

I wasn’t able to run down Jenny. She had flown to Puerto Rico to visit her family. My brother and sister were in school when I arrived. Spot and my Mother were very happy to see me. I spent as much time with them as I could, because I had to leave for Texas that afternoon. I survived my terror in the rain, but my list of ugly secrets was growing.

***

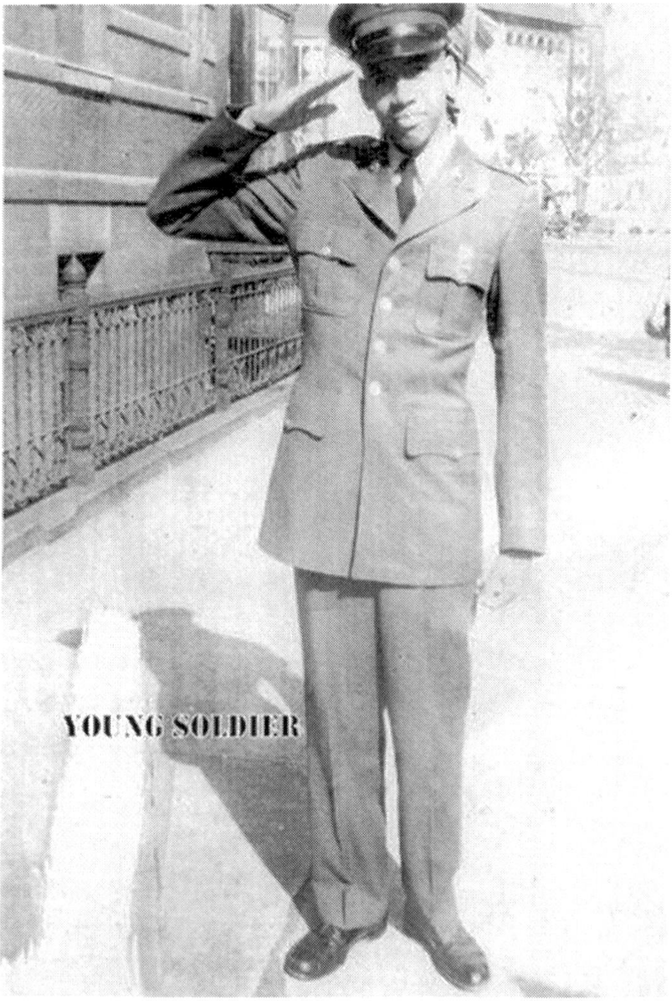

YOUNG SOLDIER

5

Milking the Snakes

I arrived at Fort Sam Houston, San Antonio, in the Great State of Texas, on December 4, 1962. It was right after Thanksgiving and snow was on the ground in New York City when I left. There were about twenty GIs, mixed in with other passengers, on the plane and most of them looked as scared of flying as I was. This was my first plane ride in my life. I was very happy that it was uneventful.

When I got off the plane in San Antonio, it was ninety degrees. I remember dust was everywhere. My khaki uniform began to wither in the heat and humidity. It was the first time I had been in a place where it was ninety degrees in December. San Antonio began as an abandoned mission that was occasionally occupied by Spanish troops. They named it Alamo "Cottonwood" after the surrounding trees. At the start of the war for Texas' independence, in December of 1835, volunteers occupied the Alamo. They were killed by Mexican troops in February of 1836. Among those who died were American legends, Davy Crocket and Jim Bowie.

An Army bus was waiting for us at the airport to take us to Fort Sam Houston, home of the Brooke Army Medical Center and the Army Medical Training School. We got off the bus in front of the WACs (Women Army Corps) barracks and a platoon was drilling in the middle of the street. The Black female drill sergeant had them sounding off for us new arrivals.

"Female "cruits" atten-hut, left fa-ace, forward arch, hut hurd, hut hurd, hurd. When I say rear hut, I want to hear sixty vaginas all snap at the same time; rear hut, rear hut."

I heard them snap too. Female basic training was separate from the men and Fort Sam Houston was their basic training camp. A large number of females went on to work in various medical jobs in the Army. They didn't have far to travel for medical training after basic. I later found out that during WWII, Black Army nurses were given the humiliating assignment of caring for German POWs here. Many German POWs refused to go back home after the war and remained in San Antonio.

After they marched pass the barracks, I noticed a tall, thin white sergeant first class standing in front of the barracks staring at me as if he had just witnessed General Grant walk out of the front door of his tomb. As he stared, I noticed the unit patch on his left sleeve was blue with a yellow sword with an Airborne-Ranger ribbon affixed atop-Special Forces, "The Gods of Fort Bragg, North Carolina."

He didn't look like a Special Forces type. Those guys were billed, as battle hardened muscle men, not thin, under-weight shrimps. He gave me a cold stare as my line marched past him. I deliberately didn't make eye contact with him. He said nothing, but the glow from his over packed mahogany pipe lit up the freckles, wrinkles and scars on his face. I could hardly read his sun-bleached nametag on his well-starched fatigue uniform, but I thought it was Jamison. He never smiled; he just gave me a look that would freeze the balls off a dead man.

We marched into the large barracks, almost identical to those at Fort Dix, except they had a second floor. The Army probably used the same interior decorator.

The Specialist 4th Class in charge of the trainees began to speak.

"Good morning, I am Specialist Coleman, welcome to the US Army's Medical Training Center at Fort Sam Houston, Texas. I am here to assign you to your bunks and answer any questions you have. Lieutenant Thomas Glover is in charge of your medical training company and he will give you a formal introduction on Monday. The NCOs will share private rooms on the second level of the barracks. The bunks are first come, first serve, respective of rank. Fall out to secure your bunks."

I simply grabbed the first bunk behind me and began to "square" my gear away in the footlocker at the foot of my bunk. It was the first time I shared the same barracks with men of a higher rank than I was. There wasn't enough space in the private rooms for all of the NCOs in the training class. SP4 Coleman told the lowest ranking corporal, James Moran, that he had to share a bunk with me. I had already laid claim to the bottom bunk, so he threw his gear on the top bunk and said to me, "I still pee in the bed at night."

"I'm used to that," I said.

Then someone tapped him on his shoulder and said, "Hi, I am Sergeant First Class Jacob Sammerson, you can take my bunk on the second floor."

He was the guy who was staring at me when I arrived. That made me really uncomfortable. As I now look back, this instant was a major defining moment in my life. If I had known what lie on the road ahead, I would have made a u-turn. I should have requested a bunk change. I should have done a lot of things different, but I didn't. Why, I don't know? My mama always told me, "Ed you are always too damn curious. Curiosity is what killed the cat." I did not realize at the time that my curiosity would almost do just that. It would inject me into the ugliest secret events in American history. Additionally, it would lead me into a personal transformation that would challenge my very soul.

I shook hands with SGT Sammerson. He had a very soft handshake similar to mine. I didn't go for all that stuff about a firm handshake is a signature of your manhood.

"I'm Private Edward Roy from New York City," I said, then turned, shook hands with the guys in the adjacent bunks and asked about chow?

The GI in adjacent bunk introduced himself as PVT John Colbert and said, "I know where the Mess Hall is. It's near the Medical Center-follow me." We left SGT Sammerson squaring away this gear as we charged off to the Mess Hall.

The heat of the day took a time out as the evening breeze began blowing gently into the leafless trees, giving you a false sense of calm and peace. I heard the crickets chirping as we walked to the Mess Hall. The airborne wings on SGT Sammerson chest reminded me of the motion picture, "The Longest Day." It was D-Day 1944, after jumping into flooded fields at night east of Normandy Beach in France, American paratroopers were trying to find one another to accomplish their mission and stay alive. They made sounds using toy crickets to identify themselves.

As we entered the Mess Hall, the mass of khaki uniforms made it look like another WWII movie. The only thing missing was the Andrews Sisters singing "Boogie

Woogie Bugle Boy." As I made my way through the chow line, I could feel someone's eyes peeling the skin off the back of my neck. I immediately turned around and standing about ten men behind me was SGT Sammerson staring at me again. My Boy Scout Master was gay and he looked at me the same way.

SGT Lonzo told me that the US Army had more faggots than "Boy's Town Reform School." He said the Army brass tried to keep it an ugly secret by simply looking the other way.

I was pissed now. I wanted to find out what was on his mind. I deliberately procrastinated on the chow line until the sergeant passed me. I watched him sit down with four other sergeants. I noticed the unit patches on their left shoulders were Special Forces. I followed him and I set down with them. I starred directly in his face with the same frozen stare that he gave me. The sergeants sitting at the table were all stunned and began to look at one another confused. Finally one spoke,

"Did you invite this cocky private to sit down and eat with us Sammerson?"

This was the first smile I got out of the SGT Sammerson. He read my mind and started to laugh as he spoke.

"No, PVT Roy, I am not a sissy. You're from New York City, right?"

"Yes, Harlem"

The other sergeants laughed.

I said politely, "What's so funny?"

Sergeant Del Vecchio, sitting across from Sammerson, introduced himself and said, "Sammerson claims he is from Harlem also. What's the name of your street again, Sammerson?"

"112 St. and 1st Ave on the east side of Harlem, Italian Harlem. Most of you farts don't know that all types of people live in Harlem, whites on the West Side, Negroes and Jews in the center, Italians and Puerto Ricans on the east. I lived on the eastside of Harlem, mostly inhabited by you guineas."

You look like you are from center Harlem."

"It must be written all over my face," I said sarcastically."

Sammerson smiled, "It's in your walk. You have that arrogant Harlem dip in your step. That dip that says I am a bad mother, so don't fuck with me."

The other sergeants laughed and I returned the smile knowing they were teasing me.

I asked him, is that the reason you were staring at me, because I looked like I am a bad mother?

He simply smiled and changed the conversation, "What's your nick name?"

"Fast Eddie."

"Let me guess, you are a pool shark?"

"Not as good as Fast Eddie Felson and Minnesota Fats, but good."

I started to eat before my food got cold, thinking at the time that Sammerson hadn't answered many of my questions. Everyone spoke during dinner; accept the dark Indian looking Soul Brother who used sign language when he spoke. It appeared that everyone understood him. Sammerson dominated the meal's conversation with the other sergeants.

He turned to me and said, "These guys sitting here are the starting five of our Special Forces basketball team, "The A-team-the Mean Machine." Say hello to Sergeants Carmine Del Vecchio-better known as Vecky, Two Feathers Norse-known as Deuce, Staff Sergeants Caley Gorge-known to his enemies as The Caveman and Norman Clayben-we call him Doc."

I wanted to ask, what happened to the rest of his A-team and why so many Special Forces soldiers were at Fort Sam Houston at the same time. The place was overflowing with them. None of Sammerson team members were the young cocky paratrooper types that I became accustomed too. They all appeared to be seasoned veterans, very laid back, confident and almost serene in temperament.

SGT Talco told me, before I left basic training at Fort Dix, that one of the most popular MOS for Special Forces soldiers was Medics. In addition to becoming Paratroopers and Rangers, they had to master three MOS, one in combat arms, one of their own choosing and usually a foreign language. Also, he said, their primary purpose was to train foreign soldiers thereby acting as "Military Force Multipliers." They could train a whole army in a year under their each one teach ten philosophy.

Only when Sammerson stopped talking did the other A-team sergeants talk or sign. They talked about the Army posts where they were stationed and how long it had been since they were home. It appeared their small talk was fabricated just for me. They referred to Sammerson by his nickname, 'the Wolfman.' I was too busy eating to ask them why.

The next morning all the medic trainees fell into formation and marched over into the training center for our medical training orientation. A tall golden haired lieutenant stumbled atop of an aging platform in the center of the large open-air classroom and introduced himself.

"Good morning, I am First Lieutenant Thomas Glover, Executive Officer Medical Training Company here at Fort Sam Houston. The motto of the Army Medical Corps is to 'Conserve the Fighting Strength.'" He began to sweat, it was only 0800 hours and it was scorching hot already. He could not hide from the low winter angle of the sun casting its orange glow over his entire body. He told us we had the weekends off, but suggested that we take the time to review the medical information that we were taught during the week.

"The beginning of the Medical Corps of the US Army wasn't glamorous, but it was heroic. During the Civil War, women started the Army Medical Corps. With thousands of wounded men lying on America's battlefields unattended to, suffering and dying, they answered the call. They were courageous women."

As I glanced out of the corner of my eye, I could see SGT Sammerson and the other Special Forces sergeants seriously and intensively whispering. LT Glover glared at them and slammed his pointer down hard.

"I am aware that you Special Forces types just returned from Southeast Asia, would you like to share the latest field medical techniques you learned there with the other medical corpsman trainees. I am sure that is what you were discussing."

The sergeants shut-up immediately, without appearing phased or intimidated by the lieutenant's comments. SGT Sammerson replied, "Sir, would the trainees like to learn about acupuncture." The class laughed, the lieutenant smiled, shook his head and continued his presentation.

"Most of you have recently completed your basic training in the military skills of taking lives in defense of our country. The rest are veterans, who have perfected the skills of taking lives. All of you must now learn to perfect the medical skills necessary for saving lives. As you move on to practice your newly acquired skills, many of you will be forced to make instantaneous decisions on the battlefield. The decisions you make will be to take a life with one hand or to save a life with the other. Outside of the Infantry, Medical Corpsmen have earned more Medals of Honor for valor than any other military occupation. Gentlemen, saving a life is just as heroic, and courageous as taking a life."

He told us that the death rate for wounded soldiers receiving medical treatment in the Civil War was 50%, in WWI it was 25% and in WWII it was 20%. But, he added that disease and accidents produce the largest number of deaths and hospitalization of fighting men.

As the lieutenant summed up the entire training program; he said, "This afternoon your training will start with immobilization of an injured patient." Then we broke for chow.

After classes, most of the other trainees played baseball in the evenings. There were baseball fields everywhere on the base, but few basketball courts. Most afternoons, after class, I would go to flag pole at the entrance of the base and watch the changing of the guard. There was a small hut in front of the post's flag-pole, where guard mount was held. It was approximately 20ft X10ft, air conditioned and always locked. The only sign on the door said, "Danger, Authorized Personnel Only." The windows were painted black so you could not see in. The constant hum of the air conditioner made it very difficult to hear the questions and commands the Officer of the Day was giving to the guards.

I loved to study the officers questioning the GIs and bet with myself on which one they would select as the Supernumerary. At times, SGT Sammerson would join me and we made small bets on which GI would be selected. He would win most of the time.

All PFCs and below were required to stand guard duty which amounted to checking cars entering the post. Most cars had post stickers; those that didn't you simply asked where they were going and provided help. SP4 Coleman pulled names out of a hat for the first weeks. The date he picked for me was in three weeks. Now, I would get another shot at winning the Supernumerary. I upped the bet to a whole dollar, with the Wolfman, that I would win.

The next day was Friday. John Colbert, the guy in the next bunk over, invited a small group of GIs to go into San Antonio with him. We were all PFCs and below and in uniform. LT Glover told all of us that the West Side of San Antonio was a very dangerous place for GIs. The West Side was the Mexican Red Light District and at least one GI out of each class would be killed on that side of town. I told John I wanted to stay away from the

West Side. I didn't even venture much on the West Side of Harlem; where I lived.

We got off the bus in the eastern part of town and walked around taking in the sights. We spotted a small bar-restaurant on the corner of a wide boulevard.

"Let's get a beer," John said, and he started to walk across the boulevard towards the bar. The rest of us followed. I didn't tell anyone that I wasn't old enough to drink. In the bar I spotted Corporal Moran, the redneck that SGT Sammerson gave his bunk too. One of the guys waved at him. He turned away without responding.

We sat at the table for twenty minutes without anyone coming over to take our orders. Finally, John waved the bartender over and asked him to take our orders.

The bartender looked straight at me and said,

"We don't serve Negroes in here."

John was stunned and replied, "What in the hell do you mean?"

The bartender replied, "Exactly what in the hell I said. We don't serve Negroes in here."

I looked over at Moran, who remained seated at the bar. He turned away from us again with a smile on his face. I looked around the large room. All the patrons became dead silent. All the customers were white and staring dead at me. The other GIs began to argue with the bartender. Some of the customers began to get up from their seats and walk towards the door.

John, now cursing loudly saying, "You SOBs, Private Roy has the same uniform on as we do and underneath that uniform is the same blood that will be shed for this country. Thereby making it possible for you SOBs to keep this shitty dive open."

Another ugly secret knot untied, Malcolm X was wrong; it's not accurate that all whites are racist.

Now! Some of the customers began to walk toward us. Corporal Moran remained seated at the bar.

"That's OK guys," I said. "I don't know who in the hell he is talking about, I am not a Negro anyway. And, my money spends better down the street where they appreciate this uniform, no matter who's in it."

I grabbed John by the arm and pulled him out of the door. All of our eyes were fixed on Moran as we left the bar. I was not willing to test my theory at another bar on that side of town, so we all went back to the base with our asses intact. The barracks were very quiet, everyone was asleep. About 2230 hours, I felt a thump at the head of my bunk. I looked up and there was Moran, drunk as a skunk, looking me in the face. He began screaming at the top of his voice "I don't like the shit the Army is doing to me, I don't like what is going on and I want out."

Some of the guys tried to quiet him down and help him to his room, but he flew back to my bunk and screamed at me, "So, you are not a Negro huh, what in the hell are you then."

I had taken enough shit off white folks that night. "Your mother knows what in the hell I am and your sister does too. Why don't you take your drunken ass over to the telephone and call-em to find out? And, while you are at it, tell them that I am fresh out of rubbers, so I can't see them tonight. They know what happened the last time I stopped over without my rubbers; they gave me the clap. And please give them my regards."

"Who in the hell do you think you are talking to, nigger."

I got out of my bunk. "I heard you say Trigger, asshole, but that's who Roy Roger screws; who's screwing you in the ass, honky."

John and other GIs managed to wrestle him into his room. I slept in the adjacent barracks for the remainder of the weekend while Moran slept it off. Sunday night the NCOs returned from their weekend passes. The Wolfman heard from the other guys what happened. He told me that Moran had been kicked out of the Marines, because no pilot wanted a drunken mechanic to work on his helicopter. He told me to stay away from him; he was a redneck racist and trouble.

Then, Monday morning, just before we fell into formation for roll call Moran approached me again and said.

"It ain't over, boy."

"You meant Roy, and yes it is."

"It's not."

"Ok, then meet me on the handball court this evening at 1900 hours and well discuss it further."

Everyone in formation heard the conversation. Sammerson just shook his head and smiled as we marched off to class.

LT Glover greeted the class with a big grin on his face. He said, "Many of you have noticed that small hut by the main gate and post flag pole. Today we are going to visit that hut and find out what's in it. But first, I would like to introduce Staff Sergeant Charles Wilkins to you. Wilkins is a world-renowned specialist in this field. Please welcome SGT Wilkins."

Wilkins removed the cover from his display charts. "Good morning men, there are over 1500 genera of snakes in the world. About 250 are venomous. Over 20 venomous species are found here in the United States alone. What is the first thing you want to do if you are bitten by a snake? "

One guy said, "Expose the wound and extract the venom."

"No, the first thing you want to do is identify the snake. Most snakes are not venomous. In that hut by the flagpole are over one hundred of the most deadly venomous snakes in the world, including ten species of Cobras.

"Why do we keep so many dangerous snakes here at Fort Sam Houston Medical Center? We milk the snakes for their venom. What do we do with the venom? We make snake bite anti-venom. We can ship anti-venom to any spot on the globe within 12 hours by fighter aircraft from Lackland Air Force Base here in San Antonio. Today you are going to watch as my assistant and I milk the snakes. And, one of you lucky trainees will assist me with the milking of the snakes as my assistant."

Most of us looked at one another saying, "Not me."

After lunch, SP4 Coleman unlocked the door to the snake hut and pushed it open, walked inside and turned the lights on. SGT Wilkins called it his Serpentarium. I didn't care what he called it. The smell of snake shit

hit you like a locomotive. SP4 Coleman said one of his assignments was to feed the snakes daily, sometimes with live food like rats and gerbils. He said some snakes could go for months without eating.

We walked into the hut single file, glazing cautiously at the critters. Some were very fascinating. Most of them simply lay in their cages unaffected by our presence. One trainee tapped on one of the cages. Wilkins hollered, "Do not tease the snakes, they are very valuable. Some of them cost the US Government thousands of dollars to acquire."

He opened a cage, reached in and pulled out a Diamond Back Rattler. SP4 Coleman uncovered a small cup with a rubber membrane on the top. SSGT Wilkins forced the fangs of the snake into the membrane. A white opaque slimly liquid ran down into the cup.

"That's how it's done, men," said Wilkins and turned to me. "Ok, Private Roy, you try it." I hadn't realized that all of the trainees standing next to me had disappeared.

"Try what?" I said.

He reached into the King Cobra's cage and grabbed the cobra in back of his head. The snake was so big that he needed two hands to lift him out of his cage. He motioned me to come around to his right side, grab the snake in back of its head and hold on for dear life.

As I grabbed the cobra, all the heat in my trembling hand seemed to be sucked into its head. I was shocked at the temperature difference between humans and snakes. The snake muscles tighten as he tried to escape. His head was so large that my hand barely covered the back of it.

Coleman wasn't very pleased with placing the milking container in front of the snake's head with me holding it. It seemed to take a year for that container to reach the snake's mouth. Finally, the snake lunged for the container and bit into it several times releasing a large amount of venom.

Most of the medic trainees had moved completely out of the hut by now and were viewing the activity through the open door and windows. Wilkins seeing that my hands were sweaty and I was losing control of the snake motioned me to place the Cobra's head on the table. He placed a long L-shaped pole on the back of the Cobra's head to hold him still. He then grabbed the back of his head again and placed him back into his cage. The guys gave me a round of applause. They all patted me on the back as I left the hut and began to chant "The Milkman, the Milkman."

I passed CPL Moran as I left the hut. He just stared, remembering we still had a date that evening to finish our business. Instantly my new Army nickname became the Milkman.

Returning from evening chow, Sammerson begged me not to go to the handball court. He felt that Moran was setting me up to attack him so that I would be court-martialed for it.

I told him, the matter had to be settled. Everyone in the barracks was very tense. No one spoke to Moran or me for the remainder of that evening. At 1845 hours, I left for the handball courts. It was muggy and very quiet, as if everyone's ears were tuned into the goings-on at the handball courts.

The streetlights automatically came alive casting their eerie, shadow-less, orange glow over the entire base as I double-timed over to the courts. On the way, I noticed an opened dumpster with a piece of 2x4 lumber protruding from its top. I stopped, inspected it and decided that it would be an excellent equalizer. As I approached the hand ball courts, I noticed a dark figure advancing from my rear. I figured that was Moran. I went to the opposite corner of the handball court from which he was approaching and hid.

I waited and waited. Then suddenly, I felt a tap on my shoulder, as I turned and stood up all those eerie orange lights on the base went out. The next thing I knew, I was sitting on the stoop of the barracks in a pool of blood. SGT Clayben, from the SF A-team, was applying cold compresses to my busted lip. I felt so stupid, but no one was laughing at me. My uniform was full of blood. He stopped the bleeding without using stitches and placed me in my bunk.

The next morning, at roll call, the lieutenant asked me what happen to my lip. I looked over at Moran; I could see sweat pouring down his brow.

"I tripped on the barracks steps last night, Sir."

"I wondered where all that blood came from. Someone reported it to the CQ (Charge of Quarters) last night." The lieutenant then ordered us to fall out for class.

As we walked into the class, John looked at me in amazement and smiled, "You didn't do well, Milkman, getting even with that redneck SOB."

I finished the issue last night John. If not, I will get better prepared for round number two, if Moran wants it. I promise you, the outcome will be different if there is a next time.

SGT Sammerson came over smiling puffing on to his pipe. He said, "You need some work Milkman; you have the courage, but not the skills for the "The Monkey Show."

"What?"

He repeated, "The Monkey Show."

The other members of his Special Forces team came over, patting me on the back, laughing and teasing me about the short ass whipping I had taken from that redneck. John didn't think any of this was funny.

"You showed righteousness, Milkman, by not snitching on Moran," Vecky said.

I tried to avoid Moran as much as possible. But, for some reason he wanted to talk with me at every opportunity he could.

"There is something different about you, versus the other coloreds I know, Milkman."

I would constantly tell him that I was not colored, a Negro nor a nigger, that I was an American, whose ancestors were brought here involuntarily from Africa and forced into slavery.

"But you are almost as white as me."

"No, Moran, you are almost as black as me. It's a scientific fact called the dominance of color, Moran. If a Blackman and a white woman, say your sister and me have four children, one will be white, two will be brown and one will be black. The white child will always be the outcast. You white folks got ran out of Africa into Europe 10,000 years ago by us, so called Negroes, your own brothers and sisters."

Sammerson was on the floor cracking up. But, Moran would not give up. The next day, as soon as I was alone, he would approach me again and start.

"You know, I do not believe in this integration stuff."

"I don't either, because it's not true integration. Most so-called Negroes think it is integration they are fighting for, but it's not. Its assimilation, not integration, the same program you white folks ran on Native Americans or would you understand better if I said "Indians." You rednecks brought about their total destruction and now you are working on Black Americans.

"What is assimilation?"

You rednecks claim you are smarter than us. Why are you asking me so many questions? You claim you want segregation from us "Negras," but you don't really want segregation. What you really want is domination, asshole. I believe Malcolm X is right, total segregation is what is needed. Blacks should have our own country in America, with our own Army, Navy, Air Force and Marines. We should have our own nuclear weapons, missiles and B52's. We should be so segregated from you rednecks that we couldn't see you SOBs, unless it is through a damn bombsite. I am going over to Lackland AFB tomorrow to learn how to use a bombsight. I hope your ass is walking around the base in full view."

"Roy, do you really feel that way?"

"Yes!"

"This Malcolm X fellow must be a communist like that Dr. King fellow."

"The problem with you dumb rednecks, is you don't even know the difference between communism, capitalism, racism or freedom."

Sammerson, who was quietly listening again, was almost dying from cardiac arrest trying not to laugh too loud.

My hand-to-hand combat training began the next evening. The SF A-team took me out into the middle of the baseball field. SGT Sammerson instructed me, "These are the conditions for your first hand-to-hand lesson. You cannot fight back or attack anyone. You can only defend yourself, evade or run to survive."

The SF team would simultaneously attack me. He deliberately didn't teach me any martial arts techniques. But my defensive basketball skills came in handy.

He said, "Most cultures of the world have developed their own forms of martial arts, whether you know it or not. Black Americans have perfected one of the most effective on the planet, boxing. In Africa boxing and wrestling was the same thing. Have you ever seen a professional prize fighter get beat in the ring by a Karate Black Belt"?

"No."

"You won't either, Milkman you have the fundamentals you need already, you just don't know it; with some slight adjustments you could be good."

How do you know what skills I have?

"I know, just leave it at that. Why did you pick up that 2x4 from that dumpster, have you ever used a 2x4 on someone in combat before?"

No, how did you know I picked up a 2x4."

"The next time you talk to Moran, you ask him some questions for a change, you might learn something. Ask him about 2x4s, maybe it will help you understand rednecks better."

From my training, I could see that the Wolfman's primary Army MOS was a Martial Artist, a Hand-to-Hand Combat Specialist; and a damn good one. During my hand-to-hand combat lessons, I never evaded the Wolfman as easily as I evaded the other team members. No one on the A-team would identify the Wolfman's or their own combat specialty. It was their ugly secret.

***

6

Pogo Sticks

In our next medical class, we began to study wounds of all types. We learned that in the Civil War, even minor wounds had major consequences. The rifle balls used by both the northern and the southern forces were so large and soft, that the wound never was a clean one. Being hit with a 58-caliber mini ball was like being hit with a sledgehammer. It just crushed muscles and bone as it danced around inside your body. Arms and legs usually had to be amputated. The instruction advanced to sucking chest wounds and the trauma caused to the body by large blood lost.

In just a few days, milking the snakes was a distant memory. The first chance I got, I sat down next to Moran at chow. He gave me a strange look, as I did so. I asked him where he grew up. He was so excited that I started a conversation with him that he started to speak almost without taking a breath.

"I grew up in the Mississippi Delta, we were poorer than dirt. In Mississippi, even dirt had some value, but "Poor White Trash" didn't. Even the coloreds got more respect than my family did. I didn't own a pair of shoes until I entered high school. I was two years behind when I did.

Times were hard in Mississippi, so I joined the Marine Corps with a negra friend of mine that I grew up with. His name was Josy, Josy Grant. My drill sergeant was Gunnery Sergeant Pat Corinne, a white fellow from......Louisiana? Yes, Louisiana. SGT Corinne had it in for both of us from the beginning of Boot Camp. He didn't like Josy or his last name Grant. He said, Josy parents must have been descendants of that race-mixing Union General, Ulysses Grant. And, that Josy and I were so close that we had the same parents. He made Josy and I fight one another viciously with pogo sticks. We had helmets and padding on, but we still felt the blows. One afternoon, he claimed that Josy and I were goofing off in our training."

I nodded and he went on.

"He ordered both of us out of the barracks and on to the parade field at 2300 hours that evening. We got into our padding and helmets and he ordered Josy and me to go at it; but instead of pogo sticks, he gave each of us each a length of 2x4-solid pine lumber. Josy was getting the best of me for a while. I was in so much pain that I thought I was going to die. Then I took a blow to the head and something came over me. I went crazy. I started to fight like I was possessed by the devil."

He paused for a long moment. "I beat Josy to death with that 2x4, padding and all."

I was stunned.

"The drill sergeant told the company commander that I'd had a score to settle with Josy and that's why I had beaten him to death. The Marines kicked me out of the Corps as unfit. I told everyone that I was kicked out for drinking too much. I had nowhere else to go, I was not going back home to Mississippi, so I joined the Army. It's been two years since I was kicked out of the Marines. I made sergeant fast in the Army, but my drinking and fighting caused me to lose my stripes. I was told that the next time I got into trouble I would be kicked out of the Army."

I didn't know what to say and he was lost in his own thoughts. Finally he went on.

"I still see Josy in my dreams almost every night, lying there in his underwear, helmet and padding, bleeding from the mouth, and his body trembling away his very life. It's been downhill for me ever since. This is my last chance in the Army, Milkman. I could have saved Josy, if I had the knowledge I am receiving now.

I saw you pull that 2x4 out of that dumpster. Lucky for me, there was another 2x4 lying in there. I could-a beat you to death that night on the handball court. I was just that mad. But, after I hit you once, all I could see was Josy lying there on the ground with blood coming out of his mouth. Milkman! The next time you pick up a 2x4 to hurt someone, you should know what you are doing and be prepared to beat someone to death with it, or you may surely die in the process yourself, if you don't."

If I had known that story, I never would have picked the 2x4 up. But, I didn't say anything.

"You know, it's alright for coloreds and whites to be friends and work, but we shouldn't live together. Josy was my friend and he lived across the street from me on the colored side of town."

I said, "Yeah, across the street on the colored side of town." I was completely taken back by his confession, his ugly secret. I looked him straight into his tearing eyes with tears running down my own humbled face and said, but, it's alright for us to fight and die together, in the same fox-hole huh. He thanked me for not snitching on him after our fight. He said he wouldn't have known what to do, if he were kicked out of the Army. We didn't talk much after that session, but I began to feel he was as much of victim of his own racism as I was and another ugly secret knot was untied, redneck racists should pitied, not feared.

The whispering among the Special Forces A-team intensified while I worked out with them. Two Feathers would sit by a bank of pay telephones at the edge of the ball field and strange things started to happen. All four telephones would start to ring simultaneously. Then start again and stop in strange patterns. Two Feathers would record the sequences and patterns. No one would pick up the telephones and answer them. I tried to answer the phones one evening and they kicked my legs out from underneath me. I asked the team, what in the hell is Two Feathers doing?

I received nothing, but blank stares in return. As the days passed, the A-team became more edgy and tense, unlike their usually quiet and confident manner. I started to ask more questions of the team. Like, why is SGT Clayben in Medic training when he already knows how to stop bleeding in large cuts without using stitches? I received nothing back, but stares.

Time was moving forward towards my turn at guard duty. All the A-team members were giving me pointers on how to become a sharper soldier, sharp enough to win the Supernumerary on guard duty. They gave me pointers on starching fatigues, spit shinning boots and super cleaning rifles.

There were two battered M14 rifles left in the rifle rack under lock and key in the barracks. When your turn for guard duty arrived, SP4 Coleman unlocked the rack for you to take a weapon. These weapons were not in the best of shape, to say the least. We were given only two rounds of live ammo on guard duty. One round was to be fired in the air as a warning shot and to alert the post MPs; the other was to be fired only in self-defense.

I wondered whether these weapons would fire at all after inspecting the condition they were in. Vecky volunteered to help me repair and clean the M14 that I was to use for guard mount.

While we repaired and cleaned the weapons, Vecky began to talk, "I lived on the West Side of Chicago; the same street where Al Capone got his start. My father came from Sicily in 1939 to avoid being drafted by Mussolini. He almost didn't make it off the boat, because he was so dark. If you ever get chance to go to Italy you'd-see-what-I-mean. The US immigration authorities preferred the white looking Italians. My father is darker than you, Milkman."

Vecky broke the M14 down in seconds, showing me where the internal parts were worn. He took parts from the other weapon to improve the working condition of my weapon. We cleaned the weapon with Q-tips, old socks and gasoline he sucked out of a Jeep. He sand down the scratches on the rifle's stock with a sock filled with sand that he got from the ball field. He polished the stock with a floor wax and shoe polish mixture he made himself. He cleaned the barrel with a bore brush and buffed it with cotton balls impregnated with gun oil and finished off the weapon with a light coat of Vaseline in the barrel and on all the moving parts. The rifle was now immaculate.

The Caveman showed me how to prepare a set of fatigues for guard duty. "Always keep a separate clean pair that you only wear for guard duty. Wash'em in cold water, no bleach, and hot water final rinse with starch."

He showed me the Argo starch that he used on his fatigues. I remembered the starch well. My mother liked to snack on it. He didn't believe me, so I ate some for him. He cracked up.

He said, "Let them air dry, but not completely, then iron them with a stream iron before the starch completely dries. Man they will stand up and salute by themselves."

Doc and Deuce helped me polish my brass and pistol belt. They recommended heating the Brasso before applying it to the metal. Doc trimmed my hair and questioned me like the Officer of the Day would. I reported to the flagpole and fell-in on the guard mount. There were four other guards from the other training companies. The Officer of the Day and Sergeant of the Guard called the mount to attention. I was looking good and felt so confident I was going to win that I bet the Wolfman five dollars. The whole company came out to see the mount including Moran. I noticed SP4 Coleman approaching the Snake Hut out the counter of my eye with a bucket of food for the snakes.

I was in the second position on the guard mount. The OD approached the number one guard. He came to attention and inspection arms presenting his weapon for inspection by the OD. The OD snatched his weapon from his hands for inspection. Then a loud scream came out of the Snake Hut and I turned to look. SP4 Coleman almost tore the door off the hinges getting out of the Snake Hut. He came limping towards us, grimacing in pain. The Officer of the Day was standing with his back to the hut and the weapon still in his hands. He violently turned to see what the commotion was behind him. In the process, he swung the weapon around and the rifle butt hit me square on the side of my head. I went out like a light for the second time at Fort Sam Houston.

I vaguely remember hearing a lot of screaming as I was coming too. Lying on my back, I could see this long thin object weaving back and forth in front of me. I heard someone holler, "Shoot it, shoot it."

Then someone said, "If you do Coleman will die, because there won't be any snake anti-venom available to give him."

"Shoot it, shoot it, Private Roy may be bitten and killed."

Then someone said, "That snake is too damn valuable to be killed, let the snake bite the fucking private."

I remember the snake's head approaching my neck a high speed. Then suddenly a fatigue jacket flashed in between the snake's head and me. I felt a thump on my neck from the snake's head, as it hit me. The two other guards pulled me away from the snake. CPL Moran had taken off his fatigue jacket and thrown it over the snake's head, just in time. SGT Wilkins grabbed the snake's head through the fatigue jacket and returned it to his cage in the hut. It was the same King Cobra I held while it was milked.

SP4 Coleman was bitten badly. They carried Coleman and me to the emergency room looking for snakebite wounds. SP4 Coleman had been bitten in the leg, but they found no snakebites on me. Moran's fatigue jacket had caused the snake to close its mouth before striking me. SGT Wilkins milked the snake again for his venom and rushed it over to the hospital to make anti-venom serum in time to save Coleman's life.

The next day, they moved the light switch from inside of the hut to the outside of the hut, because SP4 Coleman walked into a dark hut to turn the lights on. If a snake escaped from his cage, it could prove to be deadly. Yeah! Tell me about it. This incident uncovered another ugly secret. In the US Army, a private's life is worth less than a snake's. Moran and I began to talk more after that snakebite incident. Even John started to talk to him. I guess we settled down a bit and grew more comfortable with one another. The next weekend Moran invited John and me to go into town with him for a drink.

I said to him joking, "I don't want to kill any drunken rednecks this weekend."

John smiled and said, "I may go looking for some ball-head pussy."

I grinned and said, "I don't want to get killed by any wetbacks either." I remained on base.

LT Glover announced to the class that the Cadre from Fort Benning, Georgia would be coming on post to give PT Tests for Jump School. I told the Wolfman I wanted to try out.

He looked at me funny and said, "Milkman, that snake incident should have taught you every lesson you needed to know about this man's Army. Evidently, you didn't learn much. We are led by some of the most self-serving people in the world. No officer or NCO spoke up for you when that snake was about to attack you. It was Moran that spoke up for you. The officers and NCOs just care about their own asses. And there are people in high places in this country that will sell us out for nothing more than a few pieces of silver to protect their distorted vision of what America should be. Now you want to give them another opportunity to take your life by going Airborne? The extra $55 per month jump pay is not worth it."

"That's mighty strange," I said, "coming from one of the best Special Forces Paratroopers in the country."

"Be the best soldier and the best medic in the Army, Milkman. Don't volunteer for shit, don't be a dead hero. Take everything Uncle Sam is willing to give you and run like hell with it. Leave the Army after your enlistment is up; use your GI bill to go to college. You will have free medical benefits for the rest of your life. Live, Milkman, live to take advantage of them."

He paused and then added: "Most of all, stay away from Vietnam, those little slant eyed SOB's are gonna tear America a new ass hole, believe me. We learned nothing from the French defeat at Deim Bein Phu. Most Americans didn't know that we trained those "SOBs" to take back their homeland from the Japanese; who took it from the French. Ho Chi Minh was a student in France and General Vo Nguyen Giap was a schoolteacher and a poet. The French killed Giap's wife, Quang Thai, by hanging her by her thumbs and beating her to death for information on her husband?"

I shook my head no.

"Well they did. The United States' OSS (Office of Strategic Services-the precursor to the CIA) trained those guys into two damn good generals. They have been fighting foreigners for more than 20 years now; and they are damn good at it. They were about to kick the

Japanese out of Vietnam when we dropped the Little Boy on Hiroshima. We forced them further into the communist camp by helping the French reoccupy their country. We gave them no other choice, but to fight us. We sold them down the river even after they modeled their constitution after ours. Now, they are about to kick our asses out of Vietnam, Milkman"

I was stunned. It was as though I was standing on the corner of 116th St. being lectured by Malcolm X.

"They use low technology, not high technology that we over depend on. They are using primitive crossbows to shoot down helicopters, for God's sake. Anything we throw away they use. They make mines out of #5 food cans. They make some of the best jungle combat footwear in the world out of our used steel belted tires."

He was saying the same kind of things that Malcolm X said, but Malcolm X didn't know all the ugly secret details that the Wolfman knew. But, once again, my childish competitive instincts took over.

"I appreciate your advice, Wolfman, but I still want to try out for the Airborne."

I could see that he didn't appreciate my response, and then he rocked me good.

"Milkman, you want to know the secret about me and SGT Lonzo Morgan? I served with Lonzo in Korea in 1950. A few days after you left home for Boot Camp, he sent me a message to keep an eye out for you. He told me all about you. I told Lonzo that there was a hundred to one chance that our paths would ever cross in the Army. Yet here we are."

I just stood there motionless with my mouth wide open. This was the first time I ever heard Lonzo's last name mentioned.

"Lonzo told me that you would be easy to recognize, because you were the spitting image of Lieutenant Victor Masterson, our Platoon Leader in Korea. I couldn't believe my eyes when I saw you. That's why I was staring at you so."

I was stupefied, as he went on. "Milkman, Lonzo has secrets, I have secrets, the Army has secrets, and President Kennedy has more secrets than all of us put together. Many of America's ugly secrets are more troubling and profound than any secret classified as Top Secret by the government. Usually, only the president knows these secrets, and sometimes even he doesn't. Vice President Harry Truman knew nothing about the Manhattan Project until he was president.

There are lots of ugly secrets that would challenge everything I thought I knew about America. No one would ever put these ugly secrets in writing and those who know them usually take them to their graves. If such secrets were ever revealed to you, Milkman, there are three things you could possibly do with them.

One, you could reveal them.

Two, you could take them to your grave.

Three, you could take responsibly for them.

By revealing America's ugly secrets, your actions confirm you are not trustworthy, loyal or honorable no matter how despicable the ugly secrets may be. You are saying to America that your personal interests and ambitions must be placed above everyone's interest in the nation."

I looked at him in confusion, thinking of the foul things that racist Americans did to Black Americans and other peoples and swept it under the rug; especially the foul deeds that were done to Native American peoples here in this country. And he was saying I should keep quiet about it.

"The people who reveal ugly secrets are not usually believed and are written off as crackpots. The revealed secret now becomes a noose around the revealer's neck and the secret, most often, finds another rug to hide under. The revealer immediately becomes a threat to the nation and expendable. Usually, the people you reveal the secrets too are preconditioned not to believe you anyway."

He saw my reaction.

"Don't panic, Milkman. By not revealing the secrets, you take responsibility for them. You put yourself in the driver's seat, a position of action to alter or reverse the results of the ugly secrets as you see fit. In effect, you bring about change without ever revealing a problem existed. I learned this in Korea from Lonzo and LT Masterson. The choice is yours, if you so choose."

"Wolfman, I don't understand what in the hell you are talking about? Are you saying that I must take responsibility for all the foul-shit that America has done to me, my ancestors and other peoples over the past three hundred years, simply, because I want to go Airborne?"

"Yes! I see it in your eyes, Milkman. This is just the start for you, as it started for Lonzo and me long ago, the same way. Ok! Milkman, promise me that you will never reveal an ugly secret or take an ugly secret to your grave without taking responsibly for it."

"Shit, I promise, Wolfman."

"This is an example of what I mean, whether you agree or not, in WWII, the British broke the German's secret code using a captured German Enigma Machine. The British intercepted and deciphered messages traveling from Japan going to Germany that an attack on Pearl Harbor was imminent. They refused to give the information to the United States.

General Marshall received information from his staff that the Japanese fleet was sailing southeast from Japan and its probable destination was Midway or Hawaii. He informed the White House and the Pentagon. No one informed Pearl Harbor. America lost over two thousand men in one day during the Japanese attack on December 7th, 1941.

Now! You say that was a cruel act, first on the part of the British, and second on the part of General Marshall and finally President Roosevelt But, notifying Pearl Harbor that an attack was on the way may have lessened American causalities that day, but it could have cost us the war.

President Roosevelt knew that stopping the attack on Pearl Harbor would have only delayed further America's entry into WWII. Roosevelt and the British knew that stopping the attack may have revealed to the Germans and Japanese that they were able to unlock their secret codes. The outcome of the war may have been much different. Under the isolationist anti-war policies that existed in this country at that time, it was the only way for President Roosevelt to go."

My head was spinning and Wolfman took pity on me.

"I know you have many questions, Milkman, but this is not the time. Tomorrow morning at 0400 hours, you'll get up with the A-team, train with us and we will see if you are airborne material."

Monday morning at 0400 hours the Wolfman, shook me to get up. As I slid out of my bunk, I noticed that John was missing from his bunk. I mentioned it to the Wolfman. He went upstairs into the NCO's section to see if Moran had returned. He wasn't there either.

Doc said, "They must have gotten hold of some serious tail this weekend. Roll call will be at 0730 hours. They will be back by then."

The SF teams put in 4 miles of running every morning. And, that was in fatigues and jump boots. It was still dark and very cool. I guess that's why they liked to run in the early morning. The other SF teams from other training companies were also out running. We were all clad in jump boots, fatigues and white tee shirts. Now the Paratrooper cadence calls that I learned in Basic Training started to mean something.

"Here we go Airborne-here we go Ranger"

I was sounding off good with the group for the first mile or so. Then the sun began to clear the hills. The heat from the asphalt started to raise like that cobra friend of mine.

"Up the hill, down the hill, Airborne, Ranger, living a life of danger." I started to fall back as the hills got taller. The other troopers smiled as they passed me by. The sweat in my clothes began to weigh me down making it more difficult to run. I was losing sight of the group. By the two mile point, the group turned around and headed back towards base passing me by with smirks on their faces.

I was reduced to almost walking wounded at his point. My ass was dragging. I said to myself, I am one hardheaded SOB. I don't listen to anyone, Lonzo, Malcolm X or Sammerson. But, I kept moving, chanting "Gonna-be an Airborne Ranger, Gonna live a life of danger." The more I chanted the more energy I was able to pump into my body. I picked up speed about a half mile from the base's gate. I spotted the tail of the group ahead of me. They were really sounding off now.

Now, my energy level began to feed off the groups chanting. I finally caught up to them at the base gate. They began to wave me on as we all went through the gate together. Then they all ran into the ball field and started doing push-ups, sit-ups, and pull-ups. I didn't even try, I ran right pass them into the barracks. I had finished the four mile run. It was up and down hills, unlike the flat runs I completed in Basic Training. That was my accomplishment for the first day.

0600 hours was approaching, when I got back to the barracks. John and Moran still were not, "*Present and accounted for.*" I wondered if they had got into a fight, with one another, and were locked up by the MPs. When Moran got drunk, those redneck instincts began to surface big time. I took a shower and put on a clean pair of fatigues. I fell out for roll call.

0700 hours, LT Glover called us to attention with a stern face. He started calling names very rapidly without waiting for acknowledgements. When he called John's and Moran's name, he paused, waiting for them to respond with hear or present. He received no response.

I looked at Sammerson. We both knew something was seriously wrong.

LT Glover didn't say anymore. He ordered us left face, and forward march. He marched us in a different direction than we took to get to the Mess Hall. The A-team members and I stared at one another as we marched towards the base hospital. He marched us through the front door of the hospital and down the stairs into the basement. LT Glover ordered us to come to a halt in front of two large stainless steel doors.

A doctor came to the door, his face covered with a surgical mask. He wiped the small window that was frosted over by the low temperature in the room. He looked through the window and nodded his head to the Lieutenant. LT Glover ordered us forward into the large room. There in the middle of the room was a large stainless steel table with an outline of a human body covered by a bloody white sheet. Man, that room was cold.

LT Glover ordered us into a circle around the table. He then nodded to the doctor. The doctor removed the sheet from the body. Some GIs started to vomit, some knees got weak and one fainted. I lowered my head to my chest. As I raised my head, the Wolfman was looking me square in the eyes. I knew what he was thinking, but it was not true, I had nothing to do with this.

LT Glover leaned forward over the body with tears in his eyes and said, "That is Corporal Moran, Doctor, he was a good soldier, but sometimes good soldiers don't always follow orders. I instructed all of you on several occasions to stay out of the west side of San Antonio."

I heard a sound of a motor starting in the background as I glanced down at Moran on the table. The doctor pushed me aside, removed Moran's penis from his mouth and placed it in a tray. He began to cut his skull with the circular saw along a line he previously marked with vegetable ink. LT Glover ordered us to attention.

The doctor began recording his autopsy by stepping on a pedal on the floor underneath the table to start a tape recording machine. "This begins the autopsy of CPL James Moran who was killed on November 22, 1962 by multiple stab wounds to the chest, abdomen and throat. The aorta artery in the neck was also severed by a single cut from the right ear to the left ear."

The doctor then began removing the top of Moran's skull. A few more GIs fainted dead away. I rocked backward as Moran's blood and skin splattered on my face from the circulating saw blade. The doctor recorded that most of the stab wounds were on the right side of the chest and his penis was removed and placed in his mouth.

LT Glover ordered us to remain at attention during the entire autopsy. About two hours later, we all stumbled out of the morgue. We all asked about John. LT Glover said that John was in and out of consciousness in the intensive care unit upstairs. He lost a lot of blood from stab wounds. We all asked if we could be excused to donate blood. LT Glover granted us the OK. The donation room filled up quickly. The nurse told the A-team and me that we must wait to donate.

It hit us like a ton of bricks simultaneously. We all ran for the elevator. John was on the third floor in the intensive care unit. Upon arrival, we asked the nurse if we could see him.

"Only one at a time"

The Wolfman went in first. I could see him bending over talking to John, with John trying to respond. I could see John's eyes and lips move. Listening, Sam nodded his head up and down. I could not contain myself any longer, I ran into John's room with the nurse right on my heels. As I approached his bed, all types of bells, buzzers, and whistles went off like a jailbreak at Leavenworth. John had died.

I grabbed the Wolfman, "What did he say, what did he say to you?"

He said, "Tell the Milkman to stay out of Mexican bars."

The Wolfman went over to the A-team and began talking to them in sign language. They formed a circle to hide their hands as they responded in a full-blown silent discussion. I could see that they didn't want me around at this point. I took no offence as I walked towards the elevators, because these guys were always helping me out when I needed it. But, I would have given a month's pay to find out what they were discussing in sign language.

I loved Malcolm X and I respected him. But, times like this caused me to question his "All white folks are devils theory." There are many screwed-up-in-the-head white folks in this country, but John was not one of them and the same was true for the Wolfman and the A-team. My head began to pound. My eyes began to tear. I couldn't walk straight. John was for real, like a serious Brother on the block, if you know-what-I-mean. Another ugly secret "bites the dust," all white folks are not devils as Malcolm X said.

I needed a mental fix; a change in subject and the funny papers was what I needed. So I walked into the hospital's gift shop and purchased the local newspaper. Most newspapers in the country ran Snuffy Smith, that crazy, moonshine drinking country redneck, whose antics I loved to laugh at.

As I fingered through the paper, I couldn't help, but read the stories concerning Robert Kennedy. The press was criticizing him about the overseas trip he had taken to the Far East. The paper said he handled the leftist students well in Japan who heckled him, but his comments he made in Indonesia about the US involvement in the Mexican American war were downright unpatriotic.

President Kennedy was also taking a lot of heat again about a $100,000 film that was made of his wife Jackie during her trip to India and Pakistan. The paper said the film was propaganda for the Kennedy family at American citizen's expense. Another article said that Kennedy was mismanaging the economy. It said that the 1962-63 fiscal year budgets showed a deficit of $7.8 million instead of a projected $500 million surplus. It said that the total national debt topped $300 billion for the first time in US history. This debt amounted to $1600 for every man, woman, and child in the United States.

The newspaper said dwindling gold reserves were another problem caused by the Kennedy administration. For the last six years, the United States had been paying out more dollars overseas in military, economic aid, investments, and foreign imports than it was getting back in exports of American goods and from other sources.

The total American gold reserves were less than $17 billion dollars and the lowest level since 1939. All of this just added fuel to the fire for Right-Wingers, who were still reeling from Kennedy's decision to send Federalized US Troops to enforce the 14th Amendment at the University of Mississippi.

Before he died, Moran said on several occasions that he would love to put a couple of deer slugs into those Kennedy brothers. Most of his anger was directed at Bobby. He felt Bobby was the true power behind the throne. He felt Bobby was a pink-o double agent. I had heard the same sentiments in basic training. Hot damn, I found Snuffy Smith on page five.

Moran's autopsy was a very sobering experience. It caused me to revisit thoughts concerning life and death and their true meaning. You are here today and gone tomorrow. You will spend more time in a box, buried six feet under the ground than walking the face of this planet above ground. My time on this planet instantaneously started to become very precious. It must not be wasted; why did I join the Army anyway? Was it a waste of time? We were about half-way through our 8 weeks of medic training.

That evening the Wolfman said, "Milkman, your personal training has to pick-up if you still feel you are airborne material."

I replied that it appeared that all I was achieving was getting my ass kicked in a ball field on a nightly basis in place of a bedtime story.

He smiled and reminded me that a good defense is also a good offence. We continued my personal hand to hand combat training. The other A-team members finally revealed to me that the Wolfman had studied under some of the world's best hand to hand combat experts. He had studied knife fighting with British Commando units in England, Tae Kwon Do with a 10th Don Black Belt in Korea, Judo, Kendo (fencing), Kyudo (archery) and Karate with a Sensei at the Shotokan in Japan. In Israel, he had studied Krav Maga with the Mossad, the Israeli Secret Intelligence Service.

One evening I said to the Wolfman, "I think I've figured out you and the A-team members. The first thing I noticed about you was the respect the other SF Teams here have for you guys."

"What else have you figured out, Milkman?"

"That Vecky is the small arms expert on the team, probably a sniper, and probably a good one. He quickly helped me put those banged-up M14s back together in working order.

Deuce is the communications and administrative specialist. He is the first to jump when phones or radios pop off. He also gets the A-team through the Army's red tape and administrative messes. He always gets the supplies, equipment and you guys paid.

The Caveman is the demolitions and transportation man. I have seen him under four different vehicles since I have been here. I have seen him hot wire one of them by lifting it up without a jack. He is built like a Neanderthal and hair grows in the palm of his hands.

Clayben is already a medic, he fixed me up after Moran kicked my ass, and he knows more about this base than anyone on your team, because he's trained here before."

The Wolfman just stared at me with a big grin sticking out from under his pipe.

Now Wolfman, it's my turn to get some answers. Why do they call you the Wolfman? What are you guys really doing here in San Antonio? I don't believe you guys are here for medical training. What are the rest of the ugly secrets concerning you and Lonzo Morgan? In short, Wolfman, who are you guys and what in the hell is going on here?

He just smiled and said, "In due time, Milkman, in due time. You have two weeks to get ready for your Airborne qualifying PT Test. You need to concentrate on that for now."

I smiled, shook my head and assumed my hand to hand combat stance.

***

READY FOR GUARD DUTY

7

The Bitch of Buchenwald

The next segment of our medical training dealt with CBR, chemical, biological and radiological (nuclear) warfare. My antennae were really functioning now.

I learned in the Muslim bookstore that chemical and biological weapons had a long history. Most people think the use of chemical weapons on the battlefield began in WWI with gas. That's not true, after Hannibal was defeated in Africa by the Roman General Sipio in 300 BC; he became a mercenary adviser to anyone who would fight the Romans. In a sea battle against Roman allies, Hannibal ordered venomous snakes placed in olive oil jars and catapulted on to Roman Allies vessels. It took a while for the snakes to have an effect, but it worked-chemical and biological warfare rolled into one.

The Wolfman told me that we had seriously considered the use of chemical weapons on Japan in WWII. China had urged us to use them in retaliation for Japan's use of chemical and biological weapons on Chinese citizens.

Deuce added that General MacArthur made an ugly secret deal with the Japanese. He would forgive most of Emperor Hirohito and Japanese officer's war crimes, if they turned over their research of the hideous biological experiments their Unit 731 conducted on captured American and British soldiers during the war.

Now, I could see why, the United States didn't have any ethical problems conducting inhumane biological experiments using the syphilis bacterium on unsuspecting Black men in Tuskegee, Alabama. After the experiments, they were left to die untreated.

The next morning in our field medical class, LT Glover began the introduction of a female instructor from the Chemical Warfare unit. But, before he finished her introduction, she walked upon the platform and introduced herself.

"Good morning men, I am Captain Margaret Forman." She put on her gas mask and immediately began tossing tear gas grenades at us. The whole class scrambled to put on gas masks. The Wolfman reacted very ferociously. He took off his gas mask and began to curse the captain.

"Do you think this shit is funny or was it you didn't get any last night, which one, bitch?"

She hollered back, "Stand down, sergeant or I'll have you confined to your barracks."

Lt Clover asked Captain Forman, "Do you wish to file charges against SGT Sammerson?"

She said "no."

Choking and coughing from the tear gas, he began to cry. You would expect tears from the tear gas, but his cry was different, his tears were different. They were tears from a fractured soul. I had heard Lonzo cry like that once in his sleep.

The Wolfman refused help from everyone. I couldn't believe what I was seeing, the Wolfman losing his cool. He was always the steadiest guy on the A-team. His reaction to being gassed reminded me of my reaction when I was first gassed in basic training. But, his cry of hurt and fear was much deeper than mine. As the gas dissipated, she began her instruction in biological and chemical warfare. She definitely had our attention now.

"Biological and Chemical Warfare is by far the scariest and most deadly form of warfare. Casualties are usually indiscriminant, very painful and death is very slow in materializing; sometimes taking weeks. It is by far the cheapest form of warfare for the attacker and the costliest form of warfare for his unprepared enemy. Biological and chemical agents produce large numbers of casualties at one time, thereby tying up and consuming massive amounts of military manpower and resources.

"In all wars that preceded WWII, biological agents produced more casualties than any other means of warfare. In many cases, the attacker's hands did not produce the causalities, Mother Nature did. In most cases, ignorance and poor health habits assisted Mother Nature to wreak havoc on military forces.

"Today, the Russians are arming warheads with biological agents – small pox, sleeping sickness, plague, yellow fever and anthrax, to name a few. They are stockpiling viruses such as Westnile, Monkey (HIV) and others that attack the human immune system. Infected mosquitoes and ticks are some of the vehicles used to carry the diseases. Large number of mosquitoes and ticks can be bread infected with these diseases, once released they can destroy entire populations. Today both the US and the USSR are actively engaged in developing thousands of biological agents and vehicles for delivering them. The US Government has tested many of these agents, mostly on animals, but some on humans."

She showed us films of various airborne agents being sprayed from attacking airplanes that immobilized and disoriented American ground forces. The film discussed how effective or ineffective different delivery methods were.

She went on, "The Russians' chemical and biological weapons program is running at full stream. We have discovered over fifty different agents being tested and produced by them. They are testing and manufacturing gases such as nerve and mustard; nine different ones. Nerve gas kills the unprotected soldier in seconds. Mustard agent lingers in the ground for years. Some farmers in France, plowing the earth today, have become contaminated with mustard agents that were delivered by Germans in WWI. You will be taught how to protect yourself, American and Allied fighting forces from these agents."

She finished her first CBR segment by making a veiled snide remark referring to President Kennedy. She hammered, "The Cold War with the USSR is not as cold as it appears. In fact, it is a very hot undeclared war. No one talks about the number of undisclosed casualties that are taken by each side, each year. The missile race with the USSR is hotter than hell on the 4th of July and the United States barely kicked Russia's missiles out of Cuba; barely mind you. Who knows, some of those missiles in Cuba may have had chemical or biological warheads instead of nuclear ones."

She then showed us films of American soldiers on field exercises in Nevada advancing while a nuclear mushroom cloud was still rising above desert. She didn't say when it occurred. She stated it was classified. She added films of the only nuclear explosions ever detonated killing human beings, the bombings of Hiroshima and Nagasaki, Japan. Those films were horrific, 80,000 plus lost their lives instantly at Hiroshima. People were vaporized so quickly that their shadows were burned into the sidewalks and on buildings where they once stood.

The number of burn cases numbered into the hundreds of thousands and the Japanese, too this day, are still counting the dead as they continue die from the after effects.

She said, "A medic can walk on ground zero, five minutes after a thermo-nuclear blast without suffering any ill effects of radiation."

I noticed the Wolfman smile at the other A-team members when she said that.

"Our intelligence services say the Russians plan to use larger bombs on American cities. The 10-megaton plus bomb America used on Hiroshima would be too small for attacking an American city today. The Russians are building the king of thermonuclear weapons known as the Tsar Bomba with an estimated yield of 50 to 100 megatons.

"For battlefield purposes, smaller nuclear weapons are more effective. We call them Tactical Nukes. The Red Stone, Honest John, and Corporal missiles, are the latest in our own arsenal, they can deliver a 10-megaton blast or higher with-in a range of 200 miles.

"The smallest nuclear weapon in the American tactical arsenal is the David Crocket; its warhead is classified-top secret. It can be fired from a Jeep mounted recoilless rifle. The David Crockett is assigned to division commanders. These weapons would be very effective against mass troop formations, like Russian tanks. In Europe, the Russians outnumber Americans four-to-one in tanks. The David Crockett and his friends are our equalizers."

She told us, "We learned a great deal from the casualties of the nuclear blasts at Hiroshima and Nagasaki. In general, after you treat the burn and blast wounds, the difficult part begins with radiation wounds. Radiation is a very slow killer. The heat and blast itself can be stopped by well-fortified structures like well-buried caves and tunnels, but the radiation will still penetrate solid obstacles for miles pass the blast.

"Always remember that there will be no winner in a nuclear conflict, she said." "The conflict will be hot and heavy for about two or three days. Then the entire planet will become a radiological wasteland. The radiation will eventually kill most humans in a matter of weeks, even those who claimed to have won the conflict." As she ended her presentation, I became more uneasy about why I joined the Army and my future on this planet.

After chow, the Caveman, met me at the ball field for our usual workout and said,

"Milkman, the US Army hides a lot of lies and BS in the middle of the truth. Like some of the BS, the captain was shoveling today. The United States learned very little concerning maneuvering troops on a nuclear battlefield from the Atomic Bombs dropped on Japan. No American ground forces were involved on the ground to learn anything. That's why they tested A-bombs on American troops in the Nevada desert.

"The film you saw today was the 'Little Feller 1' exercises-war games of July 17, 1962 when the Army test fired our smallest nuclear weapon, the Davy Crocket, from a recoilless rifle."

He gave a short laugh. "But there's a small problem with the weapon. It is supposed to be a variable yield weapon; meaning the operator is supposed to dial up the yield of the weapon before firing and denotation. They dialed up a 10 megaton yield and upon donation, it yielded 18 megatons. In an actual battlefield scenario, the soldiers firing the weapon would have been killed, because they would have been too close to the 18 megaton explosion.

"After the blast, about 1000 Soldiers of the 4th Infantry Division advanced onto ground zero; on foot and in tanks. Soldiers are still getting sick from the radiation effects of that explosion. Some are expected to die, because of it. It was the last atmospheric nuclear test by the United States of America. The captain lied about the health effects of radiation on those troops involved. Milkman, don't believe you will survive at Ground Zero five minutes after a nuclear blast. They will be eating you instead of roast turkey for chow that night.

"Just a footnote, Milkman, Robert Kennedy and General Maxwell D. Taylor viewed the test in person. Why was the attorney general supervising an American nuclear test? Another ugly secret, Milkman, a trusted America president and his brother will also deceive you."

He told me the entire A-team was really pissed with the BS of today's class and that's why they were correcting so many of America's ugly secrets concerning nuclear weapons.

When the Wolfman arrived, I walked over to him. "Don't feel bad, man, I lost it also while being gassed for the first time in basic training."

He began to rock back and forth without saying a word.

I was stunned. "What's up, are you all right?"

He reached into his back pocket and pulled out a little black hat, a Yarmulke. He placed it on his head and started to mumble to himself. Then he turned and looked me straight in the eyes and began telling me his story.

"Milkman, I am Jewish, I met SGT Lonzo Morgan on April 11, 1945 in Germany. Lonzo's tank platoon was liberating the Buchenwald death camp. I was there. I was 16 years old, almost your age, and near death from starvation when Sergeant Lonzo's tanks rolled through the gates. I was delirious and I thought those tall black figures were angels of death coming to consume me in my final hour on this earth. I never had seen a Negro before. They handed me little packets of chocolate, but I was too weak to put them in my mouth. They hand fed me for two days before they were ordered to move on. SGT Lonzo's platoon adopted me, introduced me to Jewish resettlement organizations which helped me get to America. Lonzo sponsored me at a group home for young holocaust survivors in Manhattan. When I turned 18, I joined the Army, sought out Lonzo and volunteered to serve with him in Korea.

"I lost my parents, both of my brothers and one sister to the Death Camps. My family name was Sammerstein, but I changed it to Sammerson after I arrived in America. I now wish I hadn't changed my name, but with the work I do now, it's for the best.

My native language was German, I was German and my parents were also Germans, so we all thought. I learned Hebrew from my parents. I learned English after

I arrived in America from Lonzo and even picked up his Harlem street-accent trying hard to lose my German accent. I learned Spanish in the group home on the Lower Eastside. I speak about 9 different languages now. My language skills and my Korean combat experience got me an invitation to join the first Special Forces units being developed at Fort Bragg, North Carolina."

My eyes, already wide, got even wider, when SGT Sammerson said he remembered his first knife fight. "Lonzo and I cut up two Soul Brothers in a bar in Korea over a Korean bar maid."

"I knew there was something about you the first day I arrived at Fort Sam Houston. The way you looked at me... I saw something dark deep inside you, Wolfman."

"It's difficult to hide," he said simply.

"Lonzo never mentioned you by name, other than to say he liberated a Jewish concentration camp in Germany in his tank."

"Ah, yes. The Mighty Mouse"

He stroked me on the shoulder, "Milkman, as I said before, everyone has their ugly secrets, Lonzo has his, I have mine, America has hers and you will have yours. Lonzo only revealed the pleasant things in his life. My story is not pleasant, Milkman. I still smell the excrement the inmates released all over themselves as they fought for the last breath of their lives. I still smell the lingering odor of the gas used to kill them and the constant stench of burning bodies in the crematoriums.

"The German Guards at the camp promised me my life if I calmed the incoming Jews and carried their bodies from the gas chambers to the crematoriums. I was a

'Sonderkommando,' a Special Commando. I had to be very careful, because the Zyklon B gas was still escaping from the lungs of the dead as I moved them."

He paused, lost in very dark memories. Finally he went on.

"It took about fifteen minutes to kill everyone in the death chamber. The guards knew when the people where dead, because their screaming and scratching on the chamber's doors stopped. They waited a half-hour before they opened the doors. After we removed their gold rings, we pulled their gold teeth. We then inspected vaginas and rectums for hidden valuables. Then we pulled out the bodies and took them to the crematoriums. Sometimes we were given gas masks, rubber gloves and meat hooks, but the gas masks filters soon turned yellow and stopped working. The gloves were full of holes and the meat hooks wore dull from moving thousands of bodies."

He stopped again, then went on.

"Karl Adolf Eichmann visited the death camp with the Red Cross. Yes, the Red Cross."

"Who was he?"

"He was Hitler's homeboy from Linz, Austria, and head of the Jewish Office of the Gestapo. They made us clean the camp before he came. They gave us baths and new clothes so the stench of the inmates and camp wouldn't offend him or the Red Cross inspectors. I celebrate the anniversary of his death each month. The Israeli Mossad captured, tried and hung his retched ass on May 31st this year, God rest his retched soul."

Then he pulled up his left fatigue jacket sleeve and he showed me his Army serial number tattooed on his lower arm. I looked at it and then I raised my eyes in confusion.

"Look at it carefully, Milkman."

I lowered my eyes and pulled his arm closer. I could see that some of the numbers were different in form from the others. The lettering, height and color of the figures were not consistent. Some numbers appeared written over or altered.

"To this day, I wake up in the middle of the night, in a cold sweat, after dreaming about being gassed to death by the Bitch of Buchenwald."

"Who?"

"Frau Ilse Koch, the Bitch of Buchenwald, she was the wife of the commandant of the death camp. Crossing her very whim would bring severe punishment and most often death to any inmate. She decorated her home with our body parts. Her prized processions were lampshades she had made from the tattooed skins of murdered Jewish inmates."

I didn't know what to say, so I said nothing.

"After moving dead bodies all day from the gas chambers to the crematoriums, I stumbled from exhaustion and over turned a wheel-cart. I was so tired that I simply lay on top of the still-warm bodies and fell asleep. I felt someone pick up my arm. I opened my eyes and it was her looking for tattoos on my arm. She told me to take off my clothes. It was 20 degrees out, but I didn't hesitate. She inspected every inch of my body for any tattoos or unusual markings. When she finished she said to me, "Get dressed, if I see you sleeping at work again I will personally drop the pellets on you. Verstehen sie mich? (You understand me?)"

"Her Jewish skin lampshades were prized all over Germany. She shipped them out as fast as she could, but they were always on back order. Her prize lampshade was the skin tattoo of Hansel and Gretel. It's funny, Milkman, the SS, executed her husband for excesses. Can you believe that shit, for excesses?"

He then said a strange yet provocative thing to me.

"Milkman, sometimes I wish my parents had been slaves like your great grandparents."

My eyes got big again.

"Slaves were valuable property. You were bought, sold, insured, traded and bequeathed in wills. The more skills you acquired, the more valuable you were to your owners. Jews in Germany and Europe during WWII had no value, respective of our skills, education, financial status or commitment to the Fatherland. We were only excrement, to be worked to death in menial labor camps or better yet exterminated."

"Both of my parents were doctors and if they were American slaves, they would still be alive. No matter how poorly slaves were treated in America, you lived, Milkman, you survived. Be thankful; be thankful that your people and their descendants are still alive. Be thankful that you are still here and able to raise the righteous hell in America, addressing your right to be first class citizens."

"You are still alive, Wolfman."

"Yep, and I owe it all to SGT Lonzo Morgan and the Mighty Mouse. You know Milkman, Two Feathers described him this way, "Him tall like pine tree, him black like coal, him talk more shit than radio.""

I laughed.

Deuce was listening, he smiled and said, "The Wolfman is right, be thankful, Milkman, be thankful. Government agents gave blankets infected with small-pox to my people. Whole tribes were wiped out. There were 10 million of my people here in North America when the White Eyes arrived. Now, there are less than two million of us left. Those blankets could have been given to your people."

The Wolfman went on, "To add insult to injury, Milkman, it was a Jewish captain in the German Army that invented those hideous gases that eventually killed over nine million of his own people."

I looked at him strangely.

"Yes, a Jewish Captain in the German Army in WWI actually invented Zyklon B, the gas used to kill millions of Jews and other 'inferior' people. His name was Fritz Haber. He converted to Christianity in order to please his German superiors. He brown nosed his way into becoming an officer in the German Army. The German high command did not think much of Captain Fritz or his poison gases as a weapon. On April 22, 1915, Captain Fritz opened the valves of his poison gas on British troops and caused 10,000 causalities. The Germans did not realize they were victorious in battle until it was too late. When Britain matched his inventions with their own poison gas, he upped the ante by developing Mustard gases, Farsgenes and Zyklon B."

"His wife, Clara, was totally distraught by his activities committed suicide. He died in 1934 after being rebuked by the Nazis. His fellow Jewish assistants were all sent to concentration camps and killed by the same gas that they had invented and perfected. Too much trust in your own people can lead to your death, Milkman. I know; I lead thousands of my own people to their deaths. I committed the ultimate betrayal. Milkman, I am not going to hell, because I am already there. I live there each night during my sleep."

I was paralyzed now. I wanted him to stop. My head was pounding. The next blow sent me into orbit.

"I heard Malcolm X speak about Jews one afternoon and what he said about my people was so true. He said, "That history's most tragic result of mixed, therefore diluted and weaken ethic identity, has been experienced by the German Jews, even though they made greater contributions to Germany than Germans themselves. Jews won over half of Germany's Nobel Prizes. Jews led every culture in Germany. A Jew published the greatest newspaper. Jews were the greatest scientist, artists, the greatest composers and stage directors. But, he said Jews made the fatal mistake of assimilating; and he was right. We were increasingly intermarrying. Many of us changed our names and took on other religions. We denied our own rich Jewish religion, our Jewish ethnic and cultural roots. We began to think of themselves as only Germans and not as Jews. Our self-brainwashing was so complete that long after the gas chambers, a lot of us were still gasping, "It can't be true, it can't be true."

He did not talk anymore about the Holocaust. I was pleased, because my soul had taken an awful beating. I told him I had a confession to make. I didn't think it was a good time, but I had to make some contribution to the ugly secrets being placed on the table no matter how meager mine were.

I told him that in my younger days, my friends and I would ride the subway downtown looking for Jewish boys on the train. If we found any, we would rough them up by taking their Yarmulkes, Shawls and lunch money; just for the fun of it, because we knew they would not fight back. After I spoke, I sensed that this was definitely not the right time to tell him that. He gave me a brief glance in silence. He said no more, so we just sat there, on the bench, counting the stars.

The next morning in class Captain Forman, our CBR warfare instructor, now dubbed by the Wolfman and the A-team as, "The Bitch of Buchenwald," apologized for gassing us without warning. She said, "In combat, men, you'll never receive a warning of a gas attack. In WWII, the British were the first to try to use gas in an attack. It blew back on their forces and it was a disaster. They never tried it again."

The Wolfman had not spoken to me for two days. He was still in a bad mood, possibly from being gassed or possibly my telling him that I once kicked Jewish kids in the ass and took their lunch money. On our third day in CBR class, he told me to meet him and the A-team on the ball field that evening. I was very relieved that things were on the "up-and-up" again between him and me; so I thought.

That evening, I walked out to the ball field looking for him and the A-team. It was quiet and not a soul in sight. Someone had turned out most of the lights on the pathway. I heard a funny noise like a cricket, but I couldn't tell where it was coming from. No one was on the bench where we usually sat. But, I kept hearing this cricket noise. I walked over to the bench and I threw a candy wrapper into the garbage can. I saw nothing. I then turned around and leaned against the garbage can, trying to identify where the sound was coming from.

All of a sudden, this arm locked around my neck. "So, you like to kick defenseless Jewish kids in the ass, huh."

He had been hiding in the garbage can. I immediately went to work with what he taught me. I pulled my legs up to my chest causing all my bodyweight to rest on his arms. My weight caused him to lean forward. I then regained my footing with my hip below his and flipped him out of the garbage can, but he landed on his feet.

He was dressed all in black with a blacken face. That didn't faze me. He came at me again. I picked up a handfull of dirt and threw it up in the air. He ran directly into it blinding himself. I side stepped him and kicked him in the back of his knee. He went down and I picked up the garbage can and held it above his head. He held up his hand in submission and the other A-team members came running from nowhere applauding, stating that I was ready.

Ready for what, I replied?

They all laughed and walked me back to the barracks.

Later that evening in the barracks, the Wolfman walked up on me listening to my portable radio with my head bobbing like candy apples at a Halloween party. The Latin Jazz music from the local radio station was really kicking. His spirits had definitely picked up.

He said, "Now that's what I miss about New York City"

I turned and looked at him as if he was crazy as he went into his Latin dance steps. He continued,

"Symphony Sid, The Allegro All-stars, Joe Cuba, and of course the King, Tito Puente. I lost my cherry listening to Tito's music; just around the corner from 111th St. where he lived."

"Whooh, you Latin, Wolfman?"

"I Latin, Milkman. As slow as you are with your hands Milkman, I wonder why they called you Fast Eddie back on the block."

"Let me get my pool stick, Wolfman and I will show you why."

The Wolfman went into his footlocker and pulled out a new Latin album. "Here," he said, "it is by Compay Segundo."

I said, "I never heard of him

"I picked it up on sale in the PX. He is a Cuban legend and one of the originators of Salsa. Milkman, I never figured you for a Latin Jazz fan, most of the Soul Brothers in the Army don't know anything about this music. It is like it didn't exist in Harlem or on the planet."

"Yeah, man, a lot of Black people don't know much about Jazz or Blues either and that's our own music; also. I spent many a night, with my girl Jenny, on the dance floor kicking to this music man."

The Wolfman got so excited about the music that he started dancing again and speaking to me in Spanish.

I stopped him, "I don't speak Spanish, Wolfman, my girlfriend Jenny spoke both Spanish and English, Man. Please speak English. I prefer to talk to people in English.

"I know, Milkman, you talk too much."

"You know, Wolfman, English isn't my native tongue. I don't know what my native tongue is, because you white folks snatched my parents from underneath a coconut tree in Africa, enslaved us, bought us here, and separated us from our true culture and language."

"Whooh, don't blame that shit on me, Milkman. I barely made it to America alive myself running from white folks. If you think white folks are mean to Black folks, just pay attention to what they do to other white folks."

I smiled, "You have a point, Wolfman, and that is another ugly secret. I like all kinds of music as long as it moves you and is hip."

"I may have a few years on you, young blood, but I am surly not dead yet. I know you and Malcolm X were buddies. But, Mr. History Buff, many decent righteous white folks gave a lot of themselves, including their lives; so you and I could stand here and have this conversation. Think about it, you can't make a statement like that to me without losing a part of your ass. I lost my native land also, Milkman. Celebrate where you are going and only remember where you came from."

"Wolfman, if you don't know where you came from, you won't know where you are going." He was becoming agitated again, so I tried to change the subject. "Still, if you have a pool stick and some money to loose, I will show you how bad I am."

"Lights out," the guard said.

The guards who didn't make Supernumerary had to make the rounds checking the barracks, looking for possible fires, etc. The GIs were allowed to smoke in the barracks, but not in their beds. Some of the guys were careless, so guards checked out sleeping GIs very carefully at lights-out. I picked up the album from my bed and placed it in my footlocker, as I did, I noticed the label. It said, made in the Republic of Cuba. I turned to ask the Wolfman if the PX was allowed to sell imported products from Cuba, but the lights went out.

***

8

The Monkey Dance

The next day was Friday the 13th. The entire A-team approached me saying they wanted me to join them for a couple of beers that evening. We just finished up our CBR warfare segment. We didn't have any homework or reading assignments for the weekend. I said fine.

"1700 hours, no civvies; Class-A uniforms only"

"Why are we going into town in our dress uniforms?"

They repeated, "Class A's."

My mother repeatedly told me, "It was curiosity that killed the cat." I should have said I wasn't feeling well or something. I pressed my khaki uniform, spit shinned my low-quarters shoes and stuck my Garrison Cap in the shoulder strap of my shirt.

I was standing in front of the barracks when they all walked up. They were glistening. They had on their green berets, airborne wings, service ribbons, and spit shined jump boots. No one carried anything, but Vecky and Wolfman. Vecky had a long sack with something heavy in it and Wolfman carried a paper bag, which contained something that rattled.

We all packed into a souped-up 1960 yellow Chevy convertible that I hadn't seen them in before. It smelled like alcohol. I asked, where in the hell did you get this car from? The Caveman replied, he borrowed it from a Moonshiner. Then he proceeded to drive to downtown San Antonio. I had an ugly feeling.

All of a sudden, the Caveman pulled off to the side of the road and said to me, "We are going to see if you're Special Forces material tonight, Milkman. We are going to the Monkey Show and do the Monkey Dance."

The Wolfman chimed in, "Your assignment is very simple, Milkman. If things get out of hand, there is a 6 foot long solid oak table in the middle of the bar room. You go and hide under that table. Do not come out for any reason except one. If anyone pulls a pistol, you pick up that oak table with the top two legs over your shoulders and the bottom two legs in your hands and you ram the shit out of the shooter with that table."

I shouted, "What? Let me out of this damn car."

The Caveman pulled off and he didn't stop until we arrived in downtown San Antonio. The Caveman slowed down and the Wolfman said, "This goes for everyone, under no circumstances does anyone leave the bar through the front door. It's the back door or through the front window, understood. Milkman, I know you have been picking up our sign language, so pay attention to my hands at all times."

I smiled as the sweat began to pour down my face. The Caveman then hit the accelerator again with the Wolfman and A-team singing a familiar tune.

"Put on your red dress baby, cause we're going out tonight. Put on your high heel sneakers, cause we're monkey dancing tonight."

The Caveman zigzagged through the back streets until we arrived in the Mexican red light section on the west side of San Antonio. The street was alive with music coming out of the bars and whorehouses. To our surprise there were a few soldiers in uniform on the street. None of them should have been there.

The Wolfman nodded. The Caveman drove pass a small dinky bar. The sign said Quarto Rosa, (the Four Roses). The bar was alive with the locals drinking and partying. The Wolfman tapped the Caveman on the shoulder and he pulled into the alley across the street. We all piled out of the Chevy.

Vecky went into the trunk and took out his bag and he remained with the car. Wolfman collected all of our black Army nametags and put them in a bag on the seat of the car. He handed everyone a pair of very dark sunglasses and told us to put them on. He went into the bar first, laughing and teasing the working girls standing in the front of the bar.

A big burly Mexican was standing in the doorway. He wouldn't move as we walked in. The Caveman pushed him out of the way. The big SOB started to move toward us, but the bartender told him to stop in Spanish. We all walked to the center of the bar. Doc ordered drinks for everyone. The Wolfman signed to us not to drink them. The Wolfman walked to the middle of bar room. There were two women were sitting at the oak table he mentioned. He sat down with them and started a conversation in Spanish. He ordered an unopened bottle of liquor and had it placed in the center of the oak table.

He signed to me; "This is the table I was talking about." I signed backed that I understood and then I turned around and faced the bar. I could see Wolfman's hand movements in the mirrors. The Caveman sat down with the Wolfman and the two women.

A real short Mexican girl approached me saying she was a good time girl. She wasn't more than 12 years old. Wolfman's hands were below the table waving me off.

I said to her, "No dinero." She understood that quickly and moved on.

Then two Mexican guys came over to the bar and started a conversation with me in English. I smiled, as they asked me where was I from? I said New York. We began to talk about the New York Yankees.

Wolfman signed me to get the guy on my right to smile. I wondered why, he wanted the guy to smile? I told jokes, but they were not funny to him. The guy wouldn't smile. So, Wolfman got up, came over to me and said to the guy in Spanish. "He's a young rooster and we are going to buy him his first hens tonight."

The guy broke into a hardy laugh showing four gold teeth in the front of his mouth. We all laughed and Wolfman asked the other guy, "Where did you get that tattoo on your arm from."

The guy said, "I took it off a dead soldier."

We all laughed again. Wolfman signed to Deuce, who was nursing a beer at the front of the bar, to follow him into the bathroom, which was at the end of the hall near the bar's rear door. About five minutes had passed then Deuce walked out of the bathroom. He walked over to the oak table where the Caveman was sitting with the women and started to argue with him over the women. By that time, Doc joined me at the bar with the two Mexican guys. Doc bumped me into the two Mexican guys. The Mexican spilled his drink on his friend.

He said to Doc, "Maricon." I knew what that meant in Spanish. The shit was about to hit the fan now. I tried to get out of the way and under that table in the middle of the room as soon as possible. One Mexican swung at Doc; he ducked and came back with an elbow to his throat. The other Mexican pushed me into Doc and pulled out his knife to get at him. Doc used me for a shield.

The tactic confused the Mexican for a split second, then he got smart and he came at me with the knife. Doc pushed me to the left and the guy followed me. He moved to the right, side stepped him and kicked him in the kidneys with his steel plated jump boots. Then he arm locked his knifed hand and pulled the guy's arm completely over his shoulder breaking it in the process. The guy hollered and stumbled towards the bar. Then the bartender tried to hand him something in his good hand.

I walked across four chairs, heading for the oak table where the girls were sitting. The Caveman punched one of the girls, square in the jaw. She went out like a light. The other girl grabbed the whiskey bottle on the table and broke it over its side. As I slid under the table, she poked the broken bottle at me.

Suddenly, all the lights in the whole joint went out. The only available light came from the sign of the flea bag hotel across the street. I kept kicking chairs in the girl's way so she couldn't get to me under the table. I finally figured out why we were wearing sunglasses and pulled them off.

Then, this striped face figure appeared out of the bathroom. His silhouette looked like the Wolfman. He had some type of a long chain or chain saw blade in his hand. He lashed it around the girl's hand holding the broken bottle and pulled. She let out a horrible scream. Her hand went flying under the table where I was. Her blood was shooting from her arm splattering everywhere.

The guy with the four gold teeth came at Wolfman with a machete. Like lighting, the Caveman placed a black wire with handles around his neck and in a flash, his entire head popped off.

The patrons in the bar started to run for the front door out of horror. I heard automatic gunfire piercing the darkness from outside at the front door. Bullets were ricocheting off the sidewalk like raindrops. The bar patrons simply crammed back in the doorway, they were forced to watch the fight, because they could not get out of the bar. They were hollering, screaming and begging God for their lives in Spanish.

Then the tattooed guy, who's arm was broken, started to fire a pistol that he received from the bartender into the darkened room with his good hand. He couldn't see what he was firing at.

When the fight started everyone on the A-team took off their sunglasses, but me. When the lights went out their eyes were already adjusted to the dark. The Mexicans could only see shadows and flashes of individuals moving around. Now, I could see them good now. He mistakenly fired two shots into two bar patrons that stood next to me.

I was late on my cue, and I didn't know if I could do it. Blood was spurting everywhere from the handless woman and the guy who lost his head. I was so frighten that I started to hyperventilate. The A-team members were diving for cover on the blood filled floor along with the other bar patrons.

I managed to get to my knees and pushed up on the table. He saw me immediately and started to fire at me point blank. The oak table was stopping the small caliber bullets. That table was heavy, but I ran towards him as if four white policemen from Harlem were chasing me.

When the table hit him, the breath from every bean he ate in the past five years came out of his gut. I pinned him against the bar. His fat stomach collapsed as he coiled up like a spring. Then like the speckled Cobra that almost sent me to Nirvana, his body released its tension causing the table and me to recoil backwards. His entire body followed the table off the bar. The gun popped loose from this hand. He fell on top of the table with me lying pinned underneath. Then the striped-faced phantom pounced on his neck like a great white shark eating its first meal.

All I could see were his legs and arms hanging from the sides of the table convulsing and grimacing. Blood began to shoot everywhere. There was a fierce struggle for life going on the top of the table above me. I finally pushed enough chairs out of the way to roll out from underneath the table. As I rose, I could see the soles of a pair jump boots tightly gripping the floor. I saw the back of an army uniform holding a tattooed sponge of a man down by his throat. Blood continued to spurt in every direction. Then the lights suddenly came back on in the bar.

It was Wolfman eating the Mexican's throat out with a set of titanium incisor teeth in his mouth. Blood continued to spurt everywhere. I tapped him gingerly on his ass to let him know I was OK and to stop killing the Mexican. He didn't stop. The guy he pinned was kicking and gasping for air. Wolfman wouldn't let him go. The Wolfman put a death lock on his throat and upper body.

I backed off looking into the eyes of the bar patrons that could not escape, because of the automatic weapon fire Vecky was blanketing against the door outside. There was horror and silence in the bar as the tattooed mound went limp. I turned to find another exit, but the bartender was pointing a gun directly at me that he picked up from the floor; sheer horror filled his eyes.

The Wolfman continued to eat without lifting his head, grunting and groaning in the process with blood running from his mouth like the flow of the Texas Red River. The other members of the A-team were ready to pounce on the bartender. The bartender knew he couldn't shoot us all without one of us reaching him first.

The Wolfman finally stopped and held up two fingers in the form of a V. He did so without lifting his head to see if the bartender was going to fire his pistol at him. The Bartender began to tremble worse than I did. The Wolfman finally lifted his head from the tattooed giant's throat. I could see the titanium incisor teeth in his mouth reechoing with blood. Wolfman's face was now completely painted with red blood, black and green camouflage paint in a hideous pattern. As he turned toward the bartender, the bartender dropped the gun.

The woman who was sitting at the table with Wolfman was still screaming holding her handless arm. A bar patron began to rip her dress making a tourniquet for it. Wolfman walked over to the bar placed a twenty dollar bill on its corner.

He then grabbed a chair and threw it through the front window. He signed to us to follow him through it. We heard sirens in the distant. I could barely walk, because I was shaking so badly. He helped me through the window. Vecky pulled up in front of the bar and we all piled into the Chevy. The Caveman got into the back seat and fired a few rounds into the air from Vecky's M1 carbine as we drove off.

No one said a word until we were about a mile from the base. Vecky pulled off to the side of the road and Deuce told everyone to get undressed. He placed everyone's bloody uniform in a shopping bag and then into the trunk of the car. He gave everyone their name tags back and a clean pair of fatigues to put on.

We all piled back into the Chevy and drove onto the base singing, "Put on your red dress baby," all accept me. The guard on duty simply waved us through the gate. Wolfman slapped everyone five and said, "Low-tec kicks high-tec's ass at the Monkey Show."

I was still shaking like a leaf as we approached the barracks. Wolfman stopped and told me to put my head between my legs and take a few deep breaths.

"You did well, Milkman, you did well. We only critique the bad missions. The good ones we never talk about again. Dead men do talk, John and Moran gave us all the information we needed to locate and identify those rats that attacked and killed them.

"The autopsy showed that Moran was stabbed by a left-handed person who was shorter than he was. I watched the tattooed one pick up his drink in the bar, he was left handed. John told me, before he died; that the guy with four gold teeth and the one with that tattoo did them in. And, it was the girl who lost her hand that set them up. I don't think that any more GIs are going to die in that bar or on that side of town.

"If anymore asks, we dropped you off in town, you went to the movies at The Old Nickel Theatre that we passed on the way to the bar. What movie was playing, Milkman?"

"Gone With the Wind, Wolfman."

"Good, I wanted to see if you were still asleep. You know, you went to sleep under that table in the bar."

I smiled.

As I pulled back my GI blanket to get into my bunk, I wondered what in the hell have I gotten myself into. I had just helped a group of crazy-ass GIs kill at least two Mexicans, if not more, and maim many more. It was a difficult sleep that night.

The next morning about 0400 hours, Wolfman tapped me on my shoulder for our run. I simply grunted and rolled back over. I fell out for formation at 0700 hours with the rest of the medic trainees. LT Glover was standing in the front of the formation with two MPs. I started to sweat. I looked at Wolfman's poker face as LT Clover brought us to attention.

"Gentlemen, two Mexican Nationals were killed and others were wounded in a restricted bar in San Antonio last night. Eyewitnesses state that the killers wore US Army uniforms and green berets. The Newspapers reported that one of the soldiers was a demon, with a red, black and green face, that sucked all the blood out of one of the victim's body. Automatic weapons were fired. Although no one was shot by the alleged soldiers, they were five NCOs and one light skinned Negro private involved in the assault. The private told one patron that he was from New York."

LT Glover began to walk up and down the formation. He stopped in front of the only other light skinned Soul Brother from New York in our training company. He looked him straight in the eyes and said, "Are you from New York, Private Dickinson?" Then he stopped in front of me, looked me straight in the eyes and asked. "Are you from New York, Private Roy?"

"If the individuals who committed these hideous crimes come forward now, I will do everything in my power to assist them in getting the best treatment. If not, I will turn the matter over to the Military Policemen standing here for resolution. Those who were involved please step forward."

The sweat was pouring off my face, but I didn't move forward. He ordered the formation to fall out for class except Dickinson and myself. The MPs escorted both of us into the lieutenant's office. There was a captain and two lieutenant colonels in the room. Both of us were asked to sit down in chairs placed in the middle of the room.

The captain spoke first, "One of you guys committed murder last night along with five other Special Forces NCOs, and it's all over the newspapers. The problem privates is that both of you are from New York and only one of you did it. Which one of you did it? Now, we know that John Colbert and James Moran were attacked and killed near or in the same bar a few weeks earlier. We understand that you were probably settling a righteous score for them. Just tell us what happened and we will do our very best for you. Private Roy, where were you last night? You were seen leaving the base with other Special Forces NCOs."

"Yes, Sir, I asked for a ride into town. They dropped me off at the movie house. I don't remember their names, Sir."

"What movie was playing Private Roy?"

"Gone With the Wind, Sir."

"What was the name of Clark Gable's character?"

"Rhett Butler, Sir."

"What was the real name of maid's character?"

"Hattie McDaniels, Sir, I believe she was the first Negro to win an academy award for a supporting role."

"Dickerson where were you?"

"I was at the EM Club, Sir."

"Here on base?"

"Yes, Sir."

"So, neither one of you were involved in these murders?"

"No, sir"

"I am going to give you both a few days to think about your answers, I suggest that one of you come clean. Both of you are restricted to base until otherwise notified. Next week, both of you will be visiting one of the victims in the hospital for identification. You're dismissed."

As I walked into the class, I looked at the A-team with disdain. The medical classes proceeded to cold weather injuries, frostbite and hypothermia, etc. They appeared uninterested, as if they already knew the material. It appeared to me that I was taking all the heat for us going to the Monkey Show and doing the Monkey Dance. No one said a thing to me all day, because they knew I was in an ugly mood. They continued to whisper very intently among themselves about something.

The next morning I got up at 0400 and ran with the team. I tried to tell Wolfman what was going on with the MPs and me. He simply put his finger to his mouth, and said in a harsh voice, "Don't worry about it," and ran ahead of me.

"Milkman," Deuce said, "It's time for the A-team to jump for our extra fifty five dollar per month. We want you to come; we're going teach you how to jump."

"The last time I went some place with you guys, I learned a hell of a lot more than I intended too and I almost didn't come back."

Doc had injured his leg in the fight. If he went on sick call, he would bring attention to himself. He started to fall back from the SF teams as we ran. I fell back with him and he asked me, "Milkman, do you have a problem with the A-team or something?"

"I am very upset with the team for not telling me that you planned to kill those Mexicans."

"It was righteous, don't worry about it, it's not a real problem."

"Doc, it is a problem, I am about to have my ass roasted."

He replied, "You don't want to know what the real problem is, Milkman. Everyone on the A-team is just as edgy as you are about something else."

"Something bigger than what we did in San Antonio?"

"The west side of SA was light stuff compared to what is on our plate now."

I left it alone at that point. The next Friday, we got up before daybreak and drove over to Lackland AFB, They told me to put on Doc's fatigue shirt and make his pay jump for him, because he had injured his leg. There, I took a few practice jumps from a tower used to train pilots on how to eject from airplanes. Then we marched over to the runway where C130s were parked. There were a lot of paratroopers making their money jumps. Someone must have told them I was a cherry, because they broke out in the Airborne Song, "Blood upon the Risers." It's sung to the tune of the Battle Hymn of the Republic.

"He was just a cherry trooper and he surely shook with fright, as he checked on all his equipment and made sure his pack was tight, he had to sit and listen to the awful engines roar

Chorus:

And he ain't gonna jump no more.

Glory, Glory what a helluva way to die,

Glory, Glory what a helluva way to die,

Glory, Glory what a helluva way to die,

And he ain't gonna jump no more.

"Is everybody happy?" cried the sergeant looking up, our hero feebly answered "yes" and then they stood him up, he leapt right out into the icy blast his static line unhooked

Chorus:

He counted long, he counted loud, he waited for the shock, he felt the wind, he felt the clouds, he felt the awful drop, he jerked his cord, the silk spilled out and wrapped around his legs,

Chorus:

The riser wrapped around his neck, connectors cracked his dome, the lines were snarled and tied in knots around his skinny bones; the canopy became his shroud he hurtled to the ground

Chorus:

The days he'd live, loved and laughed kept running through his mind, he thought about the girl back home, the one he'd left behind, he thought about the medics and wondered what they'd find

Chorus:

The ambulance was on the spot the Jeeps were running wild, the medics jumped and scream with glee, they rolled their sleeves and smiled, for it had been a week or more since the last a 'chute had failed,

Chorus:

He hit the ground the sound was SPLAT! The blood went spurting high, his comrades all were heard to say, "A helluva way to die," he lay there rolling round and round in the welter of his gore,

Chorus:

There was blood upon the risers there were brains upon the chute, guts and entrails were hanging from his Paratrooper boots, for he'd caught himself a streamer and he landed on his snoot

Chorus:

Deuce sat down next to me smiling seeing that I wasn't fazed and had enjoyed the song.

As the plane began to taxi, the noise became almost unbearable. Vecky squeezed in tight next to me and he picked up the conversation revealing more of the A-team's ugly secrets. He began where he had left off when we were cleaning rifles.

"My old man was always in and out of jail all the time. My family life went from feast to famine, on a daily basis, depending on whether or not father was in jail."

"What did you do to help the family out, Vecky?"

In a sarcastic tone he said, "What in the hell do you think I did, Milkman, become a priest? My family was always preaching that family honor was the most important virtue on the earth. They said family honor was more important than honoring one's country. That was bullshit, Milkman. I took out two cousins in the name of honor, over bullshit, money bullshit. I grew tired of killing cousins, uncles and friends, Milkman; all in the name of honor. It wasn't honor, it was greed. The only people we Italians kill in the name of honor are other family members. That's the reason I joined the Army, to get away from the SOBs in my family. Only to find out, to my surprise, they have connections in the Army too."

He began giving me a history lesson.

"The Mafia came into existence in the late middle ages in Sicily as a secret organization to overthrow the rule of foreign conquerors. It drew its membership from the small private armies that were hired by the Landlords. They were better known as the Mafie. When the 1900's rolled around the Mafia families controlled the economies of their localities. From 1920 through 1944, Benito Mussolini jailed many of the Mafia families in Italy and Sicily, because the Mafia was challenging his authority in Italy.

"What we did in that bar, Milkman, was for honor, respect and country, not money. You know, Wolfman and I just got back from Cuba, not Vietnam."

"I suspected that, Vecky, because Wolfman gave me an album that read made in Cuba."

"I took out Fidel Castro with one shot, at 900 yards, through the head."

"What? Castro is still alive."

"Tell-me-about-it; the SOB was using doubles. After Castro kicked the Mafia out of Cuba, Ike gave them the OK to take his ass out. But the Mafia screwed it up. They were a joke. They ordered their people to poison Castro, and Castro's top aid ate the food. They ordered a bomb placed in the parking garage under the floor where Castro parked his car. Castro's police locked up the SOB who planted the bomb for smuggling or something before he got a chance to detonate the bomb. He had the detonation device in his bag when he was arrested. The police thought it was a portable radio. He was incarcerated for two years while the detonation device remained in the property room of the Cuban jail. The bomb, still attached to the ceiling, went undetected for almost two years while he was in prison. A storm blew in down and they found it."

Vecky told me that all kinds of Keystone Cops activities were put into place to kill Castro by the US government and the mob in Cuba:

- Inject an untraceable poison, a botulism toxin, into selections of Castro's favorite brand of cigars and present the poisoned cigars to him.
- Create a booby-trapped seashell that would explode if removed from the floor by Castro, who was an avid scuba diver.
- Manufacture a fountain pen with a hidden needle capable of injecting a lethal toxin and persuade Castro to write with it.
- Assassinate him with a high powered rifle with telescopic sights. Wow!

"After JFK got elected, Bobby Kennedy took over running the kill Castro campaign." Vecky said, "Now it was called Operation Mongoose. It was Bobby's recommendation to JFK, not to follow through with supporting air strikes that screwed up the Cuban Bay of Pigs invasion. After all that shit, Bobby orders our Special Forces unit into Cuba to take Castro's ass out without up-to-date intelligence. I risked my life to take out a stupid double. Bobby was so incompetent that he caused seven of our unit to get killed. We are the only ones that made it out alive. The Mafia hid us while we were in Cuba. I was right at home." Vecky said ironically.

He gave me more Mafia lore.

"In the forties during the war, the Navy and J. Edgar Hoover made a deal with the Mafia. They asked the New York families to help the government catch Nazi spies operating out of the New York City, Boston and Philly docks. The New York families actually helped America hunt down Germans spying on shipping out of New York Harbor. German spies were radioing sailing dates and times of merchant ships to Nazi submarines waiting off the coast. The Germans were sinking Allied ships within 5 miles of the US coastline. It was like shooting rats in a barrel.

For the families' reward for helping America win WWII and fighting Communism, the government ordered Naval Commander Charles Radcliff to run project 'Under World,' a partnership with the New York Mafia families and the military. In turn, the FBI and the New State Attorney General's Office turned their heads and looked the other way from the Mafia's narcotic traffic coming into the United States.

"Milkman, the government told the Mafia families to take dead aim at your people, the Negroes, with their narcotics traffic. This winking shit between the crime families and the US government has been going on a long time."

"That's what Malcolm X said"

"Your homeboy, Malcolm X, knows what he's talking about."

"Ugly secrets are a bitch, Vecky"

"There has been no major Mafia narcotics arrest in this country for years by the FBI. Now! What both of my Uncles Sams want me to do, I will not do and this team will not do."

"Vecky, I know that America has asked soldiers to do some fuck-up shit in the past, in the name of duty, honor and country. But, what in the hell are you talking about?"

"Not only has Uncle Sam asked us to do this shit for my country, but my family's Uncle Sam has asked me to do this for the 'family.' Wolfman knew a lot about CPL

James Moran, because he was to take the fall for it. Now their plans will have to be changed."

"What Uncle?-Moran was involved?-plans for what?"

He replied, "My uncle Sam G—."

I interrupted him, "Hold on, on second thought, I am already in enough shit, because of you guys. I don't really want to know what it is you guys are into."

"Milkman, you are right. Do not worry about that thing in downtown SA; that was a light one. It was a righteous one. You are one of us now, we have your back. What I am talking about is not righteous and it's best for you not to know."

The Jump Master hollered, "Stand-up, check equipment, sound off for equipment check, hook up, shuffle to the door, Go, Go, Go."

I was Ok until I got into the door of the airplane, then I froze. Vecky pushed me out. As I floated to the ground, my mind was still burning from doing "The Monkey Dance" in that bar. Next Tuesday, LT Glover was taking Dickinson and me to be identified by the woman who lost her hand in the bar fight. I felt the MPs were focusing in on me, because they thought I would be the weakest link in fingering the A-team.

My Airborne qualifying physical test was Wednesday and the replacements for the Special Forces B-team, that were lost in Cuba, were coming in for "medical training."

Friday was guard mount and the Supernumerary challenge. My curiosity questions were being answered too quickly. Now, I knew why they called Sammerson, the Wolfman. Where he had learned those moves, I didn't know and I didn't want to know. I could not talk openly on the subject with the A-team from fear of being overheard. Vecky had divulged his ugly secrets to me on the C130, because there were no listening devices on the plane. If they were, they would not function well, because of the plane's noise.

Our last weeks of classes were also coming up. The final two weeks we would be bed-pan-jockeys and sticking thermometers in GI asses at the base hospital. The jump went well and so did the Airborne PT test; I passed. Doc laughed and said, "Congratulations, now you have the time to really get into more deep shit with us."

I didn't laugh. My old friend, bad eyesight, bit me in the ass again. LT Glover ordered me to the base hospital to have my eyes reexamined. They issued me a second pair of black horn rimmed glasses. They looked just like the ones Malcolm X wore, so I really didn't have a problem wearing them now.

I was very concerned about the ID visit to the hospital in SA. I was pleased when it was postponed until Friday. When the time came, both Dickinson and I were placed into a Jeep with two MPs. They drove us downtown to the San Antonio General Hospital and escorted us up to the second floor ward where she was.

The MPs told Dickinson to go into the room first. Her eyes widen as he entered the room with the MPs. She didn't speak English very well. The nurse was acting as the interpreter. She said she didn't recognize Dickinson. Then the MPs took me into the room. She almost jumped out of her bed. The MPs clamped down on my arms and then she lowered her eyes and said she didn't recognize me either. The sweat running down my face immediately dried up. I knew she got a good look at me in the bar. She was too afraid to ID me.

When we got back to base, the MP Officer was very upset. He started to holler and scream at Dickinson and me. He said that one of us was going to hang in Leavenworth. Then the door of the orderly room opened and in walked this 6 foot, 3 inch Black officer. He was a captain with a well-worn Green Beret bent to the side of his face. He walked over to me and said,

"How are you doing, Private Roy? I am Captain Theodore Grumble. I've heard a lot of good things about you. I think you are going to be a fine soldier and medic." Then he turned to the MP Officers and asked.

"Is PVT Roy being charged with any offence?"

"No."

"PVT Roy has to prepare for Guard Mount this evening. He is representing his training company. Come with me, private."

I got up and walked out while watching Dickinson hold his head in his hands. The entire SF team was waiting outside including the newly arrived B-team, Frost, Unicorn, Anvil and Hook. They were all smiling and they began to pat me on the back. I turned and glanced back through the opened orderly room door. Wolfman always had the ability to read my mind.

"He will be OK, Milkman."

As we worked the hospital wards in our final days, I was upset about not passing the physical for Airborne, because of bad eyesight. Wolfman and the A-team continued to be very troubled also, constantly whispering among themselves.

Wolfman finally said to me that the A-team was being sent to Nam, Vietnam; for him his third tour. The B-team would remain here in the states with their officers. I sensed they were breaking up this team for some ugly reason. Wolfman said nothing more to me about it.

I won my first Supernumerary contest. There was $250 in the pool. They give me twenty five dollars, 10% of the pool. The two SF Teams became more distant from each other after I won and with me in the middle, things became very ugly between them.

Our medic training was winding down. I got my orders to report to Fort Rucker, Alabama's base hospital. Fort Rucker was the Army's Helicopter Training School and an express ticket to Vietnam.

Wolfman said, "Milkman, stay the hell away from those choppers, because they will guarantee that you will be sent to Nam. Remember what I told you; don't waste your time trying to be a hero. Learn as much as you can from Uncle Sam and get the hell out the Army. Promise me that you will use your GI bill to go to college after you get out of the Army. You should have listened to Malcolm X and stayed out of the Army. He knows what in the hell he is talking about. Promise me."

"That's promise number two, Wolfman, I promise."

He upset me again and I was very concerned about him and the A-team. I never heard Wolfman talk like that before. I turned to Vecky, but he and the remainder of the A-team were also upset. They all refused to talk to me about what was going on. They stopped sitting with the B-team at meals. The SF Officers ate with the B-team including their Black captain, Grumble.

I tried to question them about Grumble. They simply turned away without answering my questions. I sensed that the A-team did not like him much. There weren't many Black officers in the Army and you could count less than a handful of Black Special Forces officers in the entire Army. I was able to pull out of Wolfman that CPT Grumble had graduated from Yale University, and had gone to school with many CIA heavy weights. He might have been the only Black member of the super-secret Skull and Bones Society at Yale University. It was rumored that this fraternity dominates American politics and power.

Wolfman said he was very smart, but was an unprincipled Uncle Tom sellout. He speculated that the members of the B-team might not be Special Forces at all. That he was waiting on the information about them from his friends in Washington. He told me to be very careful with those guys. I remembered what Wolfman said about putting too much trust in your own people simply because they have the same skin color or religion as you. Standing in the Muslim Book Store, I had read that most slave rebellions in America were never successful, because other slaves usually betrayed them.

CPT Grumble always spoke to me in a kind voice, too kind. He told me to suspend the traditional military courtesy of saluting and calling him sir. He said to call him Ted, which I did. He knew a lot about me including that I thought a lot of Malcolm X and was fond of Latin Jazz. He tried to draw me into conversations about my relationship with Wolfman and the other members of the A-team.

"The A-team likes you a lot, and you are going to be a fine soldier. I know exactly what you guys did in that bar downtown and its safe with me."

"Ted, I am sorry, but I don't know what you are talking about."

Two days before graduation, Wolfman and his team left for Vietnam. The Wolfman walked me out to the ball field and gave me a black plastic bag that contained a San Antonio telephone book with its cover removed. It looked similar to the one that Lonzo kept in his foxhole.

I smiled. "What kind of going away present is this?"

"The kind that may save your life one day, keep it safe and in good condition. Don't make any marks in it. Remember your birthday; it will be the key to the code you will need to decipher my messages. Any message from me will start with the words 'A penny please.'" My foster mother Lonzo taught me this code. And yes, I am still in contact with 'her' and 'she' will be in touch with you when you get back to New York. I going to try to do what I can to get you sent to Europe."

I teased him, "But, I never met your foster mother. I don't even know her real name or where she lives. And, who said I was going back to New York anyway."

He smiled, "She will contact you."

"But you never finished telling me what happen to your foster mother, the Buffalo Soldiers and you in Korea."

He smiled again and said, "Ugly Secret, Private Roy-Ugly Secret."

The morning that they were scheduled to leave, CPT Grumble called the entire SF Team to attention in the empty barracks. I watched through the cracked bathroom door as CPT Grumble placed red scarves around each of the team members' neck. I couldn't hear what he said to them. The Wolfman did not look happy. As soon as Grumble finished, Sammerson and the A-team removed their scarves and dropped them on the floor. Sammerson then walked over to the B-team, removed their green berets from their heads and dropped them on the floor.

A truck pulled up to the back of the barracks and the A-team threw their gear in the back.

Sammerson turned to me and whispered, "I confirmed my suspicions that the B-team members were not Special Forces. These guys' backgrounds are unknown, but they definitely are not Special Forces. Mercenaries were a favorite of the NSA, CIA and Special Ops. Be very careful with these guys Milkman, and always remember that I betrayed my own people too."

"That was an unwanted ugly secret, Wolfman."

I was very, very sad to see the A-team truck off base, sensing that I might never see them again; and wishing they hadn't taught me to Monkey Dance.

***

9

The Peanut Capital of the World

I arrived in Enterprise, Alabama, on January 17, 1963, sitting in the front of the bus late in the afternoon. It was the dead of winter, but it wasn't very cold. Very few people were walking the streets as the Greyhound bus pulled in front of the only drug store in this dusty town. It was a mild sunny day providing ample sunlight for this wire headed old man to whittle on a stick while rocking back and forth on a milk crate. This town could be a Norman Rockwell painting.

Across the street was a small bank with a little white copula on the top. In the center of Main Street was a small plaza containing a large bronze statue of a woman holding a Boll Weevil. It was an insect that ate cotton plants.

A short dark skinned Brother was sweeping the plaza. I hoped the town wasn't paying him by the hour, because the broom was so small, it would have taken him a year to finish the job; but the area was spotless.

As I stepped down from the bus, my uniform caught his eye. He turned and smiled at me as I stepped up on the sidewalk. There wasn't an Army ¾ ton M37 truck waiting to take me to Fort Rucker; as I was told. So, I walked into the drug store that seconded as the town's bus station and asked the clerk about transport to Fort Rucker.

In a heavy southern drawl he replied, "The Army sends a truck every hour to pick up soldiers. The next truck is do-in in twenty minutes."

I purchased a pop, that's a soda in the South, and I walked across the street into the plaza to get a closer look at the infamous bronze insect that the local hicks apparently idolized. I parked myself on a bench in front of the statute and just stared. I guess I looked hickish myself in this deep Southern town. The guy cleaning the plaza startled me as he approached me from the rear.

He said, "I was drafted in back in 1950."

"I volunteered," I said.

"They gave us three weeks of basic training and sent us to Korea."

"You're kidding."

"Buddy, I am a Christian, I don't kid. I was at Panmunjom when the armistice was signed."

"What unit did you serve with?"

"The 24th Infantry, the Buffalo Soldiers"

"I have a friend that served in the 24th. I have heard ugly secrets about the 24th in Korea."

"They were all lies. We fought like hell when we had ammo and officers to lead us. Most of our officers were rednecks that spit on us and treated us like shit. They stayed buried in their bunkers, behind the lines, while the colored boys were in open trenches taking artillery fire, doing all the dirty fighting and dying."

He paused, remembering.

"The North Koreans would charge in human waves that were so thick that firing one round could kill three of them. Only their front charging line had weapons. The remaining lines would pick up the weapons of those who fell in front of them. They kept coming. After we ran out of ammo, we would fight hand to hand. Then we would haul-ass down the Bug-Out routes."

"I heard talk of the Bug-Out routes. Many white Army officers said Negroes soldiers were cowards for bugging out."

"Hog-wash, we learned of the Bug-Out routes from the white boys. Yet they blame us for using them also. It served no purpose for anybody to commit suicide. We had nothing to fight with, no leadership, no ammo, no artillery and no tank support. Our white officers would be the first to run and then they would say it was the Negro soldier's fault, because we refused to stay and fight. They didn't tell the truth. It was the 24th Infantry that gave the United States their first victory in the Korean War at Yechon."

"Are you sure, you guys were not a bunch of yellow livered Negro cowards?"

"Buddy, my eyes are not that good. I see your name tag, but I can't read it. I don't know your name and I don't want to know it either. I told you, I do not lie."

I knew he wasn't lying, but I wanted to tease him a bit. I decided to leave Wolfman and Lonzo buried for a while, so I didn't bring them up by name. He may have known them. I looked up at the statute.

"The boll weevil just about destroyed this town," he said. "The only crop everyone planted was cotton.

People here almost starved to death one winter, because the boll weevil destroyed the cotton crop three years in a row. So some bright-headed person came up with the idea of growing peanuts. It saved the town, the county and southern Alabama. Now we are the Peanut Capital of the World. The white folks don't want to let on that George Washington Carver, a little Negro professor at Tuskegee University, found more usages for the peanut than they could shake a stick at. Now, every year they have a Peanut Festival thanking the Boll Weevil instead of that Negro professor for saving them from starvation."

He looked up at the sound of a truck. "Here comes your ride, buddy. Good luck, and stay off those dat-blang hel-i-o-chopers. Every week, someone is in the papers getting killed in those things. If god wanted man to fly, he would have given him wings."

"Thank you, I've been told that already." I ran across the street to the arriving ¾ ton M37, tossed my duffel bag in the back and climbed into the front seat. I was the only one being picked up this trip. The Soul Brother that was driving asked me my name and what unit I was assigned to.

"PVT Roy and the base hospital."

He replied, "That's boss, man, they have the best chow on base. Some GIs go on sick call just to eat at the hospital's mess hall."

We drove north on State Route 231, a deserted highway flanked by long rolls of erect stalks of peanuts mimicking soldiers; as they dried reverently in the open fields. The rows floated gently and neatly over the red dirt hills giving off a pleasant musky aroma. The aroma attracted the birds to the fields like bees; they worked the stalks along with the local laborers like a colony of black ants storing up for the winter.

I said to the driver, "Too bad the land owners won't be sharing much of the proceeds with the ants." He simply looked at me in confusion and I didn't try to explain. The ride took about twenty minutes to arrive at Fort Rucker. As we approached the main gate, a new HU-1A "Huey" swooped down over the highway on its landing approach. There were no guards at the front gate, so that meant this was an open post. The place appeared older than Fort Dix, with similar long rows of poorly-maintained white barracks and buildings.

"You know," the driver said, "the only reason they keep this place open is that the local congressman has seniority on the House Arm Services Committee."

I nodded and asked him, "What happens around here after dark?"

"Enterprise, four blocks east of where I picked you up, is the 'Hole in the Wall,' the Black section of town. There are two bars where the guys and the gals hang out on Friday and Saturday nights. This is a dry county, so no liquor or beer is sold anywhere in this county."

I turned and looked at him with a frown on my face.

He laughed, "Except Shine."

We both laughed.

"Where are you from Roy, up north somewhere-I bet."

"New York."

"Us mud-busting farmer boys down here don't like you pretty-yellow-up-Northerners, because the girls down here flock to you like chickens to corn. Are you married, Roy, you look sort of young."

"Nope."

"Be careful, these country girls down here are looking for a ticket out of here. They don't care whose back they ride on. You have to watch out for these rednecks too. They killed a Soul Brother hitchhiking back to the Fort about two months ago. His body was found on the side of the road about two miles from the main gate with his head busted open."

"How do you know it was rednecks that killed him?"

He didn't answer, as he gave me a long stare as he pulled the truck around to the back of the base hospital where the HQ was located. He got out and opened the rear gate. "I like Ozark, Alabama myself. It's small and not many GIs go there, and boy do those country girls treat you right."

Reading his name tag for the first time, I asked, "Robinson, where are you from?"

"Mississippi."

I thought of Moran. Then it hit me like a brick, what the park maintenance man said about the 24th using "Bug-Out Routes." There were more ugly secrets to know about Lonzo, Wolfman and now the park keeper concerning the 24th Infantry in Korea. All I had to say, to put him on the defensive, was white folks said the 24th Infantry had a bad reputation for running under fire. On 115th St., if you had a rep for not fighting, you received numerous ass whippings until you did something to change it.

I reported to the orderly room. The CQ gave me a welcome pack containing everything a newcomer needed to know about Fort Rucker. It contained two sets of medic whites and the history of the Fort. The pack said the Fort was currently an Army Aviation Developmental Center for both fixed wing and rotary wing aircraft. The pack told you where to find the PX, the chapel and the MPs etc. And, the best part of all was medics were given 24 hour passes, because we worked 24 hour shifts.

My first work assignment would be in the hospital's emergency room. The CQ gave me one day to get my bunk and myself squared away and then report to the emergency room. I was scared to death. I hadn't worked on a real live injured patient before, except for taking their vital signs and removing their bed pan. I introduced myself to the other guys in the barracks. They told me that I would not see much of them, because of the funny hours everyone worked. The mess hall was open twenty four-seven, because the hospital functioned around the clock.

The barracks were very quiet, several guys were still asleep. They said they had very few inspections, but the guys cleaned up every Thursday to keep the NCOs off their backs. The hospital laundry cleaned all your clothes and you didn't pull any guard duty. I fell right into that.

It was still fairly warm in Southern Alabama in February. The only outer clothing that everyone wore was a light jacket or sweater. I reported to my work assignment the next day in the hospital's emergency room. It was busy, two doctors, a head nurse and four medics working the room. There had been a helicopter crash. The pilot had been killed and the instructor was badly burned and in critical condition. The medic driving the ambulance said he had to remove the pilot's remains from the chopper with a shovel, because they were still hot from the burning wreckage.

As soon as the introductions were over, the doctor told me to go into the back room and remove sutures from a sergeant's hand. He had received a severe cut a few weeks earlier and it was time for the sutures to come out. I went into the backroom, the sergeant stared straight at me and my knees buckled. Oh shit, a sergeant, what's going happen to me if I messed up my first patient's hand. I looked for a pair of scissors to begin my work. There was a pair in a tray on the table.

I picked them up and approached the sergeant. I asked him to raise his hand. As he raised his hand, he just looked at me with a cold stare. I started to cut and he hollered every time the dull scissors pulled up on the sutures in his finger. My hands began to shake, he hollered for the doctor. Both doctors and the nurse came running into the room.

"Where in the hell did you find this incompetent private from," he exploded. "He is about to take my finger off."

The doctor shook his head and the nurse asked me to observe the doctor remove the sutures. The doctor pulled a very small pair of scissors out of his breast packet, saturated the area with iodine, and began to cut the sergeant's sutures. The scissors that I picked up were big enough to cut through a chain link fence. I was out of the emergency room the next day. I didn't mind either. They did some heavy work that was above the head of a novice. They averaged one helicopter crash a week, two car crashes, along with the standard stuff, pregnancies, broken legs, and heart attacks etc.

I was transferred to the pediatric ward to begin my on the job training. It was much slower. I loved children and related to them better than I related to adults anyway. My first assignment in pediatrics was not a pleasant one. A child had died of phenomena during the night. When I arrived for duty the next morning, the hospital's head nurse, Captain Cynthia Morales, asked me to prepare the child for the morgue.

I asked, "Prepare what, for where?"

The nurse escorted me into the back room where the dead child was lying on the table. She instructed me to pack all orifices in the child's body with cotton to prevent bodily fluids from leaking out.

The poor child's bowels had begun to move all over the table and me. I quickly went to work with the cotton. I was feeling very sad that the child lost its life so young. But, the captain didn't allow me any time to mourn the child or feel sorry for myself.

Captain Morales was unique. She was a former Special Forces Nurse, a master parachutist and a helicopter pilot. She was good with her hands, a black belted Martial Artist, and none of that movie shit either. She had served with SGT Sammerson in Vietnam on a previous tour. She couldn't recall his name until I said the Wolfman.

She said, "I treated a prisoner that the Wolfman brought in after interrogation. The prisoner was barely alive after the Wolfman finished interrogating him and he had some unique wounds."

"Around his neck?" I asked. She just smiled at me

I learned more from Captain Morales in three weeks on the pediatric ward, than I had learned during medic school. I learned real medicine; bush folk medicine. Much of it she had learned in her homeland in Cuba, and more in Vietnam. Much of what she taught me, she taught to the doctors as well. She made many of her own remedies from plants she picked up from the side of the road or walking through the woods.

Aloe and periwinkle were her favorites. Aloe treated skin problems and intestinal problems and periwinkle caused an increase of red blood cells, very useful in the treatment of children's leukemia. She also loved to use the same phrase the A-team used, "Low-tech kicks high-tech's behind." Within two weeks, she had me giving classes to new mothers on how to care for their babies; from feeding them, to changing diapers, to what wonders apple and prune juices can contribute to regulation of their bowel movements.

In some battlefield situations, Army medics functioned in the same capacity as doctors or nurses. We gave shots, dispensed medicine and in emergency situations we were expected to perform minor surgery. Generally, Army medics take their jobs very seriously and must be prepared to put all of their skills to work to save lives. The Army doctors and nurses always shared their knowledge freely, because of that.

I was assigned to work each ward in the hospital for three to four weeks. During my last week on the job in pediatrics, two young Black girls were brought into the ward, and everyone was very upset with the girls' father. He was a tall slim sergeant who just returned to the United States from South Korea finishing an eighteen month tour; the standard tour there. In Europe, it was generally two years or better.

The girls were crying loudly and in a great deal of pain. One was throwing up a fowl smelling substance and the other's legs were encrusted with dried feces. I began to work on the young girl with the encrusted feces. I asked the medic assisting me to hold her suspended in air so I could cut the diaper off her. Each time we tried to place her on a worktable or in a crib; it would cause her great pain from the sheet making contact with her skin.

I proceeded to cut the diaper off her with my scissors. As I cut, the scissors became clogged with feces. It took me a while, because I had to wash my scissors after a few cuts. Finally, I cut the diaper into two pieces. As I started to remove the diaper, the young girl let out a scream that came directly off a Civil War battlefield. I was pulling her skin off with the diaper. The doctors and nurses came running, but this time they encouraged me to finish the job.

I took some netting from one of the cribs and fashioned a hammock across one of the empty cribs. I cut the strings away where her buttocks would rest so it would hang free. We placed her in it without her reeling from pain. Then I used warmed distilled water and iodine soap to soak the remaining diaper free from the encrusted feces and from her skin. I worked until I was able to remove the diaper completely.

When I finished, the young girl had lost her first layer of skin on her backside and upper legs. When the doctor and nurse Morales viewed the results of my work, they both went ballistic on the girls' father. To my surprise, Captain Morales grabbed him, twisted his arm and pushed him into the staff's lunchroom. She told him that she would have him Court Marshaled for child abuse. The sergeant just sat there and cried.

"When I left for South Korea," he said, "I only had one little girl. When I returned to California, eighteen months later, I had two girls. The youngest was only 6 months old, you figure it out. I only had three days to get cross-country from California and report to my new assignment here."

"The girls weren't feeling well, but I thought they were well enough to travel. So I threw everyone in my car and started to drive cross-country. Two days into the drive, I noticed bad smells coming from the children. I thought my wife was taking care of the girls, but she wasn't. Then the girls started to get very sick and they couldn't keep anything down. When I arrived here, I drove them straight to the base hospital. I left my wife in the car outside. I don't even know the youngest girl's name. I was so damn mad with my wife that I didn't say anything to her the whole trip here."

The doctor asked, "Where is your wife now?"

"In the station wagon parked outside."

They both walked outside to confront his wife, but she was gone; her suitcase and all. The kids were twenty pounds underweight and their legs were bowed from malnutrition. The child's diaper, which I had worked on, hadn't been changed in months. When the doctor and sergeant returned to the ward, without his wife, Captain Morales simply set down and cried with him.

I stayed with the girls my entire final week, day and night, sometimes sleeping on the ward, feeding them and bathing them with distilled water and aloe soap made by Captain Morales to prevent infection. I created a scab on their skin using zinc oxide ointment and an infrared heat lamp to promote healing. When I left the ward, the girls were up, moving around and the sergeant's parents were coming from Ohio to pick them up. The doctors confirmed his story and he never heard from his wife again. The sergeant gave me the honor of naming the girl that wasn't his. I named her "Hope."

Captain Morales stopped in on me from time to time to check up on my progress as I moved from ward to ward. While I was serving on the OB-GYN ward, she happened to walk in on me during childbirth. The woman having the child was a white Southerner and she was having a lot of difficulty with the birth. The doctor gave her a local anesthetic, but it wasn't having the desired effect. She had been in the stirrups for an hour fully exposed to everyone in the room.

When I pulled down my mask to greet the captain; the white woman noticed that I was black. She hollered, "I don't want that nigger in here looking at me." It caught everyone in the room by surprise including me. We briefly looked at one another and I was considering leaving. Captain Morales grabbed me by my arm and motioned me to stop in my tracks.

The doctor in charge didn't hesitate. He said to the white woman very emphatically, "It's OK. I will ask PVT Roy to leave, but we all will leave with him. And, if you wish, you can have this baby by yourself. Now, if you want us to stay and assist you with your childbirth, you will have to apologize to PVT Roy."

She thought about it for a few moments, and then she looked at me and said she was sorry for the foul remarks. She then proceeded to continue her moans and give birth to a 6 ½-pound boy. I doubt it, but I hope she tells her new son, when he's old enough, the story of how a Black Army Medic helped bring him into this world over his mother's racist objections.

When things are going really good, that's always a sign for me to look out - things are about to take a down turn. Captain Morales introduced a new medic arrival to me, Haymen Swilley. PVT Swilley was a blue blood redneck from Tennessee. His father was a retired Army colonel whose family owned a tobacco plantation there. Haymen was just out of medic school, about a month behind me. He was about as racist as they come, but he was very smooth with it.

He dropped out of VMI (Virginia Military Institute), because, as he said, he was unsure about what he wanted to do with his life. Some of his white schoolmates said he couldn't get along with anyone there, so they mistreated him so badly that he had to leave. His parents were very upset with him for dropping out of college, so he joined the Army as an enlisted man to take the heat off. Now, I was assigned to babysit him, show him the ropes on the wards and teach him as much as I could about the hospital.

For some reason, redneck white boys seem to flock to me, like flies to glue paper. It started in my childhood. He took the bunk next to mine in the barracks. Sometimes the CO knows more than they let on about GIs. That's why they do the things they do. One day, I walked in on him reading one of my Black History books by John Hope Franklin, "The Negro in America."

I jumped on him. "Who told you that you could go into my locker and take what you wanted, Swilley? I see you really wanted to get educated real bad. Keep it; maybe the book will help you ship some of your ignorance back to Tennessee."

"The worst thing decent white folks did was to educate you Negroes," he said. "Now, you people think you know it all and are as smart as white folk."

"You have it wrong, Swilley. We have always been smarter than you. That's how we survived your treachery for the past three hundred years. In fact, it was Africans who brought the first universities to Europe, teaching you Dark Age cavemen about science, medicine and philosophy. Additionally, it was African peoples that brought the first bath tubs to Europe, teaching you that soap and water didn't contain any evil spirits."

"I majored in history at VMI, Roy, and you, Mr. Smartass, don't know what in the hell you are talking about. The things you are saying ain't true. I never read anything you are saying in any history book that I ever read."

"Well, you will need to continue to read John Hope Franklin, won't you?"

We would continue our history battles for hours even at the dinner table in the mess hall. When we started our discussions, other GIs would get up and walk to another part of the chow hall. They said we both were obnoxious. Although we didn't like one another very much, we always found ourselves in one another's company for some odd reason or another.

When I got tired of him, I would pull rank on him to shut him up. I was promoted to PFC one month after I arrived. He was still a private. That didn't last too long; he was promoted to PFC within two weeks after his arrival. To shut me up, he started to point to his single mosquito wing on his shelve in defiance.

I said to him, the only reason you got promoted so quickly was that your father was a former Army colonel. During many of our contentious conversations, our medic training in San Antonio came up. I mentioned the A-team, but I didn't mention any names. He said, he'd heard about two medics being killed in my training company and it was rumored that a Special Forces Team, in my company, avenged the killings. He asked me if I knew anything about what happened.

"No."

The next day, I was assigned to pick up a group of new soldiers coming in by train to Ozark, Alabama. Haymen Swilley was assigned to be my driver as I hadn't learned how to drive yet. We drove to the Ozark train station and found five white soldiers chowing down the Jordan's Food Palace.

Swilley walked over to them and introduced himself as I checked the roster, which listed six names. One of the GIs wasn't in the restaurant. A few people in the restaurant lifted their heads staring at me as I walked into the bathroom marked "White only" looking for the sixth soldier. He wasn't there. I walked back and asked the soldiers what happen to the sixth man.

One of the white soldiers callously remarked, "He's outback."

Swilley and I walked around to the back of the restaurant. As soon as we turned the corner of the alleyway, we saw a Black soldier sitting in the backdoor of the restaurant's kitchen, next to the garbage cans, in his uniform. There were tears in his eyes and a plate of food in his lap.

I said, "Yo Brother, what's happening."

"Is this what I have to go through to serve my country?" he said bitterly.

My experiences in San Antonio hit me like a brick. "What is your name?"

Charles Ritter, "I am in charge of the soldiers inside," he said. "It was my suggestion that we get something to eat at this place. It was on the voucher list of places that we could eat at. I lead them inside this place, we set down to be served and the manager came over and said we don't serve coloreds here. We have a special place around the corner for coloreds. I am from Chicago; I didn't know what to do. The white GIs began to order their food, so I walked around back. This back door of the kitchen was it. The asshole just handed me a plate of food as soon as I walked up to him."

"Who has the voucher to pay for the food?"

"I do."

I looked at the voucher. It said to provide food service for six US Army Soldiers.

Swilley said to Charles, "Call the manager."

When the manager arrived, Swilley handed him Charles' plate. "It is unfit for human consumption." The manager took the plate and threw it into a garbage can. All three of us walked around to the front of the restaurant. Swilley asked the other soldiers, who were finishing their meals, "Did you enjoy your food?"

They replied, "Yes."

Swilley slammed his fist on the table, "But you didn't give a shit whether or not your fellow GI enjoyed his or not did you?"

One GI said, "We didn't want to get into any trouble down here and the Negro soldier picked the restaurant, we didn't."

Swilley said the restaurant owners had a right to serve anyone they choose. "But, you GIs also have an obligation to take care of one another regardless of skin color."

One of the soldiers said, "We didn't know what happen to him, he just disappeared."

"None of you went to see what happened to him. Well, you guys sit right here while we go and get him something decent to eat."

Charles said, "Look man, I appreciate what you guys are doing, but I don't want to get into any trouble either. How are we going to pay for the food"?

"Let's go," Swilley said, "You sorry asses stay here and entertain yourselves until we get back to pick you up." He grabbed Charles by the arm and pulled him through the door and we all jumped into the front seat of the truck. Swilley drove to Aunt Millie's Restaurant in the black section of town. Aunt Millie's wasn't listed on the voucher's list of places, but when I told her what happened, she laid out a king's table of food. Swilley, Charles, and I ate like it was Judgment Day.

Even a jar of sipping shine miraculously appeared, from nowhere, on the table. We gave Aunt Millie the voucher, because it couldn't be split up between restaurants. About three hours passed before we drove back to the Jordan's Food Palace. But, before we left, Swilley asked Aunt Millie to fill his canteen with water and put some uncooked grits in a small bag for him.

I asked myself, what in the hell is this crazy white boy up to. When we drove back to the Food Palace, the GIs inside came running outside to the ¾ ton, stating that the restaurant manager was upset with us and wanted the voucher to get paid for the food.

Swilley asked them, "Do you boys want to walk to the base"?

They said, "No."

He instructed four of them to put a small handful of grits in their mouths and not to eat-um. He gave each a small sip of water from his canteen. He told the fifth GI to lead the group back inside and tell the manager the voucher was on its way. About two minutes later Swilley went to the window of the restaurant and started to make funny faces at the GIs seated inside. Man, those guys started to laugh and cough up the foulest looking stuff on this planet all over the restaurant.

The manager came running over, franticly ushering the GIs out the front door. As they walked out, the GIs hammed-it-up big-time, by holding their stomachs. I almost died from laughter, all those guys walking out of the restaurant barfing and choking. We loaded them into the truck and as we drove away, the manager hollered at us, "Tell the Army we don't serve any GIs here anymore, period."

On the way, back to the Fort Swilley told the soldiers to never let anything or anyone divide them. "Unity may save your life one-day and you didn't want any fellow soldier to have second thoughts about putting his life on the line to save yours." Swilley caused you to hate him one day and love him the next. He was that kind of guy.

Captain Morales was sitting on my bunk that evening after we returned. The GIs in the barracks were all staring at us, because officers rarely came into the enlisted men's quarters; especially females. I thought she was going to scold me about the pickup and the meal voucher in town.

She led me outside looking shaken. She knew I became close to SGT Sammerson and his A-team at medic school and told me she had information she wanted to share with me about them.

She said that SGT Sammerson and his team were assigned to a Special Operations Group in Vietnam for a deep penetration mission and were listed missing. She said she believed that most of the team had been killed or were missing in action.

I was stunned.

She said that one team member had survived the mission and was scheduled to arrive at the Fort Rucker hospital in four days. She was transferring me to the Neuro-Psychiatric Ward where he would be housed and treated. We treated a lot of Vietnam returnees in that ward. Most were being treated for psychiatric problems as well as combat wounds. She felt a familiar face would up lift his spirits.

I asked who the survivor was, but she said she couldn't say and walked back into the hospital section.

Three days later, I reported to the Neuro-Psychiatric Ward. The sergeant in charge of the ward introduced me to all the patients on the ward. They all seem quite normal to me.

The sergeant told me that the ward's doors must remain locked except the backdoor, which was unlocked once a day to allow the patients to go outside for exercise.

"Every now and then, a patient makes a break for it," he told me. "We aren't allowed to run after anyone, it's the MP's job to return them. Most are caught on post. Two weeks ago a patient ran away and they found him at the PX eating all the ice cream he could stuff into his mouth."

When I grinned he went on, "You would think that sex would be on the top of Vietnam returnees list, but it isn't. Hamburgers, hotdogs are number one and ice cream is number two. "Now" he said, "They now put ice cream on the menu twice a week and keep some in the staff's refrigerator in the lunchroom at all times for the patients. Nighttime was a difficult time on the ward, because most of the patients were Vietnam veteran returnees and many had mental wounds as well as physical ones. The Vietcong operations were usually carried out at night. And most of the men in the ward were wounded at night. Because of that, most of the men didn't sleep well at night and sometimes not at all. Most of the sleeping was usually done in the daytime. Even the patients who didn't have acute mental problems didn't sleep well at night, because of their fear of Vietnam returnees patients going off."

"I won't put you on the night shift until you become more familiar with the patients," the sergeant said. "Captain Morales said you might know the new patient arriving tomorrow by Caribou. Tomorrow morning, at 0700 hours, I want you and PFC Swilley to pick him up. Pick up the ambulance from the motor pool and go to the fix-wing hangers at the north end of the airfield and wait for the plane to arrive."

After a sleepless night, Swilley and I did just that. I was very tense. I was hoping that the Wolfman would be on the plane. I told Swilley that I had grown close to these guys. I hung out, drank with them and they were a cool bunch. I told him that each of them had very distinct personalities. Then Swilley started to ask too many questions, so I changed the subject and started to talk about the weather. It was a very overcast day in the Peanut Capital of the World.

***

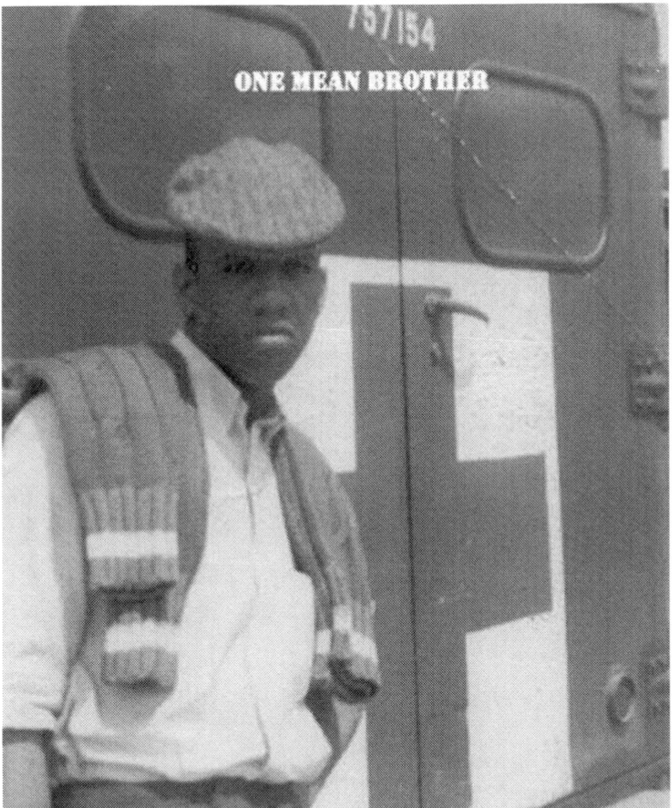
757/154
ONE MEAN BROTHER

10

Ozark Red Lipstick

The Caribou is a plane made in Canada which is popular with Special Operations Forces, because it's very rugged and can land and take off almost anywhere. About 0800 hours it landed and taxied to the front of the hanger where we were parked. The rear gate opened and this blob of humanity limped out on one crutch and I recognized him immediately. It was the Caveman, SGT Gorge.

We rearranged the stretchers in the back of the meat wagon, as the ambulance was dubbed, so he could sit in the back. He was carrying his own IV solution. When he saw me, a grin a mile wide appeared on his face. He said to me, "Damn Milkman, these rednecks down here didn't hang your cocky black ass yet."

"I am too fast for them Caveman," as I gave him a hug.

Swilley had not heard my nickname before, turned to me and said delightedly, "Milkman, Milkman is your nickname?"

We drove SGT Gorge straight to the hospital and allowed him to enter the ward through the backdoor. After registering him and checking his vital signs, Captain Morales said, no one is to know he is here or his real name. I thought that was sort of strange, but I followed orders. I assigned him to a bed by the backdoor near the screened porch. He wanted it moved to the middle of the ward. I didn't ask any questions, I just moved it.

I wheeled him to physical therapy and to the chow hall, because he wouldn't eat any meal brought to his bed on a tray with his fake name on it. He wanted to eat in the mess hall out of the same pot as everyone else, so I wheeled him to the mess hall and ate with him. I didn't push him for any information about the A-team. I knew he would tell me what happened to the Wolfman and the others when he was ready.

Captain Morales said that she wanted me to stay on the Neuro-Psychiatric Ward until Gorge was able to walk well by himself. A week passed and Gorge said nothing of the A-team. Then one Wednesday, while we were eating chow, four members of the SF B-team walked into the chow hall. I was just as shocked as the Caveman to see them at Fort Rucker. They immediately walked over to Gorge and me and started to talk trash.

"Yo, Milkman, been milking any snakes lately?"

"No, but I see a few now, and I might start soon," I said with a grin.

"Caveman, we are glad to see you back in the world, man. But, some of your partners couldn't find their way back home yet."

As they walked away, the Caveman backed his wheelchair from under the dining table, turned it and took off like a dragster doing a wheelie at the NHRA finals. He wheeled it straight into Frost and Unicorn. He hit them so hard in back of their shins, that they immediately hit the floor in pain. He wheeled around, grabbed the other two Anvil and Hook, one in each arm, lifted them on to his shoulders and squeezed them like they were dishrags. Boy did they holler. There was nothing wrong with his arms only his legs were out of action. I laughed my behind off.

Captain Morales walked in after hearing all the commotion. She ordered Gorge to release the two B-team members and ordered them all to leave the hospital grounds immediately. She scolded Gorge and told him, "If you cause any additional trouble you will be confined to your hospital ward, in a straightjacket; if necessary. Do you understand me, sergeant?"

Gorge said, "Yes, Ma'am," turned his wheelchair around, rolled it back to the dining table and finished his meal.

As I wheeled Gorge back to the ward, we went past the hospital's library. He took over the wheelchair, made a sharp left into the library and darted into one of the sound proof listening rooms with me in tow. He locked the door and said those four guys were pure cow manure.

"The Frost is from Sweden and has a head problem, because he was raised by Wolfs. The Unicorn is from Brooklyn and is a good pit fighter. Other SF-Teams have lost to him in 'Last Man Standing Pit Fights.' The Anvil was born in Cuba, but raised in Newark, New Jersey. Not much is known about Hook. All of them were members of Brigade 2506 of the Bay of Pigs invasion. They were released by Castro last December."

He then told me the whole story.

"Milkman, the A-team was set up in "Nam" by our own people. We were given an assignment to retrieve a local tribal leader in Laos, who was tagged for assassination by the North Vietnamese. We never felt right about this mission. We suspected a set-up from within the Pentagon itself. Our SOG team reported directly to the Pentagon, not even the commanding general of Vietnam knew of our mission.

"Our dog tags were collected, Soviet watches and toothbrushes were issued to us. We turned in our AR-16s for AK47s and Chinese's RPGs. We turned in our Army fatigues for tiger stripes camouflage ones. All ID and insignia had to be removed from our uniforms. These uniforms were not general American issues. In-fact we wore no American military clothing at all, including underwear. Our boots were made in Czechoslovakia, along with our pistol belts and canteens.

"Everything was going well as we choppered in from Thailand into a small village called Sop Nao, just south of the North Vietnam border near Dien Bien Phu. We felt it was bad luck to have a Special Op so close to where the French had gotten their ass kicked royally by the North Vietnamese. But, we took the mission anyway, because we had turned down the mission in San Antonio which came straight from the CIA.

"The guy we were supposed to rescue was hiding out with his family just north of the village. We made radio contact with him about fifty miles into Laos. As soon as the choppers landed, all hell broke loose. It was supposed to be a clean in and out operation. I was hit first and one chopper was knocked out of commission. We all loaded into the second chopper. It was flying overloaded and it had taken gunfire also.

"Milkman, we noticed something very strange, it was the first time I'd seen Soviet combat troops on the ground in Vietnam and they were in their field uniforms. We took off without retrieving our contact. A Soviet helicopter gunship began to follow us and it was gaining on us. Satchel Page once said, 'If you are running from someone don't look back, because they may be gaining on you,' he was right.

"We got as far as the Nam Seng River, which flowed, directly into the Mekong River. We felt we may have a better chance moving down the river at night, because the chopper we were in wasn't going to make it. The pilot had already called in our position and a May Day. He landed and they put me into a small boat. They told the chopper pilot, he had a better chance on his own to get back with an empty bird. The chopper took off smoking, but it didn't make it far. The Russian gunship shot it down.

"Wolfman and the rest of the team stayed behind to give me a head start down the river. As I floated down the river, I heard gunshots from the A-team fighting it out with the Russian Special Forces unit. Then there was silence. An Army chopper picked me up on my third day on the river.

"Milkman, the Wolfman was looking through his field glasses at the advancing Russians and he turned white, as if he seen a ghost. That's why he sent me ahead."

"A ghost?" I said, "I don't understand Caveman."

"Have I ever bull-shitted you, Milkman."

"No, what do you think happened to the Wolfman and his team?"

"I think they fought to the last man. They wouldn't allow themselves to be captured if they had anything to say about it. The last person in the world you would want to do battle with is a cornered American. Americans are generally not suicidal, but if the ability to fight and win is not there, we will take you to hell with us.

"We don't mind dying. The Japanese learned that from American naval flyers after they surprised attacked

Japanese's aircraft carriers at Midway. Many of the Navy's planes malfunctioned losing their bombs and torpedoes, so the pilots simply crash-dived their planes at the Japanese's carriers. Whole squadrons sacrificed themselves during that attack. That taught the Japanese what a Kamikaze attack was all about.

"Now, that's what honor is all about, Milkman, making the ultimate sacrifice for your country. Not the underhanded slimy shit that some in Pentagon wanted us to do."

"The ugly secrets that you guys were keeping from me at Fort Sam Houston."

"Yes. The B-team took the assignment and Wolfman took their green berets, because of it. They shouldn't have been wearing those green berets anyway. We checked with all of our sources and no one could verify these guys were US Special Forces. Only Captain Grumble was Special Forces and he was a sellout. The rest of them were made of pure scum from the Cuban Brigade 2506."

I looked him straight in the eyes to ask the home run question.

He said, "Don't do it, Milkman, I might be tempted to answer your question. The only reason you are alive is you don't know about the mission we turned down."

"I remember what the Wolfman said to me about taking responsibility for ugly secrets, Caveman. I think I understand better now what he was talking about. What are you going to do about your ugly secrets without revealing them?"

"As soon as I got here, Milkman, I put an action plan into motion to do just that."

I stared at him as he wheeled himself out of the hospital library. I was concerned about the Caveman and I spent as much time as I could with him. I asked to be assigned to the night shift on the ward. I knew fully, that some patients went off at night and I would be in danger on the ward by myself; but it was for him. My first week on the ward went well, but the third night of my second week things got hairy. It was a very quiet night on the ward, too quiet. When the guys sleep, they snore, talk, toss, turn and fart in their sleep. It was too quiet.

I took my flashlight out of the desk drawer and walked slowly down the hallway; keeping my back against the wall. I shined the flashlight into the ward and everything looked very normal until the light reflected off one of the patient's eyes lying in bed. His eyes were wide opened. He was so frightened that his body was in a frozen state. His eyes didn't blink. They were glued to the ceiling. I shined the flashlight on several other patients and they all were in the same state. Something was going on, they were all awake and petrified, yet no one made a sound. I shined my light on the Caveman's bed and it was empty.

Things were not good; there was an emergency button on the wall that would alert medics on other wards that I needed assistance. But, I tried to think my way through this. Most guys with problems returning from Vietnam retrogress back to tactical situations in Nam. When they went off, most became confused by bringing back memories of firefights and hand-to-hand combat. Captain Morales had told me that a patient went off one night after the medic ordered him back into his bed. The medic tried to restrain the patient, they struggled and the medic hit his head against the metal bedpost and ended up in a coma.

I slid down the wall, with by back firmly against it, shining my light into the ward trying to locate SGT Gorge. I had locked the backdoor earlier and it appeared still intact, so he had to be somewhere between the backdoor and me on the ward. I started to shine the light under the beds, two beds over from his my flashlight reflected off a pair of cat eyes. They were his.

"Turn off that damn light, Milkman, the Gooks (Vietcong) are coming, the Gooks are coming." I turned off the light."

"From what direction and how many?"

"That way and I don't know."

I got down on the floor and began to crawl underneath the bed with him. He pointed down the hall to the back door.

I saw nothing, but I thought of Lonzo's Phantom Platoon. I said, I see them, but what are we going to do.

He pulled a garrote from his pajama pocket. It looked like the same garrote that he used to kill that Mexican in San Antonio. I was scared shit-less.

I said, "I'll try a get their attention then you follow me and take care of them."

"Good plan, Milkman."

I crawled into the staff's lunch room and waved him to follow me. I picked up the phone in the lunchroom and told him I was calling for some backup. He said fine with the garrote hanging from his neck. I told the front desk that we were under attack by Gooks, needed reinforcements and for them to maintain tactical silence.

I told the Caveman that reinforcements were on the way. One doctor and two medics crawled through the ward's front door and rushed the lunchroom. There, they found Gorge and me sitting at the table eating an Eskimo Pie ice cream bar with his garrote hanging around his neck.

He told the doctor, "The Milkman let the Gooks get away."

The next day CPT Morales told SGT Gorge that he would have to sleep with a restraint on one of his wrist. I felt very bad about it, but where he got the garrote from no one knows. He didn't remember a thing about the incident the next day. His mother was coming to visit him from Anniston, Alabama in a few days. His father had died three months earlier from some mysterious illness. His father worked at the Army's Chemical and Biological Warfare plant there. Gorge didn't like the fact that America was involved in the testing and manufacturing of hideous agents. He felt his father's death was caused by exposure to these agents.

"God forbid," he said, "My father may have been used as a guinea pig and took his ugly secrets to his grave. I didn't learn what was happening at Anniston until I joined the Special Forces. Just, because the Russians were developing these agents was no excuse for America to develop them also. Anniston wasn't the only site in the country that produced or stored dangerous agents; there were other sites, many other sites. Milkman, if the Army mentions chemical or biological warfare to you again; run and don't stop until you get to Canada."

My ugly secrets continued to grow. The Caveman had been making excellent progress with his legs. He was wounded in the left thigh. They had removed the bullet in Vietnam. The Russians also began to chamber their AK-47s with the new American .223 caliber (5.56mm) round. The smaller and lighter round allowed American troops to carry 25% more ammunition in the field. He said the A-team liked the new round, but hated the new AR-16, nick named the Mattie Mattel, because some parts of it were made out of plastic and it functioned like an extremely unreliable toy.

The B-team was constantly hanging around the hospital. They ate at the hospital's mess every chance they got, because they said they liked eating the best chow on base. Generally, you had to get a chow pass from the induction desk up front, but they had some way of getting around that. They said they were in Fort Rucker to take advance training on the new HU-1A helicopter gunship. It had completed its testing and was about to be rolled out by the Army. We stopped talking to them altogether, but I could see in their eyes that our fight was not finished.

I didn't want to leave the Caveman alone, so I pulled double ward duty covering for fellow medics that wanted the weekend off. Everything was going well until Sunday night. At bedtime, it was my job to tie one of Caveman's hands to the bed railing with a length of surgical gauze. I tried to make him as comfortable as possible before I turned out the lights on the ward. I restrained the Caveman, locked the back door, checked on the remaining patients and cut off the lights in the staff's lunchroom.

Then about 0200 hours in the morning, I heard a noise coming from the ward. I grabbed my flashlight and walked slowly into the ward. I shined my light on a few patients. Everyone was in his bed, but wide-awake with those frozen stares again. I shined the light on to SSGT Gorge. He was in his bed with his eyes opened, but there was something awkward about him. I shinned the light on his hands and both of his hands were restrained with gauze. I had only restrained one hand, his left hand.

I walked over to his bed and touched his hand, it was cold. He was dead.

I immediately dropped down below the bed looking around the ward for any legs. No one else was out of their beds or loose on the ward. I turned on the ward's lights and none of the patients said a word. I called the duty doctor and head nurse. When they arrived, they examined him and said he had died of a heart attack. I told them that I had only restrained one of his hands not two.

"You forgot what you did, PVT Roy," the doctor said, "He simply died of natural causes."

The doctor asked me to move his body into the back area of the ward and prepare him for the morgue. I rolled his bed into the sunroom of the ward and closed the curtains behind me. I examined the body myself and started to pack all of his orifices. I noticed tape marks around his mouth and severe bruises on his wrist. He had been fighting to free himself. As I placed cotton balls up his nose, they began to absorb blood. As I pulled the cotton balls out of his nose, there was a strong odor of garlic. I looked up his nose with my flashlight. I saw a needle mark going up into his brain.

When I finished my job packing him, I went back into the ward and rolled Ziggi, a patient in the first bed near the backdoor, into the staff's lunchroom.

"What happened to the Caveman?"

"I don't know."

I reached for the freezer door, and then I abruptly slammed it. "Ziggi, I will make sure that no ice cream will ever appear on your plate again."

"The Gooks came and got him."

"The Gooks?"

"Yes, the Gooks. They came for him before, you remember, but he spotted them first coming in the back-door. He slipped out of his bed and they couldn't find him in the dark. They were all dressed in black pajamas with their faces blacken and partially covered. They come in through the backdoor again and this time they crawled to his bed. They tied his loose hand down and taped his mouth. Then they jumped on top of him and stuck something long up his nose and they were gone in 30 seconds."

I reached into the freezer, came out with an Eskimo Pie, and gave it to Ziggi. I pushed him back into his spot on the ward. I went and inspected the backdoor. There were scratches all around the lock and the latch. Small pieces of tape were still attached to it, where the latch was held back.

The next morning I called Captain Morales' office. They said she had been transferred to another hospital and they wouldn't say where. I remembered Captain Morales saying that garlic is a wonderful seasoning when applied to food, but a deadly poison when injected into the blood stream.

Swilley asked me, "What happen to SGT Gorge?"

"He died of a heart attack."

He shook his head in disbelief.

Now, I was really frightened. I didn't know what in the hell was going on, but I knew it wasn't good. Too many of my good friends were dying under weird circumstances. Their deaths were all untimely, unnatural and unexplained. Was I bad luck for my friends? I began to have concerns about Swilley's welfare.

Two days later, Gorge's mother and two guys with badges walked into the ward. They walked up to me and asked to speak with SGT Gorge. I said that he had passed away and his body was in the morgue. They looked at one another. Gorge's mother leaned back with steam in her eyes and began to cry.

They asked me my name. I replied PFC Roy. They pulled out a black book and looked down a list of names. They spotted my name. Then he asked, "Did you serve with SGT Gorge and the other members of his SF A-team at Fort Sam Houston."

"Yes."

"Did they ever discuss any of their assignments with you?"

"No, sir."

The second agent, who never turned around to allow me to see his face said, "PFC Roy, It appears you have a closed mouth."

"No, sir, I actually have a big mouth, but I simply say what needs to be said only and nothing more."

"How do you feel about the president and his brother, Roy?"

"I don't know how to answer that question, Sir, but I know a lot of good people are getting killed trying to follow the president's orders."

"Killed, how do you know they are being killed following the president's orders?"

"Don't we all follow the president's orders?"

The other agent looking at Gorge's chart with the wrong name on it said, "Here it says that a Sergeant Miller died of a heart attack. Was Miller-Gorge?"

I simply looked at them without answering their question. I looked down at the other agent's hands. He had picked up the San Antonio telephone book that was in the Caveman's nightstand that the A-team used as a codebook.

He asked me, "Have you seen this book before?"

"That's a dumb question, I just left San Antonio."

He asked me, "Do you have one."

"No."

I was glad I had mistakenly left it at home in New York City. I suspected they would check my locker for it. They gave me their card. It said they were special agents assigned to the Office of the Attorney General of the United States. They left saying, "If you come in contact with any information concerning the members of the A-team, we would appreciate hearing from you."

All of this was getting a bit overwhelming for me. Vecky had told me that Bobby Kennedy was personally supervising them in Operation Mongoose while they were in Cuba. Vecky said that Bobby ordered the assassination of Fidel Castro, but the bad "Intel" he provided them screwed up their mission.

I never heard from Captain Morales again and yes, it was that time again. I had to find a newspaper with the cartoons of Snuffy Smith to calm myself. Additionally, I made several trips into Enterprise, Alabama to party. I was trying to forget my troubles, but I never had a good time; except for once. It was during a visit by James Brown and Bobby Blue Bland. The little hole in the wall bar in which they played was sold out. Every "Country Soul Sister" within fifty miles of Enterprise was in attendance. After the show, my driver Robinson from Mississippi, and I found two girls who wanted to do the nasty. So we got a jar of shine and headed for the local hotel with both of them in tow.

I never grew comfortable with Enterprise. I preferred to hang out in Ozark, due east of the Fort. I visited Ozark many times with Robinson and Swilley. It was their favorite also. Most of the girls in Ozark were as "country" as the ones from Enterprise. But, they were better looking and the juke joints were friendlier. There you didn't have to watch your back all the time.

I met a very nice Soul Sister in Ozark by the name of Carol Thompson. She had the most incredible brown skin and body. I nicked named her Brown Sugar, because her skin tone was the same color and as smooth as my rifle in basic training. Her skin literally glowed at night, she was very intelligent with a wonderful sense of humor and she didn't have a Southern accent. She had worked years on losing it. She joined the Toast Masters at high school to better her speech. She was a senior at the Ozark High School and made it clear to me, up front, that she wasn't giving up anything- no sex.

Her father reinforced it by saying, "In addition to my daughter, the only thing I am giving up is a hard way to go and a short life to live to any Soul Brother who is too aggressive with her."

Her county recently integrated their local high school in Ozark. Some of the white students joined the KKK in protest and burned a cross into the football field. I took her to the football games on Friday evenings and walked her home afterwards to protect her from the rednecks. One Friday game ran into overtime and ended very late. Ozark lost to an all-Black high school from Enterprise, Alabama. A number of the redneck students were upset about the lost.

As I escorted her home, we hugged and kissed as we walked down a very dark road. I noticed a car pulling up slowly behind us with its bright lights on. Carol didn't pay any attention to the car. She simply kept her month running as usual, only to stop for an occasional kiss. I reached down and picked up a rock. The car was full of drunken white boys from Ozark high school.

"Hey, nigger, that's a pretty colored girl you got there."

I said nothing.

"We like colored girls too."

We kept walking. They banged on the side of the car door to scare us. I raised the rock to throw it. Carol stopped me abruptly, turned and walked up to the car. I was dumb founded. She approached the car's rear door, looked inside and said, "Cory is that you in the back seat of this car." She had recognized his voice. The white guy seating in the back slid down into the seat trying to hide his face and the liquor bottle in his hand.

"Your father works with mine and I am going to tell him that you have been drinking."

"Please don't, Carol," he said, "I didn't know that was you. Please don't." He tapped the driver on the shoulder telling him to get going.

"Don't you pull away from me without apologizing to my friend."

"I am sorry, fellow; Carol, please don't tell my father."

I began to laugh my ass off. Man, it was dark, no street lights, on a deserted road, deep into redneck country and this Sister is taking on a whole carload of drunken redneck school boys. The sweat was pouring down my face. I gave her the biggest hug and kiss I could find. We continued to talk and walk towards her house; laughing and joking about what a coward I was.

Then another car appeared with its bright lights on. This time, it was coming down the road at high speed-low level flying. She looked at me with concern this time. The car was driving down the shoulder of the road where we were walking. I only had a faction of a second to pull her out of the way. We both jumped into the roadside ditch. This car was not the same car that had stopped earlier. This was a deliberate attempt to run us over. She tore her skirt diving into the ditch.

The car came to a screeching halt, and turned around about 50 yards pass where it tried to run us over. She was really scared now, so was I. The car crossed back over the highway and proceeded to come back looking for us against the oncoming traffic. We were lying in an open field of drying peanut stalks and I felt we would be easily spotted if we tried to run across the field.

She looked at me with questioning eyes, "What are we going to do?"

I didn't get a good look at the men inside the car as it went pass us, because they covered the side windows with newspaper. But, I had seen that car on base before. We started to run back down the roadway in the opposite direction from which we came. Suddenly another set of headlights appeared in the distance in front of us. It became a race as to which car would get us first. The car chasing us was traveling slowly shinning a flashlight into the fields by the roadway looking for us. We were hauling ass as fast as we could in the darkness, putting a lot of distance between us and the first car. Then she tripped and fell letting out a loud scream. I held her down flat in the roadway to avoid being seen. The first car turned around, their headlight's hit us and they sped up until the headlights of the second car hit them.

The second car came to a stop, because the car chasing us was blocking the roadway in front of them. It was Swilley and some of his friends. Their country music was blasting from their radio. I was never so glad to hear country music in my life.

Swilley drove up and asked us, "What's going on, Milkman and who in the hell is in that car backing down the wrong way of the highway?"

"I don't know and don't want to know either."

Swilley wrote down the plate number and said, "Milkman, you get into more shit than a hair in a snake's ass."

"Milkman, that's your nickname?" Carol said. "You must be a farmer. You are not from New York City; you're a hick like me."

I laughed, looking at the other car pulling away from us. We drove Carol home and then proceeded back to the base. I couldn't figure out who would want to run me over, but I started to have my suspicions.

Swilley couldn't stop talking about the upcoming dance at the EM Club. He even told Carol about it.

I wasn't really looking forward to the dance, because the Fort's social service director told me that this would be her last try to have an integrated dance party on base. There was a near riot during the last dance at the EM Club, because a Soul Brother had asked a white soldier's girl friend to dance.

Swilley invited his girlfriend Maggie from Tennessee to take a bus down for the weekend. They never had done it before. She asked him to propose to her that weekend and she would give him some.

The social service director literally begged me to help with the getting the Black GIs to attend the dance. I told her, I would do what I could. The girls from Ozark wanted to come, but they had no transportation. I told the director that if the Army would foot the bill for a bus to pick up the girls from Ozark, it would be a good reason for the Black GIs to come. I said the last dance caused problems, because there were so few Black girls in attendance. The Soul Sisters had no way of getting on the base to the EM Club. And, the Soul Brothers definitely were not going to stand around and watch white guys dance. She said she would try and hook-up transport for the Sisters.

Later some of the white soldiers complained that there was no bus service for the white girls and it started to get out of hand. The SSD told me she didn't know if she could pull it off. I told her I would do her a favor and help with the music, if she could pull it off. But, the music would be half Country, half Soul and Rock and Roll. Swilley was so excited about getting some that he didn't care what kind of music was scheduled to be played.

Two days before the dance, a small group of medics and I were called into the HQ Orderly Room. We lined up at attention and the first sergeant told us that the commanding officer of the hospital had important news for us. Both Swilley and I knew that our time at the Fort Rucker Hospital was coming to an end. Generally, the medics were either sent to helicopter crew chief school or to Europe. If you got chief's school, it usually meant you would be in Vietnam within three months.

The death notices littered the bulletin boards at the school's entrance. The Army didn't sanction the notices, but they allowed it, because the instructors used it to motivate the students to pay attention. Some GIs got killed on their first flights in Nam. The choppers they were using were old and slow and they had very little fire support on their missions. That was the reason the Army was developing a new helicopter, the HU-1A (Huey). They were transports and gunships, but they were not in Nam yet.

Most GIs wanted to go to Europe. If you got to Europe, you would be guaranteed two years there and your enlistment would be up by the time you came back home. The only problem was the Russians, but at least they were not shooting at us yet. If we could keep them relatively quiet, you stood a good chance of coming back home walking instead of in a body bag. The NCOs said that Europe was all spit and polish soldiering, which meant you did nothing, but cleaned your equipment and stayed ready to fight. Many units in Europe stayed in the field, because of the high state of readiness required for facing off the Russians. Most Soul Brothers who were stationed there said the European women treated you like kings. Right on baby, I was ready to go to be knighted.

Swilley and I were standing at the end of the formation, as the CO come down the line handing each GI his sealed orders. Some GIs fainted dead away after opening them. Some hollered with joy, jumping up and down until the first sergeant calmed them down. You could tell who got what orders by their reactions. When he handed me my orders, I opened the envelope, the letter said the 517th Medical Clearing Co., Bad Kreuznach, Germany and I hollered. Swilley didn't say anything.

I turned to him and said, "Chief's school right?"

"Yes and no, flight school to be a pilot, my father must have had something to do with this. I didn't ask for flight school."

I patted him on the shoulders. Swilley wasn't too down about it, even though he knew that the medical evacuation choppers had the highest attrition rate in Nam. If he made it, he would be promoted to warrant officer, something his father could live with.

There was a lot going on in my mind also. I wondered if SGT Sammerson had anything to do with me getting orders for Europe. There was no confirmation of his death. He and the remainder of the A-team were listed as missing-in-action, not killed in action. Too many of my friends were getting killed or disappearing. Historically, it was the Soul Brothers who were lynched in uniform, now it was my white friends. I felt relieved that Swilley was going to a different unit than me. He had saved my ass a few times and I was worried about his.

Swilley and Moran taught me a lot about rednecks, you might not agree with their racial politics, but if a redneck was your friend; he would put his life on the line for yours. Swilley never said he was my friend, because he didn't have to; he lived it. Both of us were ordered to clear the post's barracks within two weeks.

Saturday finally rolled around and I still hadn't heard whether there was going to be a bus for the Sisters in Ozark. Swilley was about to come in his khakis. I couldn't locate the social services director, so I went over to the EM Club to find her. She had stepped out, said the DJ. Not to waste my time, I tried to work out the music with the redneck DJ. It was a waste of time and I was about to slap the SOB when Swilley walked in. He knew Swilley and we got the music arranged without killing one another.

The EM Club wasn't allowed to serve any hard liquor or beer during this dance. My first legal drink was a beer at Fort Dix on federal property, at an EM Club. The Army felt if you were old enough to die, you were old enough to drink. The Army respected local laws only when they wanted too. My eighteenth birthday was in two days and I was going to party down.

The dance started at 2000 hours. Only a few Black girls were in the EM Club when 8:00 pm rolled around.

The Black GIs were getting ants in their pants and were on my case, because I promised Soul Sisters. Swilley was in seventh heaven; his girl arrived earlier by bus from Tennessee. He introduced Maggie to me. I didn't say so to Swilley, but she looked like a veteran streetwalker to me, not the virgin that she told him she was.

He was holding her closer than "white on rice." The white soldiers got a bus for their girls. It picked them up in Enterprise, Alabama; they had already arrived and started to party. The Soul Brothers came to me again complaining about it. I told them to be patient. The music was getting hotter and the DJ started to play Motown. The Brothers were getting extremely antsy now.

Swilley walked away from his girl to get a soft drink. Before I could blink an eye, a Soul Brother grabbed Swilley's girl and took her out into the middle of the dance floor. The white Southern soldiers immediately left the dance floor, but Maggie didn't miss a beat. She was dancing her ass off with the Brother. Then Swilley appeared with two cups of pop. I tried to block his view of what was going on. I couldn't tell the Brother that he picked the wrong white girl to dance with, because she accepted the dance. Swilley spotted the Brother dancing with his girl and he went off like a Minuteman Missile headed for Moscow. I tried to stop him from attacking the Brother on the dance floor.

He threw both cups of his pop on my clean uniform. The Brother dancing with Swilley's girl saw him throw the pops on me and he took offense. He didn't give a damn whose girl it was anyway. They were playing his music and he was going to dance with any girl in the place that wanted to dance with him.

I begged Swilley not to attack the Brother in the EM Club; this would be the end of dances for everybody. He challenged the Brother to come into the bathroom and he told me not to touch him or follow him. He said that I double-crossed him and his girl.

The white Southern soldiers came back onto the dance floor as soon as Swilley and the Brothers stormed into the bathroom. A few of Swilley's white soldier friends followed him into the bathroom also. I tried to stop the Soul Brothers from following him into the bathroom.

One Brother called me a "faggot" and said, "If you aren't going to kick Swilley's ass, he was."

A few Brothers followed him into the bathroom. I went into the bathroom pleading with both sides. They started to push one another. I got between them preventing them from getting close enough to hurt one another.

Robinson called me over to the bathroom's door as they went at it verbally. I peeped out the bathroom's door and I laughed at what I saw. I went back into the bathroom and forcibly grabbed Swilley by his torn uniform and pushed him to the bathroom's door. He looked out onto the dance floor. His girlfriend was now dancing a slow-grind with a white corporal.

I said, "Swilley, I guess he outranks you."

He was about to take off after the corporal. I gently grabbed his shoulder and he just stopped and gave me a dumb look.

Then someone hollered, "The Soul Sisters from Ozark are here." All the Brothers in the bathroom flew to the EM Club's front door. I grabbed Swilley and took him with me to keep him out of trouble. The school bus pulled up to the front door. It was the same bus that picked up the white girls first. The bus's doors opened and the social director walked down the stairs staring at the both of us.

She said, "What happened to you guys?"

I said, "I spilled some soda on myself and he fell down in it."

The girls rushed off the bus. They looked so good. Carol came also and I grabbed her before she hit the bottom step. Every one of the twenty-two girls on that bus had on the same shade of red lipstick. They shared one tube of lipstick between all 22 of them. I called it "Ozark Red," the most beautiful shade of lipstick in the world.

"The Army only gave me one bus," the director said to me, "And, I had to personally guarantee the girls' safety to their parents before they would let them get on the bus leaving the high school's grounds in Ozark." She gave me a long stare and said, "They must to be back on the bus by 2300 hours. They will go home first since they came last. Do I have your word, PFC Roy that they will leave in the same condition that they arrived in?"

I smiled and said, "Yes."

Swilley didn't dance with Maggie at all. She danced with every white guy in the place. No Brother would dance with her again after the sisters came. I invited Swilley to hang out with the Soul Sisters and me at my table. A few sisters remembered him from the time we brought Charles, the newly arrived soldier, over to Aunt Millie's to eat. They danced with him most of the night sometimes two girls at a time.

Finally, Maggie convinced the corporal to take her back to her hotel, because Swilley refused to talk to her again that evening.

I didn't let Carol go the entire night. No one else danced with her either. I told her, "I received my orders and was being sent to Europe; exactly where I wanted to go."

She became very upset and said, "What about us?"

"I am not going to lie to you, Baby, and tell you that I love you and want to marry you, just to get you in bed with me before I leave. I like you a lot Carol, but I am not ready for anything that serious. I just turned eighteen. We could write one another, but I don't like to write. I will not get in your way if you want to date other guys. I will be away for at least two years and a lot could happen in two years."

We danced, hugged and kissed the rest of the evening. I kissed all of the Ozark Red lipstick from her lips. It tasted so good. 2300 hours rolled around quickly and I put Carol on the bus last and we said our tearful goodbyes. That was the last time I never saw Brown Sugar and Ozark Red Lipstick again.

***

11

A Different Kind of Hero

It was the first day of May 1963 when I arrived back home. New York City is beautiful in the spring. Central Park's trees, once bare and almost lifeless, started to break out of their depression. They discarded their boring grays, tans, and browns and transformed themselves into lush greens, yellows and reds. Freshly painted white stripes began to appear on the streets and avenues. Broken streets lights began to work again. Walking bundled lumps of humanity began to shed their manufactured skins and morph, once again, into arms, legs, necks and faces of individuals that you once knew only a few months earlier.

My orders called for me to leave via the Brooklyn Navy Yard, in New York City for Bremerhaven, Germany in 6 days. It only took a half day travel to get to the ship. This was a great birthday gift for me from the Army, because it gave me extra time to spend with Mom, SGT Lonzo Morgan, and Malcolm X. I had a lot to discuss with everyone, especially Lonzo.

I knew when I ran into Lonzo, he would be very proud of me. He couldn't tease me about the loose fit of my uniform anymore, because I had bulked-up and it looked tailored now. I knew he would lecture me on keeping my Johnson covered and watching out for those Russian bastards in Europe, because they would try to cut my throat if I gave them the chance. I would tell him that these redneck bastards, here in America, almost cut my throat at home.

It was still very early in the morning, as I walked up the subway's steps and through my deserted street looking for flowerpots to rain down on me from Sis's fire escape. There was no one in sight. This scene appeared identical to the one in the motion picture, "War of the Worlds" where the aliens were invading the town and all the streets were deserted, because the town's peoples were in hiding. With what I had been through in such a short period of time, I felt different, almost like I was an invading alien.

It was too early for Lonzo to drill his platoon on 115th St., so I went to my apartment. Everyone was asleep. I grabbed Spot's leash and took him out for a walk. As I exited my front door there stood Lonzo with a smile a half-mile wide, on his face.

He gave me a big hug and said "Eddie you have grown into a real soldier, the Milkman, the ladies' man and a true street fighter."

He stopped talking and went into a hand to hand combat stance. I reacted instinctively with a defensive move.

I smiled and said "It's against the law in New York City to beat up an old fart." I told him, "I ran into the Wolfman. I now know your last name, SGT Lonzo Morgan."

He acted like he didn't know who I was talking about.

"The Wolfman did a good job training you, he is the best. Let me see what you know."

I smiled as we walked down stairs into his Foxhole, sat down on his nasty bed and had a drink of his hot Gypsy Rose wine. I sensed that he knew all about my adventures in Texas and Alabama. He just smiled at me as he touched his wine bottle to his mouth.

"SGT Lonzo Morgan, you know more about my adventures and what's going on in Uncle Sam's Army than I do; you old fart." I gave him another hug as he instinctively grabbed his life force in his back packet. Some things change, but most things remain the same. He took Spot by the leash, walked him out of the basement's front door and we began to talk.

"The only news I received about you Lonzo, was from my mother's occasional letters."

"Like you, I don't like to write."

"My mother told me what was happening on the political and civil rights fronts in the country, as well as how you were doing."

"You know I never liked to talk about negative things, especially politics. How did the Southern girls treat you?"

"Great."

"Wait until you get a shot at those European girls."

"I haven't heard anything about the fate of the Wolfman and remainder of his team, have you?"

"Sam is one of the nastiest street fighters in the world. He was as good as me, even before I left the Army. He has five years to his retirement and he isn't going to miss that date for nothing. I am sorry for not telling you about my relationship with the Wolfman. I was like a father to him, with him losing his entire family and all. He picked himself up, got to America and followed me to Korea. I am very proud of him."

He looked at me. "The Wolfman told me about your progress as a soldier. He told me that you were developing into one of the best he ever trained, though you didn't qualify for Airborne?"

"No, bad eye sight-it is for the best. And, who in their right mind wants to jump out of a perfectly good airplane anyway?"

"I really wanted to tell you about the Wolfman, but he and I didn't believe your paths would ever cross. And I definitely didn't want him to tell you any of my ugly secrets. You know, I raised Sam after WWII. I never got married, because of Sam. He lost his whole family in the holocaust and I still had mine in South Carolina. They wouldn't ever consider allowing a single black man in the Army to adopt a white Jewish boy. Anyway, he was only two years from being eighteen and on his own, so I left it alone.

"I joined the Rangers in the meantime and I checked up on him once or twice a week. He was a good kid, a bright student like you. The Jewish home on the East Side was doing a great job taking care of him. But, he refused to trust anyone, but me.

"I remember, one time, they wanted to take him on a train ride to Washington, DC in 1947, for a support the State of Israel rally. He emphatically refused to go. The home's director couldn't understand why and told him he must go. He refused again, ran away from the group home and called me collect at Fort Benning. I knew immediately why he didn't want to go to Washington, D.C.; he had to ride on a train.

"The last time he had seen his parents, brothers and sister, they were being ordered on a train to the death camps. I told him that I wanted him to go on the trip with the other young Jewish kids to Washington, D.C. I said to him jokingly that he would meet some nice Jewish girls there.

"He told me he still wasn't going. I told him that I would pay his airfare to fly to DC, if he would go. He said yes and returned to the group home. Milkman, I encouraged you as a young man to go to Washington, D.C. to protest racial discrimination in this country.

I nodded.

"When the United Nations established the State of Israel, he was so proud of the fact that he played his small part in making it happen. When he was old enough to leave the group home, he married a Puerto Rican girl named Celita. It didn't last too long; he had bit the soldier bug like me. He went to Israel and served in the Israeli army. An Arab broke his arm in a street fight and he was sent back to recuperate in a hospital here in America. That was about the time the Korean War broke out. He joined the US Army and followed me to Korea. That fight with that Arab was the last street fight he ever lost.

He smiled at me and said, "I heard you lost a street fight also, Milkman." I laughed, then he got contemplative and began remembering; I leaned back and just listened.

"I got sick and couldn't go to the Korean front with my ranger unit. Later, I was sent to join the 24th Infantry, a previously all colored regiment, The Buffalo Soldiers. It was bad news from the time I walked into the HQ. The United States thought WWII was the war to end all wars. Where have we heard that before? They sent us into combat, in Korea, with a rifle, one band of ammo, a set of wings and a prayer. We lost Negroes left and right. The Brothers heard the white boys talk about bug-out routes. They used these routes to save their asses when their ammo ran out and they were about to be overrun by the North Koreans. Following the white soldier's lead, the Negro soldiers started to use bug-out routes too.

"Lieutenant Victor Masterson, our Platoon Leader, was one of the few Negro officers in the 24th and the only Negro West Point Graduate I ever met. He was very upset with the lack of ammunition, food, artillery and tank support the generals were allocating to the formally all Negro units. He was fed up with the lack of proper resources, training, leadership, and the blatant racism the US Army was directing at Negro soldiers.

"He was very vocal about it to our company commander. He felt the company had lost enough Negro men fighting to the North Koreans. We often fought hand to hand, outnumbered ten to one. You can't fight a war armed with tooth picks. General Patton demanded the best from his Negro soldiers and he made sure we got the best resources to fight with.

"Milkman, I saw a Brother pull the pin from a hand grenade still attached to his body and fling himself into a crowd of advancing North Koreans, because he ran out of ammo. Milkman, that's no way to fight a war. Our white officers started to call us "Nigger Cowards." They told LT Masterson the next time he ordered his men to retreat in the face of the enemy they would have him arrested and court martialed. They did that to another Negro lieutenant from C Company and no one ever heard of him again. He just disappeared into thin air after the MPs picked him up.

"The North Koreans just attacked again and again, wave after wave, non-stop for days. We would melt the barrels of our 30 caliber machine guns, killing those North Korean SOBs. One day, we were in the middle of an attack; we fell back by taking a bug-out route. Our company commander, a redneck from South Carolina, called over the radio for LT Masterson to report to him in the HQ. The Lieutenant left me in charge of the platoon. After LT Masterson left, The North Koreans began to attack again and we ran out of ammo again. I called over the field radio and asked the CO to send LT Masterson back with ammo.

"The company commander said to me over the radio, 'That uppity nigger is never coming back and you cowardly, black ass niggers better stand and fight to the last man. Pull out your dicks and piss on the SOBs if you have to.'

"I put Corporal Sammerson in charge of the platoon. I grabbed both my 1911 Colt 45 and the "Third Luger", the one that I took from that SS Bitch in WWII, and I fought my way to the HQ. My Colt-45 was out of bullets by the time I arrived at the HQ. I was mad as shit. I kicked opened the HQ door and asked the CO, 'Where is LT Masterson.

"On his way to hell were all you cowardice niggers belong."

I raised The 'Third Luger' and shot that SOB in the same exact spot that I shot that SS Bitch. At the exact same time, the North Koreans threw a satchel charge into the doorway of the HQ; as they overran it. It blew the door clean off its hinges and the door hit me square in the back, knocking me across the room. I went out like a light. They burst into the HQ with flame-throwers and torched us. I was protected from most of the flames and heat by the HQ door landing on top of me. Only parts of my back were burned.

"When I came-to, a North Korean officer entered the HQ and stepped on top of the door. He picked up the "Third Luger" from the ashes; he didn't know that I was lying underneath it and still alive. I heard him say to the XO, "Surrender your company."

The executive officer and company clerk were still alive, but burned too badly to speak. I was still lying under the door with my hand exposed. The North Korean Officer spotted my hand moving; trying to reach the spot that I had dropped the Luger. He jumped on top of the door and I hollered from the pain of my burnt back. He complimented me on the Luger, pointed it at the XO and shot him in the head.

"He ordered his men to bring LT Masterson into the smoking HQ for questioning. The Lieutenant was still in the MPs' handcuffs. North Korean soldiers had intercepted and rescued him from the two white MPs who were in the process of pushing him off a cliff. The North Koreans shot the two MP SOBs. The North Korean Officer then demanded that LT Masterson, now the highest ranking officer in the company, order the entire company to surrender to him. He said to him 'We saved your life from your own racist people, now you save the lives of your remaining men.' He handed LT Masterson the burnt, but still working HQ radio field-phone and told him to call the platoon leaders."

"The lieutenant said, "No."

"He pointed the Luger at the wounded company clerk and shot him in the head. He then said to LT Masterson, 'I will give you one more chance to save your men.' He hit the lieutenant in the face with the pistol and ordered him to provide information concerning our platoon's locations on the ridge that we were defending. The lieutenant said nothing.

"He then stepped off the door, pulled it up and pointed the Luger at my head and pulled the trigger. The Luger went click; it was out of bullets. He then un-holstered his own pistol and pointed it at me. LT Masterson said he would talk if the North Korean officer would spare my life.

"About the same time, The Wolfman and the remainder of Company B were counter attacking the command post. The North Korean Officer ordered his men to stand their ground as mortar rounds began dropping on top of the HQ; like raindrops. North Korean body parts were flying everywhere. The North Korean officer was wounded in the leg and he finally ordered his men to retreat from the HQ. He dragged LT Masterson with him; still in MPs' handcuffs.

"The Wolfman broke into the HQ, with what was left of my platoon, firing at anything that moved. The Wolfman slowly looked around the HQ for any moving enemy soldiers. He noticed the CO, who I thought was dead, trying to speak and pointing his finger at me. He died before he said anything. The Wolfman ordered our platoon out and to form a defensive perimeter around the HQ.

"My back and neck were burned badly; I couldn't say a word either. He ordered a private to find a medic for me. When they left, the Wolfman picked up my 'Third Luger', wrapped it in toilet paper and stuck it in his shirt. The Wolfman assumed I shot everyone in the HQ. I never told him that the North Korean officer shot the company XO and clerk with my Luger; and missing me by one bullet.

"I was court martialed for leaving my platoon while it was under fire. I was busted down in rank to private and dishonorably discharged from the Army in 1952 with 10 years of service. I simply refused to talk to anyone at my court martial. My platoon members were forced to make written statements that I put the Wolfman in charge of the platoon during a North Korean attack and deserted them.

"The Army noted in my court martial record that the company officers and clerk of Company B were shot with a 45 ACP pistol. The North Koreans did not use 45 ACP rounds and the rounds recovered from the officer's bodies didn't match any rounds test fired from my or anyone's 1911 Colt 45 pistol in our company. No one presented any evidence or filed charges at my court martial concerning who killed the CO, XO or company clerk. I never saw that Luger again, either. The Wolfman to this day believes I killed all of them with it. I would have. I never discussed Korea again with anybody, until now. As you know, we only discuss bad missions, because there is something to learn from them. There is nothing to be learned from this. I was wrong and my ugly secret is now yours.

"We never heard from LT Masterson again. His body was never recovered, no prisoner of war confirmation, nothing. He is still listed as Missing–In-Action. The commander of the 25th Infantry Division, Major General William B. Kean, requested that the 24th Infantry Regiment be disbanded from the Eight Army, because it had demonstrated that it was 'Untrustworthy and incapable of carrying out missions expected of an American infantry unit.'"

"American combat units that don't distinguish themselves in combat are not allowed to return their unit colors home after a war or conflict. Their colors were assigned to a foreign purgatory. The 24th Infantry wasn't allowed to return their colors home to the United States with honor.

As the tears rolled down my face, I recalled what Wolfman had said about ugly secrets and the responsibilities that go along with them. I gave Lonzo a long hug. He seemed to have lost a hundred pounds after his confession. I walked Spot back into our apartment house. As I pushed open my apartment door, my mother grabbed a broomstick, because she thought someone was breaking into the apartment. When she recognized me, she dropped the broom and gave me a big hug.

I woke up my brother and sister by tickling their noses and feet. They were also glad to see me. My mother had enrolled my sister into the Eastern Stars; the female Masons and she wanted to show me how well she would march in their upcoming parade. As usual, my brother had wet the bed and it reeked. It was one happy occasion. My mother never asked about the details of what I had experienced. She just wanted to confirm that I was well and for me to share my traveling experiences. She didn't ask about my love life. If I had brought a girl home, she would have known that I was serious about a female. So if I didn't say anything, she wasn't going to either.

I took a shower, put on civilian clothes and went looking for my friend Teddy. When I left home, he had graduated to heroin. He lived a few doors up the block. I went upstairs and knocked on his door. His father answered the door and said he was in the front room of their railroad apartment. As I entered his filthy room, I saw him bent over in a heroin nod in dirty underwear, with sores all over his body. I almost threw up.

I said, "What's happening, Brother."

He raised his head with a half-smile on his face and said, "Fast Eddie, what's going on, Brother," then immediately went back into his heroin nod. I patted him on the back and quietly left the apartment.

I walked around the corner to the Muslim Bookstore and asked Brother 17X about Malcolm Xs' whereabouts. Brother 17X remembered me from the long hours I spent standing and reading in the Muslim Bookstore. He said, "The Minister is extremely busy, but he is scheduled to speak at a rally on the corner of Lenox Ave. and 116th St. later in the month."

Another Brother, 23X, said he was in Chicago, which meant he was meeting with The Honorable Elijah Mohammed, Head of the Nation of Islam. Things had gotten ugly between them. I imagined what he would have said seeing me.

17X said, "I mentioned to Brother Minister Malcolm X that you joined the devil's Army. He said, he was sorry he lost you to the Devil. Are you a spy for the Devil now, Brother?"

I smiled and said, "Not yet, Brother, not yet."

The Muslim Bookstore was alive with reporters from all over the world. They were everywhere, including the Muslim restaurant next door. In April, Malcolm had learned of the infidelity of Elijah Muhammad and the resulting children that were born out of his sexual exploits with his secretaries. Malcolm X had heard these rumors before, but now he had proof. He was speaking openly about it exposing his ugly secrets. Both the Wolfman and I suspected he had ugly secrets and he would pay dearly for revealing them.

Additionally, Malcolm X and JFK were having a continuing running gun battle in the press that picked up in intensity. Malcolm X wrote open letters to JFK severely criticizing him for his handling of civil rights protests in Birmingham, Alabama. Malcolm X also criticized Martin Luther King for his repeated non-violent stand in the face of overwhelming violent oppression against so-called Negroes by racist white Americans.

He said, "It is easy to understand why the presidential candidates of both political parties put on such a false show with the Civil Rights Bill and with false promises of integration. They must impress the 3 million voting Negroes who are the actual integration seekers.

"The white liberals control the Negro civil rights leaders. As long as they control the Negro civil rights leaders, they can control and contain the Negro struggle. As they can control the so-called Negro struggle, Foxy white liberals think they can control the Negro revolution, by the government itself. But, only God controls the Black revolution. The same American government that is responsible for the assassination of Congo leader Patrice Lumumba and Mississippi NAACP leader Medgar Evers."

There was a great deal of tension in the bookstore and restaurant. Many Muslim Brothers felt that Temple # 7 was literally crawling with FBI, Justice Department, Defense Department and NYC Police agents.

17X speculated, "If you were to spend one dollar in the bookstore, you would get three dollar's worth of change from a FBI agent trying to turn you into a spy for the government. So many Muslim Brothers were on the government's payroll, that the Brothers have stopped collecting welfare checks and were driving Cadillacs."

I hadn't seen so much activity on the corner of 116th St. in my life. On June 29th, Malcolm was scheduled to speak at a rally there. Unfortunately, I was headed for Germany unaware that Malcolm X's prophetic criticism of President Kennedy for his lack of condemnation of the racial violence, that was sweeping America, was about to consume them both, bury them in their own ugly secrets and connect them at the hip for an eternity.

I thought a few days off would rest my mind and get my experiences in San Antonio and Ozark behind me and out of my head, but they wouldn't go away. My gorilla nightmares were as strong as ever. I felt that I was being transformed from a budding Black Revolutionary into an American Military Assassin disguised as an Army Medic.

I shipped out for Europe on one of the oldest and slowest troopships in the US Merchant Marine fleet, 'The USS General Rose.' There were guys from all branches of the Army on board the Rose, chemical warfare specialists, artillerymen, mechanics of all types, Airborne and Special Forces.

I was seasick for the first three days on the big pond. I became seasick as soon as the ship pulled away from the dock. I experienced firsthand what my ancestors endured leaving the shores of Africa for their first and final time. I never drank another cup of coffee again while I was abroad the General Rose. I felt it was the coffee that made me seasick, at least that's what I thought.

The second day out, I was assigned to keep clean one section in a flight of stairs that led to the sleeping areas below deck. There were so many GIs on the General Rose that the NCOs had to spread thin the make-busy-work duties.

The third day out, I spotted a familiar face in the chow line. It was Roger Moreland, the guy who I had met on my first day of active duty in the Army. He looked lost. He said he didn't know anyone aboard ship. I asked him if he wanted to be assigned to the empty bunk underneath me. He said yes and had his bunk changed. He was very nervous and very uptight. He was assigned to keep clean the section of stairs just above mine.

I noticed the insignia on his collar; it indicated that he was a CBR specialist. I asked him if he got his top secret clearance that went along with his job specialty.

He said, "Yes" and he just left the small, little heard of chemical and biological warfare base at Fort Detrick, Maryland. He changed the subject and went silent on me, something he never done when we entered basic training together.

At night, he was constantly writing in his fancy leather bound diary by the light of his flashlight. A lot of guys kept dairies in the Army. Me, I admit, I was too lazy and did not like to write at all. That's the main reason why I couldn't keep any girlfriends while I was serving in the Army. But, there was something different about Moorland's writing. Late at night when he thought everyone was asleep, he would get up put on his clothes and disappear below deck for hours then reappear and write in his diary.

It was our fourth day out and my first trip on the big pond was getting better. I wasn't seasick anymore. The weather was beautiful. Moreland and I began to hang out on the ship's decks together. He didn't have much of a sense of humor, but I enjoyed his company anyway. He also had problems with the war jocks aboard ship, the same as I did.

He noticed that the SF B-team appeared to be shadowing the both of us all over the ship. For some reason they were traveling to Europe on the same ship as I. I told him not to worry, that I knew of them. I didn't tell him that I felt uncomfortable around them also.

On the forth evening out, Moreland and I were standing at the stern watching the mess men throw the ship's garbage over board from the deck below. A school of great white sharks followed the ship from New York City's shores. They were attacking the garbage like lions attacking a limping gazelle.

Man, they ripped through those empty five-pound metal cans like they were tissue paper. Sometimes, one shark would accidentally bite another shark. After smelling the blood, they would go into a feeding frenzy by attacking and killing the wounded shark. Moreland didn't like watching it very much. But, there was always a bunch of GIs on the stern every evening watching and betting on the action.

Man, those sharks would clear five to six feet out of the water getting at that garbage. I bet a GI $5 that I could pick the shark that would follow the ship the longest across the ocean. I picked the most determined shark in the group. He had a nasty scar on his fin.

I named him Bismarck, because we were told that the German Battle Ship Bismarck was sunk during WWII by the British due south of where we were. You know honor to one's country is strange. I was told the captain of the Bismarck was of Jewish ancestry. He went down with his ship fighting for the Nazis, a group he openly despised.

On the fifth day out, we met a tall dark Brother, on board, who was a merchant seaman. Scampi was his nickname. This Brother didn't have one once of fat on his body, but it was also obvious that he was gay. Scampi invited us down in the hole of the ship into the weight training room where he and other merchant seamen worked out. This guy could bench press twice his body weight, about five hundred pounds. We worked out with him never taking our eyes off our asses.

Scampi also noticed the B-team shadowing us. They walked into the weight room looking around as if they were lost. Scampi asked them what they wanted. If they weren't invited into the merchant seaman's weight room, they would have to leave. The B-team didn't like being put out. After that, every time the B-team members saw Scampi, they began to mimic his feminine movements. They began to tease him in the ship's canteen, in the ship's mess hall, and in the ship's theatre about being gay.

On the seventh night on the pond, we were sitting in the ship's theatre. We had to sit on the floor, because there were no seats. Anvil and Hook of the B-team started their mimicking act. Scampi got up grabbed both of those guys, one in each arm, lifted them up and squeezed the natural shit out them. They hollered and kicked, but they could not extract themselves from his death grip. It was the exact same grip that the Cavemen had placed them in. This was the first time I saw Moreland laugh. He laughed so hard that tears swelled up in his eyes as we left the theatre. Then he started talking; the laughter seemed to have a loosening effect on his mouth.

"We shouldn't be developing, testing and building these kinds of biological weapons."

I wasn't sure what he was referring too. I said to him, "listen, the Russians are developing the same ugly weapons that we are and we won't know about them until they hit us with them."

"Milkman, what I am talking about doesn't have anything to do with the Russians. We are developing weapons to kill civilians we just don't like. We have biological weapons that will destroy the body's ability to fight off disease."

"I have heard of these weapons in medical corpsman school, but my understanding was, that they were not very effective. They take too long to kill and are not effective against the human body defenses. So, for combat purposes they are useless."

"Milkman, that is exactly what I meant; these biological weapons are not being designed and manufactured to kill soldiers. They are being designed to kill civilians. In fact Milkman, they are being developed and tested in our own back yard on Plumb Island on the eastern end of Long Island"

"Still, these weapons would be very difficult to deliver for use on humans," I said

"Milkman, just you wait and see. Just you wait and see."

I could see he was in a funk, so I changed the subject. I asked him to help me collect division patches from soldiers on board ship going to their new units. We had to cut their old patches from the shoulders of their uniforms. They had to change the unit patches anyway when they arrived at their new units. I was collecting the division patches to make a souvenir quilt of all of the current active duty divisions in the Army. The only problem was, sometimes we would cut their uniforms while removing the patches. He liked this; he took pleasure in accidentally cutting the uniforms of cocky paratroopers from the 101st and 82nd Airborne Divisions.

By the eight day out, I was starving. The ship's food was getting horrible. The ship had run out of fresh food, but Moreland kept me alive on cans of sardines and Vienna sausages his aunt had given him before he left New York City.

We were standing on the ship's stern deck watching the sharks eating the ship's garbage. I heard Moreland's name called over the ship's PA system. It ordered him to report to the bridge of the ship. He didn't return, so I went below to lay on by bunk. A sergeant woke me from my sleep and told me I was assigned to stand fire watch for him in the cargo hole of the ship. I said to him, I am not scheduled for a watch; I had already pulled my fire watches for the entire voyage. It was Moreland's watch.

He said, "We can't find him. It isn't bad duty and you must take the watch even though you weren't scheduled for it."

Looking for Moreland, I took a different route to my post. On the way, I noticed the B-team guarding some crates in the hole of the ship which read "Cholera Vaccine." I said nothing to them as I passed. The next morning was the start of our ninth day out. As I made my way back to my bunk, Scampi the Merchant Seaman, was gathering Moreland's things.

"What's going on Scampi?"

"Moreland missed role call this morning and no one knows where he's at."

"What do you mean? He has to be on this ship. He was called to the bridge last evening."

"He never reported to the bridge and we searched the entire ship. We always lose a few guys crossing the big pond."

"It's as simple as that, I was on fire watch duty all last night and no one informed me to search my area for him. There was no man overboard alarm given and the ship never stopped." Scampi turned and finished gathering Moreland's things without saying anything more about it to me. I could not believe how cool and disconnected he and the ship's crew was about it.

I asked the senior NCO, why we didn't stop the ship to see if he fell overboard. I got no response. I asked my other bunkmates, if they knew anything about Moreland's disappearance. No one knew anything, except one soldier who said that he overheard Moreland talking to unidentified soldiers about violating a secret clearance or something. The Wolfman's words flashed before me again.

I walked up to the bridge of the ship and demanded that the ship be searched for Moreland. The captain sounded the man overboard alarm and brought the ship to a stop. He then ordered the ship to be searched from top to bottom. Moreland wasn't found anywhere.

When I told Moreland what unit I was assigned too he gave me a long stare. He then said the cholera vaccine on board this ship was going to the 517th. Then he gave me a disgustingly funny look, the same look he gave to the first meal we didn't eat in the Army. I still had no idea what the 517th Medical Clearing Company did, other than what its name implied. I knew it was a company of medics. We did not have a hospital to run, nor were we assigned to support a combat unit directly. So what was it that we did? We wore a 7th Army patch, not a division patch like the 3rd Armored Division or the 8th Airborne Division.

We passed the northern coast of England, just one day out of Bremerhaven, Germany. I could not sleep anymore. I walked the decks of ship for hours. Occasionally, I was distracted by the mess men throwing garbage over board and the crouching sounds of the sharks tearing the wooden boxes and number five steel cans to hell. I won the bet. Bismarck, my shark, followed the ship the longest, all the way to England from the United States. I began to say my good-byes to the guys on the ship. I simply rolled my eyes at the SF B-team. They had rid themselves of their Special Forces insignia, all rank and nametags. The only GIs that dressed that way were members of the Army's CID (Central Investigation Division).

We arrived in Bremerhaven, Germany on June 20, 1963. Bremerhaven was a large port city in the northern part of Germany. It had taken ten days for us to cross the Atlantic Ocean. It would have taken the ocean liner, the USS United States, three days and a Pan American jet eight hours. The General Rose was truly the slowest general in the fleet.

Moreland had helped me collect almost every division patch in the US Army. I was going to sew them all on my army blanket after I arrived at Bad K. I was not going to buy a blanket, if Uncle Sam would be generous enough to allow me to misappropriate one. I felt very disappointed that he wasn't going to see it. I decided to dedicate the blanket to him. I learned at Fort Rucker that the Army doesn't give you much time to mourn anyone's death or feel sorry for yourself concerning it.

An Army band greeted us at the docks playing a medley of John Phillips Sousa marches. I guess the Army forgave him for being in the Marine Corps. As I walked down the gang plank, I noticed the cargo being unloaded. The cases of cholera vaccines were being placed in trucks marked the 517th Clearing Company.

They double-checked us for the right shots. We had all of our shots before we boarded the ship. They filled us up with so much medication that we pissed out medication like a soda machine. They handed us bag lunches for the trip ahead. I really wanted some fresh milk. I would have paid dearly for it too. My allergies started to act up as soon as the ship hit land and I was out of my allergy medicine. That wasn't a good sign for my future stay in Germany. I wasn't much good to the Army that day.

They sorted us out according to our final destinations and boarded us on trains going south. Germany was still behind the times. They were still using stream locomotives to pull their trains. Exactly like a page out of the Orient Express. I immediately fell in love with the cute little compartmented cars as we traveled south. The trip from northern Germany to Frankfurt took most of the day. The trip was boring. I saw most of Western Germany from the train and it looked good for a country that had been devastated twenty five years earlier.

It hadn't happen before in the history of human conflict that a conquering nation invested so much of its own resources into a defeated enemy's homeland. At the end of WWII Germany was divided up into four zones. The northern zone was British. The middle and south zone was the American and the western zone was the French. The eastern part of Germany was the Russian zone which contained the former capital of Germany; Berlin. Berlin was also divided up by the allies.

It was early evening in Frankfurt when we arrived; with about an hour-or-so to go for Bad Kreuznach. I changed trains in Frankfurt for Bad Kreuznach, which was 50 kilometers south or about 33 miles. You can cross western Germany in a single day's trip, if no one is shooting at you. Lonzo told me that it took almost a year for him to travel from the beaches of Normandy, France to halfway across Germany in WWII.

I started to hear Malcolm X speak again and I immediately became resentful that no Black American had much to show for years of fighting in two European wars. I felt Germany had received our forty acres and a mule after WWII in the form of the Marshall Plan. And, I was over here helping her to defend it from the Russians.

I had taken possession of many ugly secrets concerning America and the individuals that served it. I didn't fully understand them nor was I very comfortable with any of them. Yet, I said nothing to anyone about my secrets, not even to Lonzo. I questioned again, why I joined the Army and why was I putting my life on the line for America and now Europeans. Who was I loyal too?

Lonzo once said to me "My loyalty to America is an investment in the future." I was having difficulty excepting that, but he was my hero-a different kind of hero.

***

12

The Supernumerary

A deuce-and-a-half was sitting waiting for me at the Bad Kreuznach's train station. I noticed the other GI's collar insignia as I got off the train. Some were combat engineers, chemical warfare specialists, missile men and of course airborne-paratroopers, "lots" of paratroopers, but no medics.

A young, skinny paratrooper looked me up and down with distain. It was a half frowned, half-brainwashed look reserved especially for "legs" (ground soldiers). I guess that semi-intimidating look was intended to convince me that paratroopers were the sharpest soldiers in this man's army. The Ranger patch on his sleeve was new, which meant he was a cherry, he hadn't sent his uniform to the cleaners yet. He just finished Ranger School, crawling around the jungles of Panama, eating six legged creatures that he couldn't name even if you gave him an encyclopedia to look them up. I wasn't impressed.

The driver, reading my name tag, told me to throw my well-traveled bags into the back of the truck and sit up front with him. The truck looked brand new, just out of the factory, but the driver was the filthiest Brother I had seen in the Army. He had grease all over his body, face and hands. He even had dirt inside his ears and nose. As he slid into the driver's seat, I asked him his name. He said Raymond Jackson, better known to the Soul Brothers as "Nasty Jack."

I reeled backwards from laugher. He gave me a cold stare as he started the engine. As he raced the trunk's engine, he grabbed his genitals and let out a sensuous, "Uooo, feeling this turbocharged-diesel run is better than having sex."

"You must be a truck mechanic."

"Not any truck's mechanic, Mabel's mechanic. She is my new child, born in Detroit and she the fastest the army has." As he tapped the gas pedal and put her in gear, he let out another sensuous, "uooo" as he drove from the train station.

Dusk was causing the small quaint German town to light up with the movement of the residents returning home from work. We crossed charming stone bridges topped with little houses that had been built in Roman times. The petite streams and stoned ways seem to glow in the burnt tint of Germany's evening light. The singing in the guesthouses was barely audible as the sounds from the deuce-and-a-half's noisy diesel engine reverberated off the ancient stucco walls.

The houses were built so close to the road that you could kiss the Frauleins hanging out of their windows; as you passed. The truck's black veil of smoke growled from its pipes, signaling its authority to disrupt all that was in its way. Its ugly American black plume was in full flower, as the truck raced through Bad Kreuznach's winding donkey cart streets. This bull of a breast was causing pedestrians to run for their lives. Man, this was a fitting introduction to Europe for a cocky Soul Brother from 115th Street.

Nasty told me that Bad Kreuznach was one of Hitler's favorite towns, and that he slept in the BK hotel by the river as we passed it. As the truck clawed its way up Kuhberg Hill, I could see most of the quaint little German town appearing below as it displayed its gray rustic tones that squeezed the quicksilver river through the middle of its recesses. Nasty Jack didn't stop for any traffic signs or lights. It would have been a very tragic day for any non-alert VW driver to tangle with this 2½ ton US Army breast delivering its newly arrived cargo.

Nasty began my German language education by stating, "Kuhberg means Cow-Hill in German. Although most of the cows were long gone, there still remained a few resident farmers with flocks of sheep that grazed on top of the hill. The Seventh Army used the site for a helicopter landing and paratrooper drop zone. The farmers lost several sheep in surprise exercises and alerts. The Army helicopters made lamb stew out of them. Now, he's the man, he gets two hundred dollars, "US-Green," for each sheep killed by Uncle Sam's troops."

Nasty went on, "Every German, in town, knows when NATO Central Command is calling a surprise monthly alert. There won't be any sheep on Kuhberg Hill, because the Army tells the farmers not to graze their sheep there for a few days. The farmers tell their daughters who, in turn, tell their GI boyfriends. NATO calls a practice alert once a month to test all units readiness to deal with the Russians. It is assumed the Russians will start to move their armor through the Fulda Gap, a pass at the East German border, if they felt really good about starting WWIII. Even though we are outnumbered and out gunned four to one, it's our job to stop them. A comforting thought isn't it, Roy?"

The Medical Kaserne (post) rested on the side slope of Kuhberg Hill overlooking the small German town. "Bad," is a prefix that Germans add to their towns' name, designating it a resort town. So "Bad," that allied bombers spared it during WWII. The 517th Medical Clearing Co. was snuggled behind the 67th Field Hospital. The 67th was a huge five-story white building, shaped like a crescent, with three large red crosses perched on top of a slopping, frequently repaired, black slated roof.

The truck raced through the open gates of the Hospital Kaserne. There were no guards to stop or check us. The truck pulled in front of a row of sterile barracks that had been used by the Nazi Army in WWII. A large sign boldly stating the 517th Medical Clearing Company greeted me as I peered through the window of the fast moving beast. Across from the barracks were a line of jeeps, ambulances and Army trucks, some with attached ¼ ton trailers. All vehicle bumpers were marked with 7A-517th on the passenger side and CLR and truck's number on the driver side. Next to the 517th barracks was the 15th Medical Evacuation Wing. This helicopter company provided medical evacuation support for the entire 62nd Medical group of which the 517th was apart.

Nasty Jack stopped the truck in the middle of the street, jumped out and lowered the truck's tailgate. I jumped out of the front and retrieved my bags from the back. As I did so, I noticed the three cases of Cholera Vaccines that came over on the General Rose with me. Where or when he picked them up, I didn't know. I looked carefully at the cases. The labels were written in English and Russian.

There was a large contingent of GIs gathered in front the parked trucks. They didn't even say hello; they were engrossed in the goings-on in front of the trucks.

It was Friday evening and most the GIs were dressed in civvies.

Nasty escorted me into the HQ building and upstairs to the office. The sergeant on duty introduced himself as Sergeant De Voe, a heavyset Brother with a robust laugh. I handed him my orders.

"Have you had anything to eat, PFC Roy?"

"I'm starved, Sergeant."

He called in a private first class who introduced himself as Eugene Webb. He assigned him to get me settled in the barracks and show me where to get something to eat. I picked up my bags and followed him out the building. The crowd of GIs that gathered in front of the trucks and 15th Med-Evac Wing had grown larger and louder.

On the way, Webb introduced me to his friend, Mark Parsons, and then instructed me to drop my bags by the barracks' door and join him in the middle of the crowd that formed around three soldiers in formation. I squeezed through the crowd to get closer look them. They were in line and locked at attention waiting to be inspected.

Money was being passed in all directions in front of me. There was a lot of chatter about a GI named Carl Jones from the 517th, who was going to kick the ass of a GI named Pablo Perez a.k.a. "PP," from the 8th Airborne Division. It sounded like a prizefight. Boy, I was about to witness my first guard mount competition in US Army Europe. I had been on guard duty and made Supernumerary before, but nothing like this. There were more than two hundred guys there betting large sums of money.

I looked at Webb in confusion as he pointed down the street. I saw a small ¾ ton Army truck mindfully approaching the crowd. Its bumper read 8th Airborne HQ.

The truck stopped a few feet from the group. The two drivers got out, went to the back of the truck, pulled back the canvas tarp and dropped the tailgate. To my surprise, there was a soldier standing in the back as stiff as a board. He didn't move. The drivers lifted him down to the ground and handed him his weapon. The M14 weapon in his hand was just as immaculate as he was.

I could see his nametag and it read Perez. He was the private first class from the 8th Airborne Division they had talked about. He was dressed in his summer green fatigues with the flat top fatigue hat; which was now world renown due to its adoption by Fidel Castro. He walked towards the other soldiers on guard mount like one of the Rockettes wooden soldiers performing the Nutcracker Suite at Radio City Music Hall's Christmas Show.

I laughed; Perez turned and looked at me without a smile. I quickly learned that guard mount was serious business in Europe. Some of the medics in the crowd began to heckle him and call him names. One medic whispered to him as he went pass, "Perez, I purchased a blow-job from your mother last night for five dollars. She did a great job, because she didn't have any teeth in her month.

By now, one of the guys accompanying Perez had a fist full of money from the wagering. Perez joined the other soldiers on the guard mount with a confident smile. It reminded me of the goings-on on 115th St. in the

Street Games. I smiled and began to feel at home. I then heard a rustling noise in the crowd. A wedge opened up to my left and there stood another toy soldier with his weapon grabbed at the barrel. Jones was the name on his nametag. In the midst of hops and howls, he also joined the others on the guard mount. Jones represented the 517th Medical Clearing Co.

A sergeant came out of the 15th Med-Evac building behind me which served as the guard house. He told crowd to quiet down and the guard mount to be at ease. He called off the names of the units that should be represented. He then asked soldiers on the mount to call out their names and units they represented. When they finished, he did a sharp about face as the OD appeared from the same building.

Webb whispered that the OD was Major Gary McComb. He was a West Point graduate, helicopter pilot and one of the fairest officers in the medical group. The big money came out when it was his turn to serve as OD. The sergeant of the guard saluted the officer and said, "All present and accounted for, Sir."

Immediately, The OD approached the men on the mount, as the sergeant cried, "Attend-hut." A loud, crouching sound rose from the uniforms cracking the stress of the starch for the first time. Simultaneously there was the loud clicking sound from the tapped heels of jump boots breaking the silence of the evening.

The OD wasted no time in approaching the first soldier, who immediately came to inspection arms. As the major fronted the first soldier, he snatched his weapon from his hands and held the barrel up to his eyes peering down the hollow death tube looking for any signs of neglect. He followed the same procedure as he inspected the remainder of the guards. He finished the first round of inspections by throwing Jones's weapon back at him.

He then whispered to the sergeant of the guard. The sergeant did an about face and told two soldiers on the mount to fall out. The OD then started round two, personal inspections. He circled each soldier, looking meticulously at their haircuts, their shaven faces, their fingernails and even inside their ears. He checked the condition of their uniforms, whose brass was super cleaned and who had the deepest spit-shined boots. When he finished, he whispered to the sergeant again and the sergeant did an about face and told another soldier to fall out.

This left Perez and Jones as the only remaining guards in the running for Supernumerary. There was a deafening silence. Webb whispered to me that over four hundred dollars had been bet on Jones for this mount. The odds favored Perez from the 8th Airborne. The sergeant ordered Perez to take a left face and ten steps forward. The OD then began to test the military knowledge of the guards. He asked Jones several questions then Perez. Then he turned and whispered to the sergeant again. The sergeant did an about face and told Jones to fall out. The crowd went wild with boos. The OD said he would have the guards clear the plaza if the crowd didn't quiet down.

The sergeant placed an acting sergeant's armband on Perez's arm indicating he was the Supernumerary and acting sergeant of the guard for the weekend. The guards who had lost immediately approached Perez and requested the shifts they wanted for patrol. All except Jones, he just stood there and molted.

Webb said, "Thank God, there isn't any hot war to fight in Europe. The only way a soldier could distinguish himself here was by gambling, bar fighting, shooting pool, drinking liquor, screwing women and guard mount competition. All were valid measures in determining who the best damn soldier in Europe was."

I smiled.

"Perez was the best of the 8th Airborne and he didn't have to pull guard duty at all. He replaced a member of his company when he heard our sharpest soldier Carl Jones was scheduled for guard mount. It usually meant a lot of money was going to be bet, won or lost. The Supernumerary gets 10% of the pot, plus any winnings from the money he bets on himself. Perez was assigned to the 8th Airborne Headquarters Company, which was located downtown in Bad Kreuznach. Medics very seldom go to their headquarters to compete for the Supernumerary on their guard mount, because we always loose. Their officers refuse to judge "Legs" fairly.

As Webb showed me to my room, he said, "There are about 500,000 American soldiers in Europe and 300,000 dependents. If the Russians attack, we don't have a realistic plan to get the dependents back home or out of harm's way."

I was assigned to the second platoon. He helped carry my bags upstairs. As he walked up the stairs, I noticed the swagger of confidence in his step, very similar to mine. When he arrived at the top of the stairs, he spoke again.

"The second platoon's floor is divided into four large rooms with four to five men in each room. The higher-ranking men, the sergeants, generally live in military housing with their families or off base. The two rooms in the middle of the hall are for single sergeants. There are three platoons of medics and one headquarters platoon, about thirty men each in the 517th. For some reason we are heavily armed with M14s; some full automatic. Some Jeeps and trucks are equipped with machine gun mounts, but I don't know why."

"I thought the Geneva Convention says medical personnel are non-combatants?" I said, "So, why does 7th Army need a company of heavily armed medics?" No response from Webb.

"Sergeant De Voe asked me to help you get squared away. Chow is in the hospital mess and it's the best of all the Kaserne's chow in Bad-K, but the mess is closed for remainder of the day. You will have to buy something to eat at the EM Club this evening."

"What is a Kaserne?"

He laughed and returned with, "Nicht Sprechen Deutsche? You don't speak German?"

I just smiled, not knowing what he said.

He went on, "The 67th Field Hospital serves troops in the Bad-K area. Our hospital Kaserne was a former SS hospital during WWII. Some say the Nazis conducted human experiments in the basement there. The US Army took it over after the war. To keep up your medical skills, you will get a choice of the 67th or 97th. The 97th is Frankfurt General Hospital. Frankfurt is one of the largest cities in Germany and about fifty clicks away.

"Come again, clicks?"

He smiled. "Kilometers, a little more than half a mile." Then he went on.

"Or, you can go south to the hospital in Lanstuhl. Most of the Brothers go to Frankfurt where the women are thicker than mud, man." He stopped in his tracks, and stared straight into my eyes and asked. "Have you ever made love to a girl before, Roy?"

"Yes."

"What about a white girl?"

"Yes."

He could tell by the downward roll of my eyes and the tone in my voice that I was lying about the last question.

"Believe me, Brother, it's no big thing. The women over here don't consider themselves white."

"What do they consider themselves?"

"They consider themselves French, German, Danish and Dutch, etc. Only the American white boys bring that racial shit with them." He led me into the backroom on the north side of the building. There was no one else in the room.

"Where are you from, Roy?"

I said with indigenous pride, "Harlem, NY."

"The Big Apple, New York City, New York, so bad they had to name it twice, New York, New York. We're home boys."

I lit up and asked, "Are you're from New York City?"

"No, I'm from Buffalo, just up the street. And, don't call me Buffalo Bill or the Wild West Webb. Everyone calls me the Spiderman. What do they call you... what's your nickname?"

I smiled and said, "The Milkman" since corps school. Don't ask it's a long story."

He stopped by the first bunk, closest to the room's door. "This one yours; just like the ones in concentration camps down the road, the new man gets the draftiest bunk closest to the door."

"Where is yours?"

"Across the hall."

"Where is everybody?"

"Most of the guys are on three day passes."

"Three-day passes?" I said wonderingly.

"Damn, you never had a three day pass did you? Let me tell you, the First Soldier is a weird SOB. He is a German named Hans Doctor. First Sergeant Doctor is a regular asshole and a royal mother you-know-what-I-mean combined. He is Dr. Jekell and Mr. Hyde. He is Mr. Hyde during the week and Dr. Jekell on the weekends. He fucks' you over you during the week, then turn around and give you a three-day pass on the weekends. About every two months, he'll rent a bus for the entire weekend. Then authorize three-day passes for anyone in the company that wants to go with him. He may not even tell you were he's taking you, but you'll wind up in hottest tourist spots in Western Europe. Mostly the white guys go."

Where is he taking them this weekend?"

"To Luxembourg"

"No Soul Brothers want to go to Luxembourg?"

"Only a few, you get tired after working with these white guys all week and then hanging with them on the weekend too, that's a bit much. It must be the Schnaps he drinks that makes him do it."

"Schnaps, what's that?"

The Spiderman shook his head in disbelief.

"This is your locker, Milkman; a few of the guys are over at the EM-Club. Jones got his ass kicked by Perez. We lost a lot of good money betting on Jones today on the guard mount. I'll see you over there."

As I lay on my bunk, testing it out, I drifted off into a semi-sleep. The walls seemed to come alive with thoughts of Lonzo, the Wolfman, and the Bitch of Buchenwald. The years of paint that covered Germany's foul history seemed to peel off and bleed from the walls like a river of death. As I dozed, I saw jack booted, brown shirted, psychos goose stepping to marshal music; up and down the wide cobble stoned street just outside the barracks. The aromas in the room began to smell of death camps. I heard the screams of suffering young, starving, and bug eyed children. I thought of the day, when SGT Lonzo Morgan smashed his Sherman tank through the front gates of the Buchenwald Death Camp. And, a traumatized, starving kid was thinking that the Black Demons burrowing through were about to consume him and what little life he had left. The excitement of my arrival in Germany was over and the historic realities of why American soldiers were here began to set in. Every time a crazy ass European gets a hair up his ass, there is a war in Europe. The result is all the countries get rearranged and the citizenry get abused. Whoever has the biggest canons, the most horses and the meanest guy in charge gets to draw the new boundary lines; wherever he wants for his country.

I woke up immediately and I begin to unpack my uniforms, underwear and personal items that had made the long trip with me. Out came my cashmere "stingy brim" fedora that I carried in a sealed, well-protected hatbox. J&J's Hats on the corner of Lenox Ave. and 125th St. prepared it especially for me. It was dark gray with a green, red and yellow rooster feather proudly chirping out of its black head band. I proudly stroked my v-neck, All-American sweater which I had purchased from A.J. Lester Men's Wear, on the corner of 8th Ave and 125th St. I un-packed my dark brown Cordovan shoes, with a newly applied spit shine. And finally, I pulled out that lady killing sport jacket, with its large black and white hound's tooth checks. It was the baddest thing alive and it was going to be the first impression that the Soul Brothers of the 517th were going to remember the Milkman by.

I hung my uniforms in the metal locker and rolled my underwear to make them fit neatly inside of my footlocker. I reached into the duffel bag for more socks and I felt a large square leather book like object. It felt strange, because I didn't remember having such a thing. I felt around the edges in puzzlement hesitating to pull it from the bag. I felt a small buckle and edges of paper. As I began to pull it from my bag, I heard a voice.

"The Spiderman is an asshole. I see he stuck you in here with all these rednecks, huh."

"Excuse me?"

"Excuse you my-ass. You better come to attention and lock your heels, soldier."

I immediately snapped to attention. I saw a tall figure standing in the doorway. His boots appeared to be as dark as he was. I could see the outline of his pistol belt with a canteen hanging off its side and a well-polished M14 rifle at the ready.

He grunted, "CID, we don't wear rank. I am Captain Carl Jones, Military Intelligence of 7th Army Headquarters. Let me see your orders."

I quickly fumbled through my belongings scattered on the bunk and found the well-worn document with my instructions to travel from Fort Rucker, Alabama through New York City's Brooklyn Navy yard to the 517th Medical Clearing Unit in Bad Kreuznach, Germany.

He roared, "What are your name, rank and serial number?"

As many times as I was required to spit it out on command, I fumbled it miserably.

He laughed and said, "Welcome to the 517th, in Fairy Tale Land."

As he moved from the shadows, I remembered him from the guard mount earlier. I just shook my head. He "Nuked" me good. I was too dumbfounded to ask him about the guard mount he lost.

He said, "I'll take you over to the EM-Club to get something to eat. Leave your shit; nobody is here to mess with it."

I forgot about the grand entrance I had planned and the strange object I'd felt in my duffel bag. The EM-Club was across the cobblestone plaza in front of my barracks. It was a large white one-story building with a small side door with three steps leading into it. As we entered the club, it blossomed into a large dance hall with a highly polished oak floor. I could hear Country and Western music playing from the jukebox. Johnny Cash was singing, Ring of Fire. The dance hall contained about twenty tables with clean, blue checkered tablecloths surrounding the dance floor. There was a small kitchen in the rear of the building where fast foods were prepared, hamburgers, fries, hot and cold sandwiches, etc. Now that's what I was interested in.

Between the kitchen and the dance floor there was a small bar where mix drinks and beer were sold and served. Across from the bar, there was the game room which contained noisy pinball and slot machines. It was Friday evening and the place was very crowded. The crowd was mixed ranked, mostly E-4s and down. The enlisted men, NCO's and officers were allegedly not allowed to fraternize with one another. That hadn't been the case with the SF A-team and me at all.

Jones and I entered the bar area where we saw the Spiderman and a few other guys. As I approached them, Spiderman appeared very startled for some reason. I laid "five on the black hand side" on him.

"What's happening, baby?"

He returned the greeting and began to introduce me to the other guys at the bar.

"This is Sears."

"On the black hand side," Sears said.

"This is Kirk, Wade, Mumpfers, Dixon and White."

Kirk replied, "Same Soul Brother."

Then he started to introduce me to a few of the white GIs at the bar.

"This is Manor Faust or better known as Snuffy. He is the best helicopter mechanic in the 15th Medical Evacuation Wing."

He was a short thin SP5. These guys have the same pay grade as sergeants, but without the command authority. Usually they are skilled in military trades like aircraft mechanics. He barely raised his head off the bar. He was already stewed. I didn't remember the names of the remaining guys at the bar that night.

My mind started to drift back to my duffel bag and the leather book that I didn't get a chance to pull out. I did not remember owning any leather book. I felt that I'd seen the book somewhere before, but I couldn't remember where. It was troubling me. I knew I would figure it out when I got back to the barracks. Jones said he wasn't allowed to stay in the EM-club while on guard duty, so he left. I ordered a sloe-gin-fizz and a hamburger. I looked around for the Spiderman, but he had disappeared.

Snuffy lifted his head from the bar and said, "That's a ladies drink" in his strong Southern drawl. "You better get used to drinking Steinhager liquor."

He was a "Dead-Ringer" of my favorite moonshine drinking redneck, Snuffy Smith. We talked about baseball for a half-hour. He later explained Steinhager was Germany's version of a weak Russian Vodka. He offered to buy me one. I declined and proceeded with my sloe-gin-fizz.

The bartender was an off duty sergeant who was working a second job to pick up extra cash. He had four kids in Germany living in military housing with him. He requested that I pay for the drinks and food up front. The tab was two dollars. I reached in my pocket for the money and nothing was there.

"Damn, I left my money in the barracks."

Spiderman said he was returning from the bathroom. He looked at me in confusion as I walked towards the door without saying anything to anyone. I ran across the plaza, towards the barracks, pass Jones who was making his guard rounds. He didn't say anything as I passed him. There was a tall white guy in fatigues standing in the doorway of the barracks as I entered. I hit the stairs, taking two steps at a time, then powered myself onto the second floor and skated across the hall to my room.

I immediately saw that someone had moved my duffel bag from the bed onto the floor. I opened my locker where I placed my carry-on bag; it had also been moved and unzipped. I could see that my wallet was gone. I picked up my duffel bag from the floor. I placed my hand into it and felt for the leather book; it was gone also. I was pissed. I immediately ran downstairs to the front door and looked for the GI that was standing in the doorway, but he was gone also. Jones was still outside walking his guard post.

I said to Jones, "did you see anyone go into the barracks while I was in the EM Club."

"No."

"What about the white guy that was standing in the doorway?"

"I didn't see any white guy standing in the door way."

I just stood there looking at him with a disgusted frown on my face. Then I heard a distinctive sound straight out of the Spanish Harlem.

"Hey ju; wha's ju oblem?"

As I turned around, all I could see was a black arm band with sergeant stripes swinging down the street.

"Ju're che new cherry, wha ju oblem?"

"Someone took my wallet out of the room."

"Ju stupi was laughing at me earlier."

As he walked under the barracks' light, I could see it was Perez, the Supernumerary of the guard mount.

"I guess I must be stupid for letting this happen, but I want to report it stolen."

"Ju just got here and ju causing trable already."

He pointed to the 517th sign, where the charge of quarters is located. I could see he wasn't too pleased with me reporting items stolen on his watch. As I walked to the orderly room, I began to think about what he'd said. My first day in Bad-K and I was complaining already. I decided to leave it alone. I walked back to my barracks, up the stairs and secured the remainder of my belongings.

Payday was four days away and I would have to rough it until then. I suspected that Jones and the un-named white guy had something to do with my wallet going missing. The GIs said that Jones was the best in the 517th and Perez was the best in the 8th Airborne HQ in the Bad-K. I couldn't wait to get my shot at guard mount and face both of them down for the Supernumerary as pay back.

Spiderman returned to the barracks from the EM Club. I told him what had happened. He said he paid for my drinks, food and he loaned me ten dollars to purchase some personal items until payday. I was still pissed and decided to stay in my room for the rest of the weekend. Spiderman could see that I was very upset and asked if I wanted to go into town with him to a guesthouse that the medics from the hospital frequented. He said it was on him.

"As you found out, Milkman, Carl H. Jones is a crazy-ass-mother. He pulls the same shit on all the new guys coming into the unit. The white guy that was standing in the doorway was Gary E. Livingston. We called the two of them, Batman and Robin, because Livingston follows Jones move. Jones does whatever crazy shit he wants and Livingston thinks it's great and follows him. The white guy thinks he is a Soul Brother."

"What's their story?"

"The story goes; they both are from Cleveland. Livingston's mother died of breast cancer when he was ten years old and his father tried to raise him, but he was a drunk. They lived next door to the Jones' family in the slums. The child welfare agency was going to take him away from his father, because of child abuse. He was under weight and had bruise marks all over his body. Jones's mother said she would take care of him. She had five kids of her own, and she was already feeding him. She said another mouth to feed wouldn't make any difference at her table. So she raised Livingston with the rest of her kids. Jones and Livingston refused to be separated from one another.

You noticed that Jones's doesn't have any rank on his uniform. That's, because he has been busted so many times. Whenever Jones is busted down, Livingston follows in a few short days. If you ever get into a fight with one, look out for the other, because they are a dangerous duo. They went to public school together and they joined the Army together. They sleep, eat, fight, and have sex together; not with one another, but together. They are a real Batman and Robin. I gave them the name and it stuck."

***

BAD KREUTNACH MEDICAL KASERNE

NASTY JACK

13

A Date with Doctor Death

I went back into my room and put on my fineries to meet the Spiderman at the front gate. Batman was on guard there as we left the Kaserne. Perez was still talking shit. "Ju pussy leg medics, you don't know shit about soldiering. If I had my way, all ju asses would be back in basic training."

The Spiderman turned away from him as we started out the Medical Kaserne's gate. We walked about a block then Spiderman suddenly jumped off the sidewalk and began running down a steep slope into a small ravine.

I shouted, "Where in the hell are you going?"

He growled, "This is our secret short cut to downtown and back. If you ever get into trouble you should come back to the Hospital Kaserne this way."

I naively asked what kind of trouble?

"Bar fights, running from the police, an angry boyfriend or husband, things like that."

I smiled as I stooped low into a duck walk to get through a series of rain drainage tunnels. We exited the final tunnel near the edge of the Bad-K Bridge, where we fumbled our way up from the river's bank to the street. He said, "Most of the time the tunnels are dry so you shouldn't get your clothes dirty."

We proceeded to walk through the town. Occasionally he said "Guten tag" to the locals. Some of the town's people would respond back with the same, but most just ignored you. I asked about the town's people. Were they as prejudice as white Americans?

"Some are, but most get it from the American white boys who bring their prejudices with them from home. Not that the Germans don't have enough by themselves. It was white American soldiers that started the ugly rumor during WWII that America was so short of men to fight the Germans that she was enlisting monkeys to fight and Negro soldiers had tails to prove it."

I laughed and said, "Hanging in the front or the back?"

We crossed over the Bad Kreuznach Bridge, turned the corner and went down a narrow wet street to a small building with a cute little sign out front, "The Haufbrau Haus." I heard Soul Music pouring out of its opened windows. The Spiderman opened the door and I peered inside. It was one of the most remarkable sights I ever seen, all the GIs in the place were Black and all the women were white, excuse me European. Some Brothers had women sitting on their laps, some were cuddled up with them at the bar and some were dancing.

Looking at me standing there with my mouth open, Spiderman said, "What did you expect, sapphires?"

"Sapphires?"

"Yea man, Soul Sisters, remember Amos and Andy."

"That's a Black woman's put down, man."

"No, Milkman, here it's a badge of honor, Brother."

I followed Spiderman inside to the bar which was located at the rear of the building. He called the bartender over.

"Hans, zwei beer, bitte; two beers please."

The bartender reached under the bar, pulled out two frozen, gray ceramic beer mugs, and began to fill them with the town's homegrown golden brew. The Spiderman said to me, "There is no legal drinking age in Germany. Generally the whole family goes to the beer-halls and party together, children and all."

We tapped our mugs and he said, "Here's to Budweiser, who failed German brewing school. Thank god, they got rid of him by sending him to America."

We laughed and began to drink. The beers cost about one German mark each and he got 5 marks for his American dollar from the bartender. Most of the women in the place were unattractive, but as I glanced across the bar, an attractive blond caught my eye. The Spiderman noticed the attraction, he walked over to the woman and brought her over to where we were seated and began the introduction. "This is Fraulein Wolfgang."

"How are you doing?" I replied.

"Danke, Gut, thank you, well."

"Would you like a drink, Fraulein?"

"Ja" and she asked the bartender for her usual. After that, there was no need for me to ask her if she was a regular at the place. I turned around to ask the Spiderman to loan me an additional five, but he was gone. The bartender said he had gone to the bathroom. This guy went to the bathroom a lot.

Fraulein Wolfgang asked me, "Haben Sie eine Fraulein in Bad Kreuznach?"

I didn't speak any German, but I understood that. Before I could answer the question, my Johnson jumped up as hard as a brick. I immediately thought about Lonzo's first experience with a German woman. It's been over a month since I had any.

"I am new in Bad Kreuznach and you are the first girl I have met."

She replied, "Sind sie ein jungfraulich. Are you a virgin?"

I laughed, I really understood that also, but suddenly I felt peering eyes on the back of my neck for some reason. Having picked up my first German, I responded, "Haben sie eine Herr, Fraulein. Do you have a man?"

"Nein."

The Spiderman returned from the bathroom, but he was at the other end of the bar talking to another Fraulein. I asked the Fraulein to dance. My Johnson settled down long enough for me to stand up. I was in amazement that the jukebox in the corner had all of the latest soul hits from Otis Redding, Bobby Blue Bland, The Temptations, The Supremes, The Jackson Five and Junior Walker and the All Stars.

The Spiderman choked the jukebox with German marks as I slowly wrapped my arms around Fraulein Wolfgang. She slowly responded by pressing her body against mine in a submissive manner. Our bodies began a rhythmic gyration towards the middle of the dance floor. Her soft pink dress flowed with the musical breeze generated by the whispering fans cooling the jukebox.

I pulled her continuously closer to my body as we glided in perfect step in the open dance floor. Suddenly, I began to feel a throbbing object against my thigh. Initially, I was too excited by the prospect of my first score in Germany to pay any attention to it. But, as I squeezed her tighter, it throbbed more violently. I didn't want to destroy the moment by pushing her away to check it out. I slowly began a soft twirl with her. As she slowly passed under my arched arm, her soft dress revealed the outline of a very familiar object-and it was bigger than mine. I froze in the middle of the dance floor looking at her, or rather him.

The whole bar erupted in laughter. They all knew I'd been had. I drew back to knock the hell out of Fraulein Wolfgang or Frauman Wolfgang. But, the Spiderman, now half bent over from laughter rushed in-between us. It wasn't funny, or was it? The Spiderman took me over to the bar along with the other medics in the bar and brought me my first shot of Steinhager. I began to laugh as I said to the Spiderman. That guy's Johnson was bigger than mine and he was half my size in height.

The Spiderman laughed, "If you took him to a hotel and locked the door, it was going be a fight as to who got screwed first."

I was off my barstool with laughter. Wham! The front door of the beer hall flew open. Two six foot five broad shoulders Brothers walked in. The whole beer hall went quiet.

The Spiderman cried, "Oh-shit, grab your hat, Milkman."

I took the Spiderman's advice as we began to maneuver ourselves towards the door. One of the Brothers who entered went immediately to the bar. The other proceeded directly towards the jukebox, where the Spiderman and I ended up. We both tried not to make eye contact with him by making believe we were looking at record charts inside the jukebox.

He said to the Spiderman, "Play my favorite tunes, leg."

The Spiderman reached into his pocket for his last marks, inserted them into the jukebox, and selected some records. The Brother replied back to Spiderman, "Those are not my favorites."

I grabbed Spiderman arm and motioned him wards the door. The large Brother turned towards me and said, "Who in the hell are you, leg. I haven't seen you before." Looking at my snazzy clothes he said, "You look like one of them pretty sissy niggers."

I tried not to respond and continued to pull the Spiderman towards the door. The Brother snatched my cashmere fedora off my head saying. "I saw one just like it, in New York City. I think I am going to keep it."

The Spiderman was now pulling me franticly towards the door. The large Brother turned his back to me and began to walk towards the bar. I tapped him on his shoulders and as he turned, I fired my open extended fingers into his eyes. He instinctively bent over to protect his genitals as I fired again with an open hand directly into his throat. As he fell backwards, my hat slid off his head and seemed to remain suspended in mid-air as his partner flew off the bar towards me.

I took my eye off my hat to follow his partner's movement, as he approached me at light speed. I pushed a table at him San Antonio style and the tabletop caught him in his knee. The Spiderman was running for the door, as I began to look for my hat.

"I got it," I said as I rose from the floor.

There, the first brother, with his eyes bleeding and gritting his teeth started to bear down on me like a run-away locomotive. As he reached for me, "Wham," A white flash hit him from the back and splintered into five hundred pieces. Fraulein Wolfgang spared no energy swinging that chair. He fell directly on top of me, unconscious. Spiderman booted him off me and we bolted for the door.

I had memorized the route we took getting to the guesthouse. But, it wasn't the same route the Spiderman was taking getting us out. I could hear the unusual squeal of the sirens of the German police cars passing us a few blocks over. The clicking of our heels on the cobblestone streets would occasionally spring forth sparks as we ran over local pedestrians and animals alike. We wound our way up the back streets, some too narrow for a police car to pass and up the wrong way on others, so the police cars would have to slow down for on-coming traffic.

Then the Spiderman shot down onto the riverbank. I could see he had done this before, but I was getting tired. The sirens were getting closer and the reality was slowly sinking in. I would be busted by the police for fighting in a bar on my first day in Germany. It sounded vaguely familiar.

I was dead tired from running at top speed, but the Spiderman would not let up. He could see the fatigue in my eyes. He just kept repeating to me, "Milkman, we got to get to the main gate."

Then it hit me as to what he was talking about. He meant the Hospital Kaserne's main gate, which was a ½ mile, straight up this monster Kuhberg Hill that we came down.

Suddenly the Spiderman grabbed me by the collar and pulled me into a storm drainage ditch that headed directly up to the main gate. Exiting the storm drain, I could see the top floor of the hospital and its sight was giving me encouragement. The sirens of the police cars were turned off, but we could still see flashing blue lights reflecting off the houses as the police approached the hospital from about a block away.

We clawed and scratched our way to the top and stumbled across the street to the main gate. Batman, who was still on guard duty, greeted us with his M-14 at-the-ready. The police car pulled directly up to the gate and the German cops got out saying something about "Schwartzs."

I was too tired to turn around. My jacket was torn. My hat was bent out of shape. I was covered in mud and these were my best duds. Spiderman began to laugh, saying our asses were in serious trouble now. I wasn't laughing at all. All I could think about was receiving an Article 15 under the UCMJ (Uniform Code of Military Justice) on my first day in my new unit in Germany.

I asked Spiderman, please school me on what in hell is so funny and what was that shit all about?

He said, "Did you pay for your drinks."

"No, I thought you did."

His face began to turn serious by now.

Batman told the German police to go screw themselves. They got back in their police car, turned around and drove away. Batman said they couldn't come on base and arrest anyone without the US Army's permission and he was the US Army at this moment. He wouldn't give it.

Batman asked The Spiderman, "What in the hell did you stupid asses do."

The Spiderman still gasping, "The Milkman, the Milkman fucked-up DD."

"Who is DD, I replied?"

Batman replied, "DD-Doctor Death, the Golden Gloves Heavy Weight Champ of Headquarters Company of the 8th Airborne Division. You are right, man; no medic can go back into town now."

We begin to walk towards our company's barracks. I asked him, do you guys have to fight your way out of downtown every time you want to have a beer? And, what in the hell was that shit all about with the He-She.

The Spiderman started to laugh again, "It's our custom to initiate cherry Brothers with a prank when they arrive from the World into Fairy Tale Land."

"With an ass whipping too?"

"That fight wasn't on the schedule, Milkman. Everyone at the hospital knows not to mess with DD from the 8th. They are some sick, crazy, assholes and everyone except you knew that."

"What about the police?"

"We play a cat and mouse game with the German Polizei all the time. For some reason they always come after us medics first when any shit goes down in town. The Polizei never go after the guys from the 8th. They hate our guts for some reason."

"Shit, look at my clothes man."

The Spiderman replied, "Are you still breathing, Mr. Pretty Nigger, and do you still have your ass intact? You learn to thank God for the small things here, Pretty Boy."

He then stopped, turned, looked at me abruptly and smiled, "You are one fast mother with your hands."

I smiled and agreed; Cassius Clay never hits a dude by cocking or drawing back his hands. He shoots his punches straight from his chest, like a machine gun, doubles, triples, uppercuts, hooks and jabs all coming from the same place, "Hell." He gave me five on the "Black Hand" side as I savored the moment. I didn't mention that CPL Moran permanently rearranged my lip, because I wasn't fast enough. I had enough excitement for the day. I followed the Spiderman back to the 517th barracks. He motioned me to follow him to the EM Club. I smiled, shook my head no, and went straight towards barracks building C where I was housed. The lights were out and the few GIs that didn't have three-day passes were quietly staggering to their bunks. I fell asleep with my hands folded behind my head and devilish smile on my face. I was so tired that I remained in the bunk all day Saturday.

The soft blue hues of Sunday morning's light began to stroke the darkness of the room like a soft blanket being gently pulled off a resting child. A cloudy mist flowed down the side of Kuhberg Hill blending peacefully with a pallet of green foliage surrounding the Kaserne.

Then the tranquilly of the morning was fractured by the sound of a large diesel engine and the chatter of excited men. They were all complaining about the long trip and the hard seats their still a-sleep buttocks had endured. But, they were pleasant, happy sounds except for a sharp raspy voice.

"Zou're back in zour home now, formation is at 0700 hours Monday, fatigues, boots and pistol belts. Those of zou with "drippy-Johnsons" should report for sick call." It was the voice of Mr. Hyde, the mad scientist, Sergeant Doctor himself. The sounds of GIs began to fill the halls of the barracks with laugher and weird sounds of rustling clothing bags being dragged across the barracks' floor.

Breakfast was served late on Sundays. Returning from the trip, Vaugns from second platoon, introduced himself, asked if I wanted to eat breakfast and attend church with him.

Joking, I said, "Is Malcolm X preaching."

I didn't like church services in the Army, they were too boring, but I said yes. Vaugns was the only Soul Brother that went on the trip to Luxembourg with Sergeant Doctor. I heard of the small place, but I did not realize it was a country. I had met so many GIs, this weekend, that I would need an encyclopedia to help me remember all of their names.

The Soul Brothers in the 517th knew what I was in for from the rednecks of the second platoon. It was obvious; the Spiderman had no choice, but to put me into that room. The Army tries to maintain an atmosphere of integration, but many of the white GIs are not going for it; no matter what. The Brothers just wanted to make me feel comfortable with the fact that the new "Colored Boy" had to be the $517^{th's}$ freedom rider.

I asked Vaugns to give me five minutes to take a shower. I grabbed my lavatory bag and went into the shower room, which was located in the center section of the 1st floor. I walked pass the heads into the shower stalls and turned one on. Everything was fine until I began to dry off with my towel. My skin began to itch and it turned cherry red. I couldn't stop scratching. I ran into my room dancing and trying to find the psoriasis ointment that I brought with me from Fort Rucker, Alabama. One of my roommates, observing me dancing, started to laugh.

I replied, "What's so damn funny."

Before I got a sarcastic answer back, Vaugns intervened, "Many GI's have a problem bathing in the water here in Germany. It has a high mineral content and treats your skin like sandpaper."

I said, "Oh-shit," to myself, "I am in serious double-trouble now. I have to deal with acid water and DD for two years."

I gingerly slid into my clothes and followed him to the mess hall. It was huge and tastefully decorated for a military mess hall. There were a large number of German Nationals working in the back and on the serving line, all dressed in whites.

I asked Vaugns, "Do we have to pull KP?"

"You will, if you refuse to come across with five dollars from your pay each month."

"What do you mean?"

"The Army hires the Krauts to serve, clean the kitchens and the GI's pay for it; that's if you don't want to join them pulling KP."

I grabbed a tray and walked down the serving line. I was amazed at the selection of food, ham, grits, eggs, bacon, French toast, SOS and biscuits.

Seeing me admiring the food, Vaugns said, "If you really want to eat well, just wait until the 517th goes to the field. Our cooks are assigned to the hospital mess when we are on base. They must cook what the hospital's mess sergeant says cook. When we go to the field our cooks do their own thing man and the food is great."

Then he abruptly looked at my plate. "If you are a Malcolm X fan, why are you eating that swine-bacon?"

"What swine bacon?" I asked innocently?

I couldn't believe my ears. We will eat better than this when we go on field exercises. Things were happening so fast that I forgot about my stolen items. As we sat down to eat, I let loose with a thousand questions for Vaugns.

"What about our military skills, rifle, pistol and physical fitness?"

"They really don't expect much fighting out of us medics, most of the field grunts think we're a batch of pussies anyway, as you quickly found out at the Haufbrau Haus last night."

"Field grunts?"

"Most of the combat units stay in the field for months at a time. Armor and artillery units stay in the field three months at a time. You qualify with your M14 once a year and take the physical fitness test once a year. Our officers really don't care if you pass or fail."

"I bet the Russians hope we will fail. What about the heavy weapons mount on our vehicles?"

"I don't know. It is strange that we don't have the fifty caliber machine guns in our armory to set on top of them."

"Those Russian assholes just threw up the Berlin wall overnight. They out number us four to one and that's not good odds for a basketball game. It appears we are bit too laid back over here for me, Vaugns."

"I am not that gung-ho, Milkman. I just want to do my time and get the hell back to the real world in one piece. Besides these assholes, we have for officers and NCO's, couldn't fight their way out of a paper bag, even if you loaned them a razor. All except the first soldier, SGT Doctor, that little half-pint runt will bite the nuts off of a bull."

As we left the dining room Vaugns said, "I can't make church with you, Milkman. I should get back to the barracks and get my gear squared away, I heard Sergeant Doctor didn't get any pussy on this trip and that means a surprise inspection Monday morning."

"Where is the church?"

"It's the first left turn out of the mess hall."

There seemed to be quite a few GI's going that way. I followed the crowd. I was raised as a Baptist and switched to Episcopalian in my teens. My mother rushed me out of the house to Sunday school, almost every Sunday, whether I wanted to go or not. I only remembered going to church with her on special occasions, like holidays, church outings or seeing a well-known preacher who was scheduled to preach. I believed in God, but it appeared that God was someone that only children were required to believe in. Adults very seldom put in practice their belief in God; especially Americans. I was told if I didn't believe in God, I surly was going to hell. The fear of retribution, retaliation, sure punishment and possibly death by God's hand kept me in line; until I was 12 years old. After that, my prime motivation for going to church was the opportunity to dress up and look good for the girls. I only had one bad suit and one boss pair of dress shoes to profile for the girls, but they worked.

As I walked into the chapel, I noticed that many of the GI's brought their girlfriends, wives and children with them. I was surprised to see a good number of Brothers with German wives. Some children came quietly and some came screaming; as if they were on their way to hell and not the house of God. The Chaplain, Captain Louis Kress, greeted everyone at the door of the chapel. The Chaplain opened the service with hymn #154, Amazing Grace. I later found out that the author of the tune was a slave ship captain. He found religion after almost losing his life in a storm at sea, yeah, a storm of angry Africans that broke out of their shackles in the hole of his slave ship. The service quickly became boring and I politely excused myself before the Chaplain began his sermon. As I exited the chapel, there stood all four members of the B-team. They were all dressed in CID style uniforms that showed no rank, insignia or unit patches on them.

I startled them by saying, "What happened, the Special Forces ran out of uniforms?" It pissed the Unicorn off.

He replied, "I got something for you, Mr. Pretty Nigger. That was my homeboy's eyes that you punched out." He moved towards me as the other B-team members held him back.

"If I had known, I would have cut his balls off as well. We don't need any more of you SOB's breeding on this planet. Why can't I get rid of you assholes?"

Frost chimed back, "That's right, Milkman, we going to stick to you like odor to an Ox's ass."

"I must be a very important fellow for four of America's best to love me so much. I am underestimating you."

"You are definitely overestimating yourself and I would stay out of bars in Bad-K, if I were you, Milkman."

"But you are not me, thank you."

Whenever I ran into these guys, serious trouble always followed for my friends, but I didn't have any friends in Germany yet. It wasn't a comforting thought. Very troubled, I bolted over to the EM Club to listen to some music. It stayed opened late on Sundays after church. I played whatever records that was in the jukebox. I didn't like the selections much. Most of the songs were country & western, Pat Boone and a few very old Platters sides. I didn't feel like a drink, but I sat at the bar anyway. I was in an ugly mood. Snuffy from the 15th Med-Evac Aviation Company looked up from the bar. He recognized me from the night before.

"You're that boy with those fancy clothes who got into a fight downtown."

"Boy? Boy plays with Tarzan in the movies. Who do you play with-yourself?"

"Oh don't be so touchy, I bet the first thing you are going to do is go downtown a get a white woman."

"Maybe not the first thing, Snuffy, but the second thing. And besides, you forgot to fly the Black women over here in your Huey. I don't believe you left this bar the entire weekend. Your clothes smell like they were soaked in alcohol."

He pulled out a pack of cigarettes from his breast packet and placed one in this month. "If you light that cigarette, you will blow up the whole-damn EM Club."

"Very funny, Pretty Ni..."

"I thank you for stopping and adding pretty to your phase. I am very happy you are not too drunk or too crazy to finish your sentence. What's your problem anyway? I bet you don't even have a woman over here."

No response.

"What's your woman's name, maybe Lilly, Anna or Greta?"

No response.

Then he lifted his head off the bar, "That Spider Webb fellow found a beautiful colored girl over here. Every time he brings her to the EM Club, the colored boys go wild over her. Maybe you can find yourself a colored girl too."

"I tell you what Snuffy, since it troubles you that much, I will try very hard to find a colored woman. That way it will increase your chances of you finding a European one."

He simply slumped on the bar.

I paid the bartender and walked out, stopped and set on the stairs of the EM Club. I wanted to watch a German sunset in peace and quiet for the first time; and it was fantastic. The sun played a peak-a-boo game with the clouds and the mountains as it danced below the horizon. It poured its brilliant yellows, reds, and oranges all over the Kaserne; concocting intoxicating brews more potent than the ones served up inside of the EM Club.

I walked back to the barracks reflecting on DD, the Spiderman, Snuffy and the B-team. I counted how many times I had been referred to as a "Pretty Nigger" this weekend. I could not forget the leather bound book that went missing from my bag. I thought of my childhood and the mind games I played with others. Now, others were trying to play mind games with me. I quickly pulled myself together, hoping never to run into Doctor Death or the B-team again.

***

EM CLUB
KUHBERG

ONE DRUNKEN SOLDIER

SWEET WILLY READY FOR GUARD MOUNT

14

Chickens Coming Home to Roost

"Raise and shine, Princess." I rolled over and opened one eye looking at my watch which was tucked under my pillow. It read six thirty. I wasn't thrilled about going into the shower to receive another acid bath before breakfast. I grabbed my toilet kit and stumbled down the stairs to the head. The place was packed with the remaining GI's that returned to base from their three-day passes.

The Spiderman introduced Willie A. Wilson, better known as Sweet Willie. He had me beat in the Pretty Nigger competition. A GI by the name of Collins cried out, "What in the hell is that smell, somebody died in this Mother."

"Mind your own stupid ass business." Sweet Willie said. "If you don't like the smell, go next door to wash your nasty ass, Pecker Head."

Sweet Willie was stinking up the place with "Magic Shave" a depilatory that smelled like rotten eggs.

I asked him, "How does it work?"

"You mix the power with a little water into a paste, dry your skin and apply it to you face. You let it set for five minutes then scrape it off with a spatula. If you let it remain on too long, it will take your skin off along with the hair on your face. Many Soul Brothers, including me, have problems shaving, because of ingrown hair. This is my cure. Yo! You're the new guy, the Milkman. I heard you were due in this weekend, I heard you and the Spiderman had one hell of a night on the town."

"Word travels fast here." I said.

"Forget it man, everybody here will know, in one hour, what color drawers your mother wore last Saturday night. Get washed up and we'll get some chow."

I did the best I could washing with the German alligator water. I washed my face, my under arms and my chest. I left by back alone, because it was my most sensitive area. I returned upstairs and pulled a set of fatigues out of my metal locker. They were so starched that I had to kick my way into them. My boots were spit shined and blasting from the voyage over. I'd had little to do for ten days, but to shine my boots, clean my section of the ship's stairs and talk to Moreland. God bless him where ever he is.

I met Sweet Willie in front of the barracks with the others, including Batman and Robin. They were laughing, joking and slapping each other five. I didn't see the Spiderman. As we approached the mess hall, I could hear the noise coming from inside. It was packed. There must have been over a five hundred GIs inside returning from their weekend off.

"We have five units that share the mess hall. Each unit contributes their cooks."

"I know."

"Well, do ask again asshole," Willie said sarcastically.

I smiled and got on the chow line.

"Where did you go this weekend?"

"Frankfurt and the Three Pigs"

"What are The Three Pigs?"

"You do know what a pig is, don't you, Milkman?"

"Did you screw a pig this weekend, Sweet Willie?"

"You're a wise ass too, Milkman. How many college degrees do you have? The Three Pigs are the Brothers' hangouts in Frankfurt, Germany. Most of the Brothers just want to get their chest light, make love not war, Sie verstehen?"

Get their chest light?

"Get your rocks off."

Oh!

"Milkman, listen, *I am Sweet Willie Okum, the pee-hole choker, the sheet shaker, the baby maker and the heart breaker. I am known from coast to coast, the one the ladies love the most."*

He went on, "Many GIs buy love here, because they don't have the skills to wine and dine women for sex. You need at least a three day pass for that shit."

In any case, Sweet Willie, you are going to pay for it one way or another, I said smiling.

"I don't buy love, Milkman."

Oh! Wining and dining them is an investment, not a purchase. Did you get any sex this weekend?

"No"

No?

"Yes, no"

Which is it? Yes or no?

"I said, no asshole; I don't try to screw the first thing I see with two legs in a skirt. I would like to be able to look at her the next morning. You're a cherry, Milkman, cool it. Here's a spot to squat over here."

Squat?

While we were eating, Doctor Death showed up for sick call in the infirmary at the 97th Field Hospital. His left eye had become infected. He asked several medics in the hallway if they knew which medical company I was in. The medics said they didn't know me. As he walked into the mess hall, he asked a cook on the serving line if he knew me; he described me perfectly. The stupid cook pointed me out.

"I just served him; I think that's him sitting over there."

I saw him approaching me like a lion in heat, but before I could turn around he spotted my nametag. I knew it was all over now for my ass. He just stood above me with a patch over his right eye cracking his knuckles and giving me a cold stare. There were too many medics in the mess hall for him to start anything there. So, he said to me, "I know your pretty ass now. As General Mac Arthur once said 'I shall return.'"

After Doctor Death ID me, I was never comfortable going downtown in Bad Kreuznach again. I would occasionally stop by the bar to say hello to Frau-man Wolfgang and the ladies. A few of them grew fond of me and invited me home, but I said "Sorry, I have to watch my ass." I would buy them a drink and immediately leave.

The Spiderman wouldn't venture into downtown Bad-K much either. When we went out drinking, we would catch a cab outside the Kaserne's gates and travel to the next town over; Rhudesheim. Returning home on the weekends wasn't a problem, because there was always an armed guard on duty to protect our behinds. The Spiderman told me several times, following that incident, that I should find out what's going on in Europe before I got into any more fights.

I began to do just that. Staying out of trouble, I began to travel with the Mad Doctor to Austria, Switzerland and Italy. I had a very good time, after sightseeing all day, the ladies of the evening usually came out in most towns. So, if you had plenty cash and protection, you did well. A "Hard-Johnson has no conscience," especially for a Pretty Nigger in Europe.

I took up an interest in photography; Europe was very photogenic and it kept me out of trouble. There was a full photo-lab in the basement of the hospital staffed by a full time instructor. Photography became a passion of mine, so much so, that I applied to a major photography college in up-state New York. I guess I was trying to keep my promise to the Wolfman.

After running into the B-team, several times, I started to have my attacking gorilla dreams again. In my last dream, I was slow dancing with Fraulein Wolfgang and she turned into a six hundred pound attacking gorilla as I twirled her around.

Also, I was still trying to figure out why our company of medics was so heavily armed. The armory didn't contain any fifty caliber machine guns, but the buzz was we would find them from some place in a hurry if we needed them. Once again, why would a company of medics need heavy weapons?

The Spiderman and I were assigned to pick a new medic from the train station. He asked the Spiderman and me to drive him to the PX to pick up some personal items. We returned to the barracks just in time for his first alert. We formed a line at the armory to pick up our weapons, but no live ammo was issued; so we knew this was just a practice alert.

The trucks were driven to the warehouse for loading. We had thirty minutes to load all of our equipment. The warehouse contained enough medical equipment to outfit three small surgical platoons. We had surgical instruments, autoclaves, operating tables, and even special stretchers for moving patients in a CBR contaminated environment.

We had complete kitchens with stoves, hot tables and kerosene burners that heated water. Already on the trucks were huge hospital tents that weighed 500 pounds each that housed forty patients. When the tent was folded it could stop a fifty-caliber bullet, the GIs said. The guys liked to stack the tents, on the trucks, leaving a small crawl space at the bottom to hide any contraband that they picked up.

The trucks left the Kaserne in platoons. Each platoon was able to function independently, if required. Most of the time, we headed for our large assembly area on the top of Kuhberg Hill, where we would wait for our orders. When the orders came down, we would drive or wait for air transport to move us to a specified location or assembly area. Sometimes we would camp out on Kuhberg Hill for a few days waiting on our orders.

This time, we were ordered to set up a small aid station to assist the 8th Airborne Headquarters Company complete its monthly pay jumps. Suddenly helicopters appeared overhead. The choppers hovered in midair, making sure the paratroopers were over the jump zone. Then the paratroopers came floating down like giant snowflakes. If the wind became too strong, they would stop the jumps, because the paratroopers would be dragged on the ground by their chutes and injured. The jumps went well with no injuries.

When all the paratroopers were on the ground, they joined us for some hot chow. It was a surprise for them, because they expected C-Rations. Vaugns and the other medics knew what they were talking about. In the field, our cooks cooked their asses off. We ate Italian one night and Soul Food the next. SGT Ossie Gilliam and PVT Vincent Johnson were two damn good cooks.

After chow, Batman introduced his Brother Larry to us. He was a good-looking, dark skinned paratrooper, about 6 feet 5 inches of all muscle. His nick name was Jumping Jack Daniels, because he liked to drink Jack Daniels whiskey, straight; and a lot of it too. He had played football in college, but he refused to study. So, he lost his scholarship, joined the Army and volunteered for Airborne. He was soft spoken and not as excitable as his younger brother.

He was a sergeant and a no-nonsense one at that. He dressed down his baby-brother, about the condition of his uniform, while we were in the field covering his company's pay jumps. Batman liked to wear his fatigue shirt outside his pants. The sergeants of the 517th had stopped asking him to put it in, because he would act like he was hard of hearing. Larry said that his baby brother had spent 3 months in the Army prison at Mannheim, Germany for disobeying orders. Batman said, he didn't mind going back either. Most GIs said he was the best soldier in the 517th, just crazy. It was amazing how he transformed himself into the sharpest soldier in the 517th when it was his time to make some money on guard mount.

We tented down for the night in the open field. We had to play soldier by posting guards around the perimeter of the camp. There was no "supernum" in the field. We didn't have any live ammunition either. So, I don't know what spy or thief we would have stopped.

I pulled guard duty for 2 hours. Then I found a cot next to Vaugns in one of the tents. When I woke up, what a smell! Our tent was full of sheep, live sheep. The local farmer had released his flock into the field. He said he hadn't been informed that we were going to use his property for a military exercise. We didn't believe him. I think he wanted some of his sheep to get killed by our landing helicopters so he could collect money from Uncle Sam. The funniest thing was the sheep were all calling Vaugns' name, "Vaugnnnnns, Vaugnnnnns and Vaugnnnnns." The Spiderman said, the sheep were calling his name, because he screwed a few of them during the night and they liked it so much they returned for more. They refused to leave our tent.

I had to pee badly. I wanted the farmer to remove his sheep from the tent so I could get up and go to the latrine, but the sheep kept returning calling Vaugns' name. We were having a ball laughing at Vaugns. He just sat there, on his cot, ignoring us until all the sheep were chased out of our tent.

I didn't know how to drive a vehicle at all when I entered the army. So, Nasty Jack got permission to teach me how to drive while we were on alert on Kuhberg Hill. He taught me in his 2½-ton truck; Mabel. I didn't think that it was the best vehicle in the Army to learn how to drive in. I felt I should have started with something smaller, possibly a jeep. Nasty said the new M151 jeeps were death traps. They were accident-prone due to poor design. He drove his truck out into the middle of the field. He showed me how to change the gears. Then he got out of the truck and told me to get going. After a few false starts, with the truck stalling in the process, I was able to shift from first gear to second gear and get the truck moving. Then I was able to get the gears into third. Now I was motoring. He then hollered for me to practice my downshifting.

"Down shift, what's that?"

"That's how you slow the truck down. If you apply the brakes all the time to slow the truck, especially going down a hill, you would set fire to the brake shoes by overheating them." After a few rounds of up shifting and down shifting, Nasty got back into the truck and said, "Milkman, the alert has been called off. Let's head back down the hill to the Kaserne with the rest of the company. Take the last position in the convoy."

"You mean you want me to drive back?" I asked in astonishment.

It was all downhill, I mean that literally. I stopped trying to down shift while going down the steep slopes. I stayed in second gear all the way down the hill trying to keep from crashing the truck.

After a few weeks of practice, the Army gave me my drivers' license for a 2½-ton truck. I was afraid to try to drive a jeep, because Nasty was right, the new M151s had such bad reputations for turning over. Many GIs in Europe were killed in those things. Their badly designed suspensions caused the jeep to lose traction on bumps and turns making them to flip over.

Things were starting to go great. I was gaining respect for being a good soldier and I hadn't seen or been harassed by the B-team during the whole month of November. But, the month wasn't over. Boy, when things are going great, look out, downhill they go fast.

My platoon sergeant asked me to go and pick up a new arrival at the train station. I had been driving about two months now and I was getting good. I could whisk around those tight corners of downtown Bad-K as good as Nasty Jack. I parked the truck in the station's parking lot and waited for Big Old Black Smokey to pull into the station.

Oil products are very expensive in Europe. You could only get a liter of gas in Europe for what we paid for a gallon of gasoline in the States. A liter is about a third of a gallon. You could buy gas at the PX at stateside prices. The Germans said that coal was cheap in Europe, so they never switched to diesel train engines, because they would be too expensive to operate here.

Here she comes, tooting along, slowly pulling into the station and like she's in a cowboy movie. A lot of GIs come barreling off the train. Then I saw one GI step off the train that hit me like a lightning bolt. It was Haymen Swilley. I said, oh shit, I thought I had got rid of that crazy redneck.

I said to myself, "Milkman, do not panic, he may be going to another unit in Bad-K."

I looked around for trucks from other units and I was the only medical unit with a truck at the station. I dropped my head.

I waited for all the GIs to leave the station before I got out of my truck. I was hoping he would disappear, but he didn't. As I got out, I whistled a double whistle. The one Swilley used to call his Quarter Horses he owned in Tennessee. He recognized the whistle immediately. He dropped his head when he saw me and said, "Milkman, I will ask for a transfer."

"Swilley, I'm going to feed you to the hogs. How are you doing Man, looks like you lost weight?"

"Yes, I failed out of flight school, Milkman. I was throwing up almost every time I took the stick of the bird."

"Wait let's get going back to the Kaserne first, before we talk."

I threw his bags into the back of the truck and gave him one hell of an introduction ride through Bad-K; before heading up the hill to the hospital. Just like the ride that Nasty had given me. I could see that Swilley was down in spirits. I asked him about his folks?

"My father gave me a hard time about failing out of flight school, but my mother understood. Maggie and I made up just before I left for Europe, but we never got a chance to get it on."

I smiled, "Swilley, if you keep trying you will succeed in losing your cherry." I hummed that truck around those corners and up that hill.

Swilley said, "Where did you learn to drive like this."

I replied, "A little old lady from Pasadena."

After we arrived, I took him upstairs into the HQ to check in. It was late Friday evening and Captain Schmitz was waiting for him. He had known Swilley's father when he was in the Army and he wanted to welcome him personally to the 517th. He told Swilley he expected great things from him and he told me to help him get squared away. God was on my side after all; Captain Schmitz assigned Swilley to the first platoon.

On the way into his barracks, we talked, "Before I left, I saw Carol Thompson and the other Ozark girls at a second dance given at the EM Club by the base SSD. This one went much better; I had a good time with the Soul Sisters. Carol found a new fellow."

I nodded.

"Also, two weeks ago, my chopper crew and I gave the B-team a hop from Fort Rucker, Alabama back to San Antonio, Texas during a training mission of mine."

"What? They came over the pond on the General Rose with Moreland and me. He went missing one day before we landed in Bremerhaven and I never saw him again. Now, you are telling me, they are back in the States and you flew them back to San Antonio?"

"Yes, they asked me about you, because they remembered both of us and SGT Gorge. It was strange; they were carrying cased hunting rifles."

"How do you know what kind of rifles they carried in their cases, Swilley?"

"Milkman, I put those weapons in the chopper myself. I am from Tennessee not from New York City. I could tell by their weight and balance what they were. Plus, Captain Morales was reported killed in an auto accident while driving to her new assignment at Fort Benning, Georgia."

That made me sit up. "I am saddened by Captain Morales' death. Swilley."

"Things are looking bad for your friend Malcolm X. He is getting too big for his britches. He is being quoted in the newspapers almost daily criticizing the president and The Nation of Islam leader, Elijah Mohammed. He suspended him and he was ordered not to make any more statements to the press."

"Malcolm X has always been a harsh critic of the Kennedy brothers and other bleeding heart liberals for being paternalistic towards so-called Negroes," I said. "But, the Kennedy Brothers are making significant improvements in the Civil Rights arena now. Improvements you rednecks don't like. Malcolm X doesn't smile in the faces of white politicians. He feels it's their American duty to act. It is something they should be doing for themselves as well, and they shouldn't need to be coaxed or thanked for it. Everyone in America knows if you don't want to deal with the likes of Martin Luther King, you definitely will have to deal with the likes of Malcolm X or worse. I heard he is having some unknown writer, write his autobiography."

"President Kennedy has been walking on thin ice with the military for a long time," Swilley said. "My father told me that everyone is watching him – Maxwell Taylor, Curtis Lemay, even J. Edgar Hoover. And Hoover has a huge file on his love life, including a love affair with Marilyn Monroe. There is an even a rumor that he slept with an East German spy introduced to him by a senator friend."

I agreed with Swilley that Hoover and his cronies in the Pentagon were definitely no bleeding heart liberals and that the Kennedy Brothers had managed to piss off almost every right wing group in America, from the mob, through the military brass, to members of the church. All of this was in the newspapers daily; even over here.

"Joseph Kennedy bought Jack the presidency," I said. "And, I wonder if he really did him a favor. I have a bad feeling about this."

"What are you saying, Milkman? You've made insinuations like this before, it's not good to say things you don't have proof of."

I just stared at him. It was Friday, November 22, 1963.

The Soul Brothers of the 517th had purchased a case of white wine from Frau Kasser's house; which was a few streets down from the Kaserne. In Germany, it was legal to make and sell your own wine from your home. There had been uneasiness on the base all day. We had our monthly practice alert already and I was looking forward to the end of the month and payday; which was approaching rapidly. The tension with Russians was subsiding, so there wasn't much for us to worry about.

Each of us had our own jug of wine and we were drinking it straight out the bottle. I drank so much wine, that I would have made Lonzo look like a preacher. We were listening to Martha and the Vandellas "Dancing in the Streets", and that's exactly what we were doing in the middle of our cobble stone plaza. My stereo was blasting out of the barracks windows. Most of the GIs in the company were off base or in the bars downtown partying. The only white GIs left on base were Swilley and Robin, who were drinking wine with us. I still didn't trust Robin after my first day here when the book and my wallet turned up missing. We were really low-level flying by the time 2030 hours rolled around.

It was 1:30 pm, in the afternoon, in Dallas, Texas when shots rang out.

The CQ hollered out of the HQ window, "Alert, alert, this is not a drill, this is not a drill." The 517th had less than half of its company of medics on duty when the roll call was taken. As soon as they started to hand out live ammo, to drunken soldiers, I knew it was serious.

When SGT Doctor arrived, he called what was left of our company to attention and gave us the bad news. The president of the United States had been shot. At first, we thought the Russians had something to do with it. But, no one ever mentioned Russia's name. The news coming over our portable radios said they knew who the shooter was and they were going to catch him. Tears rolled down my face into my wine bottle as I tried to make sense of it all.

We tried to get into our winter field uniforms. Those who accomplished the task were to be congratulated. Most of us could only manage some part of an Army winter field uniform. Winter uniforms were a must for all alerts and they had to worn or carried. No American Army was going to suffer the same fate as the German and French Armies did in Russia.

The MPs were sent into town to tell all soldiers to report immediately back to their units. We packed the trucks in record time with half of the manpower. SGT Doctor unlocked the secure vault that contained the cholera vaccines and we loaded them on truck number one. I questioned why the crates of vaccine labels were written in English and Russian. We formed up into convoys and proceed to our rendezvous point on Kuhberg Hill.

Most of the company's mechanics could not be located, so I was assigned to drive one of the mechanic's maintenance trucks. I was so drunk that I tore down the front gate as I exited the Kaserne. My truck was dragging a ¼ ton trailer full of gasoline which I drove like a bat out of hell. If I wrecked it, I was pulling enough gasoline to get me back to hell very quickly.

It was a full tactical alert. We were driving with our headlights off using only our small slit running lights to see. I was too drunk to see anything anyway. I was driving by radar, drunken radar. And, I was hauling ass; to what and where, only God knew at that time.

As we approached the top of Kuhberg Hill, we saw things appear that we never seen before. Redstone missiles were being raised into their launching positions and they were being fueled. The sky above was ablaze with the streaking afterburners of our fighting jets dashing towards the East German border. The 8th Airborne set up its field headquarters next to our medical tents and their Davy Crockett Tactical Nuclear Weapons were in clear view next to the general's tent. The Davy Crocketts were mounted in recoilless rifles affixed to the death trap M151 Jeeps and under armed guard.

We began to sober up quickly as the remainder of the company's personnel began to arrive. Some arrived on foot and some were driven by the MPs who rounded them up in the town. The radio said that President Kennedy had made a stop in San Antonio the day before he was shot in Dallas. I just left San Antonio, a few months earlier, and my mind began to bubble with the strange goings-on of the A-team and the secrets they had entrusted to me.

I asked Swilley to tell me again, where he dropped the B-team off?

"San Antonio, Lackland Air Force Base."

He saw the expressions on my face. "Milkman, there is no connection between the B-team and the shooting of the president. They will find the guy who did it."

"Nah, you're right, Swilley, it would be impossible for the B-team to pull off something like that anyway."

I could have kicked myself for thinking aloud in front of Swilley, but I couldn't get the president's face out of my mind. Every place I traveled in the Army, people connected to me were dying or getting killed under mysterious circumstances. Now the president of the United States, could all of this be connected?

We didn't say much to one another for the remainder of the night. There was too much going on. We listened to our portable radios all night after finding out President Kennedy had died, LBJ was sworn in on Air Force One as the new president of the United States and commander in chief of the Armed Forces.

I was trying to convince myself that it had to be a coincidence. There was no proof of the A or B-team's involvement in the president's assassination or the other deaths of my friends. Even though many disliked JFK, no one in Army would ever assassinate their commander in chief; no one. I couldn't get it out of my head that this wasn't a simple assassination. This was a murder, a coup-de-tat and the first overthrow of an American government in our country's history. If my feelings were true, Kennedy had really upset some dangerous big boys in DC.

There were persistent rumors that he secretly started to bring American troops home from Vietnam. Elements of Airborne units had started to arrive in California from Vietnam. In a CBS interview, on September 22, 1963, he emphatically stated to Walter Cronkite that the conflict in Vietnam wasn't America's war. It was up to the Vietnamese to settle their differences.

Also, was this payback for him sending his brother Robert to Alabama along with federalized troops to protect Black citizens trying to get an equal education there? Additionally, this past June 11, 1963, President John F. Kennedy made a radio and television address to the American people. To me, it sounded exactly like a speech that Malcolm X would have given at the UCLA. Were these actions the final nails being placed in his coffin by the big boys in DC? I re-read the June 11 newspaper clipping I kept of his speech.

"Good evening, my fellow citizens. This afternoon, following a series of threats and defiant statements, the presence of Alabama National Guardsmen was required at the University of Alabama to carry out the final and unequivocal order of the United States District Court of the Northern District of Alabama. The order called for the admission of two clearly qualified young Alabama residents, who happened to have been born Negro.

I hope that every American, regardless of where he lives will stop and examine his conscience about this and other related incidents. Men of many nations and different backgrounds founded this Nation; it was founded on the principle that all men are created equal and that the rights of every man are diminished when the rights of one man is threatened.

Today we are committed to a worldwide struggle to promote and protect the rights of all who wish to be free, and when Americans are sent to Vietnam or West Berlin, we do not ask for whites only. It ought to be possible, therefore for American students of any color to attend any public institution they select without having to be backed up by troops.

It ought to be possible for American consumers of any color to receive equal service in places of public accommodation, such as hotels, restaurants, theaters and retail stores, without being forced to resort to demonstrations in the streets. And it ought to be possible for American citizens of any color to register and to vote in a free election without interference or fear of reprisal.

It ought to be possible in short for every American to enjoy the privileges of being American without regard to his race or his color. In short, every American ought to have the right to be treated as one would wish his children to be treated. But, this is not the case...

This is not a sectional issue. Difficulties over segregation and discrimination exist in every city, in every state of the union, producing in many cities a rising tide of discontent that threatens the public safety. Nor is this a partisan issue in a time of domestic crisis. Men of good will and generosity should be able to unite regardless of party or politics. This is not even a legal or a legislative issue alone. It is better to settle these matters in the courts than on the streets, and new laws are needed at every level, but law alone cannot make men see right.

We are confronted primarily with a moral issue. It is as old as the scriptures and is as clear as the American constitution. The heart of the question is whether all Americans are to be afforded equal rights and equal opportunities, whether we are going to treat our fellow Americans, as we want to be treated. If an American, because his skin color is dark, cannot eat lunch in a restaurant open to the Public, If he cannot send his children to the best public schools available. If he cannot vote for the public official who represents him, if in short, he cannot enjoy the full and free life which all of us want, then who among us would be content to have the color of his skin changed and stand in his place. Who among us would then be content with the counsels of patience and delay?

One hundred years of delay have passed since President Lincoln freed the slaves, yet their heirs; their grandsons are not fully free. They are not freed from the bonds of injustice. They are not yet freed from social and economic oppression and the Nation, for all its hopes and all its boasts, will not be fully free until all its citizens are free.

We preach freedom around the world, and we mean it. And we cherish our freedom here at home, but are we to say to the world, and much more importantly, to each other that this is a land of the free except for Negroes. That we have no class or caste system, no ghettoes, no master race except with respect to Negroes? Now the time has come for this Nation to fulfill its promise. The events in Birmingham and elsewhere have so increased the cries for equality that no city, state or legislative body can prudently choose to ignore them.

The fires of frustration and discord are burning in every city north and south, where legal remedies are not at hand. Redress is sought in the street, demonstration, parades, and protest, which create tensions, threaten violence and threaten lives.

We face therefore, a moral crisis as a country and as a people. It cannot be met by repressive police action. It cannot be left to increased demonstration in the street. It cannot be quieted by token moves or talk. It is a time to act in the congress, in your states and local legislative body, and above all, in all of our daily lives.

It is not enough to pin the blame on others, to say this is a problem of one section of the country or another or deplore the facts that we face.

A great change is at hand and our task, our obligation, is to make that revolution, that change, peaceful and constructive for all. Those who do nothing are inviting shame as well as violence. Those who act boldly are recognizing right as well as reality.

It was as if the president of the United States was reading excerpts from Malcolm X's column in Mohammed Speaks. Kennedy clearly paraphrased Malcolm X boldly and in some respects outdistanced the Dean of the University Corner of Lenox Ave. I wondered if there had been secret communications between the two. Maybe, I have something to fight for after all.

Malcolm X was still under suspension by Elijah Muhammad. He spoke at a rally at New York City's Manhattan Center and after the rally; newsmen asked him his opinion on the Kennedy assassination.

He said, *"That the hate in white men had not stopped with the killing of defenseless Black people, but that hate was allowed to spread unchecked and finally it struck down the country's chief of state. It was the same thing that happened to Medgar Evers, to Patrice Lumumba and to Madame Nhu's husband of Vietnam. It is a case of* ***Chickens Coming Home to Roost****."*

The New York Times only printed the last sentence of his statement. If only Malcolm X knew at the time, how prophetic his statements were and how relevant they would be to American history.

***

BOSS DUDE

15

A Desire for Sapphire

The visit which I received the day after the Caveman's death was still ringing in my ears. Bobby Kennedy was still attorney general and he definitely would not let his brother's killers get away with it. I believed he knew that both he and his brother were being stalked by powerful forces in this country.

After JFK's murder, my six hundred pound attacking gorilla dreams got worse and refused to go away. The Christmas season was horrible. I began to suspect almost everyone around me had a hand in JFK's murder. Additionally, in my gut, I felt the B-team were involved or responsible for JFK's murder and the deaths of my friends. I began to suspect that maybe I was harboring the A-team's ugly secrets concerning JFK's death. And I had a funny feeling that the B-team was still hiding in the shadows in Europe and staking me; but why?

The B-team showed up in Bad K a few weeks after JFK's murder. It was at our company's Christmas party. They definitely had a cocky attitude when they appeared. I tried to put as much distance between Swilley and me as possible. I didn't want them to reconnect Swilley to me again. It could mean bad news for him.

I had been in Germany for over six months now. During that time, I won Supernumerary on Guard Mount several times. It was very uneventful though. I was the new guy on the block and the older GIs said I hadn't established a rep yet, so no big money was bet on me. I was earning a lot of awards and commendations from the officers, but no promotions. I finally beat out Batman on Guard mount, becoming the sharpest soldier in the 517th. I made one hundred and fifty dollars doing so.

After hearing about my winnings, CPL Perez of the 8th Airborne sent word, "If I thought I was ready for him, he would oblige me, but the money pot had to be five hundred dollars minimum-up front."

I sent word back, to Perez, that the 517th wasn't able to raise that kind of money yet. But, I would come to the 8th Airborne Headquarters and challenge him on his own turf if he gave me a two dollar to one dollar handicap. He said, let's-get-it-on and allowed me to pick the date.

I mentioned it to the Spiderman and he said we would have to start to study-up for the challenge. One of the 517th's weak spots in winning Supernumerary at the 8th's HQ was our M14s. They were hand-me-downs from infantry units and not in top condition. Also, we didn't have an Armorer in our unit; someone whose main job it was to maintain, repair and restore our weapons. Additionally, our winter field uniforms were hand-me-downs. We needed brand new winter field uniforms to be competitive. The Spiderman said that correcting these problems were above our heads to solve.

We met with the "Mad Doctor-the First Soldier" and told him that our objective was to beat out the 8th Airborne for Supernumerary on their guard mount. He said there wasn't anything he could do to help us with the guard mount competition, because all the officers knew unauthorized gambling was involved. Also, medics were not authorized an armorer, because we were not a front line combat unit. After hearing that, our hearts sank.

But, he said, the 62nd Medical Group doesn't have an honor color guard to represent the group at parades and ceremonies. If it had one, let's say, headed up by a volunteer who was a proven sharp soldier, a Supernumerary, then we would be home free. The 62nd Medical Group would authorize the best uniforms for that color guard. Additionally, the 517th doesn't have a rifle and pistol team. If a good candidate could be found to organize the 517th's rifle and pistol teams, then the 62nd Medical Group would have to authorize the best weapons along with a part-time armorer for the rifle and pistol teams. Now, if those uniforms and weapons turned up on guard mount there wouldn't be any problem, would there.

I told the first sergeant that I would try to get things started. The Spiderman said he wanted no part of it. I even asked my white roommates to volunteer for the rifle and pistol team. They said no. The tension between us had reached the breaking point. That Saturday evening, one of them made a remark about my bathing habits. They said, I stunk up their room. I couldn't take a bath every day in Bad-K's high mineral content acid water. The water was driving my psoriasis skin condition crazy. I couldn't use the standard soaps and deodorants, because I developed rashes from them. By experimenting, I found that Dove soap and cornstarch body powder deodorants provided the best relief.

After I got into a shoving match with one of them, I knew it was time for me to leave the platoon. The platoon sergeant had already figured that out. He asked if I wanted to be transferred to the 1st platoon. 1st platoon was considered the best platoon of the 517th anyway. I liked the platoon sergeant. He had a different management style than my platoon sergeant. He used personal pride to motivate his troops not fear of retribution.

SGT 1st Class Nelson Byfield invited me into his platoon. He said that the only bunk space he had was on the first floor in his "Misfit Squad." These were three of his lowest performing medics. They weren't discipline problems, just a problem. He said a sharp soldier, like me, would be able to shape them up. It sounded like basic training all over again with PVT Tobin.

I wasn't in the first platoon one week, when Swilley got into a shouting and shoving match with his roommates across the hall. SGT Byfield came running into my room with that puppy look on his face. I knew what he wanted. I said yes, sergeant; move him into our room. I knew Swilley and I were going to hit it off great, "Right." I asked the sergeant for two days to get the room reorganized. He knew I was procrastinating to let Swilley cool off. He said, he would allow Swilley to go to the Third Armored Division's Ray Barracks in Friedberg, Germany. Elvis, "The King," Presley was stationed there in 1960. Swilley had requested the privilege of sleeping one night in Elvis' old bunk. He would be back in two days and that would allow me some peace and quiet for few days.

Swilley called his roommates a bunch of lowlife, white trailer trash. Gracia, one of my Misfits, said, it wasn't the first time he ranked them out. Also, he told Santos, the only Hispanic guy in the room, that Mexicans didn't go to college as frequently as white people, because they have smaller brains and aren't as smart as white folks. He told other roommates that he was a Conscientious Objector. These are guys that, for personal or religious reasons, refuse to fight or kill another human being.

I told Garcia that he was just running off at the mouth. "You just have to put him in his place and don't take him seriously."

My PFC salary was a little over a hundred dollars a month, but I was making more money by hustling pool, hustling basketball, loan-sharking and winning Supernumerary. I started loan sharking on a "Humbug" (bullshit), trying to stop GIs from borrowing money from me. I was tired of them begging money from me a week after payday. So, when they asked for money, I would snap back, "Five dollars for ten, ten for twenty." This caused friction between them and me, but they still kept coming to borrow money. Even GIs from other companies started to borrow money from me at those crazy rates. Additionally, I didn't realize that a second rate basketball player from Harlem would be a first rate basketball player in Europe. I was good enough to get an invitation to join the US Army Europe team, but there wasn't any additional money to play. So I said thanks, but no thanks, the travel and playing time would interfere with my hustling. When I won top Supernumerary honors of the 517th that put the icing on the cake. Many GIs became jealous, saying that I seldom lost at anything, because I was a cheat and I took advantage of them.

The Spiderman said to me, "Milkman, your problem is the yearling's blues, a desire for Sapphire. After a year or so, the Brothers get antsy. That's when the Sapphire desire really kicks in. It's like, not having any sleep for a long time. Not being around Black women can have the same effect. It must be something in their sweat glands, you know, the body odor they use to attract Brothers. It's almost like a narcotic habit that you are trying to kick. The Brothers that bring their wives to Europe with them don't have the problem. I don't have the problem, because I was lucky, I found a Sister over here."

The Spiderman and I had become the best of friends. We partied and traveled together to different local towns in Germany to avoid DD and other GIs in general. We met the real Germans in these places. They were relatively unaffected by American GIs bringing their bad habits and prejudices with them from home to Europe.

When I arrived in Germany, the Spiderman spoke German better than I did. But, after I took German classes, I was speaking German much better than he and almost fluently. Traveling outside the normal GI towns required you to speak German. I took every training course the army offered from German to typing classes. I started to go on every trip the Mad Doctor gave, even when he went to the same places twice. We wound up in places like Lake Como, Venice, and Milan Italy, St. Moritz and Geneva Switzerland and all places in between.

We found the small guesthouses that offered good food, good beer, good wine and, of course, good women. Most of the towns in Germany had someone local who brews beer and makes wine. Bad Kreuznach was only a few kilometers from the Rhine River and some of the best wine vineyards in the world. Our favorite small town was Rudesheim. The main highway ran directly from Bad Kreuznach through the center of Rudesheim. The town was set in a vicious bend in the Rhine River that had a history of destroying many riverboats in its dangerous waters.

Local folklore said there was a mermaid nymph called the Lorelei, who set on the rocks at the vicious bend in the Rhine River near Rudesheim. She called out to the homesick and lovesick sailors in the night. Those who were attracted by her enchanting call soon find their boat and themselves truly on the rocks. It sounded like some of the Soul Sisters I knew back home.

The castles along the Rhine River Valley were truly something to behold. They crowned the brilliant protruding green hills which framed the lush hillside vineyards in their majestic and historical spender. It is here that you really see why the American GIs called this country Fairy Tale Land. But, how could such impressive majestic beauty co-exist in a land with people who, just a generation ago, had performed some of the most egregious acts against other humans known to mankind?

Rudesheim had a number of the small haft-timber guesthouses frequented by tourist. Many come from all over the world to visit the area and sample the Rhine Valley's wines. At the end of September, they warmed up for the annual Oktoberfest. The best beers and wines in Germany are brewed and sold during this time of the year to celebrate the harvest. Other holidays during the year, the local people would dress in their traditional costumes and spend several days singing, drinking beer, and dancing to the accompaniment of local Oom-Pah-Pah brass bands with the tourists.

Also, Lenten season was upon us and Fasnacht is celebrated for a month or more during this time of the year. "That's really when the girls come out man." the Spiderman said. Fasnacht, or Karneval, is like a long Mardi Gras that starts before lent. The girls dress in the most outlandish costumes to hide their identities. This will enable them to do their naughty deeds, without their identity being revealed. So, when they returned home to their husbands or boyfriends, their robust activities wouldn't follow them. When Easter arrived, all their sins for the previous year were forgiven and they started anew for next year. We did everything humanly possible to assist every German girl in fulfilling her Fasnacht fantasies.

There was some truth to what the Spiderman said about the desire for Sapphire blues. Most German girls definitely didn't have the same personality, character or the big asses of the Sisters at home. But, I guess I had to make do with what was available. After a couple of glasses of wine, even the most obnoxious looking female looked good. We partied heavy in the guesthouses, especially those with a German Um-Pa band that played polka music; so when in Rome, do as the Romans do. I learned to dance the polka. All the old Fraus would line up to dance with spider and me. Some even wanted to take us home. There was only one problem their husbands.

But, every time I shacked up with a German woman, I was instantly reminded about Lonzo's brush with death at the hands of an SS woman. I developed a superstitious habit of checking out the Fraulein's thighs before getting it on with her. I was looking for the double lightning bolts of the Nazi SS. In one of my bad dreams, I was shot by a naked, crazed SS Fraulein that turned into a gorilla.

I would check them out so smoothly that the Frauleins thought I was an oral sex freak. I would never let them turn the lights off until I checked them out. I would slowly undress them, lay them down slowly on the bed, and start licking them at their knees, working my way up to the thighs until I hit pay dirt. After a double round of this, the girls would go wild, and if I didn't find the lightning bolts, it was time for me to go to work.

I told the Spiderman about Lonzo and the SS chick and he laughed his ass off. I finally told him about the scar that CPL Moran left on my lower lip. He died laughing about it also. I stopped talking abruptly when the conversation got close to my ugly secrets and suspicions.

"I never went into the town in San Antonio," the Spiderman said, "because some sections were too dangerous for GI's also. Between the local racist rednecks on their side of town and the wild ass Mexicans on their side of town, I wouldn't go. A couple of my GIs friends and I did go down to El Paso, Texas, on the Mexican border, to visit a friend who was in missile school at Fort Bliss. Juarez, Mexico was just across the border; a mile or so away. In Juarez, they didn't beat up too many GIs, because the GIs' money was the life's blood of the town. The Bar Girls worked the GIs like factory piece workers doing triple overtime on the night shift. You could buy sex for as little as fifty cents. Some of the girls were so young they didn't even have pubic hair."

He began to sense that I had some secrets that I didn't want share with him. He asked frequently if I wanted to talk about anything.

I said no.

"One thing you have to be careful of here in Germany," the Spiderman said, "Since there is no minimum drinking age in Germany; the guesthouses are filled with very young girls who with a little lipstick, rouge and nail polish looked grown. Some are much younger than you, Milkman."

The Spiderman was four years my senior although he didn't act like it. I had just turned 19 on my last birthday, the 26th of March, 1964. We both felt that we weren't going to get into trouble in Rudesheim. There were no military bases for miles and we very seldom saw any GIs or MPs. The girls that we partied within the guesthouses were generality clean cut, moderately dressed and attractive. Some were knock-down and drag-out beautiful. We checked their ages by their Kin Cards. All the girls eighteen on over in Germany were required to carry "Kin Cards." These cards said that a doctor checked the girl for venereal disease in the past six months. This practice was instituted in Germany after the war to knock out sexually transmitted diseases. It appeared to be working; Germany as a nation had a lower rate of sexually transmitted diseases than most cities in the United States.

The Spiderman always got lucky in Rudesheim. I never "got-over" as much as he did there. The girls were always very pleasant to me, but I seldom got anything clicking right away, except with the old Frau's, whose husbands looked like former Nazis. I always had a good time though until I saw Hook, one of the B-team members in one of the guesthouses we frequented. He froze me in my tracks. I rushed over to get a closer look to confirm it was him, but he disappeared.

The Spiderman asked me, "What's up?"

"Nothing."

The Spiderman was about the smoothest Brother I have ever met. He communicated well with women. He never rushed them. If they simply wanted to sit at the bar and nurse a drink, then that's what he would do with them. He would talk, sometimes all night with them; if we had an overnight pass. By midnight, I would give up, whether I had a pass or not. Those kinds of women wore me out. Yes, Spiderman got more than I did, but I kept more money in my pocket than he.

The Spiderman promised several times to introduce me to his Soul Sister girlfriend, who was his number two girl. His number one girl was a Swedish chick that he didn't see very often, because she lived in Stockholm. When he was able to get a three-day pass, he would meet her here in Bad-K. She would travel down from Sweden and stay at the local hotel with him. He said he wanted to take me to Frankfurt first. There we could go to some nice Jazz Clubs and possibly to a concert. That's where the hip German women go. That sounded like a winner to me, I said, let's take the train to Frankfurt next weekend.

He said bet, he had been TDY to the Frankfurt General Hospital and there were always empty beds in the enlisted men quarters. The 517th had guys stationed there on TDY all the time. We could stay there for the weekend if we didn't meet a Fraulein and go to a hotel.

Saturday afternoon, we arrived at the bahnhof in the center of Frankfurt. We walked a few blocks to the section of town that the Black GIs hung out in. Sweet Willie called them the Three Pigs, because there were three bars within a few blocks of one another that the Soul Brothers frequented to pick-up women. He teased me on the way there, by saying that I was going to meet some real Soul Sisters in Frankfurt, some real "Sapphires." I laughed at the thought.

We stopped off at a local eatery, sat down and he ordered my first bratwurst. It was a white sausage with a very subtle taste. With some spicy German mustard, hot potato salad, beans and a beer, I loved it. After downing a couple of bratwurst and a few local "Frankfurt am Main" beers, we headed out to the first of The Three Pigs.

We walked a few blocks and came upon the large timber house that was painted in very dark colors. The little sign hanging above the double doors was swinging gently in the breeze. It was called the Hexen Haus, "Witches House." I followed the Spiderman through the doors. The bar was almost empty; it was still very early for the night owls. There were a couple of GIs in the place along with approximately five frauleins. The bar was made of dark stained cherry wood with a long brass step rail hugging its bottom. Large stained wood timbers stretched the length of the entire building. The wooden floor was well worn from the dancing feet of hot-blooded GIs on the prowl. The Spiderman immediately surveyed the large room and spotted a very attractive Fraulein sitting by herself at a table.

He said to me, "Take out your note book Milkman, you are about to go to school."

I thought he knew her. He attacked her like a lion pouncing on hoofed meat. Boy, he doesn't play around I thought; he is hitting on the finest girl in the place. The Spiderman had a nose for women. He always brought home the trophies, the finest, the tallest and one with the healthiest body. We made a pack that we would never argue or fight over a woman. There had been a number of shootings and stabbings, by one Soul Brother against another Soul Brother, fighting over German women. The Stars and Stripes Army newspaper loved to print stories about Brothers killing one another over German women. It was so un-cool. We both considered it to be very primitive to fight over sex.

Both of us felt that our conversational skills were keen enough to, "Talk up on some sex" rather than fighting over some. I walked over to the bar to watch Spiderman work his show. He said, that I would learn something, I hoped he was right. I ordered a beer and I watched him through the bar's mirror for about ten minutes. He was talking a hole in the Fraulein's head. I paid no attention to the heavy set, moderately attractive Fraulein sitting next to me. Finally, I turned around and spoke to her.

"Wie geht es ihnen Fraulein, sprechen sie English?" "How are you Miss, do you speak *English?*"

"Ja, Wie sind sie? *Yes, who are you?*"

"Ich bin der Milchmann."

"I am Rose, Rose Clauz."

She said she worked at a local freight company and that her boyfriend, a Soul Brother, had just rotated back to the States. They had been together for two years and they had a big fight when he left, because he was going back to his, "Sapphire", wife in the states.

She said, he told her he divorced his wife, he was going to marry her and take her back to the States with him. I just shook my head as she told me how much she loved this guy. She was working the hell out of the bartender. She was throwing drinks down as fast as he put them up on the bar.

She said that she could have accepted the truth about his wife, if he told her the truth. But, he had lied. Finally, he told her he was going back to his wife, because she wasn't a "Sapphire"; that really hurt her. She then walked over to the quiet jukebox and put four German marks in the slot. The first record she selected was Junior Walker and the All Stars, "I am a Road Runner Baby." She then hurried back across the floor and grabbed me by the arm, and said, "I will show you that I am a Sapphire baby."

She dragged me out to the middle of the dance floor and began to dance her behind off. Now, I could get down a bit myself, but she clearly had me beat. The crowd in the bar began to pick-up. No one was on the dance floor, but Rose and me. The patrons began to holler and clap for Rose. We did The Pony, The Mash Potatoes, The Twist, The Slide, The Dog and every other dance known from Harlem to Berlin; she did them all and well.

We danced about an hour, and then finally someone played a Slow Jam. She wouldn't let me go. She squeezed me so tight that I began to see stars and she started to look like Lena Horn. She had one hell of a personality. She just wouldn't let me go. She took me back to the bar and told the bartender to keep pouring for both of us. I totally forgot about the Spiderman. I turned, so I could see him out of the corner my eye, he was still trying to talk a hole in that Fraulein's head. It appeared to me that she was starting to drink him under the table and he was buying.

Rose started to whisper in my ear, the sexual things she would do to me, to prove she was as good as a Sapphire.

She said, "Don't let the fact that I am German deceive you. I am a Sapphire, baby. I couldn't prove it to Richard, but I am going to prove it to you right now, let's go to my place."

As she dragged me out of the door, The Spiderman looked up in amazement.

I said, "1200 hours tomorrow." He knew what I meant. That was the way we looked out for one another. We would meet back at the same place we last saw one another at 12:00 the next day, no matter what.

Rose almost screwed me to death. Then she got up in the middle of the night and cooked me smothered pork chops with grits and red eye gravy; then she screwed me some more. I must have lost three pounds that night from the exercise. She woke me up early the next morning and made love to me again. The next morning she got up, took a shower, combed her hair and started off to work.

She said to me, "You stay right here, baby, I not through with you yet."

"Listen, Sapphire, you are one of the best I have ever had, but I have to go. No disrespect!"

A tear came into her eye. She said, "Thank you for that complement, Soul Brother", turned and walked out the door. Without turning around she said, "Lock the door behind you "Sweet-Thing" and give me a call when you are back in town."

I met the Spiderman with a smile on my face a mile wide. "Now, Milkman," he said, "A boss night like that can work two ways for you. The Brothers that mistreat their women get the word put out on them and they get no more sex in Frankfurt. These frauleins are tight with one another that way. But, if you treat them right and they like you, Brother, you become King Nigger in this town."

The Spiderman had spent the night in a hospital bed in the enlisted men's quarters-alone. Well, I don't know what Rose said about me or to whom, but when I walked into the Hexen Haus weeks later the girls in the bar went wild over me. Evidently, Rose must have put the right word out on me.

About a week after we returned from Frankfurt. Spiderman said he had a surprise for me.

"Yeah right, DD's brother!"

He smiled. "Meet me over at the EM Club about 2100 hours, and you better put on your best vines too."

"The last time you told me that, I wound up low crawling through a muddy rain tunnel and dirty riverbed running from the police."

About 9:30, the EM Club door opened and in walked this Soul Sister. I immediately rose from my chair and proceeded to the door with my hand outstretched. As soon as I reached her, the Spiderman walked in behind her with a devilish smile on his face. She had beautiful smooth brown skin, almost like Carol's and she was very tall with a good figure, but she wore a set of eyeglasses that would shame a Coke bottle.

"What's your name?"

"Margaret Spencer."

The Spiderman said, "If I was you, Margaret, I would not trust these hard leg GI's with my identity. They haven't seen a real Soul Sister in months. Besides, they could be Russian spies or something."

"I am Ed; they call me the Milkman, would you like to have a seat?"

The whole EM club came to a screeching halt. The entire EM Club was staring at us; it was so quiet you could hear a scalpel drop. A whisper flowed through the EM Club like quick silver, "A Sapphire, a Soul Sister." It almost turned into a quiet riot in there.

It was the second funniest scene I had witnessed in Germany after opening the door at the Haufbrau Haus. Almost every one of the Black soldiers in the EM Club, some leaving their German girlfriends, came over to our table to say hello and introduce themselves to Margaret. One Brother said to her jokingly, "What would a self-respecting woman like you want with an old rusty dog bone like the Spiderman?"

He responded, "Ok, trench mouth, go play with the rest of the Mouseketeers. This is man's work."

Most of us Soul Brothers had not seen a single Black woman in over a year. The way we stood staring at the sister like zombies verified the fact there was a "Desire for Sapphire" in Germany.

The Spiderman said to me, "That's why I don't bring her to the EM-Club much. She gets angry at me saying that I don't like to take her around my friends."

"Why don't you say something to the Brothers about it?"

"They aren't rude to Margaret, but their conduct is disrespectful to me."

He said he was going to the bathroom and simply left me at the table, alone with her to fend off an assault by a phalanx of Hard-Johnson Soul Brothers. After a while, I got tired of it myself. The Brothers would come over, introduce themselves, sit down, and rudely interrupt my conversation with Margaret; talking trash.

It was amusing at first, but after a while, she didn't appreciate it either; I could see it in her eyes. I had to figure out something. The Spiderman returned to the table saying, "What happen to all the Brothers in the Club?"

I smiled and said, I told them that Margaret was a CID officer looking for Brothers who were selling "Weed" on the Hospital Kaserne. The word circulated through the whole EM-Club inside of five minutes. It worked too well, most of the Soul Brothers booked (left) the club. Margaret was a civilian employee who worked for the Special Services Group at the 8th Airborne Headquarters. She was a social worker counseling GIs with troubled families.

I didn't realize how much I had missed the Soul Sisters or as the Soul Brothers, here call them "Sapphires." To the Brothers, the label was full of love. It wasn't Amos and Andy derogatory. To me the label meant the Sisters were prized stones. Already, I was starting to feel the need to see some long slender black legs extruding from inflated thighs with giant cantaloupes riding on top of them; quivering and trying to keep their equilibrium.

I began to think of the sisters back in Alabama, including Carol, complaining about the difficulties they were having finding boyfriends. Any Brother that could walk upright and chew gum at the same time would pass muster for them. Black women felt that Black men secretly lusted for white women. This may be true for some, to the extent that the grass appears greener on the other side of the hill until one gets there. Well, I have gotten there and I don't see anything greener. If the Soul Sisters back home only knew there were damn near one hundred thousand Hard-Johnson healthy Brothers in Europe, all looking for Soul Sisters; they would have high-jacked a plane in a heartbeat to get here.

The Spiderman was a playboy. He had joined the army, because jobs were getting scarce in Buffalo, NY. He was the envy of the 517th. He was working three women in Europe at the same time. He had a Swedish girl in Stockholm, a Soul Sister who lived in the nurse's quarters across from the hospital here in Bad-K and a Danish girl in Copenhagen, Denmark.

He said, "Milkman, there are two rules the Brothers should follow in Germany concerning women.

- One, never fight over a women unless she's your mother, sister, wife or your daughter.
- Two, don't take a woman home to America, because you can't return her and get your money back."

He showed me pictures of his other girlfriends. They both were very good looking. "Now, Denmark and Sweden is where you want to go for some first class loving. Those women don't play games like the frauleins here. They will snatch your ass off the street and just about rape you in Scandinavia."

"Rape me! When do we go?"

"I'll let you get your feet good and wet, by yourself, here first. Then we will head up north so you can see this unbelievable shit for yourself."

The Spiderman started spending more time with Margaret. He didn't have much time for a Hard-Johnson GI like me hanging around him and his girl. That provided the opportunity for me to hang and get to know some of the other guys better.

I decided to do Swilley a favor and take him to Frankfurt with me to get his cherry broken. Swilley liked New Orleans's Jazz, but the best I could do for him was two tickets to see John Coltrane at the Frankfurt Concert Hall. John Coltrane probably was too heavy for Swilley. But, John Coltrane was very religious like Swilley and maybe he could connect to his music. We were standing in a long line to get into the concert. I recognized a fine blonde standing on line in front of us, but I couldn't remember where I knew her from. Swilley recognized an opportunity to strike.

He walked over to her and said, "Hello I am Haymen Swilley, that ugly dude standing in back of you says he knows you. I bet him five dollars that he is a liar. Do you think you could help me win this bet?"

He brought her over and we started talking trying to figure out where we had seen one another. Then it hit me; she was Bridgett Heaton, the blonde who drank the Spiderman under the table at the Hexen Haus. She was fine, but a bit on the eccentric side. She liked hanging out at the Three Pigs in Frankfurt. Many German girls loved hanging out with the Brothers. Some liked the Brother's conversation, some like to party with the Brothers and some like to make love to the Brothers. Some liked all three.

She made it clear that she liked to party with the Brothers, nothing more. The Spiderman said he thought she was gay after she drank him under the table without giving anything up. She was half French and half American. Her father was an American who worked at the American Embassy in Paris. She lived in a suburb of Frankfurt about a half hour away by trolley. She was studying classical music, dance and base cello at the Frankfurt Conservatory.

She admitted that she was not very good at dancing. Her dance teacher suggested that she party with Soul Brothers to develop and improve her dance rhythm. Her eyes fell down to the left when she made that statement. I sensed she was lying about the real reason she hung out with Soul Brothers and suspected she had her own ugly secrets. On weekends, as she partied with the Brothers at the Hexen Haus, they would get into fights over her. They didn't understand that she was a tease; at the end of the evening, she wasn't going to take them home and give them some.

The Spiderman spent a lot of time and money on her when he came to Frankfurt. He was a good dancer and he loved to party with her. Once she invited Spiderman and me to attend one of her recitals at the Frankfurt Concert Hall, but I never went. There was a lot of serious music being played at the Frankfurt Concert Hall, but every time I tried to make a concert, some good loving got in the way.

I didn't have much time or money for her, because I spent my time with my German Sapphires. They were the girls who took care of me. They brought this poor-ass private all the liquor and wine he could hold, then at the end of the evening, they would take him home and screw Satan out of him. The German girls in the bar felt Bridgett was nothing but a tease and trouble. She always kept the bar in an up roar. The Spiderman kept her out of trouble by spending a lot of time with her. My weekend pass time was precious; I couldn't afford to blow a good time with my German Sapphires on entertaining Bridgett. She invited Swilley and me to sit with her at the John Coltrane Concert. John Coltrane was known very well in Frankfurt, even before his Love Supreme album started to sell well in Europe. In fact, it was the Europeans that kept Jazz music alive when Rock and Roll became popular in the States. Jazz music was losing its Black roots audience to Rock and Roll. I believe the cause was natural progression.

The Black American jazz musicians stopped playing dance music. That was the music Black Americans wanted to hear. Jazz music in the war years was just about that. Duke Ellington's Jungle Music was always upbeat and hip. The Savoy Ballroom at Lenox Ave. and 145th St. stayed packed with mixed crowds of Blacks and whites kicking to the music of Chick Henderson. The US Army closed down the Savoy, during WWII, after making false allegations that the club was an incubator for sexual diseases. The real reason for closing it down was the club was integrated. It was one of the few places in the nation where whites and Blacks partied together without any problems during the war.

Bridgett read about the Savoy, Small's Paradise and other famous Harlem nightclubs. She had even visited a few, including the Savoy's site a few years back after it was closed down permanently. She enjoyed New York City with its bright lights, fast thoroughfares and hot clubs. She loved being entertained and the entertainment business. But, she had a strange attitude towards men, especially white men. During the concert, Swilley was getting a little aggressive in his conversation. She told him that she wouldn't have anything to do with him or any other white guy. I took offence to her statement; it was like being told she didn't serve coloreds in here. I understood that some European women liked Soul Brothers and sometimes the darker the better. I had been told by several European women, "Sorry, Brother, the blacker the berry the sweeter the juice." I took it as a complement for real dark brothers. I would simply walk away saying, "You have to add milk and sugar to your coffee, baby, to make it sweet." But, I took offence to the way she handled Swilley. I told him I wanted to change our seats; I'd never really liked her anyway. Swilley didn't find her offensive, he was enjoying the concert and wanted to remain seated where we were.

During intermission, I got up and went to the men's room. That's where I ran, smack, into my gorilla dream again; the B-team. There wasn't any place for them to hide in the bathroom; especially Anvil. They were definitely stalking me. I knew that my run-in with members of the B-team wasn't a coincidence. It was starting to happen too frequently now after the Kennedy murder. The John Coltrane Concert was the fifth time I had run into those guys in a month. I never saw their former commanding officer Captain Grumble. I spoke to them in my usual sarcastic manner, whenever I could not avoid them.

I didn't say anything to Swilley about it; I didn't want him to get riled up. Bridgett apologized to Swilley for being so abrupt. Then she invited Swilley and me down to spend a weekend in Paris at her father's home. I said OK, but I wasn't going to take her up on the invitation. As time went on, things got worse between Bridgett and me. Once, I left her standing in the middle of the dance floor when my "German Sapphire" date showed up at the Hexen Haus. She didn't like that at all, and she shoved me in the middle of the dance floor. She said, she didn't see anything of any substance in the women I party with. It almost got ugly when my date felt she crossed the line and almost beat her behind.

The next night, Bridgett grabbed me by the arm and took me outside the bar. Spiderman had a nasty frown on his face when I walked out of the door with Bridgett. Finally, she broke down crying telling me her ugly secrets. Her aunt's husband had raped her as a child in France. She wouldn't give him the dignity of calling him her uncle. It happened right after her mother died. Her father was always traveling for the State Department in some foreign country, so he left her in the care of her aunt's family in Paris. She never told her father. She couldn't stand the feel of male human flesh being pressed against her body, especially white flesh. So as she grew older she wouldn't let anyone touch her, but a Black female roommate in boarding school. It wasn't anything sexual about it; it was simply a matter of trust. That was the reason she liked to party with Black guys, she felt safe. That was one hell of a story, a fine white girl feeling safe around a bunch of Hard-Johnson Black GIs. But, I guess it was true, none of the Soul Brothers ever tried to take advantage of her; in spite of her being a tease and getting drunk every now and then.

I sensed that the Spiderman really liked her, but for some strange reason he felt she was above being made love too. Also, some Southern Brothers were afraid to make love to European women, because they felt their deeds might get back home and some redneck sheriff would come after them with a rope after they returned home. Many Black soldiers had been lynched in their uniforms by rednecks after WWI and WWII after returning from Europe.

For the remainder of that evening, we just walked, talked and then one thing lead to another. We found our way to her small apartment, on the north side of Frankfurt, in a clean, but noisy neighborhood. She said that she really liked me, but that it was going to take some time for her to get over being sexually assaulted. I replied, if you really want me to help you get over it, then we should get started right now, baby.

"I don't know how to begin."

"You know how to dance don't you?"

"Yes."

She had some Miles Davis records in her collection. I went over to her record player and pulled out Miles' "Quiet Nights." We began to dance slowly. I slowly began to kiss and undress her, and then she pushed me away and asked me not to do that. But, she was already standing there, partially nude, in the middle of the floor. The mirror on the wall revealed every beautiful flaw on her body and her soul. I backed away, and motioned her over to me. I turned my back to her, facing the mirror, so she would not feel threaten and could see my every move. I put my hands behind my back and she began to remove my clothes one button at a time from my rear. When she reached my zipper, she jumped. From behind, she continued to remove my pants. She began to massage my penis and stoke it to the rhythm of Miles' music.

She wanted to take the lead, so I let her. We danced and kissed in the nude, sipping white wine and nibbling cheese which was providing the fuel for our desire. She had danced with a lot of guys before, but never one that had freed her soul. Dancing was something she felt comfortable with. I danced her over to the bed and motioned her to lie down. She wouldn't, but she refused to release me.

I moved over to the chair by the bed and sat down. She danced all around me until she set on top of my body and allowed me to enter her. She jumped up, but I wouldn't allow her to run anymore. I gently eased her back down as I licked her tears away from her face. I rubbed her neck and back as Miles played his soft rhythms to the movement her body. She began to move more violently as she began to have her first orgasms. The fluids from her body began to flow like wine. She began to glow as if the years of tension held by her body were freed to explore the heavens. It was one of the most memorable experiences of my life.

***

Fabulous Fraulein

DANISH PRINCESS

A DESIRE FOR SAPPHIRE

16

The King of the Wild Frontier

The word from back home was that Malcolm X was splitting from the Nation of Islam over the fact that Elijah Muhammad had fathered several children by his secretaries. Malcolm X flew to Frankfurt on his way to Saudi Arabia to make his first hajj. A hajj is a trip to the holy shrine of the Ka'ba located in the holy city of Mecca, in Saudi Arabia. It's a trip that every Muslim should make once in his or her lifetime. Malcolm X left the United States under his new name of Malik El Shabazz. He had changed it after leaving the Nation of Islam and converting to an orthodox Sunni Muslim. He stopped over in Frankfurt, but by the time I heard about his trip, it was too late for me to get the airport to see him.

The Rochester Institute of Technology wrote me back wishing me well in my future endeavors, stating that I didn't meet their standards for admission. That really brought this cocky Soul Brother back to earth. Maybe I wasn't as smart as I thought.

Captain Schmitz, CO of the 517th and his incompetent XO lieutenant were transferred back to the states after a shooting incident in the pay line. The dumb-ass lieutenant went to pick up the company's payroll, in cash, from the paymaster armed. He forgot he had chambered a round in his 45 pistol. It accidentally discharged and the bullet missed our heads by inches while we were standing in line being paid. Even as paranoid as I had become, I knew this incident was an example of stupidly on a grand scale on the lieutenant's part. It was made worse when the captain tried to cover it up.

A former 82nd Airborne First Lieutenant, by the name of Garry L. Biggs replaced him. According to Jumping Jack Daniels, LT Biggs had been stationed at Fort Bragg, North Carolina serving as an infantry officer in his previous assignment. He lost his nerve to jump after being in the unit for about three months. This assignment at the 517th was his last chance to make captain. He had been passed over for promotion twice already. As soon as he arrived at the 517^{th,} the B-team members paid him a visit. They knew him from Fort Bragg. I knew that meant trouble for me.

I did some free portrait photography work for two sergeants and their families, so they volunteered to be my color bearers. That honor was usually reserved for NCOs. They were Sergeants Moore and Cummings. The only problem was their tours in Europe were almost up. Guarding the colors were Swilley and me. President Kennedy had complained about the lack of Negro servicemen serving on military color guards at his inauguration. Now you very seldom see military color guards without Black service members represented.

But, I didn't let my paranoia overwhelm me. After a month of begging, bribing and brow beating, I was able to pull it off. I had enough volunteers for my rifle and pistol team. Most of the guys in the Misfit's Squad volunteered. In addition, we picked up Raymond Jackson, a.k.a. "Nasty Jack", the truck mechanic.

Private Vincent Johnson also volunteered for the rifle team. He was our assistant cook and a good one. Vincent bunked with the Misfits, because there wasn't enough room for him in the headquarters' platoon barracks. He liked to bunk with the Misfits Squad, because he said, it kept him out of the mess sergeant's eye. At that time, I really didn't understand what he meant.

Vincent was fanatical about cleanliness. He was also a very precise Brother. Some GIs felt he was gay. He vigorously denied the accusations, but we never saw him with any women the entire time he was in the unit. He developed into the best rifle shot on the 517[th's] team. He soaked up the training by mastering every technical aspect of shooting. The Army policy in dealing with homosexuals was simple. Look the other way until you catch someone in the act, then look the other way again if you can. There were a large number of homosexuals in the US Army both men and women. Most of these individuals, generally, were very good soldiers.

At the height of the Greek Army's dominance as a world military power, their whole system of training recruits was based on homosexuality. So, there was no correlation between skill, courage and homosexuality, because the Greeks had the best fighting machine in the world at that time.

In addition to Nasty Jack, Vincent and Swilley, a surprise volunteer stepped forward, Gary Livingston a.k.a., Robin. He was someone that I definitely didn't want on the team, but it was open to all. Anesto Garcia, also a Misfit, volunteered to be the part-time armor.

I couldn't fill-out three teams, so I asked the Mad Doctor if he could find other GIs to head-up the small-bore squad of the pistol team. The pistol competitions were held in two classes, small bore 22-caliber and large bore- 45 caliber. I liked the large bore weapons, they were the most popular and the same weapons we used in combat. The Mad Doctor complimented me on the good job I did in organizing the team and said he would find others for the small bore unit.

My team and I were sent to the US Army's Advanced Marksmanship School in Lanstuhl, Germany. Instructors were flown in from the States to train us. We trained and fired for about two weeks on the shooting ranges under their instruction. Our marksmanship instructors taught Zen breathing techniques which allowed the weapon to rise and fall in the target area as you inhaled and exhaled. The worse thing in the world for a good shooter to do is try to hold the weapon still on the target. In a long shooting match, you will tire yourself out trying to do so.

We all finished the course and graduated as advanced marksmen. Our first shooting competition was against the Air Force team from Wiesbaden Air Base, Germany. We kicked their butts with our M14 rifles and 1911 45 ACP pistols. Our small bore team lost. But like the rest of our weapons, our pistols and rifles were old and needed a lot of maintenance. Garcia returned from armor's school which was held at the 3rd Armored Division in Kaiserslautern, Germany where he graduated with honors. Garcia was the worse medic in the company. He knew his medical stuff, but hated the sight of blood. Garcia was sent back to the 517th from TDY at Frankfurt General Hospital, because he almost killed a guy when he fainted during a blood transfusion. Garcia was very distraught about it and was always depressed.

We teased him about being a "Wetback", because his parents were illegal's. They crossed the Rio Grande River into Arizona when his mother was 8½ months pregnant.

She wanted him to be born in America as a citizen of the United States. He almost didn't make it. His Mother gave birth to him in the middle of the desert, but he lucked out when the border patrol picked them up. He was born 500 feet inside Arizona's, United States border. He became an excellent armorer.

Seeing our progress, the Mad Doctor called us into the HQ and allowed us to witness the first lieutenant and him signing the requisition for new M14s and new "Match 1911-45s", solely for the team to use in competitions. The Match 45s were some "Bad Dogs"; they came in cold blue steel with Red Oak handles and adjustable sites. They cost over five hundred each and this brought huge smiles on our faces. The 1st LT signed the requisition and said he wanted to see some results from his investment. After the signing, he asked me to stay in his office as the other members of my team left.

He said to me, "I have heard good things about you PFC Roy and I want you to take up the Supernumerary challenge given by CPL Perez at the 8th Airborne Headquarters."

I saw deceit in his eyes that said he was up to no good. I replied, yes, sir, and added, "I didn't know Perez had received a promotion. As soon as we get our new weapons and uniforms, Sir, I will throw down the gauntlet to CPL Perez. "

"Keep me informed as to when it's going to happen."

"Yes, Sir."

I saluted, did an about face and left his office. About two weeks later, the supply sergeant sent word to me that our new uniforms and weapons had arrived.

I gathered up my team and we all stormed into the supply room to pick the stuff up. Everyone was very excited, we helped Garcia unpack the weapons, and to our surprise, there were two specially prepared M14s in the box of ten. They were immaculate; they were fitted with Brazilian Walnut stocks. All the machined parts and barrels were polished, blued and never fired.

Garcia said to the team, "These two will be our parade weapons. They will be used for the color guard and guard mount only. We will never fire these two specially prepared M14s, because it would be sin."

Swilley looked directly at Garcia and said, "What in the hell do you think weapons are for, the movies." Our new set of match 45 pistols hadn't arrived, but we felt Swilley's comments where strange.

I opened the box of the new winter uniforms and I gave each member of the team a new set including myself. I took my pants immediately to the laundry to have them starched. Garcia went to work on the new weapons degreasing, cleaning and checking their functions. I notified LT Biggs that I was ready to take on CPL Perez on his own turf. The date was set for next Tuesday evening at the 8th's HQ. The 8th Airborne held guard mounts every evening, because their base housed top secret weapons that had to be guarded 24 hours a day.

I was ready. My boots were spit shined to a mirror finish. I applied two light coats of "Clear" floor wax on the top of the triple spit shine, just like the Wolfman had showed me. The barber cut by head clean and razor trimmed a sharp hairline around my entire head. He even trimmed the hair in my nose and ears.

When the time arrived, I placed cardboard inside my field pants legs to provide a straight-leg-blouse over my boots. I lay down on the bed for Swilley to slide my starched field pants on. After he slid them on, he stood me up straight so I would not break the starch. After I put on my winter wool shirt, Swilley slid me into my field jacket without opening it to prevent the starch from cracking. Then he folded the excess waist material of the jacket into the back and held the folds in place as I tightened my pistol belt around my waist. Garcia had worked on my new M14 most of the day.

He brought it to me wrapped in brown paper saying. "Never put this weapon in a case, because the moister in the barrel can't escape causing it to rust from its own sweat."

The Spiderman pulled the ¾ ton around to the front of the barracks. They carried me out by my armpits and lifted me into its back. We were running a bit late for the mount. The Spiderman was driving and he wasted no time in getting me to the 8th Airborne Headquarters; which was near the center of the town. Their MPs stopped us at the gate. When one looked into the back of the ¾ ton, he couldn't believe his eyes. He called his duty sergeant over and said, "Serge, a leg medic is coming here to challenge us on guard mount."

The sergeant said, "Provide him with a special escort, this is the first time in over a year that a leg medic has challenged paratroopers on guard mount."

The MP patrol car led us to the HQ building with their lights flashing. Perez and three paratroopers were already in formation. A large crowd of paratroopers gathered. The odds dropped to $3 to $2 that Perez would win. My personal money which I bet with Perez was $2 to $1, for $50 dollars total. I didn't know what the total size of the money pot was, but Perez was happy with it. Swilley acted as my second. He handled the betting with Perez's second; who demanded to hold the money. They opened the tailgate and lifted me out of the ¾ ton. Then the heckling started.

"Who shinned your boots, leg, your mama?"

"It will be a cold day in hell if you take down, Perez, Fart."

"Look at him, he so scared that he's shaking all the polish off his brass."

Swilley handed me my weapon and I stiff-legged over to the mount. Without warning, this huge figure appeared out of the crowd with a coffee cup is his hand. As he stepped on by boots, he said "Ups" and spilled his coffee on my uniform. Then he said to me with a smile, "Like MacArthur said, I have returned. Good luck, Milkman."

It was DD-Doctor Death, he had finally struck. Swilley took out his handkerchief and spit on my boots trying to re-shine them, but the damaged DD caused to the shine was too deep. Then he tried to spot clean my jacket with water from my canteen, it was too late.

The sergeant of the guard called the mount to attention. He read off the names of the units that should be represented. They booed loudly when he read the 517th Medical Clearing Co. He simply stopped reading the names, looked at the crowd and they went silent.

Where had DD come from? He had really pissed me off. DD stood in front of the crowd making faces at me and running his index finger across his neck, like it was a gang fight in Harlem. The officer of the day, a major from the 8th's Combat Engineers walked out of the HQ. He introduced himself and welcomed the 517th Medical Clearing Unit to the 8th Airborne Division's guard mount.

He also said, "The inspection of the guards on this mount will be conducted with the highest level of integrity."

It was a little late for integrity. I clearly had the best prepared weapon on the mount, but my boots and jacket were not going to make muster. Maybe my weapon would balance things out. The first round of inspections went very well. The Sergeant of the Guard told two paratroopers to fall out. Now, it was Perez and me going head to head. The officer asked us military questions and inspected us twice again. Then he whispered to the Sergeant of the Guard. The sergeant told me to fall out. The paratroopers went wild.

The OD pulled me aside and said, "You did well, PFC Roy, it was very close. Your weapon was the best prepared I have seen since I arrived in Europe. Clearly, your boots and jacket needed some work. The military knowledge was even between Perez and you. It was your gas mask that decided the completion. Your filter canister was not screwed on tight." Since basic training, my gas mask and I never got along very well.

Perez walked over to me, counting his money saying, "ju're bad man, Milkman, I have much respect for you coming over here to challenge me. I told the OD I wanted a fair one, "Man-O, Man-O." I am giving you the first pick for the tour you want."

I gave him a hug, a pat on his back and said 0200 hours.

He said, "ju hod it mange."

I gave the parade weapon back to Swilley, in exchange for an older one to use on my guard tour. The sergeant of the guard drove us around the headquarters area showing us the areas to be patrolled. He pointed out a set of bunkers that were marked "Authorized Personnel Only." The sergeant said they were kept locked at all times and no one was to enter them under any circumstances unless the OD and he accompanied them. Perez told the first guard to get out of the jeep and start his patrol. I asked Perez what was in those bunkers.

He said, "Milkman, ju don't want to know."

"Where have I heard that before?"

Then Perez got out of the jeep. He handed the guard two clips of live ammo. As he got back into the Jeep, he started to whistle, "Davy, Davy Crockett the King of the Wild Frontier." I knew then, that I would be guarding the 8th's Airborne Tactical Nuclear Weapons. We drove back to the guardhouse and I went to sleep until it was my turn to go on patrol. About 0130 hours, Perez woke me up and drove me back to the bunkers. The guard who I relieved handed me the two clips of live ammo.

Perez said to me, "Here, Milkman, we go locked, loaded and live; which means you fire first and ask questions later. Keep one round in the chamber at all times." He ordered me to lock and load. Then he asked me, "What is the password and color of the day?"

"The password is dogfight and the color of the day is red." I then asked, why wasn't there any lights around the bunkers?

"Because, we don't want the bunkers to be visible from the air at night."

I started my patrol, which included the motor pool as well as the bunkers. The total patrol route was about a ⅓ mile in a semi-circle. I made two rounds of my patrol when I heard a noise that sounded like mental doors opening. I double-timed back to the bunkers to check it out. The area was completely dark accept for a light shining out of one of the bunker's doors. I took the safety off my weapon as I crept through the bunker's doors. I heard talking. One of the voices sounded very familiar, but I could not place it.

I called out, "Halt, who goes there?" There was no response. I hollered again louder, "Halt, who goes there?"

The muffled response was "Dogfight, Red."

Then I saw two figures standing by the Davy Crockett Tactical Nuclear Weapon mounted on a recoilless rifle attached to a M151 Jeep.

I said, "Halt."

I saw two figures, with their backs to me, dressed head to toe in sealed white overalls. I told them to put their hands on the back of their heads and kneel down on one knee. They followed my instructions. I walked to the front of the jeep, where I saw that they were wearing gas masks. Instinctively I reached for my gas mask. With one hand holding my weapon and the other fumbling for the gas mask, it wouldn't come out of its case. The OD had unscrewed the filter canister off my mask completely, inspecting it, and he hadn't screwed it back on property.

I walked in back of intruders where they could not see what I was doing. I laid my weapon down while I tried to put my gas mask back together and put it on. That's when the lights went out. The next thing I knew I was hearing voices calling my name "PFC Roy, PFC Roy", and feeling cold water being poured on my face from my canteen. When I came too, I was sitting in the bunker's door. The Davy Crockett was gone.

Perez was saying "Ju fucked-up Milkman, Ju fucked-up."

The OD told Perez to keep quiet and that no one was to say a word about this until further notice. I was taken into the Post Provost Marshal's office.

"What happened?" the provost marshal asked me.

I told him, that the bunker's doors had been opened by someone and I had gone into the bunker to check it out. There, I saw two men dressed in white radiological suits standing around the Davy Crockett. I told them to halt, but they gave me the password and color of the day. I told them to put their hands on their heads and kneel. That's when I saw that they were wearing gas masks. I thought poison gas was released in the bunker and I reached for my gas mask and it wouldn't come out of its case. I walked to rear of the intruders to un-case my mask and put it on and I was blacked out.

"Do you have a history of blacking out PVT Roy?"

"I didn't black out. Someone blacked me out."

He said, "PFC Roy, you better tell me the truth; a nuclear weapon is missing on your watch. I don't want to say stolen; yet, all you can tell me is, "I saw two men dressed in white overalls, gas masks and I blacked out."

"There is a bump on the back of my neck, Sir."

"You could have received it during your fall after you blacked out. We have information that you blacked out on guard duty before PFC Roy."

"What in the hell are you talking about, Sir."

"In medical corpsman school, you were on guard mount and you blacked out there."

"Bullshit, I was hit in the head with a rifle butt by the OD that time."

"That's not what we heard, PFC Roy. You are ordered not to discuss this situation with anyone until our investigation is completed. Do you understand me, private?"

"Yes, Sir."

"You're dismissed."

The next morning they drove me back to the 517th. Some guys at home started to tease me. "We heard you got your ass kicked by Perez on guard mount."

I was ordered to immediately report to the 1st lieutenant's office. As I walked into his office, he locked my heels at attention. The first soldier was standing and watching from the corner.

"I was informed, PFC Roy, that something of great importance you were guarding went missing under the 517th's watch. That doesn't make the company look good after all the effort and resources that were extended to you."

"I was ordered not to discuss it, Sir."

He said that he understood that and he then dismissed me. Things went further downhill from there. A lot of whispering began in the company about me. The lieutenant started a rumor that I was a Black Muslim, a disciple of Malcolm X who hated white people and wanted to take over America. Some of white guys started to harass me. My footlocker would mysteriously overturn. My bed sheets would mysteriously short. Finally, one evening, a redneck from my former platoon called me a "Nasty Nigger", because, as he put it, I didn't bathe enough. We went at it verbally until one of the sergeants broke it up.

Some of the white GIs stood by me, the Misfit Platoon, the rifle and pistol teams, but not without consequences. Their support of me caused all of them to come under attack by LT Biggs in an effort to isolate me. Additionally, he called Swilley into his office and told him that he was promoted to Specialist 4th Class and as a junior NCO he was expected not to associate with privates. He told Swilley that I was in a lot of trouble that he couldn't talk about. He mentioned to Swilley, that he took the liberty to write his father to let him know about his promotion. Also, he was recommending him for an appointment to the West Point Military Academy in New York State.

When Swilley returned to the barracks, he said nothing to me about the news. He began to sew his new rank on his uniform as the rest of the Misfits and I watched. I could see he had an attitude about it. I told him that his father had something to do with it and he was promoted over all the GIs in the company who had higher ratings and more time in grade than he had.

He became very angry with me and said, "I am a better soldier than you Milkman, and the rest of the soldiers I was promoted over."

"Bullshit Swilley, by what measure, your white skin?"

"You people always have to fall back on skin color when you don't measure up."

"Swilley, you have never measured up to anything in your life. Put your money where your mouth is and we will see who the best damn soldier in the 517th is. You name the measurement Swilley; pick your own damn poison."

"The bet is on, Milkman; you pick your own damn poison, Supernumerary on guard mount or rifle shooting."

I knew Swilley was a good shot with a rifle. He had hunted with his father as a child and both of us had fired "Expert" in our last rifle-qualifying shoot. I hollered back, guard mount and pistol shooting, fifty dollars each contest; even money.

"You pick the time and place, Swilley. No officers or NCOs from the 517th can judge the contest. The judges have to be neutral."

Swilley wouldn't pick a medical knowledge challenge, because he knew my medical test scores in the company were higher than his. He said, "I want to get this over with as soon as possible, so I can study for the West Point Academy's entrance examination."

"He promised you West Point also? I must be a very important nigger for him to give away so much to get me. Next Friday's guard mount, Swilley, no matter who the officer of the day is."

I knew the OD was going to be an officer from the 97th Field Hospital. When Friday arrived, I beat Swilley's behind on guard mount. He was very nervous and couldn't remember a thing. I made him walk the graveyard shift 2 am to 4 am. There wasn't anything LT Biggs could do about it, either. The day before, I had beaten him at pistol shooting on the US Army's range on Kuhberg Hill. At 0200 hours, I handed him one M14 chip with four rounds of live ammo as he handed over the one hundred dollars he lost to me in the bet.

He said, "You are a predator, Milkman, and predators usually get eaten by other predators."

"That may be true, Swilley, but I definitely won't be eaten by you."

He didn't need any instructions from me to walk his patrol route. He had walked it many times before. Swilley won supernumerary several times, but he never beat Batman or me. I saw improvement every time he stood guard mount. It would just be a matter of time before he would take both of us down. Swilley still hadn't cleared up the serious conflicts going on in his head with his father; the retired colonel. His father still felt he wasn't up to his standards as a soldier. Swilley was definitely missing the fire in his heart, that killer instinct you need to finish on top. He was very bright and I could see the fire slowly building inside of him. I could see the increasing glow in his eyes, but he was walking the fence on many personal issues that he didn't want to talk about. He was carrying his own ugly secrets.

It was about 0300 hours when Swilley and the charge of quarters woke me up as I slept in the guardhouse. I asked, what in the hell was going on that's so important that it required you to wake me up. It had better be WWIII.

"I helped PVT Vincent into his bunk half an hour ago. He had been drinking at the EM Club and was stone drunk."

"So!"

Swilley grabbed me by the arm and said follow me. He took me into our barracks and he placed his finger to his mouth telling me to be quiet. Our room door was already cracked. I peered through the door and I saw the outline of two men. One was screwing the hell out of the other from behind on Vincent's bunk. I couldn't see their faces. I turned to Swilley and asked?

"Who are they?"

"Private Vincent is on the bottom and Sergeant Ossie Gilliam is on the top doing the work."

"How do you know?"

He simply turned and looked at the CQ and said, "I don't want to be the one to rat them out; PVT Vincent is a good soldier and the best rifle shot on our rifle team. But, Vincent was drunk and alone when we placed him in his bunk."

I looked at the CQ and said, "I didn't see anything."

We turned on the hallway lights and I deliberately dropped my flashlight on the floor, making a loud clang, as we walked out of the building. SGT Gilliam ran out of our barracks, half-naked, and into his own barracks two doors down.

The CQ said he was going to report it Monday morning before roll call. Monday morning, after roll call, Swilley and I were called into the Lieutenant's office.

PVT Vincent was sitting in Sergeant Doctor's office as we walked in.

The lieutenant asked Swilley, "What did you see at 0300 hours Saturday morning?"

"I don't know what I saw, Sir. I helped place PVT Vincent, who was drunk, in his bunk at 0230 hours. When I was checking the barracks with the charge of quarters at 0300 hours, I saw two figures in the same bed that I placed PVT Vincent in earlier. What they were doing, I cannot say, because it was dark in the room, Sir"

The lieutenant said, "The charge of quarters saw two men engaged in a homosexual act."

He turned to me and asked "Is that what you saw PFC Roy?"

"I didn't know what I saw, Sir, it was too..." Before I could finish my sentence, we heard a commotion in back of us coming from the armor's cage where we kept the weapons. We all ran into the hall to see PVT Vincent running down the stairs with two magazines of live ammo and one of our new M14 rifles in his hands.

PFC Garcia was lying on the floor of the cage. He had been cleaning the weapons with the door opened when PVT Vincent pushed him down and took the weapon. Swilley helped Garcia up from the floor as I ran to the window to see where in the hell Vincent was going. He was headed for the hospital mess hall.

"I replied to Swilley, "Oh shit, he is going to kill Gilliam."

We both took off down the stairs after Vincent. As we approached the mess hall, we heard the crackle of automatic rifle fire. GIs were running and diving for cover everywhere as we tried to make our way into the mess hall. As I charged through the doors, Vincent was standing on the top of the steam table firing at SGT Gilliam. SGT Gilliam had taken refuge behind a steam kettle and steam was escaping everywhere. Vincent was crying, cursing and firing all at the same time. He emptied one chip and was starting to reload. I hit him from the rear with a flying tackle before he could reload. The M14 went scooting across the mess hall floor that was covered with water spilling from the steam kettles. I hugged him as tight as I could.

He was trying to get to the rifle saying, "I am not a faggot, I am not a faggot."

"I know you are not a faggot, Vincent," I said.

Swilley ran into the kitchen grabbed SGT Gilliam by the collar and dragged him out of the kitchen's side-door. His white cook's pants left a trail of shit from the kettle to the exit that he released all over himself.

The MPs entered the mess hall with their weapons drawn. I waved to them to put them away. They placed both Vincent and Gilliam in handcuffs and took them away. Swilley and I were ordered to pack their belongings in their duffel bags. I thought they were on their way to the US Army Prison in Mannheim, Germany, but the next day they both were returned to the 517th Headquarters by the MPs. After a brief meeting with the 1st lieutenant, they were placed in different staff cars and sent to new units. The lieutenant said nothing more to Swilley or to me about the incident again. A day later a reporter, by the name of Mark Coben, from the Stars and Stripes Army newspaper, came to interview Swilley and me concerning the incident.

We told him that PVT Vincent's weapon accidentally went off in the mess hall. He said he didn't believe us. But, we read in the Stars and Stripes newspaper a week later that an automatic weapon was accidentally discharged in the 97th Field Hospital's mess hall and no one had been hurt. I was hurt; I lost a friend and the best shot on my rifle team.

Sweet Willie replaced Vincent on the rifle team. Our team started to do very well again. We beat all of the teams in the 62nd Medical Group and we started to compete against Seventh Army units, like the Signal Corps and Quartermasters. I wouldn't let us compete against front line combat units yet, because those units had more field and practice time than we did.

Lieutenant Biggs tried to have me removed from the 62nd Medical Group's honor color guard, but Major McComb, of the 15th Med-Evac Wing said, I was one of the best soldiers in the 62nd Medical Group and I deserved to be on the Honor Guard. I was the only experienced soldier left on the color guard. The sergeants that I trained rotated back to the states. LT Biggs didn't like Major McComb very much for supporting me. I felt that I was being set up, big time, by LT Biggs and I had to think of something quick. I knew the next assignment that he ordered me on, could be my last.

Back home, the Kennedy Murder Investigation was going nowhere. There were all kinds of rumors, reports and counter reports being leaked to the press, as if someone was deliberately trying to confuse the American public. Almost no one believed that Lee Harvey Oswald was the lone shooter or acted alone.

The B-team was always coming and going. I would spot them in my travels one week and then they would disappear for a few weeks. Then I would read in the newspapers about mysterious deaths of people who were associated with the Kennedy murder and investigation. Then the B-team would reappear in Europe.

The Defense Department refused to release the complete military records of Lee Harvey Oswald. They wouldn't state where he had learned to speak Russian or why. They wouldn't say whether or not, he had been trained at the elite Marine Corp's Scout Sniper School. The FBI said the rifle he allegedly used to kill the President didn't match any of the bullets fired or recovered from the bodies or scene. Oswald's pistol, which was allegedly used to kill police officer Tippit near Oswald's home, didn't match the bullets recovered from the dead policeman's body.

The first police officer, who ran into the Texas Book Depository seconds after the shots were fired, said Oswald was seated in the cafeteria, and that he hadn't issued the all-points bulletin with Oswald's description. No other police officers saw him at the scene or knew who blew the whistle on Oswald, or why at that time. Oswald told the Dallas police that he didn't shot the president and I believed him. But, he probably was involved somehow and became the scapegoat.

During the winter of 1963-64, several individuals who played roles in the events of JFK murder, died unexpectedly or fell victims to unexplained violence. Warren Reynolds, a used-car lot employee who allegedly witnessed Lee Oswald's escape, after the shooting of officer Tippit, was himself shot in the same Dallas used car lot on January 23. His rifleman shooter was seen, but never found. One man was picked up, but released on the testimony of a woman who allegedly hung herself in a Dallas jail cell after her subsequent arrest on a charge of disorderly conduct.

The general who had welcomed President Kennedy to San Antonio on behalf of the Air Force, the waiter who served him his last breakfast in Fort Worth and the advertising director of the Dallas News all dropped dead suddenly. The ad director was forty-five years old and was in excellent health.

The twenty seven year old captain, who was in charge of the farewell ceremonies for President Kennedy, suddenly died. The captain took the day off and toppled over at his dinner table; the victim of a heart attack ten days later after JFK's burial in Arlington. The previous September he had passed his regular physical; his cardiogram was normal.

There were all sorts of strange deaths associated with the Kennedy's murder; taking place back home. It appeared that The FBI was deliberately bungling the case.

Moreover, the FBI was infiltrating all the major civil rights organizations, the NAACP, The Southern Christian Leadership Conference, the Nation of Islam, and many more. Malcolm X, on his Hajj to Saudi Arabia, said he was followed constantly by CIA agents who didn't even try to be discreet. The CIA, FBI and NSA were instigating all sorts of internal trouble in all of these organizations. Malcolm X, in his speeches, would acknowledge the presence of undercover police, FBI and their paid informants seated in audience of his meetings.

I suspected it, but didn't want to believe it. It was looking like the B-team and possibly the Wolfman's team had played some role in the murder of the president of the United States. But, what was the San Antonio connection? The president had stopped there one day before he was murdered. The Wolfman and his team may have taken their ugly secrets to their graves. If so, why were the B-team and the first lieutenant coming down on me so hard?

I decided to cause some mischief of my own to flush them out, but I needed someone to watch my back while I did it. I wrote my congressman, Adam Clayton Powell Jr., and told him that the $517^{th's}$ officers were promoting white soldiers over more deserving Negro soldiers.

I didn't know what a hornet's nest I was going to stir up. A few weeks later, a staff car drove into the Kaserne flying the flag of the major general of the Seventh Army. As soon as the staff car cleared the gate, you heard nothing, but "Attent-hut" all the way into the 517th Clearing Company's HQ.

A tall Black lieutenant colonel got out of the staff car and walked into the HQ and "attent-hut, attent-hut" rang out. He walked unto LT Biggs office and told him he was temporarily assuming command to the 517th. That he was conducting an investigation of racial discrimination in his unit. He ordered the lieutenant to provide him with a lockable office, a lockable desk and a lockable file cabinet. That he would be staying in the officers' quarters in downtown Bad Kreuznach and he could be reached there after hours until his investigation was completed. The word got around the company very quickly that a Black officer locked the lieutenant's heels. No one said a thing to me for days as he conducted his investigation. I never saw him and I didn't know his arrival was in response to my letter I wrote. All I saw was his staff car coming and going. On the third day, I was called into the HQ by the Mad Doctor. I was told an officer from the general's staff of the Seventh Army wanted to speak to me. I walked upstairs into his office. He had his head down reading a copy of the letter that I sent to Congressman Adam Clayton Powell Jr.

He looked up at me and I almost fainted. It was Captain Grumble, the Special Forces captain of the B-team, but he had been promoted to lieutenant colonel. I knew my ass was in serious trouble now.

I saluted him and said, "Do you wish to see me, Sir?"

"Come in PFC Roy, close the door and have a seat."

"Thank you, Sir, it's been a long time since we talked."

"I have a copy of your letter you sent to Congressman Adam Clayton Powell Jr. You said Negro soldiers are being mistreated here in 517th. Did you write the letter?"

"Yes, Sir."

"Did you type the letter?"

"No, Sir, it was typed by a friend at the 67th Field Hospital."

"Do you wish to tell me what's going on here?"

I proceeded to tell him my story without revealing my true intensions or any of my ugly suspicions. I said that Swilley and other white soldiers were promoted over more deserving Black soldiers. After I left his office, he called in Swilley and PFC Callus who typed the letter for me. Two days later, he called me back into his office and said he was sorry to hear that SGT Sammerson and his SF-Team were missing in Vietnam. That he completed his investigation and that he found no evidence of mistreatment of Negro soldiers in this unit. I had accomplished what I needed. Someone besides my mother knew I was in this unit and I could bring attention to myself and the 517th if I needed to.

Swilley stopped speaking to me altogether. That was great; I was bad news for my white friends anyway. My dreams about the six hundred pound gorilla attacking me intensified. I knew it was just a matter of time before they would try to take me out again. I was a cat running out of lives. I didn't mention anything to Colonel Grumble about the missing nuclear weapon, but his voice remained ringing in my ears like a flashing stoplight. I couldn't help, but feel that I was in the middle of the eye in a hurricane while riding on top of a run-away German locomotive.

NATO called its spring alert early in April this year. This was the big one and marked the start of the annual NATO exercises. Troops and reservists were flown into Europe from several points in the United States. Elements of the 82nd Airborne were flown into Germany from Fort Bragg. They jumped into a large field near Kaiserslautern, Germany. It was a disaster. Their drop plane arrived late from the states and dropped the paratroopers into the wrong field. NATO Command realized they were in the wrong location, but it was getting dark, so they ordered them to bivouac at their current location. Their transport was at the right location and could not get there in time. It started to rain and visibility became poor. About 0200 hours in the morning, there was a loud rumbling noise. 30 Army M60 Patton tanks came charging across the field running over men as they slept in their sleeping bags. They didn't dig any fox holes, because they were ordered not to damage the farmer's fields. Four paratroopers were killed and 14 lost limbs.

The second platoon of the 517th was ordered to fly in, by chopper, to triage and med-evac them out. Bodies were laying everywhere and the field turned into one large pool of red mud. LT Biggs response was, "Shit happens." The NATO exercise continued as planned.

1st LT Biggs was ordered to send a reconnaissance team to inspect a landing zone next to the Rhine River so the first platoon could set up our aid station to support the remaining paratroopers. He flew in by Huey and inspected the site himself. If the weather cleared up by the next morning, our platoon would be airlifted to the site by helicopters. The air-lift was designed to be a fast insertion, because of reported aggressor sniper fire in the area. Even though the shit had hit the fan, we still had to play soldier.

The Rhine River is beautiful at that time of the morning with the sun sharing its warmth with the cool mist flowing down the river valley, giving life and color to the grapes in the hills. The choppers arrived about 0600 hours to pick us up. Each medic was carrying about eighty pounds of gear. The flight took about twenty minutes.

The choppers circled the landing site once and the sergeant said to get ready to disembark. Then LT Biggs hollered "Gas." In a rush, we donned our gas masks as the chopper began its decent. The chopper hovered for only a few seconds as I followed Thomas Good and Batman out of the door with the eighty pounds of gear strapped to our bodies. The river grass was tall and you really couldn't tell where the ground was. We immediately began to sink into eight feet of water and muck. The rains upstream had caused the river to flood its tall grassy banks overnight. We began to holler, but no sounds were escaping from our gas masks. The pilot wanted to hover to retrieve us, but the lieutenant said "No." The other choppers had started their decent and there was going to be a mid-air collision if our chopper didn't pull up. So they left us fighting for our lives in the marsh. I didn't know how to swim; my gas mask and other equipment were too difficult to remove. Additionally, the water clogged the gas mask and I couldn't breathe through it.

Swilley immediately jumped out of the chopper into the marsh as our chopper was pulling up. The other choppers simply passed us by like a seat-less Ferris wheel. The Wolfman's comments began to ring true again. By the time we were picked up, Thomas Good he had drowned. He had become tangled in the river grass and couldn't get his equipment off in time. With Swilley's help, Batman and I were able get out of our equipment and made floats using our medic bags. Swilley saved my ass again.

The remainder of the 517th air-lifts was called off and we all were flown back to Kuhberg Hill with Good's body. Batman and I were lucky. As soon as he got back into the HQ tent, Batman went at LT Biggs with both fists swinging. He beat the hell out of him. Batman said the lieutenant knew damn well that the river rose during the night and he deliberately set-us-up to get rid of his two headaches.

The 1st Lieutenant had Batman restrained to a chair and said he was going to have him court martialed. I called the lieutenant a sorry-ass SOB and I didn't give a shit if I was also restrained with Batman. At least Julius Caesar had seen it coming, "Et Tu, Brute?"

Swilley had seen enough. This was the second time he'd saved my life. Not all of this stuff could be coincidental. Now, he knew for sure that I was in deep shit, realty deep. He stayed very chose to me for the remainder of the NATO exercises. When they wanted to medevac me out, he refused to let them fly me out. He said he would take care of me at the aid station there. Swilley was my King of the Wild Frontier.

261

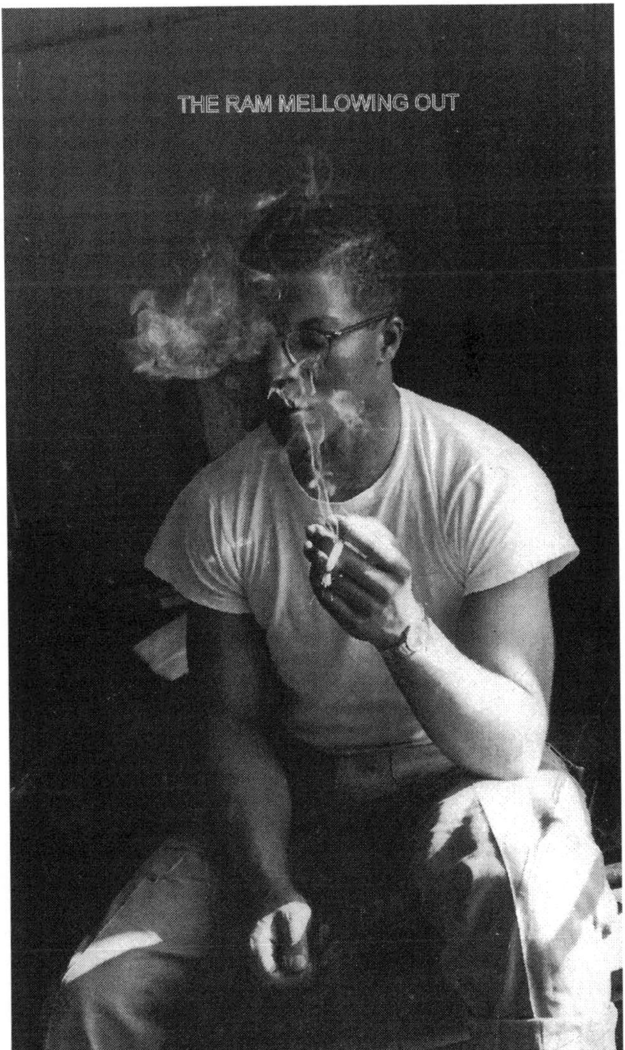
THE RAM MELLOWING OUT

17

Blood on the Risers

The NATO exercises lasted for two weeks with the 517th in the field. The combat units were still in the field when we returned to our base. Thank God, there weren't any more deaths or accidents. I remembered what LT Glover said in medic school, "More American GI's get injured or killed from accidents and diseases than from enemy fire."

A few weeks later, I received a letter from the Commanding General of Seventh Army confirming that no evidence of racial discrimination had been found during his investigation of the 517th and to contact him personally if there were any repercussions. But, I did notice that the week after LT COL Grumble ended is investigation, Vaugns, "The Ram", was promoted to Specialist 4th Class. LT Biggs called me into his office and asked me if I wanted a transfer out of the 517th to a new unit. I said no, I had less than six months left on my enlistment. The truth was I felt safer here, because I knew the people and this Kaserne like the back of my hand. I still had a few fellow GIs who were still watching my back and Swilley was now one of them. I apologized to Swilley for using him to get some attention to myself.

"Milkman, I am accustomed to being used by you, even after saving your ass on several occasions, so what else is new. You are the most ungrateful SOB on the face of this planet. But, you should come clean with me concerning the deep shit you are in."

"I would love to, but that would draw you into something that I really don't understand myself. The knowledge could cost you your life; like it cost many others their lives-don't laugh, Swilley."

My rifle and pistol team was doing very well. We beat all of the non-combat units in Seventh Army. Now it was time to take on all comers in Seventh Army including the Special Forces and Airborne units.

Major McComb informed me that Colonel Philbury, commander of the 62nd Medical Group, was rotating back to the States. He was turning over his command to LT COL Stern. They were planning a "Passing of The Colors" ceremony and parade of the entire 62nd medical group in two weeks. He wanted me to train and head the new color guard. He told me to spare no expense, because he wanted the sharpest color guard in 7th Army.

I went to see CPL Perez who was the captain of the color guard of the 8th Airborne Division. He gave me pointers concerning the ceremony and loaned me all of his unit's parade accessories, chromed helmets, white Croix-de-Guerres, white pistol belts, white gloves, white M14 rifle shoulder straps and white bayonet sheaths. The only thing we had to purchase were the white shoe laces for our boots. I personally cobra stitched each color bearers' boots after CPL Perez showed me how. The entire 62nd Medical Group was on the $8^{th's}$ parade grounds; over 1500 men strong for the parade. Swilley and I protected the colors and we put on a show. Major McComb personally thanked us for our excellent performance.

Things were getting very ugly back in the World (States). Malcolm X had formed his own organization,

The Organization for Afro American Unity. Cassius Clay, now known as Muhammad Ali, defeated Sonny Liston for the heavy weight championship of the world. Also, he announced that he was a member of the Nation of Islam and a friend of Malcolm X. Malcolm X had grown mistrustful of almost everyone except his biographer Alex Haley and his wife Betty. The cat was out of the bag. Black America was taking its fight for justice to the streets peacefully or violently; and as Malcolm X said, "By any means necessary." He could do little to stop or control it.

The bodies of three murdered Civil Rights Workers were found on a farm near Philadelphia, Mississippi. They were James Chaney, Andy Goodman, and Mickey Schwerner. Eighteen whites, including several police officers, were charged with federal conspiracy to deprive the victims of their civil rights. Federal charges were filed, because no local white jury would convict them of murder. Turmoil was breaking out all over America and major cities were in flames. The turmoil in America was developing into the most tumultuous domestic events since the Civil War. In July and August, there were race riots in New York City, Rochester, Jersey City, Paterson, Elizabeth, Chicago, and Philadelphia. Events back home were starting to overwhelm the Soul Brothers and me in the 517th. Swilley suggested that we all take some leave time, because we were starting to look at him with suspicion.

I had about a month of accumulated leave time left. One of the sergeants rotating back to the States was selling his 1957 Black Ford Fairlane. He was asking six hundred dollars. We talked him down to five hundred and raised the money by coming up with one hundred a piece. We christened it, "The Black Hornet", by pissing on the tires like our dogs did back home in the real world. This car would allow us to get as far away from the Bad Kreuznach as possible, and that's what we needed. The car had a V8 engine and after Nasty Jack worked on it; it ran its behind off. We all jumped into the Black Hornet, and headed North on the Auto-Bahn. We were low-level flying, sometimes hitting speeds over 100 miles per hour or more. We were not breaking any laws, because the German Autobahn doesn't have any speed limits. We really thought we were moving until a Porsche zoomed pass us like we were standing still.

We were headed straight for Copenhagen. The women in Denmark treated us even better than the Spiderman said. After two weeks there, we had to drag Sweet Willie back to Germany kicking and screaming after a six-foot tall, blonde haired, blue eyed Danish princess pussy whipped him into almost marrying her. We made our way back from Denmark one-day early. We all had smiles on our faces that a funeral director couldn't remove.

As we parked the Black Hornet, LT Biggs called me into his office and said PVT Jones plea-bargained for six months in Mannheim Prison for striking him. "I'm ordering you to drive him to the Army prison in Mannheim, Germany under arm guard."

I asked, "Why me?"

"You are the best pistol shot in this company. You will be returning to duty by bed check tonight. Pick another member of your pistol team to be the driver. PFC Garcia will issue you weapons before breakfast chow. Jones is a flight risk and I don't want him on this Kaserne one minute longer than it is absolutely necessary. I want him out of my company's area before roll call tomorrow morning and I want a receipt for him from Mannheim Prison; do you understand me PFC Roy."

"Yes, Sir."

This was the same shit that Lonzo had experienced during the Korean War. I couldn't believe it. It was a different time, a different place and different circumstances, but the same shit. If I had that "Third Luger", I would have shot his ass. The next morning, Swilley and I picked up our 45 pistols and two clips of ammo each from the Armor. Swilley volunteered to be the driver for Batman and me in one of the company's M151 deathtrap jeeps.

I asked Batman if I was going to have any trouble out of him. If so, I was going to handcuff him. He said no, but he wanted his partner Robin to ride to Mannheim Prison with him; to see him off. I said OK, if I don't have to place you in handcuffs.

The drive down was going well. We were about 15 minutes out of Mannheim, Germany. Then we passed an US Army Mobile Atomic Cannon that pulled off the road. It was having mechanical problems. We pulled off the road and asked the cannon's crew if they needed any help. They said no, that help was on the way. Man that was the biggest piece of equipment that I have ever seen move.

Suddenly Batman pulled my 45 out of my holster.

"You lying ass dog, you have no honor at all," I said.

Swilley pulled out his 45 and said, "I don't know what your plans are Batman and I don't want to know them either, but we are going to get a receipt for your ass, dead or alive from Mannheim Prison."

"You talk a good game Swilley, but the word on you is, you are a closet conscientious objector and you wouldn't kill a fly."

Swilley couldn't pull the trigger and the Batman saw it in his eyes. Robin was begging Batman not to do it. "The most you have to do is three of six months for punching out that faggot officer, Batman."

"I am tired of prison, Robin," he said.

Robin begged him again, not to do it.

The GIs operating the Atomic Cannon were going nuts. They didn't have any small arms at hand.

"Batman, put the damn gun down now," I said.

"Milkman, you think I won't shoot your Pretty Nigger ass? Yea, that is what you think. I see it in your eyes; you think I won't shoot you."

I could see the tension in his trigger finger increasing. I calmly said to him again, "Batman, put down the gun."

He pulled the trigger and the gun went click. I reached in my pocket, pulled out seven bullets and threw them at him. As he reached down to pick them up, I tackled him. Swilley and I applied the handcuffs with help of the Atomic Cannon's Crew. We completed our run to Mannheim Prison and received a receipt for him. I didn't say anything to Swilley coming back; I could see he had serious issues to deal with personally. I had serious issues to deal with also, how to stay alive long enough to take responsibility for my ugly secrets.

As for Batman, he felt he was the best soldier in our company. Batman and I developed a rivalry from the first day I arrived in Germany. He accused me of bringing him bad luck the day I arrived on base. That was the day he lost the Supernumerary to CPL Perez of the 8th Airborne Division. He wanted to bet me in every competition we undertook. The outcome, most of the time, was me taking his money. It made no difference whether we were in the company's pool room shooting nine ball, or in the gym playing one-on-one. I got over wanting to compete against him. But, if I didn't, he would call me all kinds of things, like a faggot or a pussy; so I just beat the shit out of him. Beating him all the time just made his conduct worse and the drugs he and Robin were consuming weren't helping the situation either. He was a good soldier when he wanted to be. And, when he competed for Supernumerary on guard mount, he was like a knight in green armor with Robin as his second. Batman could command money pots up to five hundred dollars for his guard mounts. GIs would travel miles from other Kasernes and barracks to complete against him.

One of the NCOs said, "If I could get hold of a backhoe, I would become rich from the drugs and money that Batman buried in the ball field across from the barracks."

It was also rumored that Batman's brother, Jumping Jack Daniels, was a major drug pusher in Europe. No one could figure out how he owned so many fast sports cars on a sergeant's salary. He had a 1965 Cobra 427SC, the exact copy of the one that beat Ferrari, "The Italian stallion," at La-Mans, France earlier in the year. There were all kinds of rumors flying around about him. One rumor was; he was the chief pusher for the CIA and he was Mr. Untouchable here in Europe. Another rumor was; Jumping Jack Daniels' connections kept his Baby Brother from doing any serious time in the Army's prison in Mannheim, Germany.

I didn't spend a lot of time on rumors. My motto was, "Seeing is believing." If I didn't see it, I didn't believe it. But, after what I had gone through in this man's Army, it wouldn't take much for me to believe just about anything. A week later, Jumping Jack Daniels drove his Cobra SC GT into the Kaserne with his fine Dutch girlfriend sitting in the front seat. He said she was from Amsterdam, Holland. Amsterdam was the European drug capital. He handed me two little packages, one was weed and the other was a match box containing cubes of sugar with little red dots on them. I didn't ask any questions, because this was his way of thanking me for not killing his crazy-ass brother on the way to Mannheim Prison. I had given up weed long ago, because I was allergic to it and it was the gateway drug that my friend Teddy used as his excuse to move up to heroin. I refused to try anything else. I hid the packages under the tents in my truck; why I didn't throw them away, I didn't know.

I didn't see Jumping Jack Daniels again until we covered his next pay jump. Both of us were unconscious as they med-evaced us to Frankfurt General Hospital for emergency care. I only stayed in the hospital for three days. After I recuperated and returned to the 517th, LT Biggs sent me back to Frankfurt General; TDY. I didn't want to go at this time, because my pistol team was competing against the best in 7th Army. Lieutenant Biggs was getting reports that our company's pistol team was very good, so he ordered me to go TDY to get rid of me. I asked to be assigned to the orthopedic ward where JJ was recuperating. He was a pitiful site as I walked in on him in the Orthopedic Ward. He was in full body traction; iron weights were hanging from everywhere.

"How are you, JJ?"

"How in the hell do you think I am, Milkman. The doc said that I will never get full use from my hand again. That redneck SOB, you wait until I get a hold of his ass."

"What happen on the jump, Man?"

"I am sorry Milkman, thank you. My jump buddies told me what you did to save me, man. My head is just a little screwed up now. They keep me drugged up for the pain. I knew that Barry Jobs, that redneck asshole, was going to give me trouble on the jump. So I ordered him to the back of the jump line. We were jumping a NATO, West German C-130 with an all-German crew on board. It was supposed to be a simple monthly pay jump from a NATO plane. They opened the side door of the plane and I looked out to see if I could spot the Kuhberg Hill drop zone coming up. I had made eight Kuhberg Hill jumps before this one. The yellow ready light came on and I ordered my platoon to get ready.

When the green light came on, I hollered "Go." Everyone was exiting the door smartly. Everyone in the platoon had exited the plane except Barry and me. When he got to the door, he stopped, turned and smiled at me. I smelled liquor on his breath. I ordered him to exit the plane. He turned around in the door and started to make false jumps movements with his ass and giving me a hard time. Then it hit me like a brick. This asshole was deliberately delaying my jump so I would miss the drop zone and land in the trees.

I said "You drunken redneck" and I shoved him out the door. He grabbed me as he exited the plane and he pulled me out with him. I was so upset with him that I hadn't checked my static line. His chute opened without a problem. But, my static line was wrapped around my arm and it could not release my chute. There I was dangling on the outside of a C130, 1200 hundred feet in the air and going three hundred miles per hour. The plane's propeller wash was banging my head against the side of the fuselage like a dog's tail wagging against a car door.

"I was losing consciousness. I had to do something quick. I was hollering as loud as I could, but the German pilots had closed their cockpit door. They said the co-pilot opened the cockpit door to see if anyone was still in the plane and closed it when he didn't see anyone. They pressed the side door close button from the cockpit and the side door started to close. I felt the plane starting to bank to the left. I knew I wasn't going to make it if I didn't do something drastic.

"I had no choice; the plane's side door closed. I had no way to get back into that plane. I pulled my bayonet from my shoulder scabbard and started to hack at my tangled static line. As I cut the line, I was also cutting my wrist as well. I whacked and hacked and the blood was flying from my wrist into my face. The prop blast was causing my spilling blood to blind me. I couldn't see what I was doing. I felt I was committing suicide in order to save myself."

"I know, JJ, the blue sky turned into a red rain from hell that day."

"Finally, I hacked through the tangled static line. I don't know how, but I managed to release my reserve cute."

"I don't know how you did it either, man, but you did. There was blood all over your risers."

"Milkman, why didn't the copilot walk to the back of the plane and check?"

"I don't know. We were on the ground covering the jump and watching every bit of it; like it was a horror movie. We were trying to radio the plane to tell them what was going on. But, the radio frequencies used by the German plane were not on our radio set. We had to radio 8th Airborne Headquarters for them to radio German Air Force Headquarters in Heidelberg; asking them to radio their plane."

"I wish the co-pilot had looked harder."

"He said he opened the cockpit door and looked down the plane, saw no one, and heard no one. Then he pressed the side-door close button and told the pilot to start the turn. By the time we radioed the pilot, you had cut yourself loose a half mile passed the drop zone. I saw your chute go into the trees. I jumped into my deuce-and-a-half and followed your red rain trail of blood through the woods until I spotted your chute in a tree."

I paused, vividly remembering the scene.

"I had no way of getting you down," I went on. "I tied the truck's wench cable around the tree and tried to pull it down, but the cable snapped and it crashed back through my windshield. So, I put the truck into four-wheel drive low-range and started to push the SOB over. It leaned enough for me to grab you and cut you out of your chute.

You were a Black man who had turned white. Your pulse rate was almost gone. You had lost a lot of blood and if I waited for help to arrive with the blood, you wouldn't have made it. I looked down at your blood type on your dog tags and it wasn't the same as mine. So, I cut the palm of my hand, then placed some of your blood with it and mixed the two together with my finger. They coagulated in my hand and that told me that the two blood types were compatible. I tied your belt as a tourniquet around your arm and then my belt around my arm. With two needles and a rubber pipette tube, I transfused blood from myself to you directly. I kept pumping until I blacked out."

"Milkman, thank you, I broke my hip, five ribs, two legs and one arm. The doctors said they didn't know why I was still alive. I lost two thirds of my blood from my body. I cut all the tendons in my right wrist. I lost all ability to close my right hand and I will walk with a limp for the rest of my life, if at all."

It was difficult watching Jumping Jack Daniels eat. He took his left hand and closed his right hand's fingers around his fork in order to eat. All while hanging suspended above the bed in a full body cast with his arms and legs in traction. I did the best I could to nurse him back to health. The Sister Head Nurse on the ward, Captain Agnes Carter, took a special personal interest in JJ's recovery; if you know what I mean. He needed a lot of daily physical therapy and she made sure he got it. God Bless him, like the paratrooper's song, there was blood on his raisers as was well as his Soul.

I started to see a lot of Bridgett while I was TDY in Frankfurt. She glowed each time we made love. She seemed more relaxed now. We hung out in Jazz Clubs instead of the Three Pigs. They were more intimate and she was really getting into the music. The Spiderman called her from time to time. She told him that we were running into one another every now and then. I don't think he "put two and two together." She never met him at The Three Pigs again. She always made an excuse not to. I knew he liked her, but Spiderman liked all fine women. He had three and they all were just trophies to him.

My three mouths TDY at the Frankfurt General Hospital came to an end quickly. Jumping Jack Daniels was out of his body cast and he was up and walking with a cane. His brother, Batman, was still in Mannheim Army Prison and I missed all of the Misfits of the 517th. The 517th sent a truck to pick me up. I rode in the back of the truck, all by myself, all the way. I did so, because I was thinking about the mess that I was still in and how I was going to get out of it without splattering my blood on the risers.

***

Cool Soul Brothers

Infantry personnel of the 101st Airborne Division preparing to fire a Davy Crockett during a training exercise at Fort Campbell, Kentucky, May 14, 1962

Soldiers conducting tests of the Davy Crockett at the Aberdeen Proving Ground, Maryland, December 16, 1959

PICTURE COURTESY OF THE BROOKINGS INSTITUTE

ARMORER AT WORK

ON HIS WAY TO JAIL

18

Cries of A Wounded Soul

When I arrived, I was very happy to see the guys again. The first thing many of them asked me, even before I climbed down off the truck, "Please loan me ten dollars for twenty."

My biggest surprise was that our pistol team took third place in the 7th Army shoot out without me. I was so proud of my guys. It wasn't important who beat us; it was more important who we beat. The 3rd Armored Division took first place, 7th Army Headquarters took second place and the 517th Medical Clearing Co. took third. Swilley, who led the 517th's team, beat the 8th Airborne Division, a Special Forces Unit and the CID; which included members of the B-team. The B-team didn't like getting beat by Swilley and our lowly medical company pistol team.

I was extremely proud of Swilley. This was the first time he had led, competed and succeeded on his own. He was still studying for his West Point entrance exam when I arrived back at the Kaserne. He said going to West Point was what he really wanted to do. As soon as we were alone, I talked to him. I asked him, what was he going to do about his ugly secrets? I didn't think Swilley was going to make it at West Point without dealing with them. He had the courage, the motivation and the intellect to succeed as an officer. But, could Swilley actually take a life? That was the issue.

"Swilley, you are one of the most courageous guys I know. I would not be standing here if it were not for you. On more than one occasion, you saved my life by risking yours without thinking once about it. But, there may come a time when you will have to take an individual's life. Will you be able to do it?"

He didn't immediately answer me so I went on. "It's not a matter of courage; it's a matter of conscience. You can't hide from the question. We have been trained to save lives with one hand and take lives with the other."

"You are right," he said. "I must deal with that now. But, I don't know the answers, Milkman. About the only thing Martin Luther King and I agree on is non-violence."

He continued how his father forced him to go deer hunting as a young man.

"Sometimes we would track a deer for three days. Then BAM! He forced me to kill it. Sometimes I would miss deliberately. But, if I missed, he would simply make me track that same dear until I killed it. Then we would drag the deer out of the woods bleeding and then hang it up by its hind legs. Then I had to slit its throat, so all of its blood would drain from its body, skin it, butcher it, and cook some of the meat for my brother, sister and I to eat for dinner."

He looked a bit sick just remembering it.

"He made us all eat it, Milkman, which was about as close as you can come to cannibalism. My father said the motto of a sniper is one shot one kill. Sometimes, I would place one round in my rifle and point it at him out of my bedroom window as he went to work in the morning. But, I couldn't pull the trigger."

"Fortunately Swilley, I had parents who were very happy that I made it through high school without going to jail or being strung out on drugs. Who in the hell are you man. Do you know what I am saying to you? Whose shoes are you wearing man? You have many questions to ask yourself and the answers you get can't be influenced by your parents or blamed on them either. You need to take a week off, go into hiding by yourself and deal with those issues, like we did."

Swilley agreed and said he was going to take a week's leave and he wouldn't tell anybody where he was going or why. Four days later, I ran into him at the Haufbrau Haus in down town Bad-K; half drunk. He was sitting in the kitchen with Stella who was trying to sober him up. Stella was the bar owner's very attractive daughter, her father was a Black GI who was killed in a rollover of a M151 jeep. Her mother used his insurance money to purchase the Haufbrau Haus. She didn't allow Stella to work out front in the bar or date GIs. Any soldier caught trying to talk to her usually was thrown out of the bar.

The Soul Brothers pulled him out of the kitchen, on too the dance floor and taught Swilley the latest dance craze. He was "Doing the Dog" and they gave Swilley his first nickname in the Army, "Top Dog." They made him "Do the Dog" with all the frauleins in the bar. I left Swilley and Nasty Jack in the Haufbrau Haus dancing. I went to meet Bridgett at the Bad-K train station. She was coming in from Frankfurt. She said she had some serious issues to talk about, and she didn't want to discuss them on the phone.

Nasty Jack and "Top Dog" Swilley left the bar soon after I did to return to the hospital Kaserne together. As soon as they exited the Haufbrau Haus, they were jumped and severely beaten by Frost, Unicorn and the others from the B-team. They stepped on their hands which prevented them from holding pistols and told them that I was the reason they were beating them. Both of them were half drunk and couldn't defend themselves. The only help they got was from Stella and her mother. They made so much noise that the B-team stopped beating them. Swilley suffered a broken hand and Nasty lost a tooth and suffered a fractured jaw.

The German police refused to help them after they found out they were from the hospital. Stella walked Swilley and Nasty back to the Hospital Kaserne. She propped both of them up all the way. They were a bloody mess when they were admitted to the hospital. Nasty Jack said Swilley refused to fight back again. Yet, he also refused to run. He just stood there and let the B-team beat the devil out of him. Normally Jack would have carried his razor, but he was naked that evening.

On the way to the train station I ran into Claus, a "Shwartza Kin" (a Black German child), hanging out in my favorite short-cut alley. His father was also a Black GI who had rotated back to the states leaving him and his mother to fend for themselves.

"Hi, Claus, I haven't seen you in a while."

Claus spoke perfect English, but he answered me in German.

"Haben sie eine Pfennig, bitte, Do you have a penny for me please?"

"Was, what?"

I couldn't believe what I was hearing. It had to be a mistake. After asking me for a penny again, he handed me a folded piece of the paper. I opened it and it was a page full of sequenced numbers. I immediately recognized three of the numbers being my birth date. I could not believe it was a coded message from the Wolfman. As I looked up to ask the young Claus were did he get this note from, he was gone. I double-timed back to the Kaserne and pulled out my San Antonio telephone book, forgetting completely about Bridgett at the train station.

No one was in the room, but me. It was a simple code to understand. First, you found the number indicating the phone book's page, then the number indicating the line and then the number indicating the word on the line. My birth date, March 26, determined the location of the number sequence to use. For Example, March is the third month. So, I would use the third row of numbers and so forth. No one could ever break the code without knowing the right number sequence to use and the right telephone book as the code breaker. After putting the words together, I read the message. I could not believe it was truly a message from the Wolfman, it said.

"You can't keep a good Jew down. I know you won't believe this message, but you need to contact Bridgett's father at the American consulate in Paris as soon as possible. He asked Bridgett to invite you to come and visit him in Paris, but you wouldn't go. He knows you are dating his daughter, but he won't kill your Black ass. He has some very important information for you concerning someone you know very well. Don't inform Bridgett about this message. She doesn't know what her father truly does in Paris. Also, After Paris, I want you to come to Berlin to meet me. I am well; do not worry about me, the Wolfman."

I was very late meeting, a very upset, Bridgett at the train station. I apologized and she finally said, "I received a letter from my father telling me to bring you home to Paris for a visit. It was a strange note. He just about demanded that I bring you immediately. I haven't seen my father in two months and he wants us to travel to Paris immediately together. I am concerned about him."

I got a three-day pass from the Mad Doctor and we immediately left for Paris. The B-team was following my every move now and was difficult to lose. But, I left the Kaserne through a hole in the back fence.

We arrived in Paris in the late afternoon. We were scheduled to meet her father that evening about 9 p.m. We were early and took a cab for some sightseeing before dinner. We traveled down the Champs-Elysees pass the Arc de Triomple-du carrousel. Bridgett knew Napoleon was one of my favorite generals. The Arc de Triomple was built by Napoleon to celebrate his victories and the Grand Army that won them. Napoleon actually built two monuments; the other was the Arc de Triomple-at Etoile; all around 1808. He followed the model of the Arc of Constantine in Rome. In 52 BC, the Romans began the first permanent settlement in Paris on the left bank, Sainte Genevieve Hill and Ile de la Cite, island in the middle of the Seine River. The town was named Lutetia. By 400 AD, it was largely abandoned. Paris passed hands several times under various kings and suffered greatly in 1832 and 1849 from cholera epidemics. In 1832, 20,000 people died from the decease. Today Paris is the cultural capital of Europe, if not the world. The Invalides Museum is the burial place of many great French soldiers including Napoleon. If we had the time, I wanted to pay him a visit.

Paris is beautiful in the winter with a light coating of snow covering the ancient streets and buildings. The Seine River has a pleasant stench engulfing the tourist boats as they travel beneath the Eiffel Tower. The French have a special place in my heart. They have always treated Black Americans with respect and dignity.

Finally, the cab drove us to her father's home. As we approached his house, we saw flashing lights and French policemen all over the place. She opened the cab's door before he stopped and ran into the house. The police were removing her father's body from the rear courtyard. The police said he committed suicide by jumping out of the third floor window. She broke down and cried. Even though her father was always on the move and she didn't see much of him, she loved him dearly.

Then her aunt and uncle walked into the house. She stood straight up with tears in her eyes and told him to leave her house, now. She was inconsolable. This was the uncle that molested her as a child. Before he reached the front door, I stopped him and asked, what happened here. He said, he didn't know, but he thought there was more to his brother–in-law's job at the American Embassy than what he said. This was not the time for me extract revenge on Bridgett's behalf.

After she calmed down, I said to Bridgett, let's go to the American Embassy and check it out. We hopped into a cab and got out one block from the embassy's entrance. We stood in a cold doorway across the street for two hours watching the goings on as I tried to console her. My worst fears were confirmed. Unicorn and Frost along with other members of the B-team exited the US Embassy.

I started to rock back and forth and shaking my head, "No."

She asked, "What is wrong?"

I knew at that instant, that she was in serious danger and that her father definitely was more than a support attaché at the American Embassy. I told her, I was having a bad day with all the goings-on. We went back to her father's apartment and I started to look around. I went into his bedroom where I spotted a cup of tea he was drinking before died. There was a small box of sugar cubes next to the teacup. The box was new and it looked familiar, I opened the box and there were three sugar cubes missing from it. I picked up one of the sugar cubes and looked at its bottom. All the sugar cubes had little red dots on them. They were exactly like the ones that Jumping Jack Daniels gave me. Someone slipped her father a box of LSD laced sugar cubes and he didn't know that he was taking three doses of it. It caused him to freak-out and jump out of the third floor window. I put the sugar box in my pocket, because I didn't really know what was going on yet. It was like I picked up Lonzo's "Third Luger" and wrapped it in toilet paper. I stayed with her the entire weekend in Paris. I knew very little about LSD, other than a professor named Timothy Leary at UCLA started a cult based on the use of the drug. But, a common practice was the user required an anchor person to be with them when he took the drug. It was said, the drug caused you to see and do crazy things, like try to fly.

We drove back to Bad-K, Germany in her father's convertible VW bug. We were upset and frustrated. I was fed up; it was time for me to start to take responsibility for my ugly secrets now. The first thing I did was to have Bridget drive me to Mainz, Germany to see Jumping Jack Daniels. He had been released from the hospital. Mainz was his home base, just up the road from Bad-K.

I entered his barracks alone, there was an armed guard sitting in front of his room.

"What's going on?"

"Who do you wish to see?"

"Sergeant Jones."

The guard opened his door and I walked into his room. He was sitting on his bed. I looked at his sleeves. His sergeant stripes were gone. He looked up at me, smiled and said.

"What's happening, Milkman, you came to see me off."

"Off to where."

"Back to the World Man."

"No, I need a big favor."

"I am not in a position to grant many favors now, Milkman."

"Why not?"

"When I got well enough to return to my unit, the first chance I got, I placed my entrenching tool in my right hand and used my left hand to close it. I sat on my bunk for two hours with that entrenching tool in my hand, counting the number of times I whacked at it trying to cut my static line lose. I came up with seventeen times. It was 0200 hours when I went into that SOB's barracks. That was the number of times I tried to hit that SOB with that entrenching tool."

"Did you kill him?"

"No, but I beat the hell out of that redneck. The other GIs pulled me off him at twelve licks. He is in a coma at Frankfurt General now. He is on same ward that I spent three months on. They don't want me on the same continent with that nut, because I will send his drunken ass to hell; if I get a second chance."

I pulled the Sugar Box out of my pocket and showed JJ the sugar cubes.

"Where did you get these?"

"Are they yours?"

"Don't say anymore, Milkman, there are too many ears here. My jig is up in Europe. I want to cash in my chips and head back to the world." He pulled me close to him and said, "I sold those cubes to a CID brother by the name of Unicorn last week."

"My Lady's father jumped out of his window after taking them. I believe they used them to kill her father."

"I doubt that, because I deliberately cut the dosage on those cubes to prevent the white boys from killing themselves with it. Dead customers do not return to buy again. I think they pushed him out of the window. When the autopsy is completed they will find LSD in his body and they will say drugs caused him to commit suicide."

"I think they are planning to kill someone else that is very important to me."

"Who?"

"I don't know."

"What do you need?"

"I need a reliable contact in France, because I have a suspicious feeling that an attempt on the person's life is going to take place in Europe, probably in France, and very soon."

"I feel it too, Milkman, France."

He wrote down a name on a piece of paper with a French telephone number on it. "When you call, tell him that Jumping Jack Daniels sent you. If he can't help you, he will find someone who can."

"Is he with French intelligence?"

He smiled and said, "Better than that, Milkman, he is French intelligence."

When I arrived back at Bad K, the Misfits were very upset with me, because I wouldn't discuss any of my activities with them. They said Nasty and Swilley had been attacked and beaten, because of me and my secret dealings with the B-team. I said that I couldn't discuss it with them.

I asked them, "What do want to do about the beatings." They didn't know what should be done. After Top Dog was released from the hospital, he was restricted to base until further notice. Stella came to visit him almost every day. LT Biggs was very upset with Swilley, because Swilley had totally ignored his wishes concerning me. He told Swilley he wasn't going to make it to West Point if he continued associating with me.

Swilley couldn't go anywhere so he replaced everyone on the 517$^{th's}$ guard duty roster and won Supernumerary two outings in a row. We were all hanging out in the EM Club partying with Top Dog on his birthday. He was throwing them down with the best of us. Stella was dancing with him "Doing the Dog." Then the EM Club's door opened and in walked an elderly couple. Swilley froze, I thought he'd seen a ghost, but there was a facial similarity between him and the elderly couple.

Oh shit, it was Swilley's mother and father.

They walked over to our table and his father gave everyone a very stern look. Swilley introduced his parents to us and then Stella as his "Fiancé." She blushed, my eyes got big and I wondered how I had missed that one. His father almost fainted. His mother extended her hand and said. "I am pleased to meet you, Stella."

I was in total shock. I looked at Stella and she couldn't stop laughing. His father asked him to step into the next room so they could have a private conversation. From the looks of it, it wasn't very pleasant. The lieutenant had written and told Swilley's father that his son had asked the Army for permission to marry his girlfriend after he graduated West Point. His parents were so upset that they flew to Europe to talk to their son in person.

His father tried to dress him down, but he wouldn't have any of it. Then Swilley said something to his father that shut-up his mouth quickly. His father ran back to the table, grabbed his wife, and left the EM Club.

Swilley sensed that I wanted to ask him the home-run question and said, "Yes, Milkman, I have my ugly secrets also, but unlike you, I am going to share mine with you. I told my Father that I knew about my half-Black younger brother who was conceived out of wedlock. My father had a second life going, with a Black woman in Tennessee; for a long time. My "Soul Brother" is two years younger than I am. I wrote him and he sent me a picture."

He then handed me the picture of his half-Black Brother.

"I suggested to father that if he wanted to pursue any issues with me concerning my half-Black fiancé, then we should bring mama in to help us to discuss them, all of them. Stella and I have been seeing one another secretly for weeks now."

I contacted Bridgett and told her to call the telephone number concerning her father's death. I reminded her whose name to mention. She made the called the same day and said the number was in Marseille, on France's southern coast. The person she talked too wouldn't give his name. After mentioning Jumping Jack Daniel's name and telling him who her father was, he said someone would get back to her in two days. She received a call a day later saying that we should be in the Bad Kreuznach tourist hotel lobby, the one that Hitler slept in, next Thursday night at 7pm.

We arrived on time and sat in the lobby. The concierge approached us asking our names and told us to go to room 376. We rode up on the elevator and knocked on the room's door. Two Frenchmen opened the door, invited us in and searched us for weapons as we entered the room. Then we were asked to take a seat at the window overlooking the river. We were asked not to turn around when we were being spoken too. Then a person walked in to the room from our rear. Without any greeting and without asking us any questions, he began to speak in English with a French accent.

"Madam, your father served America and France well. I am sorry for your lost. Mr. Roy, Black Americans fought in two wars on French soil and their sacrifices are buried in our cemeteries, all over France. Black American regiments served longer, in France, during WWI than any other American units. While serving in France, the 369th Harlem Hell Fighters never gave an inch of ground in battle. A grateful French Nation gave them their proper recognition by awarding them France's highest honors. France's respect for the courage of Black soldiers goes back for hundreds of years. Napoleon had many respected Black generals and soldiers; his most prized regiment was his Grand Africans. Now, America wants to use French soil to kill a courageous Black American hero who simply wants to free his people. Mr. Roy, I will assure you that this act will not happen on French soil and especially not by the same killers of your beloved president. Be at the Paris, France airport on February 9, 1965."

The room went silent and when we turned around no one was in the room. My worst fears had been confirmed, but there were still some serious unanswered questions. On February 9, 1965, El Hajj Malik El Shabazz, a.k.a. Malcolm X, flew into Paris, but was told by the French government that he was an undesirable and they denied him entry. He would not be allowed off the plane for his speaking engagement there. He was confused, because he had been allowed to speak in France; just a year earlier. We left Paris on the 10th thinking we had foiled the attempt on his life.

On February, 13th Malcolm X flies back to the United States from England and his home is fire bombed at 3:00 am.

On February, 14th He flies to Mississippi to speak to the Mississippi Freedom Democratic Party.

On February, 19th while there he speaks directly to Mrs. Martin Luther King.

On February 20th, Malcolm X takes his Wife, Sister Betty Shabazz, to visit a possible new home, in a Jewish neighborhood, on Long Island then drives himself, alone, to the New York Hilton and checks in without telling anyone. At 8:00 P.M., someone calls him and says "Wake up Brother."

On February 21st, alleged "Black Muslims" shoot and kill Malcolm X in the Audubon Ballroom of uptown Manhattan. Malcolm X said several times to Alex Haley, his biographer, and others that he suspected forces were at work to kill him that were far stronger and had further reach around the globe than the National of Islam. The President and now Malcolm X were Americans I respected and adored. I would have substituted my life for theirs. Now, I questioned what took me so long to stand up for theses Americans and their American values.

Twelve days later, Mark Coben, reporter from the Stars and Stripes newspaper visited the Medical Kaserne, allegedly covering a news story concerning another GI who was killed in a M151 jeep accident. He tried to interview me by stating that a lot of activity was taking place in downtown Bad-K with respect to feuds between medics and paratroopers. He asked me if I knew anything about it.

I said, "No."

"Your name keeps coming up. You are from New York City right?"

"Yes."

"Then you know about Malcolm X."

"Know what about Malcolm X?"

"He was killed in the Audubon Ballroom yesterday."

I froze. LT Biggs walked pass me with a smirk on his face. I could feel him gloating inside. I wanted to beat the devil out of him. He said nothing to both of us. He was very familiar with Mark from the Stars and Stripes. He gave many slanted first handed reports of what went down in his company, all glorifying him. I sat down on the curb and held my head between my legs.

The Mark asked, "Did you know him."

"Yes. He always encouraged me to grow into an intelligent self-thinking human being, to stand up for what I believed in; no matter what anyone said or thought about it. I tried, but I couldn't keep up with his spiritual growth. He didn't want me to join the Army, because America abused its Black soldiers and it was time for us to stand up and fight at home for our freedom, not here were I am now."

I looked at the Mark as he started to write what I was saying down on his pad. Then abruptly I stopped talking. He begged me to continue. I said, I had to get ready for an inspection tomorrow, so I couldn't speak to him anymore. I walked inside the barracks and I set down on my bunk. I didn't say anything to anybody for two days. I didn't say anything to Swilley when he walked into our room stating that he heard the bad news. I reported to sick call with a stomach virus. I didn't want to be in Europe any longer, because I should have been home doing something positive to help EL Hajj Malik El Shabazz accomplish the real work for Black America. The loss I felt was of missed opportunity. I missed witnessing Mother Nature helping a caterpillar morph into an American butterfly. It was, as if I was blinded by my own cries of a wounded soul.

You will have never known that you have walked with greatness, until you are forced to walk alone.

***

NATO 517TH HEAVY LIFT

517TH IN THE FIELD

LOCK AND LOADED

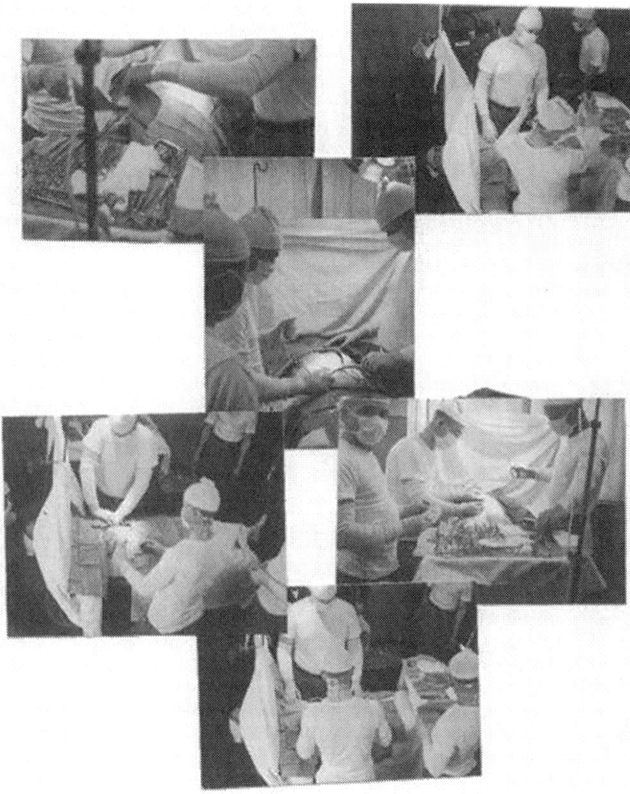

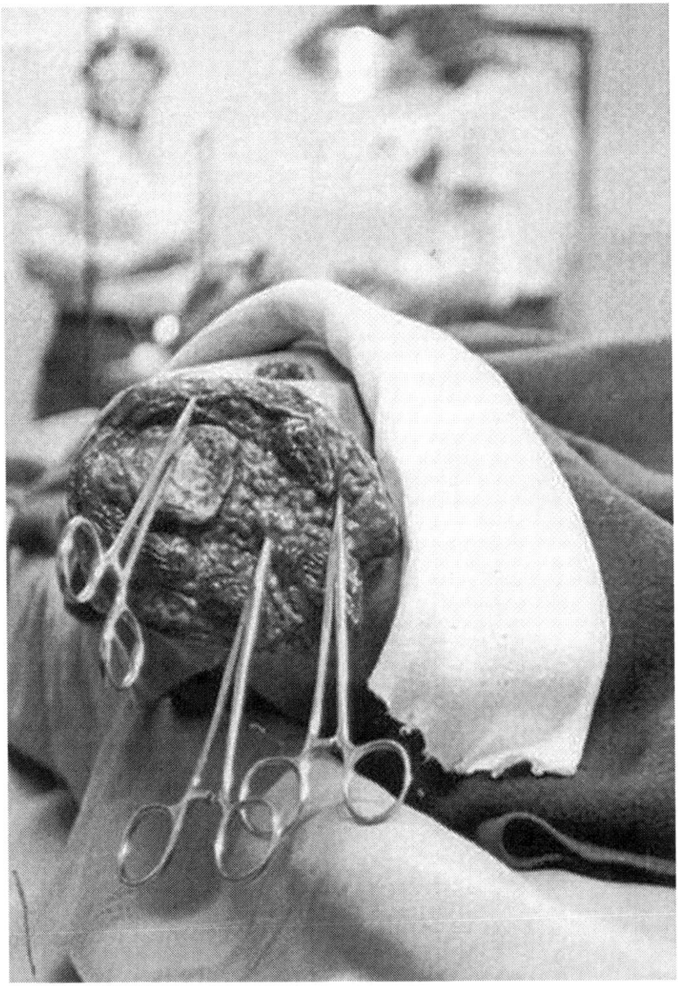

19

The American Praetorian Guard

It took almost a month to get permission to travel to Berlin to meet the Wolfman. But, I had to wait for word from the Wolfman before I left. You traveled by train through the East German Red Zone controlled by the Soviet Union. The ride took most of the day to reach Berlin from Frankfurt.

I wasn't a nice person to be around after Malcolm X's death. I got into arguments with the Misfits, the Spiderman, Swilley and Nasty Jack. They didn't want to be around me much either. Then on my 20th birthday, March 26th 1965, they threw me a surprise stag birthday party at the EM Club; to cheer me up. Swilley dressed up as a stripper and he was funny as a shit. All the guys were dancing with one another, "Doing the Dog," "The Twist," and being rowdy as hell. Then I spotted the cook from the mess hall that pointed me out to DD. He was with another GI and their German girlfriends. I staggered over to their table and asked, in English, one of their girlfriends to dance with me.

She said, "Ja, yes."

The other girl sitting at the table said to her in German, "Tanze nicht mit dem Schwarzen, Don't dance with the Blacks."

I replied to her in German,"Sagen sie ihr, sie soll nicht mit mir tanzen, weil ich ein Schwarzer bin? (Did you tell her not to dance with me, because I am black)" The girl was shocked that I understood and spoke German so well. The two cooks sitting at the table didn't understand a word of what we were saying. The only thing they knew was-it was getting very ugly. One of them started to stand up and challenge me. I slapped him before he could say or do anything to my drunken ass.

The rest of the 517th kept him off me, as Swilley and Nasty bum-rushed my drunken ass out the door and into my barracks. Swilley stood guard at my door all night, because the cooks came over to my barracks calling me out to do battle. The next day, after sleeping it off, I shook my head in discuss, because I knew that was what LT Biggs was waiting for. It was going to cause me my prized stripe that he coveted for long time. I immediately put in for a three day pass to go to Berlin before the cooks and their girlfriends made their official complaint. I went down town looking for the Claus, the Shwartza Kin and he also was looking for me. He gave me a second note from the Wolfman. His instructions said to be in Berlin by next Thursday.

I called Bridgett to let her know that I was ready to go. She was very anxious to find out more about her father's death. "Top Dog" Swilley wanted to go. I told him, once again, that I was bad news for white guys. Everyone I became close too was either missing in action or died mysteriously. I told him I would keep in contact with him by calling the EM Club's public phone in the evenings. I met Bridgett at the Frankfurt bahnhof. She was very tense, almost as tense as the night we first made love. We only carried overnight bags, because we wanted to travel light. Sam's second message said he would meet us at a nightclub that he wouldn't name. He said to take the 10 p.m. trolley that passed in front of the hotel where he told us to stay and the trolley driver would tell us where to get off.

I didn't see any members of the B-team at the train station in Frankfurt. We tried very hard to cover our tracks before getting on the train. As we crossed into East Germany, the countryside appeared very stark. Much of the damage from the allied bombing raids in WWII was still present. It seemed that God didn't want his sun to shine on East Germany. Most of the homes near the train tracks were in disrepair, along with roads and streetlights. The trip was a long one, because the train had to slow down at the crossings, because the crossing gates were not working in many places. Bridgett and I laughed and joked with one another to past the time away. We arrived in Berlin about 1600 hours. We had an uneventful ride through East Germany.

Although it was a dreary evening, there was a lot of activity in the Berlin bahnhof. The hustling baggage handlers were busy assisting people getting off the train. Other people were feverishly getting back on the train for the return trip back to West Germany. Some vendors were selling souvenirs and fruit. As I exited the train, I noticed Frost and Hook from the B-team following us. I was very concerned now, but didn't say anything to Bridgett. I tapped her on the behind to get her moving. We jumped into a taxi and I told the driver to take us to the Berlin Museum; she looked at me strange. I smiled and said I would like to see the bust of Nefertiti, Queen of the Egyptian Pharaoh Akhenaton before I left Germany. When we got out of the taxi, it became apparent to Bridgett that we were being followed.

I said to her, "I want to lose these guys, baby."

As we entered the museum, it was about to close. We took our time looking at the bust and artifacts. I told Bridgett to go to the ladies room to see if they would split up and follow her. They didn't, they both followed me. I told her to leave the museum by herself and take a taxi back to the train station, then get out to see if she was being followed. Then take another taxi to another hotel that was two blocks away from the one we are staying in. Then walk to our hotel; making sure she was not followed. As she left the museum, I watched for a minute to see if the B-team would split up and follow her; they didn't.

Now, how was I going to lose these farts? I noticed a set of stairs that said employees only in German. I made believe I was engrossed in the artwork across from the stairs. As soon as the B-team members turned their heads, I ran down the stairs through the locker room and out the back door, but I noticed that I could be seen from upstairs. So I backed up and hid, yes, you got it, in a garbage dumpster. I put a bag full of garbage on top of me, boy did it smell.

I could hear the B-team running down the stairs looking for me. They ran out the back door; thinking I made my way out. I was lucky there was a third B-team member, Anvil, waiting outside. They began to argue with him that I had gotten pass him. I waited for a half-hour, and then left dressed in someone's maintenance uniform.

I walked most of the way to the hotel and then took a trolley the rest of the way. Bridgett had registered in her mother's maiden name "Martel." When I arrived, she pushed me into the shower, clothes and all, and turned on the water. Then she got into the shower with me-butt naked; taking off my clothes and bathing me. Wow, she made me so hot, but we had to keep our heads straight. I said to her that we would be easy to follow together. We should leave the hotel one at a time to go to the nightclub.

She agreed and I said that I should go first; just in case I was followed. If I was followed I wouldn't go to the club at all. Then she would meet the Wolfman alone.

Dark fell about 1800 hours and I left the hotel about 1900 hours to make sure I had enough time to lose anyone that was following me. It went smoothly and I wasn't followed. I met the streetcar as planned. As soon as I boarded, I almost had a heart attack. The driver was a Soul Brother who spoke perfect German and looked exactly like me, only about twenty years older.

"Wie gaten si, mein freund? How are you my friend?"

"Gut, ich gehe in den zoo, Good, I am going to the zoo.

"So spat. So late."

"Bin eine nachteule, I am a night Owl."

The driver told me to sit in the rear of the trolley, which I did. I could see it was the best place to sit if you didn't want to be seen on the ride. I rode to the end of the line. He told me to stay put, the trolley turned around and started back. About two stops into the ride back, he told me to get off and walk two blocks north to the nightclub.

As soon as a got to the nightclub, I called Bridgett and told her where to come. I told her to take a cab to the train station, get out, walk around the block, wait a few minutes to see if she was followed, and then take a cab to the nightclub. I waited across the street in a dark doorway for her to arrive. About 2030 hours she pulled up in a taxi. I give her Swilley's Quarter Horse whistle and we both entered the nightclub together. The place was jumping with a lively crowd. The band was playing

Junior Walker and the All-stars "I am a road runner baby." We didn't want to be seen, so we stood in the corner with large mugs of beer in our hands covering our faces.

In the opposite corner of the club, I spotted those cold steel gray eyes staring at me. The last time I had seen those eyes was at medic school. I dropped my head in joy that the Wolfman was still alive. I could see a tear in his eye, as he stood motionless. His head nodded towards the side alley exit. A few of the smokers had gone out into the alley to smoke there. He was limping, as I followed him with Bridgett in tow. As I cleared the side door, I immediately give him a big hug. I was so excited that I didn't know where to start with my questions.

I introduced Bridgett and he said, "Your father was a good man. He was a CIA agent assigned to the American Embassy and had gotten the word that members of the Kennedy murder team were hiding out in Europe. He'd learned they were still conducting hit and run murders back home; as well as planning other assassinations here in Europe."

Bridgett didn't betray what she was feeling, but she listened to him with rapt attention.

"Your father had become very distrustful of his supervisors so he asked a KGB agent friend to confirm the story and he did. When your father learned of a plot to murder Malcolm X on a speaking trip to Paris, he made the mistake of telling his superiors; it was bad idea. They told him to calm down, and then they went about having him murdered."

Bridgett gasped and tears sprang to her eyes. She threw me a glance that at first I couldn't interpret. Wolfman looked questioningly at me, but then went on.

"I met your father during a raid we completed in 1958 to steal an enriched uranium shipment for Israel's first atomic bomb. The United States couldn't openly give the nuclear material to Israel, so, they allowed Israel to 'steal it' from them. Many of us on the team were former Israeli soldiers."

Bridgett looked at him, obviously stunned. "I don't believe it. It's not possible."

The Wolfman smiled at her. "It was a piece of cake. The truck driver stopped overnight at a hotel in the middle of the desert in Nevada. We drove up, changed trailers, drove to a deserted airstrip, loaded the material on an Israeli cargo plane and then we all disappeared."

He held up his hand and said, "Milkman, you both are in deep trouble."

"What else is new, Wolfman?"

Bridgett began to curse me. "Why didn't you tell me my father was CIA? You knew this and never told me?"

I told her, "I wasn't sure, and I couldn't say anything to anybody after I received word that the Wolfman was still alive. It was the Wolfman who asked me to go to Paris to see your father. I didn't know what your father's connection to all of this was. The contact was made by Jumping Jack Daniels connection to a French intelligence official who told us that Malcolm X was to be assassinated in Paris by the US government. I didn't know which agency your father worked for."

The Wolfman went on, "Your father met Malcolm X when he was assigned to follow him on his trips to Africa. Malcolm X spotted him trailing him in Egypt and engaged your father in a conversation that your father found to be very intriguing. He realized that Malcolm X was not the crazed radical that his superiors portrayed him to be."

Bridgett still remained very upset with me.

"The French simply refused to allow Malcolm X to get off his plane in France when he arrived. They told Malcolm X that he was unwanted in France. What they really were saying was, "America, we will not allow you to kill a Black American Patriot on French soil. Too many Black American men have died fighting for France.""

"Milkman," Bridgett said furiously, "You used me like you use all your women. You caused the death my father."

The Wolfman shook his head. "Not true. Your father found out about the Milkman from me. He wanted to alert Malcolm X through him, but you could not persuade him to travel to Paris with you so your father never got the chance. He knew he was in trouble and didn't have a lot of time so I risked everything to get in touch with the Milkman."

"Who in the hell are you anyway, Milkman," Bridgett said angrily, "some kind of spy?"

She walked away.

Whispering to me, the Wolfman repeated himself, "You two are in serious danger."

"What are we going to do about it, Wolfman?"

"I don't know yet, Milkman, but you need to know the ugly secrets that I couldn't tell you in San Antonio. The A-team was originally given the assignment to kill Bobby Kennedy."

"Bobby Kennedy?" I was startled.

"Yes Bobby, he was the tail that wagged the dog. We refused and then the target was upgraded to kill the dog. The A-team turned that assignment down also. That was what all the secret chatter was about. While we hated Bobby's guts and lost good men in Cuba, because of him, we refused to take both assignments. It was un-American and we weren't gangsters. We are soldiers and disciplined military men, who didn't want to be remembered by the American people as assassins and traitors."

He paused once again and seemed to be pondering how to make me understand. "After the target was upgraded to President Kennedy, the B-team accepted the assignment to execute him. That is the reason they were on the same ship as you. They were on their way to Ireland to take the shot, when the president was schedule to arrive on June 26, 1963. The Irish Government got wind of it somehow. So, the B-team was sent back to San Antonio to take the shot there when he was scheduled to arrive. He was supposed to be killed in San Antonio and James Moran was slated to be the fall-guy."

He had my full attention.

"Moran's death in San Antonio caused problems for the San Antonio shot, as well as their Secret Service sell-out inability to confirm the removal of the president's plastic top from his limo during his San Antonio visit. Because, the B-team screwed-up the shot in San Antonio, they were assigned to the clean-up garbage killings after the Dallas shot was taken. Oswald was just the back-up fall-guy for the Dallas shot, only if it was necessary. And yes, it was necessary for another team to take the shot in Dallas."

My head was spinning. I suspected a lot of this, but the fact that it was the Wolfman stating this that made me realize just how ugly the truth was.

"I suspected the B-team had accepted the assignment, because we were sent to Vietnam. There my team was isolated from the goings on in Texas and we were scheduled for elimination also. Milkman, as you figured it out, this was not a simple assassination or murder. It was a coup d'etat. It was hatched in Texas, executed in Texas, with Texas money. It was carried out with the expressed approval of J. E. Hoover himself, head of the American Praetorian Guard."

I looked around for Bridgett. She was standing several feet away with her back to us. I wanted to go to her, but the Wolfman was still talking.

"Now they have their fellow Texan in the White House. He was an uninformed co-participant whose real job it was to cover it up. President Eisenhower warned President Kennedy and the American public about the uncontrolled military-industrial complex in his farewell speech, but no one paid much attention. The American Praetorian Guard, headed by J.A. Hoover is real. He orchestrated this murder with the help of many of his close friends; who are among America's infamous and powerful. The only thing they will get out of the exchange will be riches from the Vietnam War. The war they will lose and lose big time."

He paused to make sure I had his full attention.

"Milkman, who did you tell, that you suspected that the B-team was involved in murdering President Kennedy?"

"I told no one, Wolfman. I was sworn by you not to divulge my ugly secrets. I didn't say anything to anyone, in spite of the fact that almost every person who got close to me disappeared or died at their hand. I tried to keep Bridgett as far away from this as possible, but her father pulled her into it by trying to connect with me."

"Your silence is the reason you're still living, Milkman, but that has changed now."

"Bullshit, I think they tried to take me out several times. What happened in Nam, Wolfman, how did you get to Germany and what in the hell is the American Praetorian Guard?"

"I vowed never to return to Germany, Milkman, but I remembered one of our conversations. I told you that you must take personal responsibility for your ugly secrets. I must take responsibility for what I did to my Jewish people here in Germany, Milkman. Additionally, it is up to me to make sure that these foul deeds will not happen to another American again as long as I live. I am just as responsible for the death of President Kennedy, Malcolm X and the others as you are. You remember what Lonzo did to the Nazi and the CO? It was for American Soldiers that would follow him."

"My team was ambushed on a mission in Laos, set up by our own people. The only one we got out alive was the Caveman, because he was wounded first. Ambushing us was a training mission for the North Vietnamese, Special Forces being led by a Russian Special Forces team. I was wounded and about to put a "Third Luger" round through the top of my mouth when the Russian Special Forces intelligence officer training the North Vietnamese walked up to me and said, 'Put on your red dress, baby, cause we's going out to night.' Guess who it was?"

"I don't have a clue."

"Our Korean War Platoon Leader, Lieutenant Victor Masterson."

I looked at him in confusion. "The Black trolley car driver-Lonzo said I looked just like him."

I wanted to tell the Wolfman about SGT Gorge's death, Captain Morales and the visit from the investigators from the Justice Dept., The disappearance of Moreland, his diary, and more, but he wouldn't let me get a word in.

"Milkman, you would think that it would be out of place to see a Black trolley car driver in West Berlin, but a lot of Black American GIs receive their Army discharges here and remain in West Berlin. Even before WWII, Berlin was a popular place for Blacks Americans. In the late thirties Black musicians topped the charts here with the "Flat Foot Floogie with a Floy, Floy." Hitler hated it. Did you register for college, yet?"

He confused me with the quick change, but didn't give me a chance to answer anyway. "Now you want to know about the American Praetorian Guard..."

In that instant, the Wolfman saw flashes in back of me and two bar patrons standing next to me went down. The Wolfman pushed me aside as all hell broke loose in the alleyway. Bullets were flying everywhere. The Wolfman went down. Bridgett ran back to me and we grabbed him and pulled him back into the doorway. He was fumbling in his belt for something. Bridgett reached into his belt, where he was fumbling and pulled out the "Third Luger."

He mumbled to her, "Its Lonzo's and its locked, loaded and live." To my surprise, she instinctively released the safely and started firing back into the dark alley.

The Wolfman mumbled to me, "Milkman, get to Checkpoint Charley, and please don't let them bury me in Germany; please. I want to be buried at home, in America, in Arlington-not here."

We pulled him further into the nightclub's doorway, as far in as we could. I started to administer first aid. He just looked at me and smiled, as if some huge burden had been lifted from his shoulders.

I said to him with tears in my eyes, "This is why you wanted to meet me. You wanted me to get you back home with dignity, honor and return the Third Luger to Lonzo." He smiled again, then his eyes glassed over and his body lost its tension.

In that instant, a shooter began firing at us from inside the nightclub, apparently trying to drive us back into the alley. The patrons in the nightclub were running in panic like those in the Mexican bar in San Antonio. I pulled Bridgett back into the doorway and pointed at the front door of the club. We ran through patrons on the dance floor in a low crouch, like fleeing thieves at night in a neighbor's cornfield. Patrons were dropping like flies around us.

We made it to the front door. I grabbed the bouncer and pulled him in back of me for a few steps to stop any bullets from behind. I heard the familiar sound of German Police cars approaching. I had no idea where Checkpoint Charley was. I knew it was the famous crossing between East and West Berlin; but where? A few years earlier, American and Soviet tanks faced off there during the Berlin crisis.

We just ran as fast as we could. I saw a sign a block away that pointed the direction to Checkpoint Charley.

But, we also saw headlights of a speeding car coming at us a few blocks away. They could hear the sound of our shoes clicking against the cobblestone street where Adolf Hitler had walked twenty five years earlier. We ran the opposite way down one-way streets and through alleys. We saw a brightly-lit area with smartly dressed US Army MPs on one side of a barrier and Soviet and East German troops on the other.

A car turned down the alley in between the checkpoint and us. We couldn't turn around, because the B-team was hot on our heels. Bridgett put the "Third Luger" in her pocket book, because she was out of bullets. We ran straight towards that speeding car coming at us. She looked at me as if I was nuts. I pushed her to the side then I jumped as high as possible. I cleared the front hood of the car and landed on the roof sliding down its back. Luckily, the car continued straight when I pushed her to its side.

As we hit the ground tumbling, she said to me, "You must have done this before with another woman-you two timer."

As we turned around, we heard a squelch, as the speeding car hit two members of the B-team chasing us. We just couldn't walk up to the MPs without attracting notice. So we made believe that we were two drunken lovers not knowing where we were going. The remainder of B-team pulled up, in their battered car a block away, smiling, knowing that the MPs would stop us. As soon as we got close to the MPs, we pushed them aside and ran towards the Soviet Troops. The MPs were so surprised they didn't draw their weapons. They were not use to people trying to escape to East Germany. Boy, what kind of trouble have I gotten myself into now? The East

German guards raised their AK 47s and they motioned us to get down on the ground. They searched both of us, took Bridgett's purse and then they pulled my military ID out of my pocket. The B-team was talking to the MPs.

The MPs then said to the East Germans and Russians, "He's a drunken US soldier; please return him to us."

The East German guards began to talk among themselves giving it a lot of consideration. They grabbed Bridgett and me and began to march us back to the American side of the checkpoint. The Wolfman instructed me how to identify myself, if I got into trouble.

I began hollering,"Bin eine Nachteule, Bin eine Nachteule, I am a night owl."

The Soviet officer at the guard post, hollowed back to the East German guards, "Halt, kommen sie heir, stop come here."

The guards marched us back to the East German side of the checkpoint. There, the Soviet officer made a telephone call and then he called for a Soviet military car to come and pick us up. As we got into the car, I could see the disappointed faces of the B-team. We drove for a half-hour into East Germany. It was very dark, because many streetlights were not working. Then the car stopped in the middle of nowhere. We were told to get out of the car.

I said to Bridgett, "I guess we're in deep shit now."

The drivers blind folded us and placed us back into the car. We couldn't see anything anyway; so it didn't make any difference to us. Where, in the hell, were they taking us? They drove us to an airport and directly into a large hanger. I could tell by the sounds what type of a place it was. They helped us out of the car and they placed us in an office and removed our blind folds. The guards asked us if we were hungry. I said yes.

They asked, "What would you like?"

"Haben sie eine Bratwuesh?"

The guard was a bit nonplussed that I knew German and told the other guards not to speak German around us; to speak Russian. Then they placed a set of rusty hand huffs on me and placed me in a separate room from Bridgett. They brought the food in and released one handcuff for me to eat. The other was attached to the chair. After a glass of beer, the door opened. There stood a tall figure back lighted in the doorway staring at me. He said to me in perfect English with a slight Southern accent.

"So you like to hang out in zoos at night, Milkman."

Then he walked into the light. It was the trolley driver. Opening Bridgett's handbag he said, "I haven't seen this "Third Luger" since 1950 in Korea. Now I am seeing it too much."

"LT Masterson," I said.

"No, Colonel Snow White, Milkman. Lieutenant Masterson died in North Korea in 1950. I am Colonel White of the KGB. I took that name as the North Koreans were dragging my Black frozen ass through the white snow; while I was still in a set of US Army handcuffs. The same ones you are wearing." Then he laughed and asked how, SGT Lonzo Morgan is?

"Barely living, Sir."

"Lonzo was the bravest damn soldier I ever had known. He had nerves of steel. When that North Korean Officer pulled the trigger of that "Third Luger" pointed at his head, he didn't blink."

He then ordered his men to remove his handcuffs and he dangled the set of rusted handcuffs in front of me.

"I keep them to remind me of what America is truly about. I begged the Wolfman not to meet you. You are hotter than Satan in hell on the 4th of July. Both of you are and you didn't know it."

"I know it now, Sir."

"All these years, I still don't know whether Lonzo shot that SOB of a CO of ours. Being a good soldier meant so much to the Mighty Mouse. I hated to see him suffer on my behalf, but there wasn't a thing I could do for him. If the North Koreans turned me loose, I would have seen the same fate as Lonzo or even worse. I grew tired of fighting both America and America's enemies at the same time. Something had to give. Now, I simply fight America's evil impulses."

He gave an intense look before he went on. "Milkman, I don't want to waste your time or you mine. I will offer you life over death, respect over disrespect. It's the same exact offer that I made to the Wolfman. I pulled the Wolfman out of a rice paddy in Laos. He was wounded, half dead and about to commit suicide with this 'Third Luger.' You know now, that he simply wanted to go home with honor and dignity. Somehow, he felt you could figure out how to get him back home. Fate is a bitch isn't it.

"He trained you. He saw you grow from a cocky young Soul Brother into a mature Super Soldier here in

Europe. He monitored your progress as you developed into an outstanding military man. One of the best medics in the 517th Clearing Company, soldier of the month, Supernumerary, Honor Guard, and you completed the 100-mile Nijmegen Marches. The Pistol team you trained took third place in the 7th Army completions. You qualified Expert in shooting both rifle and pistol. You have the reputation as one of the best bar fighters in Europe. I want you to work with me."

"Me becoming a Soviet Agent? America enslaved my great great-grandparents, mistreated my great grandmother, grandmother and my mother. And, now America was definitely giving me a hard time. It wouldn't take much for me to say yes. Most of the American founding fathers definitely didn't have my ancestors or me in mind when they wrote, "All men are created equal." But, less than a hundred years after they wrote those immortal words, their grandchildren paid dearly for their hypocrisy to the tune of 600,000 of their sons dead and wounded in the Civil War."

"One hundred years after the Civil War," I said, "We are still battling in the streets of America for our freedom. I don't know if we will ever finish the job, but there is a serious crack in the door of justice and equality in America. Somehow, I am going to walk through that door, dragging the rest of America kicking and screaming with me, if necessary. I owe that to all those who suffered so much before me"

I grinned at him and added, "I am glad you didn't run that Commie crap on me, about the best system on the face of the planet, because you guys are doing the same shit to people that Americans are doing; rule by the bullet not by law."

"I never believed that stuff either, Milkman. What I signed on to do was to put an end to America's hypocritical impulses; to abuse other people on this planet. Americans do not treat others in the same manner as they wish to be treated themselves; especially peoples of color. There is a big difference between what Americans say they stand for and what Americans really stand for. We tried to stop the murder of Patrice Lumumba, but we were too late. We did stop the assassination of Fidel Castro.

"When I learned that Wolfman's team was assigned to carry out the Fidel Castro assassination mission, I asked for the assignment to find and stop his ass. I almost did too. The Wolfman, Caveman and Vecky all left their calling cards in Cuba. Vecky killed a Castro look-a-like-double with a clean single shot through the head at one thousand yards. One of my men had his throat ripped out and another had his neck broken by the Wolfman and Caveman. They killed another two of my best men in a shootout before they all escaped on a boat owned by the Mafia back to Florida. I was hot on the Wolfman's tail for years and he didn't know it was me tracking him.

"Their Cuban mission failed, because Robert Kennedy was micro-managing it from the Attorney General's office. RFK screwed up operation Mongoose. They were not well prepared, nor supported. Now you understand why the American Praetorian Guard offered them the job to take RFK down. Bobby Kennedy's stubbornness was responsible for John Kennedy's death. He refused to take care of the people who handed them the presidency. Joe told both of his sons that they were making too many enemies in powerful places. Enemies that helped them steal the 1960 presidential election. They caused their father's stroke by their stubbornness."

I said to myself, "He sounds rehearsed and I wondered how many times he made this speech."

"Unfortunately, The American Praetorian Guard, headed by Hoover himself, isn't one you double-cross." He grinned adding, "Both JFK and RFK were banging Marilyn Monroe. Hoover uncovered that she was one of our principal agents in America. But, she was so popular that even he could not touch her. It didn't help her situation after Hoover discovered that it was Marilyn Monroe who had alerted Fidel Castro to the Bay of Pigs invasion; even though she wasn't the only communist agent bedding down JFK. The Kennedys were making Top Secret telephone calls from her bedroom which she overheard."

He told me a lot of things that I never heard at the UCLA or read in my high school history books.

"Hoover handed President Kennedy his personal FBI folder containing a long list of all of his illicit love affairs and his ugly secrets going back to WWII when he was a young naval officer. In 1942, Jack was having an affair with a suspected Nazi agent, Inga Advad, who was still married. She was a Danish beauty queen who was hosted by Adolf Hitler at the 1932 Olympic Games. Hoover told Ambassador Joe Kennedy about it. Joe had his son transferred from Washington, D.C. to Charleston, South Carolina to get him away from Inga. She followed him until he was ordered to command PT-109 in the South Pacific. Hoover and Jack had a running gun battle going on for over 40 years. They hated one another with a purple passion.

"JFK looked at the file and just smiled. Then he handed Hoover the file that the Kennedy brothers were keeping on him, documenting Hoover's homosexual activities with his long time FBI associate director Clyde Tolson. The Kennedy file also suggested that J.E. Hoover had attorney general select, Senator Thomas J. Walsh, poisoned on the train to Washington, D.C. in 1933; one day before he was to be sworn into office by the newly elected President Franklin D. Roosevelt. Walsh's first act as attorney general was to fire Hoover. Hoover had a fondness for untraceable poisons that produced heart attacks. As you can now see with all of the mysterious deaths surrounding President Kennedy's murder; it's an effective tool. Killing someone is easy, Milkman; getting away with it is difficult, unless you are head of the American Praetorian Guard."

He spoke of Kennedy almost with fondness.

"In spite of JFK's weaknesses for women, he was a great president. We didn't get much useful information directly from him, although we admit, we did help seal his fate. An American president sleeping with Soviet and East German agents could only mean death in a land of paranoid fascists.

'It also sealed Malcolm X's fate and many others, Milkman. Hoover figured out, if he could get away with murdering the president and others close to him, then it was open season on all opposition leaders; especially Black ones-including you. It's the American peoples fault, because the American people never demand the truth from their political leaders. The unfortunate thing is RFK was working just as hard as the American Praetorian Guard trying to cover up the truth about his Brother's murder. Why, you ask, would he protect his brother's killers, Milkman? Just think about it, what would a hardheaded, vindictive Irishman want to do to the people who killed his brother? Especially when he knows who is directly responsible. That's why those agents from the justice department showed up to question the Cavemen at Fort Rucker. RFK knew then that someone was trying to take both of them out."

I had a million questions, but the colonel didn't give me a chance to talk.

"Malcolm X was an early opponent of the Vietnam War," he said, "even earlier than Martin Luther King. Malcolm X wrote to President Kennedy, but Hoover was intercepting the massages. JFK's speech on June 11, 1963 revealed that he was secretly paying attention to Malcolm X and other Black leaders. The speech could have been written by Malcolm X himself; it sealed both of their fates.

"I am proud of you for helping to stop the murder of Malcolm X here in Europe, but neither you nor I had the reach that was necessary to get into the Autobahn ballroom to stop the American Praetorian Guard. Malcolm X also knew the Big Boys were stalking him. He confided that to his biographer Alex Haley. The Brothers that pulled the triggers in the Autobahn Ballroom were simply mindless idiots; not knowing the very people they despised was using them as a tool.

'I trained North Vietnamese soldiers to kill my own American Brothers. Over fifty percent of the men they killed were Black and Hispanic. That rides high in my soul, Milkman, but America betrayed the North Vietnamese People after WWII. Not Russia, not China and not me. Don't follow the BS, Milkman. Follow the treachery and the money. There is no money to be made in opposing the civil rights movement in America. But, there is big money to be made in the Vietnam War."

He finally stopped and I got to ask a question. "Why have you continued to support the Soviet Union, Col. White?"

"America is not ready for me to return; she is not ready for the truth. Why are you here in East Germany, Milkman? Is it, because there is over whelming love for you in America and the righteous stands that you take?"

"That's bullshit, the only way Russians change leadership, is by assassination and they tolerate no dissent at all. The assassinations in America should make Russians feel very comfortable."

"I am not making much headway with you. The SOBs you are protecting are eating their own children in the name of some misguided superiority complex. The murders of JFK, Malcolm X and others are just the beginning. These things scare the hell out of me and the leaders in the Soviet Union."

He took me into the adjacent room of the hanger and my eyes lit up. There was the Davy Crocket that had disappeared while I was guarding it. Its W54 Nuclear Warhead was still mounted on the same M151 death trap jeep. I walked around it, inspecting it in amazement.

"You want it back?"

"I only have only one soul to sell to the devil. This would require three souls, Sir."

"Open up the war head."

I looked at him as if he lost his mind.

"Go ahead and open it up."

"But those guys had on radiological protection suits when they stole it."

"Those were not radiological suits, they were biological warfare suits. The stealing of the Davy Crocket was just a ruse to hide and move the real booty, which was the newly developed, weaponized HIV virus that they thought was air transmittable."

"Is that the auto-immune virus that attacks the body's immune system that I was told about it in medic school?"

"Yes and no. Do you remember a young fellow by the name of Roger Moreland?"

"Yes, he was my seatmate during our first days of basic training and I shipped out with him on the General Rose. He disappeared one day before we docked at Bremerhaven, Germany."

"He was thrown overboard by your B-team. They knew about the diary he was keeping. The diary disappeared the day before he was thrown overboard. It was his job to transport the virus to Europe aboard the General Rose. People in your unit were assigned to releasing the virus. When, what, where and how, I don't know? I would like to find out."

"Col. White, I believe Moreland slipped the diary into my duffel bag and it was stolen from me the first day I arrived at the 517th. I never had a chance to read it. I did see crates marked cholera vaccine in the hold of the General Rose and they were the same crates that I loaded on our trucks during NATO alerts. The strange thing was the vaccine labels were written in both English and Russian."

"The B-team never knew how much you knew about Wolfman's or Moreland's secrets. They had to assume you knew everything and was just keeping quiet about your secrets. They needed an insurance policy and that's why they set you up in the disappearance of the Davy Crocket. They killed two birds with one stone. Remove the top plate from the containment area on the weapon, its safe."

I removed the plate.

"That is where the fissionable material goes. It's not there. What you are looking at is the crucial top secret timing mechanisms and explosive core that detonate the nuclear material. The atomic material was never there. They have the atomic material, what they needed was the tactical nuke. But, they were also interested in stealing a much deadlier weapon, the HIV virus. They used the war head as a ruse to hide and transport the virus. We intercepted the Davy Crockett on a tramp freighter in the Mediterranean Sea. They got away with the virus. The nuclear weapon was too heavy for them to flee with."

"I believe they killed Roger Moreland for telling you that the HIV virus was stored in cholera vaccine containers in Bad Kreuznach and how they were going to be used."

"But, he never told me anything about the virus and I don't know when or how they moved it from the warehouse where it was kept under lock and key; I told you that. I do know the 517th was trained to respond to natural disasters like the earthquakes in Yugoslavia, and Eastern Europe where the population would have been immunized for cholera by us."

"A cholera vaccine, that's a stroke of genius," Col. White said. "The Russians and Eastern Europeans would be killing themselves with immunizations supplied by you; if that was the case. We know your commanding officer and at least one enlisted man of the 517th were involved in transporting the virus."

"But Moreland didn't tell me anything."

"That is why he left you his diary, to let you know that the 517th was not the place you wanted to be and who was involved. It makes sense now, that's how these assholes were planning to release the virus in Eastern Europe. We don't know where or when, but it could be released tomorrow. We must be prepared to respond. Someone close to you is double crossing you, Milkman."

"No."

He slid back the large curtain in back of the jeep. There were five small suitcases on the table. He motioned me over to the table and he opened one of them. They had instructions written in English and Russian on how to arm the devices.

"They are 1 megaton each; much like your M159 Nuclear Land Mine, but ours is smaller and lighter."

I jumped back from the table.

"This is no joke, Milkman. The Kennedy murder wasn't a simple assassination and Malcolm X's assassination wasn't a simple murder. They were all well integrated and orchestrated to look like something they weren't."

"I know that now."

"Hoover is the alpha dog in this pack."

"What else is new," I said wearily.

"Milkman, I told you what my job was here. Do you remember the joke that the Wolfman told you about American and Chinese Generals arguing about who had the best nuclear weapons delivery systems? The American General said, "I have 250 Atlas Intercontinental Missiles, 300 B-52 bombers and a host of other high tech means for delivering over 5000 nuclear warheads to China." What did the Chinese General say in response, Milkman?"

"Sir," he said, "I have over six hundred million people, we can hand-carry all five of our damn nuclear warheads to the United States, low tech kicks hi-tech's ass."

"If these crazy individuals, your American Praetorian Guard are not stopped, the whole world is in jeopardy, not just America or the Soviet Union."

Looking over at the nuclear weapons, he continued, "If you were in my shoes, what would you do for insurance? These weapons can be activated electronically from a plane, satellite or a simple telephone call. There is no maintenance required. PVT Roy what would you do with these nuclear weapons if you were me?"

I held my head down, shaking it in disbelief. He turned around a large black board in back of the table. On its back was a large map of the United States. He said to me again in a calm voice, "What would you do, Milkman?"

I remained silent, just shaking my head no. The more I shook my head no, the more he nodded yes, yes, and yes. He ordered me to go to the blackboard and pick five cities, as if I was he.

I said, "No."

He nodded his head to two of his agents. They picked me up and threw me against the blackboard. He hollered, "Name them, Private Roy, name them; as if you were me."

I said, "Washington DC, New York City, Chicago, Boston and Los Angeles."

He said, "Very good, I know you are from New York City so we shall remove it from the list. The last one should be for your murdered president; Dallas."

"They will be deployed, in America, within 72 hours. Since I couldn't convince you to stay and work for justice for all people. You will have to earn your keep. You have a few days left. You will stay at the Wolfman's parent's private villa in East Germany. It was taken over by the Nazis during the WWII, after they sent the Wolfman and his parents to the death camps. It's now used as a visiting Soviet Officers quarters. You will have the honor of packing his things. Then you and your lady friend will turn up at the Frankfurt bahnhof courtesy of the Soviet Union.

"By next Tuesday, your Sergeant Doctor will receive a call indicating the location of a shipping container. This is the lock that will be on the container and here is your key for it. Inside the shipping container will be a wonderful surprise. I hope this will cause those SOBs to pause, think carefully about what they are doing and possibly convince them to spare your life; but I doubt it. I want you to tell those SOBs, what you saw here and tell them if that virus is released in Eastern Europe or the Soviet Union, American cities will go up in smoke hopefully with them in it."

For a moment I stood there in stunned silence. When I found my voice, I screamed at him, "No one is going to believe this shit, because I don't believe it myself. This really isn't happening, a Black KGB agent with 5 suitcase sized nuclear bombs that he is deploying in five American cities that I picked? And, he will accomplish all of this in 72 hours. They will ask me to share with them the Weed that I am smoking."

"Milkman, you are exactly right. Those officers that do not know any better and had nothing to do with the deaths of President Kennedy, Malcolm X, and others will not believe a word you will spit out of your mouth. But, those that do know may stop the infection of millions of innocent human beings with the most hideous weapon ever devised. But, still, they will try their best to kill you. Your odds are not good if you go back. I will ask you the same question that Malcolm X asked you. Who is your real enemy? Given that your enlistment will be up in a matter of weeks, they would rather you simply disappear; like I did. Additionally, I have a personal gift for you to take back; it may provide additional insurance on your life. It will be our ugly secret."

He rolled in an old US Army footlocker in front of me and opened it. It was the Wolfman's footlocker. It had the Wolfman's personal effects in it, shaving cream, bars of soap, shoelaces and socks, etc. He told me to inspect the items carefully. I picked up the shaving cream can it was heavier than normal shaving cans. I started to push the top, he told me to stop, because it was a CN gas grenade. I picked up the Ivory Soap. He told me to smell it. It smelled like C4 explosives. I picked up his socks; the toes were loaded with buck shoot. It was a homemade hand grenade. I picked up the shoelaces and pulled the end of the laces. A garrote blade began to come out, like the one that took the head off the guy in San Antonio. Now, I know where the Cavemen got his from in Fort Rucker.

"There is more there, you should learn how to use it all before you get back to your base. Maybe this will buy you some time and respect, not much, but some."

He placed Lonzo's "Third Luger" in a box marked cookies and stuffed it in the bottom of the footlocker. He shook my hand as his men snapped to attention. I tried to get up from the footlocker to salute him.

He said, "No, Milkman, Caesar must salute those who are about to die, because you are about to take on the America Praetorian Guard."

"Who or what in hell is the American Praetorian Guard?"

He paused and obviously decided I needed a history lesson.

"In the 2nd Century BC, the Praetorian Guards were the bodyguards for Roman emperors and generals. Their name was taken from the general's tent (praetorium). The Emperor Augustus created a permanent corps to guard the emperor and stationed its members around Rome. They gained political influence and had an important voice in appointing Roman Emperors for almost 300 years. The Emperor Constantine disbanded the body in 312AD. The Guard that made and broke Roman Emperors is now making and braking American Presidents."

***

20

The Ugly Secrets of Private Roy

Bridgett and I arrived back in Frankfurt two days late. I was AWOL. I wasn't worried about losing my stripe, because I didn't have one to lose. The one on my uniform sleeve was living on borrowed time. We took the first train back to Bad-K. Bridgett questioned the wisdom of us going back. She wanted to turn around, head directly for Sweden and ask for political asylum.

"I can't quit like that," I said, "Too many of my friends have died that were more deserving of life than I. I only had two weeks left on my enlistment and I will not leave the Kaserne until then. Then we can go to Sweden. I don't want to be a quitter or a deserter. I will figure out a way to stay alive in the meantime and address my ugly secrets later. I always have."

"You know what people say about going to the same well too often."

"I know, Bridgett, but you have to work with me on this one."

"I can't live without you, Milkman, if something happens to you. I will never forgive myself."

"I want you to go back to Frankfurt and cool out. I will call you every day to let you know I am all right. You have to trust me."

She got off the train with me in Bad-K and we watched the sun set together, at the train station, until the next train going back to Frankfurt arrived. I kissed her and took a taxi back to the Kaserne. LT Biggs was waiting for me in the HQ and he was steaming.

He said, "I am going to have you jailed."

I said, "Possibly, Sir, if you are not jailed first."

His eyes opened wide as I handed him my copy of the letter from the Commanding General of seventh Army addressing the conclusion of my racial discrimination charge which ended with "Call him if I had any additional concerns." After a lot of blustering, he finally made the call and handed me the phone.

I said, "Sir I may have found something we lost." When he told the general, who I was, he immediately jumped into his helicopter and flew to the Hospital Kaserne. He stormed into the 517th's HQ and ran upstairs. Attend-hut poured down in the building's hallway like acid rain.

He opened the door and ran straight into me, asking the lieutenant, "Where is PVT Roy?"

The lieutenant said, "Standing in front of you Sir."

He said to me, "You better have something good for me private or I will hang you by your balls from my chopper at three thousand feet."

"Sir, with the wind and prop wash, that would be one hell-of-a-blow job." He almost split his hip from laughing.

"What do you have for me, Son?"

I began to whistle, "Davy, Davy Crockett the King of the Wild Frontier."

He asked the lieutenant, to leave the room with all of the officers and NCOs.

"Son, this is very serious, you could disappear from this room and no one would ever find you."

"That is very true; Sir, but I have a hardheaded mother. She wouldn't give up until she found every hair on her pretty brown skin boy's head."

He smiled and asked, "What do you want, Private."

"Sir, if I deliver the piece of equipment you lost under my watch, I want all of this bullshit to stop."

"I don't know what bullshit you are talking about, Private, but if I did, what else do you want."

"If that piece of equipment turns up, the next day, I want all your divisions' commanders to be in this office to hear what I have to say."

"Is that all, Private, what about a million dollars or two?"

"Now, that was not funny, Sir. There are some people that can't be bought, Sir. Maybe I should put it another way. I can be bought Sir, but they haven't printed enough money yet in the US to buy me. Sir, Sergeant Doctor will get a call here at the HQ tomorrow. He will give you a series of numbers that I will decode. It will tell us the location of the piece of equipment we lost."

He called in LT Biggs, the lieutenant told him I assaulted a cook before I left, the cook and a German national had filed assault charges against me. Before the general could say anything, I said, "Sir, I am guilty, willing to give up my stripe and be placed under armed guard."

The general said, "Place him under armed guard and restrict him to base."

The lieutenant nodded his head yes, that he didn't have any problems with that, saying he would order SP4 Haymen Swilley and PFC Eugene Webb to place me under armed guard immediately."

LT Biggs called in Gracia and ordered him to issue 45s to Top Dog and the Spiderman. The lieutenant then ordered me to my barracks. Swilley went and got me my dinner from the mess hall while the Spiderman stood guard. I gave the general the key to the container before he took off in his chopper.

The next evening, SGT Doctor got the telephone message and gave it to me. I went into my room and locked the door. I pulled out my San Antonio phone book and decoded the message. It said there would be a large metal shipping container located in the Bad-K train station's parking lot. It would contain the equipment we were looking for. The general sent two truckloads of MPs downtown to the train station's parking lot. They unlocked and inspected the container and radioed back that it was the lost piece of equipment that we were looking for.

The next morning, there were three choppers circling the Hospital Kaserne. They were the commanding general of the Seventh Army, and his division commanders. I was sitting at the lieutenant's desk when they all entered the room. I rose, saluted and started speaking:

"Sirs, I have an important message for you. There are very important and powerful people in this world outside of those standing in this room. They are extremely concerned about the unprincipled behavior and the lawlessness acts of some individuals in the government, the military and industry in the United States. Their blatant disregard for international law, human life and liberty can't continue and their egregious acts cannot go unchallenged. The principles that you took an oath to uphold are now being discarded."

"Private Roy, who in the hell you think you are talking too. You can't talk to us like that. You're on very dangerous ground here. And what in the hell are you talking about anyway?"

"Sirs, there are five nuclear weapons being placed in five American cities; as we speak."

That got their attention.

"I don't know under what circumstances they will detonate. I can say that they were placed there as insurance policies in case US forces attack the people of Eastern Europe and the Soviet Union with biological weapons."

Before anyone could answer, LT COL Grumble entered the room.

"The commanding general of seventh Army said, LT COL Grumble, I understand that you had some dealings with Private Roy, is that correct?"

"Yes, Sir."

"What do you think?"

"I think PVT Roy wishes to be the center of attention, Sir. He has a large ego, probably a bit too large; in fact illusionary. The returned nuclear weapon probably wasn't stolen at all, Sir. Maybe it was just hidden nearby by PVT Roy and others."

"If, it was hidden nearby, Sir, why didn't you find it?" I asked. "And while you are at it, tell the generals where the B-team and you were on November 22, 1963 about 1:30 P.M., Dallas time."

"First, there is no B-team. Second, I don't know what you are referring too."

The Commanding General of the Seventh Army jumped in, "Private Roy, we appreciate the return of the nuclear weapon. We are not going to ask any questions as how it was removed from the 8th Airborne's HQ, how it got back to the Bad-K's train station's parking lot, or where it was in between those two time points. I understand you have about a week before your enlistment is up. I am ordering you restricted to the barracks under armed guard until you are released here in Europe; as you requested. Is that correct, Private Roy? You requested a European release."

"Yes, Sir."

LT COL Grumble eyes rose when the general said that I asked for a European release from the Army. LT COL Grumble was clearly irritated. I sensed that this was working out just as Colonel White had predicted. I said nothing more as I left the HQ under armed guard. I dispensed with all military protocol. I stopped saluting officers. I wore my shirt outside of my pants, like the Batman did. I didn't starch my uniforms anymore. My boots were not shined. I didn't shave and I started to grow an Afro. No one said a word to me, because I was a short timer and I proudly displayed my short timer's pin on my uniform.

I thought about Batman in Mannheim Army Prison. Robin was lost without him, but at least he wasn't doing anything stupid. He approached me and wanted to talk, so I brought up the theft of my wallet and Moreland's diary that was taken over two years ago.

He said, "I was standing in the doorway the day your wallet and the diary were stolen. Batman and I didn't take it."

"Robin, you don't have to lie about it now, it's over. I am leaving the Army, if I can stay alive until next Saturday."

"I know who went into the building, but I am not going to rat him out. The CQ overheard your conversation with CPL Perez. He told the officers of the company; they know also."

"They definitely know who took the diary."

"Yes, it was someone you know well."

I left it alone at that point. Col. White suspected that someone close to me was double crossing me; the ultimate betrayal.

CPL Perez sent word that he wanted to take on the new Supernumerary of the 517th. Top Dog-Swilley had worked his way up to being the best in the company now. He said, he was ready to take on either Perez or me, but I told him I had retired from the Army; I was just waiting on my release orders. Swilley smiled, called me a pussy and said he would take on Perez this Friday evening. It was the evening before I was to be released from the Army. I told Swilley, he could have all my new winter uniforms. He was about my size. They were already starched and ready to go for guard mount.

He said, "I would be proud to wear them Friday."

I told Bridgett that we would go directly to Sweden and apply for political asylum. Then I would be free to talk about all of my ugly secrets, but I remembered what the Wolfman said, who was going to believe me? I didn't have the smoking guns for most of my ugly secrets. So, what was I going to say? At least someone else would know that America is under attack from within by a bunch of crazy-ass nuts under a supporting jaundiced eye of the American public.

LT Biggs invited the entire medical company and medical air-wing to a beer blast and barbecue at a guest-house and racetrack just outside of town next Friday evening. All the guys that didn't have duty were invited to go. I was restricted to base until I left, so I couldn't go and that's the way I wanted it.

Bridgett drove down from Frankfurt in her father's ragtop VW Beetle and stopped by the Kaserne to confirm our plans. I couldn't talk openly to her, so I small talked her. Earl Wade sold me his new Sony reel to reel tape recorder for me to ship home. They ran out of them at the PX before I could purchase one. I sent it and most of my personal thing's home by Army sea transport; it would take a month for my mother to receive my things back in the States.

One thing I didn't ship was the Wolfman's footlocker which I kept at the foot of my bunk. I didn't know how the footlocker had got here, I walked into my room one evening and it was setting at the foot of my bed. I opened it up and sitting on top was the box containing Lonzo's "Third Luger." I set there, cleaned it, and loaded its clip. I looked through the other equipment in the locker. There was a crossbow, flares and other equipment. Lying on top of the equipment was a note "Low tech kicks high tech's ass." I smiled and put the items back in the locker.

LT Biggs ordered all the soldiers in the company to avoid me like the plague. It was difficult to get a hello out of anybody except the Misfits. As my final weekend approached in Germany, I began to get antsy. My seven hundred pound gorilla dreams got worse again, sometimes appearing twice in one night. I didn't have any assignments; the sergeants wouldn't let me touch any equipment, drive a truck or anything. So I went upstairs and hung out with Garcia in the arms room.

CPL Perez knew now that we had the best weapons in Seventh Army and an armorer who knew how to keep them in top condition. He would lose the guard mount if he didn't level the rifle playing field. Friday rolled around and Top Dog asked me to be his second. Surprisingly the pot was $400 dollars that Top Dog would beat "PP" on guard mount. I put another $50 into the pot. Major McComb was scheduled to be the OD. CPL Perez knew it would be a fair, but difficult contest.

I was still very antsy. It was overcast all day. My bags were packed and Bridgett was coming to pick me up at 1000 hours the next day. About 1500 hours, one hour before the guard mount, the odds suddenly changed. Now it was almost two to one that Top Dog would lose. Someone added an additional five hundred dollars in the pot. I asked around, who placed the new bet. No one knew. I saw the Mad Doctor going over to the mess hall. I pulled him aside and told him I had enjoyed traveling Europe with him, it was nothing personal between us, and I was sorry that things hadn't worked out for the best.

He said, "You were one of the best soldiers that ever served under me." Then he whispered to me, "It was LT Biggs that bet against one of his own soldiers."

I told Top Dog about it. He just stood there giving me a devilish smile. The crowd started to build. All the GIs were in civilian clothes, because they were going to the lieutenant's beer party after the Supernumerary was selected for the guard mount. Some of the guys had already started to drink at the EM Club and they were very rowdy. I fully understood what Top Dog was saying with his smile. He had graduated into a hustler now. I took off my dingy uniform and I ran into the shower and cleaned every crevice in my body. When I returned to the room, Top Dog was waiting on me with a pair of hair chippers and he shaved my Afro completely off leaving no hair on my head at all. I put on a pair of his brand new underwear for good luck. Then he slid me into my winter uniform and a brand new, Korean issue, Army rabbit fur winter hat that I had found in the Wolfman's footlocker. Top Dog gave me his brand new field jacket that he had not placed any rank on yet. I kept my parade boots in top condition always. They had a deep triple spit shine with melted candle wax on the top. I learned that trick from PP after DD stepped on my boots at the guard mount at the 8th Airborne's HQ. The candle wax was very hard and it protected the shine on my boots from any nasty competitors who wanted to uneven the competition. Garcia came in the room and smiled at me as he handed me my weapon. It was "The Brazilian, my specially prepared M14." I checked my gas mask thoroughly. I knew the only thing that would differentiate us would be our military knowledge and weapons, so it would be a fair one.

I could hear the crowd heckling Perez outside. They were calling the paratroopers, "Flying Females," too afraid to fight the enemy straight-up from the ground. His seconds kept the crowd away from him. They knew they were overdue for payback from the 517th, for what they had done to me on my last guard mount at the 8th's Headquarters.

The first three guards fell in at attention waiting for the 517th's guard to arrive. Major McComb quieted the crowd of half-drunk GIs with a stern stare. I walked out of the barracks and I deliberately didn't turn around, because LT Biggs would recognize me and order me off the mount. He didn't notice me, because Top Dog and I were about the same size and stature. I walked towards the mount with my head held down trying not to attract any attention. A wedge formed in the crowd to let me through. When the crowd saw who I was, they went wild. They started to chant, "The Milkman, the Milkman."

With the crowd making so much noise, LT Biggs come barreling out of the HQ Building running towards the guard mount. Major McComb saw him running towards the guard mount. He looked down at his roster that showed Swilley's name. He immediately called the mount to attention and began to read off the names of the units and individuals. He called Swilley's name. I said, "Private Roy replacing Specialist 4 Swilley, Sir."

Then he began his inspection. It was considered rude for anyone to interrupt an officer while inspecting a guard mount. So the lieutenant just stood there and watched. After the first round of inspections, the sergeant asked two soldiers to fall out. CPL Perez and I were left. The second round of inspections began with Major McComb whispering to the sergeant of the guard to order me to take ten steps to the right. Then he began the verbal competitions. He started by asking Perez to name all of the generals in 7th Army Europe and the chain of command up to the president of the United States. Then he asked me the same questions.

I just completed my US Army division's blanket that Moreland helped me prepare. It had all of the 7th Armies' division patches sewn on it. Major McComb saw the ball field loaded with helicopters with general stars from all over 7th Army. He didn't know they were there at my request. That question was a piece of cake for me. After he completed the last round of inspections, Major McComb whispered in the sergeant's ear. He did an about face and told Perez to fall out. The GIs went wild. Major McComb smiled at LT Biggs as he placed the sergeant of the guard stripes on my arm and dismissed the guard mount.

LT Biggs walked back to the HQ in disgust, as Top Dog collected the money. The total pot was over eleven hundred dollars and it was the largest pot of any guard mount in the 517th's history. Top Dog handed all of it to me. I gave it back to him and said it's a wedding present. A small helicopter known as a little bird began to circle the Kaserne. I asked, Major McComb, if he knew whose bird it was.

He said, "No and it's strange, because it doesn't have any markings on it."

PP came over to congratulate me, and I said thanks. He said he wanted the last shift as we looked at the chopper circling the Kaserne. I said to him, as a going away gift, I am going to walk your tour for you.

He looked at the chopper, smiled and he gave me a hug saying, "Milkman, good luck and good bye Bro."

I told the other guards that I would walk their tours also. Top Dog was staring at me. He saw the chopper circling also. I said to Top Dog, the Spiderman and the Misfits that I appreciated their support and the drinks were on me at the party tonight. I gave Nasty my last $300 dollars to buy drinks for everyone as they loaded up in five trucks.

The LT Biggs told the first sergeant that he was staying behind to take care of some paper work and he would be along shortly. The Mad Doctor gave me a long stare and I knew instantly what it meant. Garcia felt uneasy about the situation also. He slipped me the keys to the armory as he collected "The Brazilian" and replaced it with an older M14. He also handed me two full clips of live ammo. Normally there would only be a few rounds in one clip.

The trucks pulled off heading for the racetrack. If this was going to be it for me, I was going out in style. The helicopter came back circling the Kaserne again, but there wasn't anyone home, but the empty trucks, the lieutenant and me. As the bird hovered, I pulled down my pants and mooned him. He flew away.

It was just about dusk; you could cut the tension in the air. The air was very heavy and a dense fog began to roll down the side of Kuhberg Hill. There was no wind at all. I went back into my barracks, went into The Wolfman's footlocker, and pulled out a few things that I might need. I opened the candy box, unwrapped the "Third Luger" and I placed it in the small of my back. I hid some of the other items at strategic points on the Kaserne and in the trucks.

Then I felt it was time for me to get some answers from the LT Biggs. I walked into his office and closed the door behind me. I walked over to the windows and pulled down the shades.

He said, "What in the hell are you doing Private Roy?"

"Sir, it is time for you to shed some light on our ugly secrets."

"Private Roy, you are supposed to be on guard duty, I suggest that you resume your duty."

I pulled out the "Third Luger" and said to him, do you know anything about the chopper that is circling the Kaserne, Sir."

"No, I don't."

"Sir, do you know anything about the secret biological agent, a virus that America developed that attacks the human immune system, and is secretly being stored here in the 517th's warehouse."

"No"

He was moving slowly towards the phone. I chambered the first round in the "Third Luger" and fired, "BAM," hitting the telephone which shattered into pieces and wounded his hand; causing it to bleed.

"Excuse me, Sir, that round went off by accident. Why is the 517th, so heavily armed?"

Trembling he said, "It was simply standard procedure."

"Sir, who stole my wallet and Moreland's diary from my duffel bag; over two years ago on the day I arrived?"

"I don't know, but I will forget about the shot fired, if you leave the office now, Private Roy."

"Sir, for a commanding officer, you appear not to know very much of anything. That means you are either incompetent, ignorant, stupid, lying or all of the above.

But, I think you have another problem also, Sir. You must be hard of hearing." I pointed at his head.

"Sir, I would like to know if you can hear this."

He said, "No, please."

I fired one round, grazing his left ear.

He hollered from the pain.

"Sir, can you hear me now? Let's start again. Why is the 517th Medical Clearing so heavy armed?"

"It's top secret."

"Yes, an ugly top secret, so why don't you share it with me, Sir." I raised the "Third Luger" again.

"Our job as a medical clearing company would be satisfied after we treated the causalities of a nuclear, chemical or biological weapons attack. The reason the Russians would use a weapon of mass destruction on us would be to create a hole in our defenses. That would mean they would want to move heavy forces (tanks) through the hole they created."

"Yes, go on."

"The only combat ready forces that would be standing in front of them at that time would be the 517th, a company of medics or what was left of us."

"Let me see if I can help you out, Sir. Here is a bandage for your ear and hand. What you're saying Sir, is the 517th would be re-designated as an infantry company as soon as we finished our job as medics. Then we would be responsible for plugging the hole created by the Russians. Which means we would be going up against Russian tanks with M14s and other small arms?"

"If war broke out, our combat models say there would be enough heavy weapons left on the battle field and combat unit survivors to augment us. We have heavy weapons stored in another location. It is against the Geneva convention for medics to be armed with heavy weapons."

"Sir, what does your high tec combat model say about the survival prospects of the 517[th's] men facing Russian tanks?"

He didn't answer and I raised the "Third Luger" again.

He replied, "Slim to none."

I shook my head saying, 'Do you feel good, Sir, commanding a company that will be ordered to commit suicide. I bet you and the headquarters platoon will be located in a safe place."

He gave no response.

"Now, answer some hard questions concerning our ugly secrets. Sir, what about that virus that was moved? Is it a form of the Monkey Virus, HIV?"

"Yes, it was field tested on Plum Island, off the coast of Long Island in the State of New York, as an aerosol deliverable, weaponized version of the Monkey Virus. It was later proven to be ineffective as an aerosol deliverable weapon."

"Which Island, Sir?"

"Plum Island, Eastern Long Island, State of New York"

I raised my weapon again, "Where are they taking the virus, Sir?"

"The 517th was scheduled to administer the virus embedded in 'cholera vaccines' by injection during the next natural disaster in Eastern Europe. We couldn't get it into Eastern Europe or the Soviet Union as planned. They are taking it to the Middle East or Africa, for further testing as an injectable agent hidden in cholera vaccine."

"That means you want to test it on Black and Brown peoples."

He didn't respond.

"Sir, you are getting better. Who was ordered to steal Moreland's diary from me?" He remained silent and I raised my weapon again.

"PFC Eugene Webb was ordered to go through your personal affects looking for the dairy. He took your wallet to make it look like a theft. I ordered him to transport the virus to the 8th Airborne's HQ in the same truck that you rode in for your guard mount. He has been working with us since you arrived."

I held my head down from the pain that reeked through my heart and body. The Spiderman and I had grown so close. He attempted to open his desk door and I fired again hitting him in the right hand. He grimaced again from the pain.

"Take a seat Sir. I am sorry, Sir, the weapon went off by accident again. Now for the final ugly secret, why is that chopper circling the Kaserne?"

After a long pause, he said, "There are possibly two to three B-teams on the way to take you out. You have ugly secrets, Private Roy, which I have no knowledge of. Now answer me, what are your ugly secrets?"

At that instant, two choppers flew low over the Kaserne. I handed the lieutenant a second bandage for his hand, then I said to him, "If I told you, Sir, I would have to shoot you. You hung around to see the fireworks, well you stay right here. You are going to see the performance of your life."

I pulled out all the phones in the office as I left. I walked across the hall and quietly opened the armory door, took two Match 1911 Colt-45 pistols that just arrived for the pistol team and placed both of them in left and right shoulder hostlers. Garcia had ordered 50 round drums for the 45s. I asked him why? He said you never know when you will run out of ammo at a pistol match. Normally, the 1911 Colt-45 only holds 7 rounds.

The fog continued to roll down the hill into the Kaserne, making visibility poor. I walked out in to the middle of the street dragging a duffel bag. I waved at the one of the choppers and gave the pilot the finger. The little bird started to hover again, I didn't move as it hovered closer and closer to me. Then I saw a sniper's rifle pointed straight at me out of the chopper's side door. But, he was having difficulty sighting me, because of the fog. I reached between my legs and pulled out Wolfman's crossbow from my duffel bag. I fired a bolt with an attached piano wire trailing it. The bolt began to sing as it made its way into the helicopter's blades. The pilot tried in vain to pull his bird up, but it flipped over and crashed into the side of Kuhberg Hill.

I looked up at the lieutenant staring at me through his office window with blood trickling down his face. I called to him saying, "Low tech kicks high tech's ass." At that time, two more HU-1B Huey's approached the ball field with men riding on their skids. They were armed to the teeth with automatic weapons and all dressed in Wolfman's favorite color, Special Ops Black.

One chopper landed in the ball field and dropped off five guys. The other landed near the downed chopper. It dropped off its 5-man team, picked up the one survivor and flew away. From under a parked truck, I dropped two men with my M14, but I had only wounded them. They must have been wearing the new third generation body armor. I took out the next two with headshots. Only one of the five made it to the truck line. It was Flash.

I climbed into my tent truck, but I procrastinated so Flash would see me. I waited for him to climb into the tent truck behind me, but he stopped and radioed the chopper that he had me trapped in a truck. I crawled through the maze of tents that we set up inside the truck and out through a side exit. The chopper pilot ordered him to go in after me. The voice over the radio sounded very familiar. As he climbed into the back of the truck after me, I cut both tendons in the back of his legs. He hollered as I pulled him back out of the truck and I kicked him in his kidneys. I watched him crawl away in pain.

One of the wounded B-team members rose and came stumbling towards me. I saw a muzzle flash and returned fire, dropping him with a perfect shot. I called out to the last wounded guy who was hiding under the ball field's bench. "One shot, one kill, mother fucker." He refused to come out.

The second B-team, which was dropped off near the crash of the first chopper, spotted their wounded men lying in the middle of the baseball field. They retreated and went around the side of the Kaserne using the buildings for cover.

The door gunner of the third chopper opened fire with his M60 machine gun, firing at my shadows in the fog. Finally, the pilot got up enough courage to come in close to the ball field attempting to pick up their wounded. I jumped from the back of the gasoline trailer and threw a Molotov cocktail at the chopper, courtesy of Vyacheslav Mikhallovich. The chopper"s down draft caused the wick to come loose from the bottle. It hit the side door and the gasoline spattered on its side. Immediately, I pulled out the Wolfman's shaving cream can and popped the top. It started to spark as the tear gas began to escape. I threw it and it hit the trailing gasoline of the chopper before it gained altitude and it exploded in flames. As it crash landed, flaming bodies jumped out running aimlessly in any direction trying to escape the intense heat.

I didn't know it at the time, but Top Dog was having an arduous conversation with the Misfits at the party. He was very upset that the lieutenant hadn't shown up. He knew something was up. The Spiderman told him, don't worry about it. Sweet Willie said "The Milkman is too secretive about his affairs, he is in shit over his head and I didn't want to get involved in it. Nasty didn't say anything.

Top Dog became very upset with all of them. "You are some ungrateful assholes." They were about to jump him, when Nasty said, "We respect you Top Dog, but you have gone too far now."

Sweet Willie said, "The Milkman wouldn't give me a break on the money that I owed him."

Faust, a.k.a. "Snuffy" then entered the conversation and said that he would allow Top Dog to fly the guys back to the Kaserne in Major Macomb's chopper which was parked outside in the middle of the race track. Major McComb had driven off with two other officers and wouldn't miss the bird for a while. Top Dog, Nasty and Snuffy climbed into the chopper and took off.

There were still five members of the B-team left on the ground coming at me slowly from behind the barracks buildings. Then I heard a chopper returning from the west. It was returning with another five assassins on board. The lieutenant was following the whole show in amazement from the HQ's window. The bleeding from his ears slowed as he looked on. The last chopper landed outside the Kaserne's gate blocking anyone from entering or leaving. The chopper's pilot was in total amazement that two choppers had gone down and so many men were dead or wounded. Five fresh men jumped off the chopper. One of them was the Unicorn. I couldn't get a clear shot at any of them. They were moving in to surround me.

I began to toss smoke grenades in front of the trucks. This would take their vision away. Their night vision goggles couldn't see well through the sparks, smoke and fog. Low tech kicks high tech's ass. I had placed C4 under the gas tanks of two trucks on the north side of the line. Three B-team members were using the trucks for cover, and then I set the C4 off. It lit their asses up.

I heard the fourth chopper coming. Those SOBs really wanted my ass; they were sending the entire damn US Army.

About this time, Top Dog landed the fourth chopper on top of HQ roof, and Snuffy took off in the chopper.

What a relief. The lieutenant met him in the hall as he pulled the Brazilian-M14 out of the armory. The lieutenant ordered him to put it back and leave. He told the lieutenant to go fuck himself. He climbed back on to the roof and placed a poncho over himself to conceal his sniper position. I retreated back into the tent truck. I stuck my hand out of the top and signed to Top Dog, that the assassins had body armor on and he had to take them out with headshots. He gave me the OK sign. I still didn't know whether Top Dog could pull the trigger to kill a human being.

BAM! He dropped one of the assassins climbing on top of the truck in back of me. I gave him the Black Power fist and he gave it back to me. Then I heard "BAM"; he dropped another one outside the truck. As I climbed out of the truck, I became cornered by one of them between the trucks. He turned, but his weapon was hung up on the truck's fender. I finished his ass off with a "Third Luger" shot to the head.

I didn't know how many were left. Then I spotted someone approaching Top Dog from behind on the roof. It was the Unicorn, but before I could warn him, he grabbed Top Dog by the head slashed his throat and pushed him off the roof onto the street below. I went running through the smoke and fog towards Top Dog as the remaining assassins fired at me. I couldn't see very well in the smoke and tear gas, but neither could they. All I saw were muzzle flashes. I opened up with two of my 1911 Colt-45, with 50 round magazines, until I didn't see any of the flashes anymore. I held Top Dog in my arms, bleeding badly.

He frowned and said, "Milkman, I am tired of saving your Black ass. You are the only Negro in the world who is smarter than me; but you don't act like it. Apply to another college. Being turned down isn't the end of the world, Milkman. Tell Stella that I love her."

As he went limp. The second chopper that blocked the entrance to the Kaserne took off and began to hover against the ground trying to blow away the smoke and tear gas. This chopper had one of the new mini-guns on board. I made a beeline for the tent truck again. It opened up on all of the trucks including the tent truck. I heard explosions all around me as whole trunks rose into the air exploding from the fire of the mini-gun igniting their gas tanks. The medics were right; the folded tents in my truck were stopping 50 caliber bullets. Thank God, low tech kicks high tech's ass, but the remainder of the truck was coming apart. The tires were exploding and the gas tank was in flames. I had to crawl out of the truck.

Unicorn was talking to the chopper over his radio, telling it to move off, so he could come in and finish me, if I wasn't already dead. Now, I remembered the voice in the chopper. It was the same voice that I heard inside the bunker the night the Davy Crockett was stolen. As he walked in between the smoking trucks, I pushed a five hundred pound tent on top of him with my legs. He moved quickly, but the tent caught his right leg breaking his ankle. He was moving badly, but he continued to stork me. Then suddenly I felt Unicorn pulling my legs out of the side of the burning truck. I didn't fight him, because he was stumbling as he pulled me out.

"Milkman, no more of this low tech shit, it's going to be me, you and your maker now baby."

I could see that his legs were in bad shape. I replied, "No, Soul Brother, I am Jack, you're the bean stalk motherfucker, and you are about to come down."

I rolled up into a ball, as I had been taught to do in San Antonio by the Wolfman, and I hit him rolling at full speed. It knocked him over, but he recovered quickly on one knee. He punched me in the ribs and I went down. I never had been hit that hard before in my life. I couldn't get up, but he couldn't either. He rounded over on me and started to choke the life out of me. Then a razor flashed under his chin and he didn't move. His eyes looked at me in confusion. Then I heard a friendly voice.

"This is pay back mother fucker. Let's see if you bad mother fuckers know how to monkey dance."

I could see blood starting to drip from his neck as he released me and began to rise. Nasty had his razor under his neck and he was in no condition to do anything about it. I looked up and there stood Sweet Willie, Vaugns, Garcia and the Spiderman.

I picked up the "Third Luger" and stumbled over to the Spiderman and slapped him in the face with it; barrel first. As he picked himself up off the ground, I pointed the gun at his head, told him to kneel and open his mouth. As I placed the gun barrel in his month, Nasty begged me not to pull the trigger.

I said to the Spiderman, "Prostitutes simply sell their bodies, you sold your soul, and you can't live without a soul."

I pulled the trigger and the gun went click. I rushed back over to Swilley, but I couldn't do anything for him. He was gone. Over my shoulder appeared two headlights in the smoking ruins of the 517th's truck line. They slowly approached me as I picked up the lifeless body of Haymen "Top Dog" Swilley. I carried his body towards the approaching vehicle. With his body in my arms, I stopped the car from going any further. I placed Swilley on the hood of the car. I reached into my pistol belt, pulled out a single clip and clicked it into the "Third Luger."

I heard a familiar voice. "Milkman, there comes a time when combatants must resolve issues of great concern with dialogue instead of violence. Let's sit down in the car and talk."

As, I cocked the "Third Luger", I recognized that it was LT COL Grumble who was flying the helicopter gun ship, it was his voice I heard in the bunker when the Davy Crockett was stolen and it was him in the car that had tried to run me and Carol over in Ozark, Alabama. He opened the rear door of the staff car for me to get in. I motioned to Nasty to pull one of the few remaining trucks off the truck line to block the staff car from leaving.

I slid into the back seat saying, "You SOB, after you killed the president of the United States, Malcolm X, my friends and tried several times to kill me, you now say you want to talk? I am going to put your sorry Black ass out of your misery."

"All thoughts of ugly secrets must be placed behind us now, Milkman. What we must arrive at now is what direction we are going, not where we came from."

"That's bullshit, am I supposed to trust you. You have sold yourself and America down the drain. You are a prostitute just like the Spiderman. How much did you pay him to rat me out?"

"Do you really think this whole thing is about money?"

"Isn't it?"

"No! When people become a threat to the nation, someone must act."

"Who makes that determination, you, J.E. Hoover and the American Praetorian Guard? Ted, with all your education your mind still has the chains of slavery locked around it. If I didn't kick your assassin's asses, you wouldn't have shown up. Now their mangled bodies are lying all over the Kaserne in a pitiful mess and you say let's start over. We should have started over in San Antonio, we should have started over at Fort Rucker, We should have started over on the General Rose and we should have started over in Dallas, Paris and Berlin."

Then suddenly another chopper landed and the men on board started to remove the bodies from the Kaserne. Nasty released the Unicorn and allowed him to flee.

"Is that what this talk is really about, for you to buy time, so you can wipe your ass clean?"

I pointed the "Third Luger" at his head as he reached into the seat pocket on the back of the front seat, pulled out a large envelope, and handed it to me. I opened it, inside was a picture of Bridgett and me that was taken in Paris. He just stared at me.

"Oh! Now this is supposed to be a veiled threat?"

"President Kennedy lost it. He committed high treason. He was sleeping with communist agents and listening to Black radicals like Malcolm X and Martin Luther King. He was shrinking from the fight against the communist. He secretly ordered American troops to begin their withdrawal from Vietnam. He put the whole country in serious jeopardy. LBJ seem to be the best alternative to the

Kennedy's. LBJ is from the Texas old school. He knows how to deal with the "Pinkos" in this country and abroad. Hoover warned the Kennedy Brothers several times, but they would not listen. President Kennedy knew he was going to die, so did Malcolm X. Great men choose the time of their deaths. Meager men, like us, die at random.

"We weren't sure of what you knew. Therefore, we assumed you knew everything. You have demonstrated your loyalty by not revealing your ugly secrets. Therefore, I am making sure you know everything. Private Roy, the people that I represent would like to end this now. They want you to return home to New York City. Not to go to Sweden with Bridgett as you planned. If you go home PVT Roy, all of this will end as you wished. You promised the Wolfman that you would go to college on the GI bill; go."

He then placed a red scarf around my neck as he did the A-team. I immediately pulled it off. I now know why, it was the symbol of the American Praetorian Guard. The Roman Praetorian guard wore scarlet red capes over their armor. He was trying to recruit me.

"Ted, I have not demonstrated my loyalty to you. I have been loyal to myself and those who were loyal to me. You are not afraid of me going public with my ugly secrets. You aren't concerned with me running off at the mouth at home. I would just be another disgruntled Black American male, with another conspiracy tale to tell, surrounded by a few, excitable and untrained Soul Brothers carrying rusty 32 caliber pistols in their packets. But, here in Europe, I have credibility, people here will listen and believe what I have to say. The people here have resources, people that can do something about you and your cronies. You are paying me a compliment. You have more belief in me than I have in myself, that's why you are making this offer."

"What do you believe in, Private Roy?"

"First, Ted, I am no longer a private as of tomorrow. I will be promoted back to Soul Brother First Class and a graduate of the UCLA. I believe in Mighty Mouse, Superman, the Green Hornet, and Snuffy Smith. I believe in Crisps Attucks, the former slave who led white patriots against British Soldiers on the Boston Commons in 1760. I believe in our Founding Fathers, even though they didn't believe in themselves. I believe that birds and men have something in common. We must die if we can't fly free. And, that goes for all birds, no matter what color stripes are on their wings. I believe I must challenge your twisted ideology, your misguided morality and your corrupt spirituality. I also believe that a vindictive Irishman is going to do the same thing to the people who killed his brother."

"He may not get the chance, Milkman, please help us bring this to a halt? Let's put aside all the assassinations, murders and bitterness."

"I will have to think about it."

"Milkman, we don't have time for you to think about it. If I drive away it won't happen."

"Who is saying you are going to drive away, Ted?"

"Milkman, my life has no value at this point. I am already a dead man. You would be doing me a favor by pulling the trigger of that "Third Luger." I am offering you life over death. The next time it will be a battalion of men coming to get you and Bridgett. Is that what you want, to be running and hiding all over Europe and possibly in Soviet Union?

We know that Lieutenant Victor Masterson made you an offer and its BS that he planted nuclear weapons in the United States. Is that what you are counting on, that he will set them off? I am surprised at you, Roy. You have been had by LT Masterson. You don't really believe he planted nuclear weapons in the United States; do you. I am counting on you. I know, when you make a commitment you keep it. Just like you did with the A-team in San Antonio. What can we help you with, Milkman? What do you want, it's not money?"

"I am surprised at you, Ted. You are one ignorant, arrogant asshole. Graduating from Yale doesn't mean you learned anything about life. LT Masterson sent you back your own tactical nuclear toy and you question his integrity. I want you to find the HIV contaminated cholera vaccines and destroy them. I want full military honors for "Top Dog" Swilley and the Wolfman. I want to personally inspect the Honor Guard myself and escort their bodies' home. I want both of their bodies buried in Arlington National Cemetery with full Military Honors."

"Consider it done, Milkman, but the virus is out of my hands. I don't know who has it or where it is. I know it is not in Europe anymore. But, I will give you one that you have not asked for. President Kennedy was paying a lot of attention to Malcolm X; as you suspected. He had the president's ear although he didn't know it and that was the final nail that was placed in both of their coffins. The nail was placed there by Alex Haley; who wrote his autobiography. Malcolm X confided in Alex Haley that he suspected someone outside of the Nation of Islam was setting him up to be killed. It was Alex Haley; he was the prime informant for the FBI. He was the ultimate betrayer. You must be on the 0900 hours Pan American fight tomorrow going back to New York City. Both of the bodies will be placed on board with full military honors before you take your seat."

At that time, Major McComb knocked on the side window of the staff car. LT COL Grumble rolled it down.

The major said, "What in the hell went on here, Sir."

The colonel said, "Major, I will take care of this."

"No you won't, Sir. I am ordering Private Roy out of your car now. He's on guard duty."

I got out of the car, but as I exited the car, I noticed the sergeant who was driving resembled the Justice Department agent that came to question me at Fort Rucker after the Caveman's death.

The colonel said, "0900 hours tomorrow morning, Düsseldorf Airport."

I looked up at the HQ as they brought LT Biggs out and placed him into an ambulance along with Swilley's body. Major McComb ordered Nasty to move the truck and let LT COL Grumble leave.

Then he asked me, "What are you going to do, Private Roy."

"I am going to take the plane back to the states in the morning."

He ordered Sweet Willie to pack my remaining things. He told Nasty to take the HQ Jeep and back it up to the guard house door to prevent anyone from entering. He ordered all of them not to let anyone in the guard house and that they were to drive me to the airport tomorrow morning. He ordered Gracia to issue everyone full automatic M14s with 5 clips of ammo to each. I wasn't to say good-by to anyone nor have contact with anyone. I had to remain in the guardhouse all night. He took all of my weapons and handed me back the "Third Luger" without a clip of ammo.

After and sleepless night thinking about Bridgett, I didn't say anything to anyone the next morning; including the Spiderman who was leaning against the wreckage of my tent truck. Then we took off heading towards the airport with me riding in the back of a ¾ ton fronted by a M151 jeep mounted with a M60 machine gun. Where the armed jeep came from I do not know. We arrived early and they drove me directly onto the tarmac to the plane's ramp. There was an Honor Guard of two hundred soldiers representing all the units in US Army Europe. The 8th Airborne band began to play a drum funeral dirge as I walked towards the plane. An ambulance pulled up to the plane with two caskets. I saluted as SGT 1st Class Sammerson and SP4 Swilley bodies were taken out of the ambulance and placed on the plane. Major Macomb was there as the officer of the Honor Guard and personally escorted me to inspect it. I wore SGT Sammerson's Green Beret and Swilley's Specialist 4th Class rank out of respect for these two fine soldiers. I walked over to the formation and inspected the Honor Guard and I found several minor imperfections. Then I walked up the stairs to the plane.

Then, I heard the horn of a VW beetle. It was Bridgett. The guard at the gate had stopped her and she was pushing and fighting the guards to get through. I asked the major to allow her through. She started running, screaming and crying at me.

She said, "When I didn't hear from you, I knew something was wrong. So, I drove to the Kaserne and the place looked like a volcano. They placed a guard at the gate, it was Robin, but he let me through. No one would tell me anything. They were talking to the reporters from the Stars and Stripes. They told the reporters that the gasoline trailer exploded and ignited the ammunition truck. I knew it was all a lie. I saw the Spiderman, I begged him to tell me what happen to you and he said they took you to Düsseldorf Airport. I thought you were dead. Baby please, please don't leave me."

Before I could say anything, LT COL Grumble's staff car rolled up to the gangplank and stopped. I quickly handed Bridgett a brown envelope and told her aloud that it contained secret information and to look in the envelope. She opened the envelope and looked back at me in confusion. In the envelope was a new "Ruby and the Romantics" album, "Our day will come."

I whispered that I was going to send it to her when I arrived in the States. She then turned around looking at the staff car with its windows blacked out as the driver opened the front door and got out. I was sure now; it was the investigator who visited me at Fort Rucker. My heart started to pound as he winked at me as he opened the rear door for LT COL Grumble to get out. I told Bridgett that she had to leave, that I was leaving so she could live. She understood as she gave me a big hug and kiss, then she walked down the plane's stairs. LT COL Grumble got back into his staff car and left.

The plane filled up quickly with soldiers returning home to the states. As the plane took off, I saw smoke on the side of access road of the airport. LT COL Grumble's staff car was on fire. The driver was walking down the road and there was no sign of LT COL Grumble.

When the plane landed in New York City, I kissed the ground in thanks that I made it back alive. I watched them remove the bodies, and then I rushed home to my apartment building and down stairs into the basement. The basement was clean, almost spotless. I opened the door to Lonzo's foxhole, looking for him and his battered Eisenhower Jacket hanging on the back of the door; it wasn't there. I turned to look for the hot plate with the crusted pot with fossilized food; it wasn't there. I turned towards his sheet-less bed; it wasn't there. I immediately flew upstairs and banged on my apartment's door. I didn't even kiss my mother, say hello to my brother or to my sister.

"What happen to him, Mamma?"

My mother couldn't look me in the eyes as she stared at the wall.

"He fell asleep, drunk, one very cold night this past winter. The coal in furnace burned out. It was too late by the time we began to complain to the landlord about no heat. By the time, the landlord sent someone to check on him, he had froze to death in his bed. I couldn't get up enough courage to write and tell you about it."

I began to shake my head continuously as the tears forced their way through my eyes. She said that the landlord had found a package with my name on it under his mattress. I followed her into the bedroom. She kneeled down, reached under her bed, pulled out a Garden Supermarket paper bag, and hand it to me. I gave her a kiss on her cheek. I turned and hugged my brother and sister and walked into the bathroom with the unopened package. I closed the bathroom door, pulled down the top lid on the toilet and sat down. I slowly opened the package. In it was his Eisenhower Uniform Jacket with all of his ribbons and metals. There was a note folded underneath the jacket. It read.

"Dear Milkman, if you are reading this note, you have succeeded as a far greater soldier than the Wolfman or me. Everything anyone or anybody really needs to know about me is contained in this paper bag. Most doctors, given sufficient time, can diagnose most illness, but no doctor can cure every illness that he diagnoses. Therefore, our ultimate worth as humans must lie in our ability to solve problems and to explore locations in the human spirit where no other human has endeavored to trek; all while not succumbing to our human frailties.

I served America faithfully, honorably and to the very best of my god given ability. I only asked America to serve all its soldiers faithfully, honorably and to the very best of her god given ability. Now, it is up to you to make sure that America faithfully serves herself and not shrink from her principles again. You understand that it will be difficult at times for America to stay focused on that goal. Follow your instincts and do not allow America to sellout or compromise the principles that she was founded on again. It is OK for America to stumble, but she must not fall. When she does stumble, you must be ready to steady her immediately. Much is expected of you, because those who came before you have given much for you.

Soldier on,

Lonzo Morgan

Sergeant First Class

US Army Rangers/Buffalo Soldiers"

I began to reflect on what Lonzo said; that we Americans are a great, but flawed people, full of potential, energy and hope. Yet arrogance, ignorance and greed have caused us to succumb to the dark forces buried deep within us. Sometimes we exhibit behavior that can be considered, at times, no less than cannibalistic. While we try to define ourselves and relate to one another, we would be well advised to listen and not try to destroy all those who dissent or criticize. Our history is full of examples of our strengths as well as our weaknesses. But, in spite of our country's weaknesses, I have learned to kiss the very earth that I walk upon and cherish those who have beaten down the path before me.

As I began this American tragic adventure, it was not clear to me if I would complete this journey, or what or where my final destination would be. I wanted to grow, gain knowledge and experience. I have accomplished that and much more. But, the acquisition of knowledge also brings responsibility. America opened its soul to me, its past and its future. My journey has unlocked a new vision of America. I must now pause and tell others where I have been and what I have seen. I must explain why I have traveled in silence facing the dangers I have encountered.

As I look back now, it's crystal-clear to me that my personal journey is continuing and is not over and neither is America's. In fact, America's journey is just beginning, for she is one of the youngest nations on the face of this planet; and definitely the youngest to attain such a powerful status.

So now I speak, because it's as if I personally pulled the trigger on the most cataclysmic domestic events in American history since the Civil War. It is as if I shot myself, I feel the pain almost daily. I have learned that America's wisdom is not universal and others can provide the answers concerning the difficulties we Americans face as a people. History has not been kind to superpowers and it has shown that absolute power will corrupt the soul of any nation, including ours-mine.

THE END

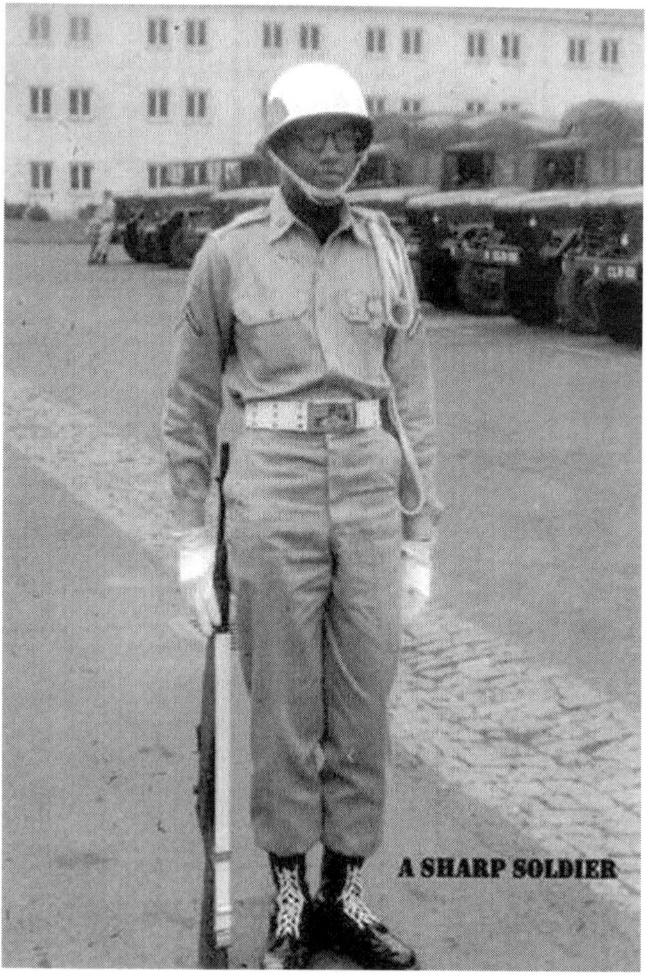

A SHARP SOLDIER

Epilogue

On October 9, 2002, the Pentagon announced that experiments using Chemical, Biological and Radiological Weapons were tested on humans and soldiers alike; some without their knowledge during the sixties.

In 2004, open letters written by Malcolm X to President Kennedy were found in the Estate of Alex Haley, Author of the Autobiography of Malcolm X. Also, the Freedom of Information Act has produced documentation that Alex Haley and associates were FBI informants.

In December of 2006, the government of Ireland released information that JFK had received death threats on his visit to Ireland on June 26-29 1963. One informant claimed a sniper would target Kennedy as his motorcade traveled from Dublin Airport to the residence of the Irish president. This was just five months before his actual murder.

On June 26, 2007, the CIA released a document entitled "The Family Jewels." This document exposed a host of ugly CIA secrets including their bumbled attempts to assassinate Cuban Leader Fidel Castro.

The members of the previously all Black 24th Infantry Regiment, The Great Buffalo Soldiers, haven't had their record cleared concerning their performance in Korea and their unit flag returned home with honor. The proud and famous Buffalo Soldiers unit was disbanded on October 1, 1951.

After more than 50 years, over three quarters of the American people feel the murder of President John Fitzgerald Kennedy in Dallas, Texas in 1963 was not the act of a single individual and this pusillanimous act grew to consume Malcolm X, Dr. Martin Luther King Jr., his brother Bobby Kennedy and others.

The French government has yet to adequately explain why they denied Malcolm X entry into France on February 9, 1965; when they had allowed him entry just a year earlier.

In the past 40 years, in Sub Saharan Africa, over 28.5 million people have been infected with the HIV/AIDS Virus. Of that number, 15 million people have died. Worldwide, 65 million people have contracted the HIV/AIDS Virus; of that number, 28 million people have died. Clearly, the HIV/AIDS virus is the vilest weapon of mass destruction ever perfected by human kind.

In 1962, the number of people in the world identified as infected with the HIV/AIDS Virus was **zero.**

Malcolm X's most severe criticism was reserved for Americans who were descendants of African Slaves, not European Americans. His criticism is just as potent and relevant today as it was over fifty years ago.

From adversity springs achievement
From truth and knowledge springs enlightenment.
From achievement and enlightenment
springs human progress
By
Edward Roy

About the Author

In August of 1965, Edward Roy (pseudonym) received an honorable discharge from the United States Army after serving three years. Twenty six months was served in Europe during the most tumultuous period in American history since the Civil War. PVT Roy was rated as one of the best medics in the 517th Medical Clearing Company, Soldier of the Month, Supernumerary, 62 Medical Group Honor Guard, and completed the 100-mile Nijmegen, Holland Marches. He fired Expert in rifle, and the pistol team he trained placed in the 7th Army completions. Major portions of his Army military records have mysteriously disappeared. In 1966, he was accepted to the State University of New York at Farmingdale where he graduated with an Associate of Applied Science Degree in Photographic Technology.

In that same year, Rochester Institute of Technology (RIT) Rochester, New York accepted him into their College of Photography with 2½ years credit and a scholarship after rejecting him 3 years earlier. In 1970 he graduated with honors and a Bachelor's of Science Degree. In 1977, using the remainder of his GI Bill Educational Benefits, he received a Masters of Business Administration Degree from Fordham University-Lincoln Center, New York City. In 1994, Edward Roy retired from corporate and civic America to pursue his long time passions.

34461828R00279

Made in the USA
Charleston, SC
09 October 2014